CONSIDER YOUR WAYS

KIMANI LAUREN

DEDICATIONS

For Shateek, who is exactly 3 weeks younger than the rough draft
of this work that is 13 years in the making.
For Jeanette, without whom this book's completion never would
have been possible.
And for Matthew, my angel in Heaven watching over me. I tried
to capture my love for you in the essence of Rize, but there will
never be enough words that can capture all that you will always
mean to me.

The buried parts of your past always resurface.

LOVED ONES DON'T DIE; THEY JUST CHANGE THE WAY THEY WALK WITH US.

KIMANI LAUREN

CRUSH ON YOU

In the warm softness of her bed, Shatima Thomas lay hoping that Heaven's door would open for her. The moment before opening her eyes signified whether it would be her favorite part of the day or the most dreaded. If she didn't make it through the night, it meant she could be reunited with her deceased father and brother. Registering that the sound of the morning news meant that her wish was denied, she sighed and rolled over to focus on the television.

"I'm Malcolm Jefferson."

"And I'm Hope Thomas, and this is *Good Morning, Sanford County*."

The peppiness of the delightful duo on the television caused Shatima to cut her eyes and frown at them. She listened to their banter woven between the traffic and weather reports. Her frown deepened as they reported the local news. A severe lack of emotion was present as they spoke about the rise in homicides. To balance it out with some good news, an entrepreneur named Malachi James just opened his seventh factory. He was handing out jobs like hotcakes. He also offered to pay for the funerals of the slain murder victims.

Then just like that, more startling news aired. Hope spoke

about a rash of kidnappings in the city's impoverished areas. Parents of African-American boys in low income neighborhoods were warned to be on high alert. That she said this so calmly with a twinkle in her eye angered Shatima. Every five to ten years, poor black boys in Sanford County were ripped from their families. Very few of them returned alive. Some of them turned up in obscure parts of town as defiled corpses. It was rumored that they were sold as sex slaves. Hope ended the report by advising all parents to be on high alert.

As a twenty-one year old single mother of a young son with a limited support system, Shatima was always on high alert.

Shatima looked at the paintings on the walls surrounding her bed as she prepared to face the day. The goddess Oshun was perched across from Isis, reminding her of who she was and why she was still here. She didn't have to wish she was dead. She had a purpose. Into the bathroom she walked and turned on a stereo with a three disc changer. Every morning she listened to Soul II Soul's *Keep On Moving* followed by Groove Theory's *Keep Trying*. Singing the hooks as she showered was like giving herself instructions for the day.

Back to her room she went to smooth cocoa butter all over her body. As she looked at herself in the full length mirror on the back of her bedroom door, she admired the contrast between the turquoise bra and her ebony-toned skin. Then she looked down further and frowned. The newborn footprints tattooed on her lower abdomen didn't do much to conceal her c-section scar. Her fingers traced the footprints, lingering over one. She pulled a set of cartoon character scrubs over her body.

After securing her hair in a simple updo, Shatima went down the hall to check on her purpose. Jabez was the reason she breathed for the past five years. She didn't know what she did to deserve that beautiful brown boy, but she cherished him. Looking at him made her feel guilty for her nightly wish. At the same time, looking at him fueled her nightly wish. She didn't do him justice as his mother, she felt. If she did, she wouldn't have given birth to him when she was seventeen. But if her wish was granted, and she went to Heaven, then who would protect him from the world?

Mornings were a complicated time in the mind of Shatima Thomas.

"Good morning, Mommy," a voice said from under a pile of Power Rangers blankets and sheets on the floor.

Shatima went to him and smiled as she unwound him. "Good morning, my love. How did you get trapped in the covers?"

A fit of giggles erupted from the sheets and blankets. "I dressed myself, and then I sat down on the bed to put my shoes on, and then I got tangled up in the covers."

Shatima had to giggle herself. In her five year old's mind, that explanation made perfect sense. She helped him to untangle himself, make his bed, and brush his teeth. She put some oil on the zigzagging parts between the cornrows going down his back. They sat at the television in the living room and watched the rest of *Good Morning, Sanford.*

The anchorwoman seemed to be holding back giggles while the anchorman reported that the citizens of South Sanford continued to complain about wanting more than one point of entry and exit. When the anchorman read a report about the people of South Sanford feeling like they were being punished or held captive, the anchorwoman lost it.

"Mommy, the lady on the news has the same last name as us," Jabez remarked.

Shatima nodded absently, wondering how someone could be so awful yet gainfully employed.

"And she has long hair like yours," Jabez continued.

Again Shatima nodded. "Yup, but she doesn't have dimples like us, and I would never wear my hair in curls that big like it's the eighties. She needs a new stylist."

Shatima turned off the TV. "Let's go so that we can get your bus. Mommy has to go get breakfast before work."

Hand in hand, they left their apartment and descended four

flights of stairs before reaching the exit to their building. It was an atypically warm day for October in Upstate, New York. Their stoop was filled with people pushing through loiterers to get to their various destinations. A woman fussed at her boyfriend for not helping her carry the stroller downstairs. He ignored her and encouraged the other men on and boys out there to marvel Shatima's ass with him. One man called to her that he'd pay her to let him use her ass as a pillow. She wished they wouldn't say such crass things around her son. Sometimes she expressed that. That day, she let her scowl speak for her.

"Ay what's wrong with y'all? Learn some respect."

Shatima stifled the wry smile that was forming on her face before the 6'4" owner of the commanding voice fell in step beside her. Dressed in coveralls and work boots and carrying a cooler, Rahshaan was the only man within the Nat Turner Projects Shatima said more than two words to the entire time she lived there. When she first moved in, he introduced himself as "Banger." She agreed to be cordial to him on the condition that he give her his government name rather than his nickname. Outside of his grandmother and his mother, she was the only woman who called him by his first name.

"Good morning, gorgeous."

"Good morning, Rahshaan," she said in a flat voice, her slightly bulbous nose stuck in the air.

Though her demeanor was snotty, Rahshaan was turned on by it. Something about her carrying herself as though she were too good for him excited him. "I'm about to go up to this factory for this orientation."

"That's nice. Good luck with your new job," Shatima told him.

He hoped she would ask him more about it, but when she didn't, he turned to Jabez. "What's up, little man? That's a dope jacket. Mommy got you looking fly as usual."

Shatima nudged Jabez. "What do you say when someone pays you a compliment?"

"Thank you," Jabez said shyly.

The three of them stopped at a corner where Jabez's bus was to pick him up. Rahshaan crouched down so that he was eye level with the five year old. "Pay close attention in math class this morning. Math is important. When you're grown up and making money, you're gonna need to make sure your money is right and make sure no one is short changing you. So pay attention, okay?"

"Okay," Jabez told him with a nod. He looked past Rahshaan and up the street. A bus was careening toward them as the driver yapped into a Bluetooth. "Mommy, here comes my bus."

Shatima clutched Jabez's hand. Every morning, she felt apprehensive about letting him board the bus. She knew she was being slightly ridiculous, but the man was always talking on that phone. Shatima doubted he knew what his passengers looked like or how many of them there were. She embraced her son, and he hugged her back until the doors on the bus swung open. The driver made no eye contact with either one of them. It incensed Shatima that he never verbally acknowledged them. She complained to the school district many times since the beginning of the year, but nothing changed. She stood there and watched the bus until it was out of sight. Then she headed back to the parking lot where her Nissan Maxima was parked.

"So what we doing today?" Rahshaan's voice made her jump. "What? You forgot I was here?"

She nodded and kept walking.

"You didn't answer my question. Where we going?" he persisted.

"*I'm go*ing to work," she replied. "I thought you said you had a job to get to."

"I make my own hours." Rahshaan took in Shatima's figure 8 frame as she walked. "You know you wouldn't have to work if you'd let me make you my girl."

"I'm nobody's girl," Shatima snapped. In a calmer voice she said, "Even if I were to get into a relationship, I would still work.

It's bad enough that I'm depending on a boss to sign a paycheck every two weeks instead of running a company. I have to be there when they say so, and I don't get to leave until they say so. It would be even worse if I let a man control my money. No thank you. I'm nobody's slave."

Dumbfounded, Rahshaan marveled at her. She sounded a lot like someone from his past. He just couldn't remember who. He couldn't help but grimace as they approached her car. In his mind, she should have been driving a more expensive vehicle, something flashy and eye-catching, just like her.

A small group of women in their 20s posed by Shatima's cranberry colored 2000 Nissan Maxima. Some of them ran their fingers through long, bright colored weaves. Others poked out glossy lips and licked them. Through their heavy stares, they communicated how much they craved the attention Rahshaan gave her. Every now and again, he would choose one, use one, and then throw her away. Never was he seen in public with any of them. He certainly didn't walk them to their cars and hold conversations. The women observed that there was even a hint of a smile on his face. Usually, it was balled into an expression that said he was angry at the world. It drove the women crazy that Shatima kept Rahshaan sniffing after her while they practically threw themselves at him without receiving half the attention he gave her. His rejection of them earned dirty looks from them when Shatima walked by herself.

To Shatima, the concept of being hated over a boy in whom she showed no interest was something she thought she left in high school. For the most part, she tried to ignore them. However, something in the air told her that one of them was going to test her that day.

"Banger, that's your wife?" one of them asked. Several times her eyes roamed the length of Shatima's 5'9" body. "Is she the reason you don't call me no more?"

Rahshaan barely looked in her direction. "Back the fuck up away from her car," he barked.

Immediately the flock obliged.

"Think about what I said," he told Shatima as she climbed into the driver's seat.

"No thank you. I'm nobody's slave." She turned up the radio and heard another news story about Malachi James and his contributions to the community. This time, he was hosting a coat drive for children in the Nat Turner and Frederick Douglas projects. For a split second, she wished she could find a man like him. Immediately the wish departed. She didn't have time for him or any other man.

As was normally the case on Friday morning, her gas light illuminated on her dash. She headed to the gas station for fuel and breakfast. The radio went from a news report about the former chief of police going to hospice due to an advanced case of throat cancer, to playing *Back and Forth by* Aaliyah. Behind the steering wheel, she danced along to the woman singing in celebration of it being the last day of the work week, *ta*king the same route she took every Friday. In a week there was a change that she didn't notice until it was too late. She hit a pothole so hard that she jerked forward. Mentally she cussed. She already was behind on car maintenance with its need for an oil change and snow tires. She didn't know where she would get the money for one more thing.

Sure enough, when she got out of the car to inspect the damage, the air escaping her tire made a hissing sound. That made her cuss out loud. She couldn't even repair that with the Fix-A-Flat she kept in the trunk. With a groan she punched on her hazard lights. Then she walked around to the back of her sedan to take out the toolbox and start putting the spare tire on.

"Get your sexy ass out the street before you cause an accident. You know that body you got stops traffic." Rahshaan walked by and tried to joke with her, but it fell flat. He paid closer attention to what she was doing. "You about to fix that yourself?"

"I used up my Triple A last time I hit a pothole the lazy city won't come down here and fix," Shatima grumbled. She slammed her trunk door and took the jack to the side where the flat tire was. With a sigh, she grumbled, "I guess I'll send another e-mail to the mayor that won't get read or replied to. You'd think that it being an election year would make people listen."

Rahshaan's face folded into an expression of doubt. Without commenting on what she said, he told her, "You could've called me to do this for you." He reached for the jack and the toolbox that she held in her other hand.

"I don't have your number," she said absently, keeping the toolbox out of his reach.

"Would you use it if I gave it to you?" he asked.

"More than likely not," she replied.

Ignoring her rejection was something he learned to do well over the past four years. He reached for the toolbox and jack again. "Let me do this for you, please? I'm glad you can do it yourself, but I don't want you to get your work clothes dirty. You look so pretty in them."

Shatima gave up the supplies and went to her trunk to get the spare. He motioned for her to stop. Instead he called out to two men walking by. The three of them pushed her car to the side of the road. The two men left Rahshaan to fix the tire. She thanked them and offered them both money, but they declined and went about their day. Within ten minutes, he had the spare on it.

"Do you know if I'll be safe to drive on this for two weeks?" she asked him.

"You should really change it as soon as possible, but you'll have to get two," he told her.

"Why?" she asked, feeling ready to cry.

"Balance," he told her. "Riding uneven will make your car have to work harder and cause more problems down the line."

"Your new job must be something having to do with cars?" she guessed.

"I just paint them," he said humbly.

She reached into her pocket and tried to give him the money she just tried to give the two men, but he looked at it like it was the ugliest thing he'd ever seen. "Please take it, Rahshaan. I already made you late for work."

"I already told you I make my own hours," he reminded her. "If you're worried about the tires, I'll buy them for you."

For a minute she stood there and looked at him. She understood why his fan club was as big as it was. Despite the fact that he looked like he rarely combed his long hair, and the fact that he walked around looking like he had a personal vendetta against the world, he was fine. He had a face set with chiseled features that included a square jaw and eyes that only seemed to light up when he spoke to her. His skin was a dark shade of brown. His back and shoulders looked like they were made of stones. She noticed that in the summer months when he wore A-shirts. She shied away when she realized he noticed she was staring at him.

"No, thank you," she told him. "I'll work some overtime or something to get them. Thank you for the offer, though. I appreciate you always being nice to me." She went to get into her car.

He opened her door for her and asked, "How come I've never seen you with a man?"

"Because y'all are trouble, and I have a son to raise and school to finish," she told him. "Thank you again." She sped to the gas station, this time more mindful of the potholes that filled the streets.

Again she said cuss words in her head when she got to the gas station. The parking lot and pumps were full of people and cars, and she was even more upset about hitting the pothole. As warm as the weather was on that Friday in October, she expected the crowd. She parked behind a red truck and waited her turn for the pump. The line moved quickly. Within ten minutes, she was able to pay for her gas, grab a glazed donut and an iced tea for breakfast, and fill her tank.

Just as she was getting ready to pull off, a white Mitsubishi Montero Sport pulled in front of her. The driver locked eyes with her and folded her arms. Shatima's eyes fell on the braids. She remembered them because she thought they were cute but too tight around the edges when she first saw them. Shatima decided she would try to play nice with the woman. She tooted her horn and then stuck her head out of the window. In a sugary voice, she said, "Hi. Can you back up please? I'm going to be late for work."

The woman's response was so sharp that it blew Shatima backward. "Bitch, I don't give a fuck what you about to be late for. I ain't moving shit! I saw you with my man!"

Still in shock, Shatima watched the woman jump out of her car and storm toward her. A puzzled look fell over her face. The woman was empty-handed, stomping toward her like a little kid who'd just had her bike stolen. She wondered what the woman planned to accomplish. It took seconds for her to come to terms with the fact that she might have to use her car as a weapon just to make it to work on time. Shatima put her hand on the gear and prepared to shift into drive. She didn't have time to fight a stranger over not moving. Drivers in cars behind them laid on their horns. Someone yelled for them to fight or get the fuck out of the way. Shatima's eyes stayed fixed on the girl. She wondered how close the woman would come. The woman continued toward Shatima, calling her every variation of bitch her mouth could conjure.

Just as Shatima released her foot from the pedal, she saw a dark brown hand grab her braids and yank her out of the way. Shatima slammed on her brakes. Anger took over her. She leapt out of her car and went around the gas pump. Her mouth fell agape when she saw Rahshaan had her in a headlock. "The fuck is you gonna do to her? Huh?" he demanded through clenched teeth.

"You ain't gonna fuck me and not call me no more, Banger! I told you I ain't no ho, but you played me for the next bitch!" she screamed.

"You a fuckin bird. Don't you ever approach her again. Get

back in your baby daddy's truck, and don't let me see you again." Rahshaan shoved her away from him and then mushed her in the back of her head for good measure.

She shot Shatima a nasty look before getting back into the truck and driving off. Shatima glared at her and then at Rahshaan.

"You shouldn't have put your hands on her. I can handle myself," she told him.

"I just defended you!" he protested.

With an index finger raised in the air she repeated, "I can handle myself. Stay out of women's business, and keep your hoes away from me." She added, "I'm really disappointed. You were just so nice to me. How can you then turn around and be abusive to a woman?"

Behind Rahshaan, a small crowd had formed. Shatima felt her insides getting hot. She liked staying low-key. It seemed that being around Rahshaan brought her life center stage. There she stood in front of people labeling her and snickering at her. To the crowd, she was another one of "Banger's" hoes, fighting over him as usual.

Beyond the crowd, her eyes fell on a wall of political ads posted on the convenience store's exterior. Her eyes first landed on one of a woman, but she was more interested in its neighbor: a poster of a tall, ruddy-complected man with saltwater colored eyes wearing a navy blue suit. Her brows furrowed and her eyes narrowed. The man on the poster stared back at her. Over his picture was an announcement that he was running for mayor. It took everything out of her not to get back into her car and ram it into his diabolical image. The only thing that stopped her was the crowd. With all of those witnesses, she'd surely go to jail for whatever damage came to the property.

Rahshaan noticed the change in her demeanor and followed her line of sight. His eyes darkened. He spun around and stalked through the crowd, demanding to know who allowed that sign to be posted in "his" neighborhood. Everyone else turned to see what had him in such a rage. Several people cringed at those devilish blue eyes, that black wavy hair, and that creamy yellow skin staring down at them, taunting them in picture form.

Shatima stood there, frozen, until someone laying on a car horn jolted her back to reality. Getting to the bridge out of her neighborhood was a blur to her. She didn't even remember rolling down her window to answer the normal interrogation from a member of law enforcement after handing over her license: "What's your name? What's your address? Why are you leaving South Ridge? How long do you plan to be gone? Is traveling outside of South Ridge necessary?" If there was anger from the ridiculous line of questioning, she didn't remember feeling it. She drove to work on autopilot. For once she didn't notice how much smoother the roads were once she left her South Ridge neighborhood and crossed the bridge. Instead, her mind stayed fixated on the blue eyed devil. There was no way he could become mayor.

The worst part of not getting to work early was having to ride the elevator with the rest of her coworkers. It was almost impossible to shut out the gossip that happened there. Not to mention the male population used the elevator ride as a speed dating service. That morning, a man who was the same height as Shatima and smelled of a wonderful mix of coconut oil and cologne breathed on the back of her neck while whispering to her about how nice she looked in scrubs.

"You just need to get rid of that perm, and then I'll be able to take you seriously as a woman," he whispered to her. "You already got all the other qualities I need: a good job, a pretty face, a fat ass, and a nice car."

Shatima scrunched her face for what felt like the millionth time that day. "Please don't ever speak to me again," she said without turning to him.

"You need to change your attitude, Sis. You're gonna miss out on a good man being stuck up."

The elevator could not have reached the tenth floor at a

better moment. Shatima practically ran from the elevator to her place at the receptionists' desk. She spread a napkin on her desk and put her donut on top of it. Before she could bite it, a shadow loomed over her.

"I thought you would be here earlier," Loretta, her supervisor, huffed.

Shatima looked at the clock and rolled her eyes. She still had eight minutes before her shift was supposed to start.

"Staffing called and wanted to know if your CNA credentials were up to date," Loretta told her.

"They are. Staffing has a copy of my license," she replied.

"Yes, they confirmed that," Loretta said.

'Then why did you ask me a question you already knew the answer to?' Shatima thought while drumming her fingers on the desktop and staring into Loretta's eyes while waiting for her to state her business.

"Well, I told them you could work a few evening-overnights at the nursing home. You'll be working 3pm-7am Monday, Tuesday, and Friday for the next two months or so."

Shatima looked at the yellow wall. Its bright hue was supposed to help people remain positive. They must have painted the wall that color in anticipation of hiring Loretta. "I wish you would have consulted me prior to altering my life. My primary position is to work here in the medical center as a receptionist, Monday through Friday, from 9 am until 5 pm. I have a 5-year-old son. While I do have reliable childcare during my working hours, your committing me to an alternative schedule may or may not have placed a burden on my caregiver. I also go to school Monday evening through Thursday evening. Our employer pays part of my tuition and requires a certain attendance percentage in order to continue doing so. Lastly, I know you don't expect me to work 24-hour shifts. That's not only illegal; it's physically impossible. Were you going to adjust my shift here to compensate this?"

Loretta glared at Shatima through icy blue eyes. "You need to call staffing and settle this. Mark my words. You *will face* disciplinary action if you refuse to take shifts in that nursing home." She stormed off to make someone else's life miserable.

Shatima's line rang when Loretta was out of sight. "Good morning. This is Shatima Thomas."

"Hey, Tima. It's Claudette," the chipper voice announced.

Even though Claudette was the gossip ringleader, she was one of the only people at that job who Shatima actually liked. She said she went to school with Shatima's father and talked about the big crush she had on his best friend. Hearing stories about her father at lunchtime was a source of comfort, no matter how many times Claudette told the same story.

"Hey, Claudette! What's the word this morning?"

"Slavery apparently," Claudette replied. "Do you know that bitch Loretta just came down here and signed you up to work 9 million hours of OT?"

"Yeah, she told me. I just told her to take it and shove it." Shatima paused. "I do need some new tires, though. And Jabez needs a new jacket for the fall and then a winter coat when the two weeks of Fall are over. And maybe I can finally get rid of this garnishment they put on my check for my childbirth bill."

"You gave birth five years ago. Why are you still paying for it?" Claudette wondered.

Shatima sighed instead of answering.

"I know. I know. It's not my business, and I haven't been able to help you get to the bottom of it like I said I would. It's just so strange that they use a separate collection agency for childbirth than they do everything else, and..." Claudette's voice trailed off. "There I go running my mouth again. What you want me to do about this overtime?"

"I need it. I can't do it without asking my babysitter first, though." After a few more pensive moments Shatima said, "Sign me up for Friday & Saturday for the next few weeks, starting next week. I'll see how tired I am and let you know if I want more."

"Bet. I'll see you at lunchtime."

Since it was going to be her last free Friday for a while, Shatima made sure to go to the grocery store before picking Jabez up from the sitter that night. She went to Costco and stocked up on snacks to send with the sitter after school. As usual, the elevator was out of service. Walking up the four flights of stairs in the high rise she lived in was a pain in her ass. When the boys on the stoop saw her coming with the first box, they dutifully ran to the car and helped her with the rest, telling her that Banger made them do it. She never saw them do it for the other women in the building. The gesture made her grateful. Skipping multiple trips up four flights of stairs was a relief.

Rahshaan's friend named Squeak sat on the stoop, barely moving while they carted the groceries upstairs. She always wondered how he got that nickname. Everything about him was so large - his fat face and pudgy nose especially. To Shatima, he looked like a dark brown ogre.

"Hey, sexy," he said to her. When she declined to respond to him, he grabbed her jacket. "I'm talking to you, girl. You got a hearing problem?"

Shatima snatched her sleeve from his grip and snarled at him. "I'm trying to get upstairs. Excuse me, please. Don't touch me again."

"Don't touch you?" The bulkiness of Squeak's voice made his nickname an even bigger contradiction. "Who the fuck you supposed to be?"

"Someone who asked you not to touch her. Now move so I can get these groceries upstairs."

She stormed up the stairs. That was just one of many endless unpleasant encounters she had with Squeak that made her wish that he would just disappear.

———

"I hate him!" Detective Kimborough declared to her partner,

Miguel Santarez, as she emerged from Chief Lyles' office. She marched ahead of her partner, her face ripening like a tomato.

"South Ridge isn't that bad of an assignment," Santarez said, strolling behind her. "It tends to get very interesting to the right person."

Kimborough slowed her walk and turned to her partner. "Oh yeah? How so?"

Santarez looked around for eavesdroppers and then pulled her toward his desk. He opened his top drawer. "It gets profitable if you play on the right team."

Kimborough's small green eyes grew wide and round at the sight of the envelope full of cash. There was enough in there to hire a divorce lawyer. "Whatever it is, I'm in!"

"Well, as you know, Emeritus Chief Jones is running out of time on his clock, and there is a criminal who can expose some information the chief wants to take to his grave. Montell Drayton faked his death years ago, and Chief Jones is paying top dollar to whoever can prove that he's still alive and bring him to justice."

Kimborough smacked on a piece of gum, smiling as she thought about all the cash. "You know, I heard a rumor about the old chief getting outsmarted by a scumbag years ago. I always had nothing but respect for Chief Jones. He's nothing like this new guy. I'll tell you what: if you can guarantee that I'll have that kind of residual income regularly, then I'm in."

Santarez smiled. A white woman with an innocent face was just what they needed on their team.

DISTANCE, DISTRACTIONS, &WHY DATING SUCKS

Sunday was Shatima's favorite day of the week. After church, she spent quality one-on-one time with Jabez. There were no distractions, just him telling her about his world. She listened to his every word. If there was a sign that someone was threatening to harm him, she didn't want to miss it. Seeing that poster of the new mayoral candidate rocked her. His return made her want to take Jabez and relocate, but where could she go? Her vanished family probably hated her. Even if they didn't, she had no money to get to them and imagined they were just as broke as her. She asked him questions about the people he saw at school, the people on the bus stop, and the people who came in and out of the babysitter's house. Today, however, Jabez wanted to talk about the animals he'd learned about in school instead. Shatima backed off her intense questioning when she realized she sounded like a lunatic for asking for so much detail from a child.

The two of them walked in royal blue and yellow Sanford University hoodies to the corner store to get snacks. They stopped and admired the mural on the side of the store and wondered about its artist. Shatima let Jabez get as much junk food as he wanted for the movie they planned to watch later that night. Jabez loaded his selections onto the counter. Shatima reached into her pocket to get money, but a long arm reached over her shoulder and handed the store owner five dollars. She rolled her eyes.

"Jabez, say thank you," she instructed him.

"Thank you," Jabez's tiny voice said and reached for the bag.

They went to the park. In just two days, the weather turned more brisk and Autumnal. Their feet crunched the leaves, which delighted the five year old. Halfway to their destination, Rahshaan fell in step with their quick pace. Shatima built a wall between the two of them.

"Why you acting like you ain't got nothing to say to me?" he demanded.

Shatima kept walking, so Rahshaan repeated himself.

"What do you want me to say to you?" she snapped.

"Say thank you for saving you from getting your ass beat."

Shatima guffawed. "You and me really don't know each other, because if we did, you'd know that I'm the last one who needs saving. You put your hands on women all the time? Am I supposed to be happy you're a woman beater?"

"It wasn't like that," Rahshaan protested. "I just put her in a little headlock. She was coming at you because of me."

"That happens a lot around here," Shatima retorted. "So why don't you find one of them and bother them? Let them know that I ain't no threat or no competition. And stay away from me. Every time you come around, there's drama. I'm good on that."

Rahsaan paused. His jaw tightened. He looked into her tight, unblinking eyes. "That's what you want, then I'm out."

"Good. Make sure you get the message out to your little friends so they don't have to make me late for work anymore." She watched him stomp off before continuing to the park. For a split second, she felt heartbroken. Then she shook off the feeling. Rahshaan was nobody to her except the man who flirted with her before work every morning. It was good to cut that out of her life. It sent the wrong message to her son.

At the park, Jabez found a friend and abandoned Shatima to play tag, so Shatima sat on a bench and watched them.

"Your son is so cute!" A white woman with fiery hair pulled into a French braid gushed as she sat down next to Shatima.

Shatima's skin began to crawl. She scooted away from her. "Why are you in the park watching kids if you don't have any out here, lady? You're creeping me out. Do you spend every Sunday in the hood watching black kids? I know you're not here for the scenery." She motioned toward all the playground equipment that had been vandalized over the years without being cleaned or replaced. Every election year some politician promised to do better by that park, and every year that promise was proven empty, just for votes.

"No, I actually spend every Sunday watching you. Every day, actually," the woman replied.

Shatima's eyes narrowed.

"I don't know if you remember me, but I'm Detective Shannon Kimborough. You came to the police station to press charges against the father of your son some years ago, and I'm the one who took the report."

Remembering how nasty the woman was to her back then, Shatima rolled her eyes. "Get away from me."

"You know, your mother told me you'd be apprehensive around me. She told me you've been afraid of law enforcement since you were a little girl," Detective Kimborough said.

Shatima's head jerked in the woman's direction. "My mother?"

Detective Kimborough nodded her head. "Your mother has been giving us tips having to do with the murder of your father. She seems to believe that you moved down here to get these same answers. These were his old stomping grounds, weren't they? I mean, back when this was Blueberry Hill. Before the fires."

Shatima kept staring at the woman, but offered no information. She was trying to wrap her head around her mother going to the police and mentioning her name.

"I see you with Banger every day, and I know the two of you are romantically involved. I also know that you know that those coveralls and riding down to that plant every morning is just a cover up for what's really going on. I know there's something really interesting going on in those factories, and I know that you can help me uncover it."

Shatima's heart raced. Her hands began to tremble. Before the woman could say another word, Shatima yelled for Jabez to come home.

"But, Mommy, it's not even dark yet," he whined.

"Come on, Jabez! It's time to go!"

As she cooked dinner that night, Shatima processed all Officer Kimborough said to her. She thought that after all those years, her mother would reach out to her to salvage their relationship. It was disgusting to her that she would put Shatima in the middle of something so serious. What if the police went from looking at her as bait to looking at her as an accomplice? Her mother was no stranger to using her daughter to get what she wanted. It was best, Shatima felt, that she didn't find out what her mother's latest scheme was. She was glad she and Rahshaan severed whatever ties they had.

And why was she being tied to Rahshaan anyway? It was bad enough that his little fan club was up in arms about him walking behind her to her car every morning. She passively rejected him since the day she moved into the Nat Turner Projects. Did she not have a say in whether or not they were together? She thought she lived her life in a way that made it clear that her only priorities were her son and finishing school. In less than a year, she was set to graduate with her Bachelor's degree.

As for the factories, she rarely thought about them. They were among the only employers in all of South Sanford that paid a decent living wage. There was a waiting list to even apply for employment with them, although the men in her neighborhood seemed to get hired there quickly. The news portrayed them as a good place to work. Everyone who worked there bragged about their good health insurance and hefty pensions.

There were some rumors from people who didn't work there about what went on in there. The stories always changed. Sometimes, it was a sweat shop. Other times, there were drugs being cooked and distributed there. A lot of people seemed to think there were strip clubs in the basements. No one had concrete proof. Shatima shook her head at them all. She hated the trouble that gossip caused. As the one person to stay away from it, why was she being sucked in the middle?

"Excuse me, Shatima? Can I talk to you for a minute?"

Tuesday evening, Shatima made her usual stop at the soda machine before heading to her Marketing lecture. She felt someone stop behind her and stare at her ass. Watching her bend over in scrubs to get that Mountain Dew was a favorite pastime of some of the male student population.

She stood up and turned around to see Tommy, a boy from her Statistics class. He was a couple of inches taller than her and okay to look at with his sparkling green eyes and smooth, caramel skin. His mouth seemed to never stop smiling. Conversations with him felt hollow. His biggest care in life seemed to be his Nike Uptowns getting scuffs on them.

"I don't really have time to talk. I have to get across the bridge to my Marketing lecture," she said in a dry voice.

"Then I'll be quick. I think you look good. I wanna take you out to dinner. On a date. Soon."

Shatima chuckled. "I don't have time to date; I have a son."

Tommy cringed at the mention of a child. When it looked like she was going to walk away, he quickly asked, "Please. Just think about going out with me tomorrow night since our class is canceled. Here's my number. Call me."

Shatima looked at the piece of paper he placed in her hand. "I probably won't call you, but thank you for the offer."

She mentioned the date to her babysitter anyway. Since the police were watching her, being seen with a man who wasn't from around there would be a good way of getting them away from her. Using Tommy was probably wrong. She hoped the sitter would say no.

Mother Charlene Glover or "G-Ma," as everybody called her, wasn't letting her get out of it. She met Shatima in church five years ago and thought she and her son were the sweetest little family. For years, the woman prayed a man would come into Shatima's life and love her. She felt Shatima deserved all the happiness in the world. According to G-Ma, happiness for Shatima included a loving man. She thought Jabez needed a father figure, and Shatima needed someone to help her raise him. To her, it seemed that Shatima's life was dedicated to raising the little boy. G-Ma would have loved to have seen a man put a smile on the young woman's face. She was too gorgeous to be wasting her twenties alone.

Looking around the woman's apartment always upset Shatima. Mentally, she called it The Land of Misfit Children. The woman practically ran an orphanage. It seemed that people dropped off the children they didn't want and rarely returned for them. If the Housing Authority ever found out how many people were there at any given time, they would evict her. The older kids didn't help clean, so the house always looked like a tornado ran through it until Shatima got there and helped her straighten up. G-Ma claimed to have a grandson who paid the bills and helped her get the kids ready for school every morning, but Shatima never saw him. G-Ma said it was because he worked a lot and didn't come home until late at night.

The sink was full of dishes, so that was where Shatima started. She pulled a chair out for the woman to sit and talk while she poured salt and water into a cast iron skillet and scrubbed it.

"Shatima, look at me," G-Ma said with a slightly sharp tone to her voice.

Since G-Ma was so much shorter than her, Shatima had to look down to look into the woman's brown face. Her dark brown eyes were accessorized with thick, gray lashes that fascinated Shatima. "Yes?"

"Shatima, are you a gay?" G-Ma asked. "It's okay if you are. I'm just curious."

For a second, Shatima's voice got caught in her throat. A thousand negative emotions passed through her. She got herself together before responding to G-Ma, but she was insulted. "No, ma'am. I am not gay."

"Then why are you so mean to these men around here? I watch you all the time, and you're rude. I know you're probably used to the attention. I've seen you stop rush hour traffic with that face and body of yours, but you act like it's a sin for anybody else to notice."

That got a chuckle from Shatima. "I'm mean because they're stupid. Do you hear the things they say to me? No woman should be okay with being approached the way I get approached."

The woman considered this for a minute. "How did the young man approach you at school?"

"He asked me on a dinner date. He told me he thought I looked good, and he said he wanted to take me out to dinner. That's the first time a man has kept it short and simple. Usually, they have to say something about my butt and how much they want to have sex with me. Or they tell me what I need to do in order for them to want to be with me." Shatima moved from the cast iron skillet and emptied the sink. She scrubbed the sink with bleach and poured baking soda and vinegar down the drain before filling it with clean, soapy water.

G-Ma laughed. "Well gee. No wonder you're so mean to the mens. I guess you ain't a gay; you just fed up." She let out another chuckle. "It's a woman that lives downstairs named Moosie. She gots lots of womens. *Moose! Th*at name just make her sound like a gay.

"Don't be like me, Shatima. Don't be an old lonely lady. The highlight of my week is you coming here to curl my hair on Saturdays. I had a husband once. Obviously, you can tell that from all these grands and great-grands I got running around here, but my husband hurt me, and I kicked him out and closed up. I'd almost cut any man who came sniffing around me, and that was a waste. I was a catch. Them hips you swing around here ain't nothing compared to the Coca Cola bottle I was back in my day. You see these big ole tits I got? They stood up straight until my oldest graduated high school. And ain't nobody but the doctor touched them since I left my ex-husband. Found out he had a couple families around the corner from where we stayed. I shouldn't've let him win. I should've lived my life. I was too worried about people calling me fast. His ass was the fast one." Her voice trailed off. Her eyes moistened.

"Go ahead out on that date. Have you some fun. Have dinner with somebody besides me and Jabez..." Her lips twisted into a sinister grin. "Of course, my grandson's gonna be jealous about you going out with somebody when you told him to stay away from you."

The plate Shatima was washing slipped out of her hands and back into the soapy water. In an effort to hold back a smile, she pursed her lips. "Why would your grandson care who I went out with? How would your grandson know who I am?"

G-Ma smirked. "He sure was sad that he didn't get to walk with you to your car this morning."

Shatima balled her face and frowned. "*Rahshaan* is your grandson? How did I not know this? You've been watching Jabez for all these years."

"Jabez knew," G-Ma said with a shrug. "He helps Jabez with his math homework on nights when I can't."

"I thought that was you all this time. I'll have to thank him for giving me one less thing to worry about when we get home at night," Shatima commented.

"Shatima, look. I know my grandson ain't worth shit," G-Ma

leveled with her. She got up from her chair and started wiping her counters.

Shatima giggled at the elderly woman's profanity.

G-Ma joined in because she knew her young friend wasn't expecting her to curse. "He really likes you, though. He's really guarded because his mama ain't shit, and ain't no excuse for her. I raised her myself, but one day she just left Rahshaan and his brother and never came back."

"What? Why would she?"

With a shrug of her shoulders she said, "I don't know. She just did. Rahshaan was a little older than Jabez, pushing his baby brother in a stroller, looking for someone to feed them because they were out of baby formula, and he was tired of eating dry noodles. And then his son's mama did him wrong and then took their son away, and he hasn't been able to track them down. So he's a little cold, but he means well. That's a lot to have to deal with, though, so I understand you wanting to go out with a... slower paced man. Go ahead and have fun on your date tomorrow. Don't be too mean."

Tommy was twenty-five minutes late picking Shatima up. Tardiness annoyed her. She had taken off her boots and was on her way upstairs to get Jabez when her phone rang.

"Shatima, I'm so sorry. I didn't know I had to sit in line at a bridge and answer police questions to get to you, and my GPS took me to this place that I don't think you live in. It looks like a project or something."

"I do live in the projects," Shatima snapped, her neck rolling with each syllable.

Tommy paused. "Well, I'm on some street called Ida B. Wells Court. You want me to come upstairs and get you?"

"No, I'll be downstairs in a minute." Shatima pulled her boots back on over her jeans and descended the stairs. The usual suspects stood on the stoop, staring at her and making comments about the way her jeans hugged her hips and ass. She wished she'd worn a longer jacket. Arms folded across her chest, she tapped her foot while waiting for him to pull in front of her high rise apartment building.

Minutes later, Tommy's champagne colored Toyota Camry came careening in front of her building. He barely stopped the car while honking the horn and motioning for her to hurry up. Shatima jumped in the car with the boys on the stoop staring at them.

"You should've told me that you lived in a neighborhood this bad," Tommy told her.

Shatima sucked her teeth. "Hello to you too," she said as she tugged the seatbelt over her. She glanced around the inside of the immaculately clean car. It smelled of citrus and leather. "Nice car. I almost bought one of these, but fell in love with my Maxima."

Tommy snorted. "Why would you buy a Maxima living in the projects? Shouldn't you take the money from your car payment and try to get into a better neighborhood?"

A groan erupted from Shatima's throat. Her eyes rolled to the back of her head. "Let me out the car."

"What? Why?" Tommy's eyes darted between the road and Shatima tugging on the passenger's side door handle. "Stop before you break something in my whip."

"Man, forget this car!" Shatima snapped. "You have made one too many insults about my neighborhood tonight. If you had a problem with dating someone from the projects, then you shouldn't have asked me out."

He took a breath and thought about how he could regain control of the situation. She looked so pretty with her long mane hanging down loose and free for once. Her makeup accented her strong bone structure perfectly. Tommy couldn't let her leave. "I'm sorry. I've just never been to this part of the county before, and I've never heard anything good about it. A lot of people get killed over here. It's on the news every morning. When you see an area portrayed in a certain way, you get certain ideas in your head about the people that could tolerate living there. I apologize if that's making me come off elitist. I just want better for you because you carry yourself better than that."

Her war with the door stopped as she listened to Tommy's words. There was something endearing about him admitting his fear. She set her attention on the scene outside of the window. There were people standing outside peered inside of the car as they passed by. All of their faces contorted into confusion when they recognized her.

After a while, Tommy relaxed. "So where do you want me to take you? Somewhere Italian? Probably somewhere French."

She thought for a minute and then said, "There's a place on Sundown Boulevard called Peter's Kitchen that I really like."

"Sundown Boulevard?" Tommy repeated, his tone dripping with disgust. "Why don't you let me take you out of South Ridge for tonight?"

"Tommy, I have a car. What makes you think I don't get out of South Ridge? I just really like this place's catfish. Since it's a weeknight, it probably won't be packed."

He shrugged his shoulders and obliged. During the drive, he tried to fill the ride with sweet talk. She tried to pay attention to what he was saying, but their conversation was forced. Inside of her head, she kept telling herself that this was a good thing. Going on this date with Tommy would get the police to stop looking at her. It might even get Rahshaan's hoes off her back. She gave up on the idea of it being fun. She could tell that Tommy thought himself superior because they were from different sides of town. It seemed his nose went higher in the air every time she answered one of his questions about what she did in her spare time and where she recently traveled. He kept telling her she carried herself a lot different than what her résumé said about her, whatever that was supposed to mean.

The restaurant's familial theme made it Shatima's favorite. Tommy went from acting stuck-up to strange when they entered. First, he complained that the wooden floors would scuff his white sneakers. Then, he grabbed a napkin from one of the tables and stooped to rub his footwear. After holding the door open for her and pulling out her chair, he insisted on sitting by the window so that he could watch his car. His Toyota Camry and its aluminum rims were completely safe, but Shatima didn't have the heart to tell him that no one wanted his car.

"Nah, I just read something where sometimes chicks will lure dudes down here to set them up to get robbed. I just found it weird that you wanted to stay down here. My money is long. You could've had anything you wanted, including Red Lobster."

With her menu held to her face, Shatima cackled into the laminated material. She snorted between laughs and then looked directly into the green eyes she suddenly suspected were contacts. That just made her laugh even harder. "Red Lobster?" she repeated. "You're a bird."

Tommy frowned. "Why would you call me that?"

"Because you've been turning your nose up at the hood every chance you got tonight, but you think Red Lobster is upscale. You are a pigeon. Do you see where we are? This is a family owned restaurant. Their history is displayed all over the walls and in these menus. Did you read any of the stories that they tell? No, because you're too busy showing how tacky your taste is."

For a moment, Tommy considered the menu. There was an announcement on the back welcoming the newest addition to the owners' family, a baby girl named Mercedes. He scoffed at the name and made a comment about how "Ghetto Blacks" always named their children after things they couldn't afford. Shatima ignored him and instead marveled at the bocote flooring and bamboo furniture that the menu boasted of being crafted by a member of the restaurant owner's family. She couldn't put her finger on it, but there was something about that restaurant that enamored her. The pictures on the wall showed a close-knit family that was also very proud of who they were. They bragged about their children's academic accomplishments. There was even a picture on the wall congratulating Aunt Darlene on a year of sobriety. Their family was what Shatima longed for her own son to have.

The atmosphere softened. The family theme made Shatima curious about Tommy's family. She asked him a few questions. He lightened up and told her about his life. He was an only child. Both of his parents worked for the city bus company. They owned a three-bedroom home in East Sanford. He never lived anywhere but in that house. They took a vacation to Disney World annually until he turned 18, and then they started going to Hawaii. He looked forward to taking a woman there with them that year.

"And I assume your father isn't in your life, since you live in the projects," Tommy said.

Just like that, the mood hardened again. At that point, Shatima just assumed he thought being an asshole was a talent.

"My father is dead," Shatima said.

"Oh. How did he die?" Tommy asked the question as though it were not at all impolite.

"I hope you choke on whatever you order." Shatima twisted her face into disgust at his presence.

Tension brewed between the two of them. They sat there glaring at each other. She grabbed her butter knife and wrapped her fist around it. She only saw a facial expression so bold when she was attacked. She wasn't going to let that happen to her on a date she didn't even want to be on in the first place. Tommy was the first to break the stare. He excused himself to go to the bathroom, taking a brush out of his pocket and vigorously brushing his hair all the way from the table to the mens' room door.

"Leave, girl," the waitress came by and whispered. "That nigga is lame, and you look ready to kill him."

Shatima took a swig of her sweet tea. "Not before I get him to pay for some of that bangin' catfish that y'all make."

As Tommy walked back to the table, Shatima's heart

dropped. This wasn't worth it. She found herself mentally picking him apart. He was a shallow person who couldn't dress worth a damn. A brief glance at his feet showed that the Jordans on his feet were fake. Fake eyes, fake rims, and fake sneakers, yet he had the nerve to make negative comments about where she lived. This was dating. It seemed that men thought she was supposed to flex to suit their tastes, even though they approached her. Here she sat with this man who interrupted her routine to ask for a chance to spend time with her, yet he wasn't even making it enjoyable. She was only there to prove to someone else that she wasn't mean. It was a confusing situation to be in. Shouldn't a man who wants to spend time with her be able to handle her meanness? Shouldn't he want to dig deeper and find out why she was so mean? It was only a first date, but she knew that Tommy could never be that. She wanted to end the date there. If only catfish wasn't on the line.

The trip to the bathroom seemed to brighten Tommy's attitude. He returned to the table and amused himself by staring at his reflection in one of the spoons. When he looked down at his glass, his attitude instantly soured again. His fingers raised and snapped. "Uh...Homegirl!"

The waitress cut her eyes at him. "You need something?"

"Yeah. I need the drink that I ordered," he snapped, holding his drink out to her. "That's grape soda. I ordered strawberry."

"You ordered grape. I wrote it down," the waitress argued. "I'll bring you strawberry though."

"It's too late now. You've already messed up my palette. Now I gotta order something that goes with grape. Just forget it."

Shatima snarled at him. "You ordered grape," she hissed. "And don't ever snap your fingers at someone who's handling your food. It's not smart."

For a split second, the staring contest returned. This time Shatima clenched her fists.

"If you're gonna be my girl, then you're gonna have to support me in everything I'm trying to do."

That sent Shatima into another cackling session.

"So I don't feel like we've gotten a chance to get to know each other," Tommy said when her cackles subsided. "So let me ask you a question: where's your son's father?"

"He's not here. Don't ever ask about him again. Don't ask about my son either. He's not your business." She shifted her body away from him.

"Oh, don't tell me you're one of those bitter shorties. You can't be mad about who you chose to have a baby with."

"I can be mad about whatever the fuck I want!" Shatima snapped.

"Well, be mad with yourself, and stop pushing us nice guys away with your stank attitude." He leaned back in his chair and placed his hands on his chest to emphasize that he was talking about him. "I'm a catch. You see the kind of car I drive. You see the way I dress. I'm in college, and I don't have any kids. You should really be happy that I gave you a chance. You come with a lot of baggage. I normally don't date project chicks and single mothers, but I'm bending the rules for you because you're so pretty to be so dark. That's a compliment. Say thank you." He paused as though he was really waiting for her to grovel at his feet. "You know why I gave you a chance? Because I recognize struggle. My mom makes me pay my own car insurance *and my* own phone bill. You know how hard it is to stick to this plan when I can only really talk on nights and weekends? And now that you're my girl, it's gonna be hard to stay off the phone with you."

"Tommy, we haven't said four sentences to each other without looking at each other like we wanted to fight each other this whole night. What could we possibly have to talk about on the phone?" Shatima cut her eyes at him while sipping her sweet tea. "And stop calling me your girl. This ain't that."

"This is what's wrong with Black women: I'm giving you a chance to do better, yet you're so hurt by the past that you don't recognize a good thing when he's sitting right across the table from you. I advised you to choose better. *I'm the* better. Let go of your baby daddy. So what if the child support is late this week? Think about how you'll get yourself into a better situation so that you don't need his money."

Ironically, Shatima often thought about getting herself into a better situation. She thought about being somewhere other than out with the most condescending jerk in the world.

"Look, I don't need you lecturing me about any part of my life. You don't know shit about me," she snapped, trying to keep her tone hushed.

"But look at your attitude," Tommy said again. "How can I want to get to know you when you don't even want to take advice from the male perspective?"

"How about you stop trying to give advice and move out of your mama's house?" Shatima argued.

Their food came. Tommy was temporarily distracted as he inspected his plate. "This ain't what I ordered," he said to the waitress.

"Yes, it is. This is what you ordered the third time you changed your order." The waitress slammed her pad down on the table as though she was waiting for that moment all night.

"Well, I'm changing my order again. Get in the kitchen and fix it. You want this tip, right? Then *serve me, server.*"

"You need to watch how the fuck you talkin' to me. I'm sick of this shit," the waitress snapped.

Shatima buried her face in her hands and started counting. She hoped that when she reached ten she would be at home in her bed. When she opened her eyes, the only thing that changed was that the waitress had backup. Three of them were screaming at Tommy while he dangled one dollar bills in front of their faces. Shatima wondered how dirty her jeans would get if she slid out of her chair, down to the floor, and crawled away. She wasn't leaving without her catfish, though, so she sat there and shoveled the perfectly seasoned goodness into her mouth while Tommy yelled about his rights to change his mind as often as he felt. She shifted her chair away from the table and turned her chair to the door.

Upon turning, she linked eyes with Rahshaan. He and Squeak were coming in from the cold wearing their coveralls. The glare in his eyes could have burned two layers of skin off of Shatima's face. His jaw tightened. For a minute, he remained in one spot as though he was waiting for an explanation. He and Squeak made their way over to the scene.

"So you told me you didn't want to see me because you out here dating lame as niggaz like this?" Rahshaan demanded. Flames shot from his eyes and feet.

"I don't have to explain myself to you," Shatima retorted.

Tommy looked from Rahshaan and Squeak hulking over him to Shatima's frowning face. He started laughing. "Oh! So I was right? You're setting me up to get robbed?" He yanked a gold watch from his wrist, but Shatima knew it was fake at first glance.

Shatima's head whipped hard and fast in Tommy's direction. She pointed one of her fingers at him, exposing a turquoise and silver nail. "You shut the hell up. You ain't got nothing worth stealing, not them fake Jordans on your feet, not that girly ass car, and not those tacky green contacts, so shut up about somebody robbing you." She glanced down at her catfish. Less than half of it was gone. Her heart sank. She'd never get to eat her catfish, and this would never stop being the worst date of her adult life. It was also the first date of her adult life, so she felt even worse.

This food could have been better as a takeout order along with a DVD from Blockbuster and Jabez by her side. When he went to bed, she could either go to sleep or watch one of those movies where a man came in and rescued a woman from her horrible life as a single woman. That story was told much better in the movies. Neither of the suitors standing before her were cut out for rescuing. Embarrassing scenes in public places? Yes. Making her feel as though she was some purchase they'd be writing a review on later? Absolutely. But rescuing her? They failed. Rahshaan was drama, and Tommy was more concerned with looking at himself in spoons than making himself interesting. Shatima never appreciated her single life more than she did at that moment, in between those two men.

She pushed in her chair. The white wooden piece of furniture was barely heard above all the yelling between Rahshaan, Squeak, and Tommy. Shatima put her jacket on and announced that she was ready to go home. She was sure that if they walked away, Rahshaan wouldn't do anything. Tommy continued arguing. Shatima tugged at his sleeve and instructed he take her home.

"You wanna go home so bad after setting me up to get robbed? Walk home then, *bitch!*"

He may as well have punched her in the face. That would have hurt less than being equated to a four-legged creature. By that time, the entire restaurant staff was standing in the dining room watching the scene. Regret tugged at her heart as she remembered being talked into this stupid outing because she was mean. Well, why shouldn't she be mean? The world certainly wasn't nice to her. She stood on the tiled floor, shifting her weight, trying to figure out where the night went wrong. Then she started fishing around in her purse. When she withdrew her hand, it was covered in a sock. In her fist she clenched a bar of soap. Eyes glazed with tears, she glared at Tommy as he and Rahshaan continued to trade threats. It was obvious that Rahshaan was stalling to give him a chance to walk away. Tommy kept testing him with empty threats. Off to the side stood Squeak, waiting for a sign from Rahshaan.

Tommy turned to Shatima. "Why the hell are you still here, bitch? I told you to walk home."

The soap was heavy in her hand. She drew back and punched Tommy in his jaw. When the soap connected, she heard and felt the crack. Tommy yelped in pain and dropped to his knees. Squeak and Rahshaan stood over him, staring. Shatima stormed out of the restaurant. It had been years since she had to resort to such tricks. She'd be damned if she spent another Tuesday like that. She started the trek down Sundown Blvd back to her apartment. It was unclear to her why there were tears in her eyes. She let them flow as she stormed home. Fuck Tommy and his superior attitude. Fuck Rahshaan and his coincidentally being present in every area of her life. Fuck Squeak because she just didn't like him. Fuck dating. Fuck everybody and everything.

———

"I thought you said you were sure she was dating Banger?" Santarez hissed at Kimborough as they sat in the back of the dark restaurant, waiting for their party.

"I was. Still am," Kimborough said quickly. She took a swig of her Miller Lite. "That guy she was with tonight was just a decoy."

"Didn't look like a decoy to me. Banger looked pretty upset that she was with him." Santarez took a swig of his own Heineken. "If she's not with him, then we have no way to prove that he's the one who took over after Mont died, *if Mo*nt really is dead."

"He isn't dead." A woman who resembled a chocolate Barbie doll stood over them, sounding sure of herself. "I can't stress enough to you that you have to get it out of your mind that Mont is dead. Montell Drayton is alive, and he owes myself and Chief Jones a sizable amount of money. Bring him to us, and we'll split it with you."

Santarez caught himself drooling over the curvaceous beauty. He stood up, helped her into the chair beside him, and introduced Kimborough to Hope Thomas.

"You know," she husked, her eyes full of lust as she locked eyes with Santarez and locked Kimborough out of the conversation, "the best part of fucking someone is knowing there's more than one way to go in."

"That's true," Santarez agreed, staring at the rise in her bosom.

Kimborough fake vomited. "So what do you suggest?" she asserted herself into the conversation when she tired of watching Santarez and Hope eye-fuck each other.

The goddess of a woman turned her attention toward Kimborough, annoyed that she insisted on being heard. "You're a woman." She frowned at the redhead's haggardly appearance. "See if you can doll yourself up and use some girl power to get the information we need."

NUT PUNCH

CHAPTER Three

Working overtime at the nursing home reminded Shatima why she no longer regularly worked as a CNA. One would think working overnight would afford the luxury of quiet studying time, but that proved to be a myth on the first night. Shatima was on her feet from the beginning of her shift until the end. It was demanding labor that did a number on her muscles and joints. The entire building smelled of soiled adult diapers and people whose hygiene depended on a short staff. She listened to the grumbles of her co-workers as they asked how people could leave their parents in a place like that. Shatima couldn't wait to put her mother in a place like that and leave her there.

Knowing her mother, Shatima would probably never get that opportunity. Some man somewhere would pay for her to retire on some private island.

She was exhausted when she got home. Jabez stood over her and whined about them not spending the weekend together. G-Ma came downstairs to get him to give Shatima a chance to rest and get her homework done. They ate pizza for dinner, an ungodly act in Shatima's house on a Sunday, and they spent the evening watching movies. Shatima was asleep by the opening credits. Jabez nestled himself on top of her, and they slept on the couch until the sun came up on Monday morning.

Come payday, it was time to reveal the fruits of her labor. She logged onto her account to see a copy of her paycheck. Her mouth dropped open. It took everything out of her to not throw her computer across the room.

"They took out more money in taxes and garnishments than I made in OT!" she exclaimed to no one in particular. She called to see how much more she had to pay on the hospital's bill from her childbirth. As usual, no one could give her an answer. Immediately, she told Claudette in staffing to cancel the rest of her overtime in the nursing home. Forever. She still needed extra money, though. There was no way around that. Getting a part time job at the mall would be just as pointless as working at the nursing home since she'd probably be forced to buy a uniform. She needed to be in control of her income.

"Why aren't you wearing your t-shirt?" Loretta came to the receptionists' desk and barked at Shatima. Loretta was wearing a sky blue t-shirt with the medical center's logo on it. She pulled her auburn hair into a ponytail as she fussed. Their male co-workers whispered about how fine Loretta's light eyes, skin, and hair made her. Even though she was a bitch to everyone, they were willing to overlook it for a black woman with those features. Shatima couldn't see past the evil to see what those men found so attractive.

Shatima looked the woman directly into her eyes. "Let me apologize to you for being out of uniform, Miss Loretta." She waited for the 'Miss' to sink to Loretta's dermal layer. The woman hated being called "Miss", even though Shatima did it out of respect for the woman's perceived age. It was hard to gage how old Loretta truly was, though the crow's feet around her eyes gave a hint. "I received an e-mail saying that the t-shirts would be issued to the staff today. May I be directed to where I am to retrieve mine?"

Loretta picked up a pile of t-shirts and tossed one in Shatima's general direction. It landed on top of Shatima's computer monitor. "I'm glad that you're in a sugary mood. Today is a very important day. My father— the emeritus chief of police— is moving into to our hospice facility today, and you are in charge of his admission. Try to look presentable."

That comment was laughable. Shatima always looked flawless at work. Not a hair on her head was out of place. Not a wrinkle was in her clothes. She went into one of the examination rooms to change from her scrub top to her t-shirt. The way Loretta announced Shatima was in charge of the admission was strange. Loretta's tone suggested that it was an honor to check some man into a place where he'd be spending his final days. She knew her boss was up to something.

When she returned to her desk, Loretta was still standing there. A smirk was on her thin lips. She and Shatima locked eyes. In Shatima's mind, Loretta had the eeriest pair of eyes she ever saw. She'd only seen eyes that freaky shade of blue on one other person, someone she wanted to forget.

"Today is going to be an interesting day. We're having Daisy's BBQ for lunch as a thank you from the Sanford County Police Department." Loretta skipped off to cause hell in another employee's life.

Shatima would rather choke than eat food provided by the police.

At 9 am, Shatima was summoned from her desk to the hospice building. She took her necessary supplies down to the lobby to meet the Emeritus Chief Jones and the rest of his family. Inside, she was shaking as she walked, though she wasn't sure why. The near-dead didn't make her nervous. A lot of times, they sent her to do the admissions simply because she was able to hold it together so well while talking to families who were preparing for their final goodbyes. Something else was wrong. The smirk on Loretta's face made her stomach turn.

The elevator doors opened, revealing that a camera crew was there to welcome the new admit. Loretta contorted her face into an expression that made her look constipated. It occurred to Shatima that Loretta was trying to smile. Evil made it nearly impossible for the corners of her mouth to turn upward.

"Hope! Hi! It's been too long!" Loretta ran to a chocolate-dipped Barbie doll wearing a tailored skirt suit, and they embraced.

"Hello, line sister!" Her teeth were as white as the string of pearls she wore around her neck.

Shatima stopped dead in her tracks. Directly in front of her was the woman whose voice woke her up every morning: Hope Thomas.

"Hello, Shatima," Hope said to her.

Her body turned to stone, Shatima did not reply.

Loretta looked from one woman to the other with the weird smile-like expression imprinted into her face. "Oh, you two know each other?"

"Shatima didn't tell you that she's my daughter? Well, I'm not surprised. She made me a grandmother way too soon and then just abandoned me." The flashy smile never left Hope's face.

"I never would have guessed in a thousand years that the two of you were related," Loretta gushed. "Shatima, you and I have to trade stories about Hope here. She was such a trip while we pledged."

The two women flitted around the room throwing up hand signs and letting out screeching noises. They spoke in high pitched tones about "that trippy thing she did in sophomore year" and squealed about how Shatima should have been there. A miniature invisible man squeezed at Shatima's brain and twisted it. Suddenly, the lights were too bright for her dark eyes. It made perfect sense that these two women knew each other and were friends. They were horrible people who sought to make her life hell.

A man came in and tapped Hope on her shoulder and whispered something in her ear. She sobered. Loretta followed her lead and straightened an imaginary wrinkle in her t-shirt.

Through one of the picture window frames, Shatima saw a police processional pulling in front of the entrance led by a limousine. It contradicted the story about the budget cuts the police department needed to make that Hope reported on that morning.

Hope looked over her shoulder and sneered. "Shatima, that hairstyle isn't newsworthy. You should have gone with a bang to hide your forehead."

Shatima snapped, "It's your forehead."

After the fiftieth police car was announced, an entourage of men in crisp navy blue suits and shiny black shoes exited the limo, walking in sync. Their backs were to the window as they helped someone out of the car. On cue, two police exited each car and stood saluting on either side. When Loretta prompted her, Shatima took a polished black wheelchair outside. Two men took it from her and pushed it over to the limo. She stood to the side and awaited the end of the unnecessary production. Her eyes stayed focused on the ground as she could feel herself being watched. Her tunnel vision was on the tiny man as she and someone from the entourage transferred him from the car to the chair.

Hope stood flashing the string of pearls she had as teeth, narrating the scene. Somehow her eyes were on the camera as well as on Shatima, judging her every move. Shatima wanted her mother to be curious about her, to know how she was doing after years of not seeing her. She wanted her mother to ask her about Jabez.

Hope's body was noticeably tipped away from her daughter as she dazzled the camera with her narrative. They were in the same space, yet there was a whole universe between them. A small tear went down the middle of Shatima's heart. With every second that her mother didn't hug her or call her baby or act interested in her wellbeing in general, the tear grew. By the time Hope's interview with the chief was over, Shatima's heart was in a million pieces.

Forcing herself to speak over the lump in her throat, Shatima let out a half cheery, "Welcome, Chief Jones. My name is Shatima, and I'll be checking you in," before she pushed his chair into the elevator.

Being in a space with that many police made the hairs at the nape of Shatima's neck stand on end. She stood shoulder to shoulder with Loretta and looked at the floor. The air felt very thin as they rode to what was known as the Penthouse Tomb. It was a running joke amongst the staff that the people who stayed there were treated like pharaohs and buried in their own personal tombs with their most prized possessions. Rich people came to die in that space surrounded by way too many luxuries.

"Where is my son?" Chief Jones seemed to wonder out of nowhere. His voice sounded like someone raked his vocal cords across a cheese grater after years of smoking five packs of cigarettes a day. It made Shatima's skin crawl.

Loretta was grandiose with her reply. "He's already upstairs making sure everything is to your exact specifications."

"*Now h*e decides to do this? I couldn't have a more useless offspring," Chief Jones remarked. "My last days are in the hands of an idiot."

Shatima's eyes bucked at the roughness of Chief Jones' statement. She pursed her lips. The elevator stopped. When the doors opened, Loretta held Shatima's wrist to prevent her from getting off before the entourage.

"Father, we just have one quick stop to make just to get you checked in, and then we'll leave you in the hands of our very capable care team," Loretta announced.

The tiny man grunted.

Shatima took the man's vitals and then opened a questionnaire. It was strange to her that the place was called a hospice. This man was still capable of walking, feeding himself, and making his end of life decisions, according to his paperwork. She guessed it was just another frivolous thing people spent their money one when they had too much of it.

"I have your forms here, and I just need you to sign some final paperwork," she told him. "One question, though. Your paperwork says that you're 6'4"."

"Yeah. So?" he snapped.

Shatima looked down at the top of his head. "You're not 6'4"," she replied.

"I was back in '98," he said to her.

She let that go, making a mental note to tell someone to correct that in their own time. She wanted to get out of the room with the tiny man and his entourage. They were all staring at her, and his frosty blue - almost white- eyes creeped her out. He looked so fragile. She couldn't believe that once upon a time he was responsible for keeping the city safe.

"Mont ain't dead like your daddy, is he?" The way he sat straight up and made direct contact with her when he asked that question jarred Shatima.

"Excuse me?"

One of the men in the entourage stepped forward and cleared his throat. "Chief Jones, are you getting tired?" He held up his hand in Shatima's direction, and tried to stifle an embarrassing smile while mouthing "Please don't mind him."

Chief Jones' stare lingered a bit longer. "I suppose I am," he said without removing his eyes from Shatima's face.

She stared back at him for a moment, trying to brush off the odd question that he asked. Everything about his posture said that he wanted an answer. Through the frosted glass, she could make out Loretta followed by a man coming toward the door.

"They're ready for you, Chief Jones. You are in my prayers," she lied and then pinched herself for telling the lie. She didn't want to think about this bizarre man ever again, let alone talk to God about him.

"Your son is in my prayers." What he said was barely a whisper, but she heard it. She stiffened. Before she responded, Loretta burst into the room as though she were on a high dosage of Amphetamines.

"Father, I can't wait for you to see your suite. It is divine!" Loretta reached for the handles of his wheelchair. She turned to a man who was coming behind her. "Tell him about his suite!"

"Father, your suite is what dreams are made of."

The man's coarse voice made Shatima's head jerk upward immediately. That voice made her blood boil. She knew of only one person who spoke as though he were reading a letter. Her hands went limp as she looked into the eyes of a man she swore she would kill if she ever had the chance. He winked at her.

"Looks like you were in pretty good hands here." A sinister grin was on the man's face. He winked at Shatima again. Her blood curdled. She gripped the pen she was holding.

"What are you talking about, Andrew? Go check the room again and make sure they got everything I asked for. I know your simple ass missed something."

It seemed to take them forever to pass Chief Jones off to the next person. As soon as the wheelchair and the entourage were out of sight, Shatima made a beeline for the staircase. She couldn't risk getting stuck in the elevator with that man. She didn't stop until she was back on her floor and in the ladies' room. Once she secured herself in a stall, she doubled over. Her chest closed. Every breath was a struggle to grasp. It got hot then cold then sweltering then freezing. She willed herself to get it together. Her mind told her to count the tiles on the floor around her. She repeated this until she was grounded. Then she went back to the front desk and busied herself coding medical bills until it was time for lunch.

Not even the smell of food relieved her. She felt nauseous and asked if she could go home. Loretta quickly denied her request with the smuggest smile on her face. She commanded everyone to meet in the conference room for lunch and to possibly be interviewed by the media.

"Tima, are you okay?" Claudette asked. She was convinced that Shatima would combust if she ate lunch by herself every day.

"You look pale. That bitch could've let you go home. You never call in."

Shatima asked Claudette to stay close to her. Claudette was glad to oblige. She doted on Shatima, making her a plate and forcing her to eat and drink before going to retrieve a cold cloth for her. In her absence, a shadow loomed over her.

"You don't look happy to see me, Baby Girl."

Shatima glared at the man wearing the same navy blue suit and shiny shoes that Chief Jones' entourage was wearing. She told him that he was lucky that she needed the job, because she would have killed him the moment she heard his voice earlier.

At that, Andrew just laughed. "You and I have a rich history. You wouldn't kill somebody who knows you as well as I, not where you make a living to support your son. Now, where is he anyway? What school does he attend? I need to lay eyes on him."

Not even a second passed between the end of Andrew's sentence and Shatima's fist forcefully connecting with Andrew's crotch. It took two security guards to pull her off of him. They ripped her from the conference room and through the office. The people were a blur except two distinct faces: Hope's and Loretta's. Both stood off in a corner with smug expressions on their faces. A strange feeling of betrayal washed over Shatima. It morphed into sadness. She wanted a hug. A longing to be comforted was replaced with a kick in the ass when she saw her mother motion to the camera man to get a picture of her being carried out.

Outside seemed colder than just a few hours ago. A consider-able wind blew around her as she was dragged to her car. One of the security guards surmised that charges probably wouldn't be pressed. The other disagreed, noting how Andrew was still grip-ping the table from the numerous nut punches Shatima deliv-ered. They laughed and made jokes about how he must have dicked Shatima down real good and then left her for her to react to him like that. The other guessed that he owed her child support. She was silent as they had their water cooler conversation. Her body went limp while they continued to carry her to her car.

"The cranberry Maxima, right? This is one sweet car. You keep it up pretty well for a woman."

The statement was carried off in the wind without being addressed.

Without keys, a purse, or a coat, Shatima stood shivering in the wind. She had no way to call anyone and no one to call. G-Ma didn't drive. Catching the bus wasn't an option. She'd have to walk home for miles in the cold. For the first time, she wished there would be someone at home to talk to about this. Days like this weren't meant to be kept to herself.

Minutes later, Claudette came out with Shatima's belongings in a small box and a plate of the barbecue Shatima refused to eat. Another of their coworkers stood behind her with eager eyes. They planned for Claudette to drive Shatima home and the other woman would follow them. It was a ploy to get the gossip on who this man was who made quiet Shatima react in such a way. Claudette was cool as a coworker, but at the moment she couldn't even remember the other woman's name. There wasn't a chance in the world Shatima was letting them into such an intimate part of her life. She sat in the car and composed herself before making the journey home.

Once again, she drove on autopilot and couldn't remember the questions that were asked or how she answered them when she got to the bridge.

"What's your name? Where do you work? Why are you entering South Ridge? Who do you know there? How long are you staying?"

"Shatima, you was on the news! What happened?"

G-Ma reached for Shatima's coat and tugged it off of her. She remarked about Shatima's frigid skin. The house was abnormally quiet. She was watching "her stories" before the kids came home from school. A tea kettle was on the stove.

"Come in and get some tea to calm your nerves. I'm glad you're here. I thought they was taking you to jail." When Shatima didn't move, G-Ma pulled her to the couch. "Everything is gonna be fine. Jabez is gonna come over here after school just like always so you can look for a job or take some more classes or do whatever it is that you need to do. Today, you're gonna go downstairs and take a nap until it's time to go to school. You're not gonna let this defeat you."

"What about money? What am I gonna do about money? I was so close to getting out of these projects, and now I gotta stay here."

G-Ma patted Shatima's leg. "Everything is gonna be all right. I ain't gonna give you no clichés about God. You know the God you serve. He'll fight that devil you attacked too."

"I don't think it works like that. I'm supposed to turn the other cheek."

G-Ma scoffed at Shatima's statement and went on a rant about the things White men put in the Bible when they didn't like the original text. As she poured tea, she pontificated on how the nonviolent parts of the Bible didn't match the chapters where people went to war over sand and sheep. She stirred honey in their tea cups and talked about how the parts of the Bible that told people who were being attacked were made up because a man who flipped tables over in a church, who said that he was the way, the truth, and the light, and the one who said follow him wouldn't tell people to lie down and be walked all over.

"And you don't have to tell me what he did. I know that man. I know him and his demon daddy. I'm sure he deserved every time you punched him in the balls. Hope he can never use them again."

A burden was lifted from Shatima's shoulders. Finally someone understood without digging into her personal business. She let out what was left in a half-hour's worth of sobs. Then she did exactly as she was instructed. She went down to her apartment, took a long soak, took a nap, and went to class. When she got home, she tried to sleep, but she tossed and turned violently. Giving up on the idea of sleep, she pulled a chair into Jabez's room and watched over him all night. Andrew Jones would have to kill her to get to him.

————

"Use some of that girl power..."

Hope's words mentally taunted Kimborough as she looked in the mirror. After birthing two children for an ungrateful man who cheated on her with her best friend, she felt like her "girl power" evaporated long ago. Nevertheless, she sat in her car, waiting for an opportunity. She felt silly when she looked in the mirror and saw how much makeup and hairspray it took to make her look somewhat enticing. She much preferred her blue uniform and hair pulled back into a bun, but Hope promised more money if she could get them an internal contact. After weeks of studying them, she knew who her victim would be. When she saw him walking down the street, she sat at attention.

"There's your boy," Santarez commented, noticing the hulking man coming down the street.

As he did every night, Squeak stopped and bought a bag of weed. Santarez and Kimborough hopped out and arrested him while the little boy who sold him the marijuana got away. They took him to the police station, booked him, and took him into an interrogation room.

"You kinda sexy," Squeak told Kimborough when she entered the room alone. "I be seeing you around the way. I know you seen me wink at you."

Kimborough was taken aback that a man that large would notice little old her. She tried to think of how Hope would respond to such a remark. "Sorry. I don't notice guys unless they're driving expensive cars, and you don't have a car at all. Not worth my time."

Squeak frowned. "Am I gonna get to speak to my lawyer or what?"

"Oh, am I not sexy anymore because I don't find men who walk attractive? That's too bad. I was hoping we could be friends..."

CHURCH SERMONS, TAX SEASON, AND FIRST KISSES

That Sunday, it felt as though Pastor Candle spoke directly to Shatima through his sermon. She sat between G-Ma and Jabez, clutching both of their hands and shouting amen every time he told her to lay down other people's crosses and rely on her own gifts and talents. Pastor Candle was never a fire and brimstone preacher. Usually, he was about teaching and making sure his congregation understood their duty as Christians in a black church. That day, however, he hollered about how Corporate America used black bodies and spat them back out into the belly of the beast when they got tired of them. He spoke about how he saw many of his congregation members put in compromising positions until their fight or flight kicked in. Briefly, he touched on how evil was raised into positions of power while the good ones were stuck working under demons for bosses.

"Now faith without works is dead. You can't keep going to that job you hate, thinking things are gonna get better. They know you hate your job, and they're only gonna make you hate it more. And they'll find a way to break you. That's when it's time to stand on your own. Stop hoping for that promotion and promote yourself. I know everybody can't own a business. If everybody owned businesses, who would buy from them? But you know what you can do. You know you can do it well. So why aren't you using the church for what it's for? Why aren't you linking up with people who can help you do what it is that you want to do? Every fourth Sunday, we get in that kitchen and eat good food, then the people who cook it go to jobs at the phone company with bosses that talk to them like garbage. You can do better. You deserve to get up, get out of your bed, and enjoy what you do with your day! What happened to unionizing and organizing for better working conditions? Your peace of mind don't matter no more?"

The sermon continued to fall on deaf ears with a few obligatory amens, but Shatima took the message for herself. She was making a list of everything that she was good at, everything she enjoyed doing, and everything she never wanted to do again.

"I know you all hate when I go back to my Black Panther days," Pastor Candle wrapped up his sermon. "I just want y'all to stop coming in here so weary from trying to earn a living every Sunday, especially since half of you don't make enough to afford a car to be able to get here. Not that Pastor minds driving the church van to come get you. If we run out of room, then the Lord will make a way for us to get another van, and He'll make a way for First Lady to get her license so she can help do some of the driving."

The congregation chuckled.

"But for real, church. I'm tired of these jobs harassing you, not paying you worth the harassment, and breaking you.

"And I'm gonna say this before I close, because I know I'm gonna be called out on it. I don't care either. Monday through Friday, I get up, and I go to my office, and I spend the first ten minutes of my appointments listening to my patients beg me to get an office on the other side of the bridge. They don't wanna answer the police's questions about why they're traveling over here and where they're going. I tell them to write a letter to they mayor, or put themselves in the shoes of the people who live on this side of the bridge. We answer those questions coming, going, walking down the street, leaving our houses, getting out of our cars to go into our houses."

The church went silent. Pastor looked around and said, "From the lack of response I'm getting, I guess I shouldn't propose we come together for another letter and email writing campaign about South Sanford's single point of entry. I'll dismiss us then. Y'all don't wanna get together and organize, then we ain't gotta do it. Just come to me and let me know when you're ready to act. You all need out of these abusive, oppressive jobs that you're working. God doesn't want that for you, and neither do I. Let's say a prayer for that shift."

It was as though an assignment had been given, due immediately. At home, Shatima sat at her desktop and got to work compiling a picture book and price lists. She made lists of things she needed, lists of things she wanted to do, and a plan to get these things done. At the end of the night, she was confident with starting a fledgling business as a hair stylist. She'd also make dinner plates, since she was sure that Pastor Candle was talking about her cooking during his sermon.

One thing that Shatima didn't fully prepare for was her environment. There was a rumored rule that proprietors in the projects paid Rahshaan and his boys a percentage of what they made. It was affectionately referred to as street tax. Shatima was done with giving anyone except Jabez any of the money she worked for. If Rahshaan or anyone else wanted her money they'd have to take it in blood.

For weeks, waking up wasn't the dreaded event that it normally was. People raved about the meals she sold and delivered during lunch hours and the way she did hair. The money that she made was enough to make her final car payment, so that was one less burden on her shoulders. It looked like Jabez's Christmas would be the best she was ever able to give him. She was so busy buying gifts and decorations that she didn't feel that normal holiday loneliness and longing for her family. These things combined with not having to make a dehumanizing commute lifted her spirits for the first time in a long time.

On a Thursday in November, a group of girls sat in Shatima's living room, looking through her hair book and selecting their styles for that night. There was a huge party going on at a club. They were trying to convince Shatima to come with them. Since shedding her antisocial disposition for the sake of her business, people found her charming. Sometimes, they even found her funny when she opened up enough to tell stories about the crazy things that happened at the medical complex. She still wasn't relaxed enough to consider any of them her friends, since they came in there and talked about each other terribly.

"Why you and Banger broke up?" the one sitting in her chair asked while Shatima wound a human hair track around her real hair, which was parted on the side and gelled into a tight bun at the top of her head.

The other two girls who were waiting to get their hair done perked for the gossip.

"He was never my boyfriend," Shatima said quietly.

"Then why does he walk you and your son to the bus stop every morning and you to your car?" the girl in her chair asked.

Shatima's insides heated. She shrugged in the mirror so that the girl could see her response in the reflection.

Her client smirked. "I heard he caught you out on a date with some lame nigga from East Sanford and beat his ass in a restaurant."

"That never happened," Shatima said. "*I p*unched the guy in his nuts and left. Well, maybe Rahshaan did beat him up after that. I don't know. I was gone. I haven't spoken to either one of them since then."

"Rahshaan," they chorused, teasing her about the way she slightly sang his name.

"*We d*on't get to call him by his real name," one of the other girls said. "I didn't even know that was his real name until you said it just now. That nigga was fixing your tires and buying you shit. You can admit y'all was together. It's cool. What you got in that pussy, though? I fucked that nigga twice, and all he did was give me some money to get my nails done."

"A banger is a gun. I'm not about to walk around calling a grown man 'gun.' Besides, we were never together," Shatima insisted, reserving her judgment. That girl's statement was a lot to digest.

"Girl, quit frontin'!" the third girl shrieked. "That nigga been walking around trying to fight every damn body ever since he saw you out. You ain't gonna sit here and tell me y'all ain't never did nothing."

Shatima kept a straight face and stood in her denial.

Her clients invited her out with them again, but she didn't feel partying was appropriate with her being a mother. This didn't translate well with the ladies.

"We got kids, and we still party," one of them snapped.

Shatima shrugged. "That's cool. That's just not what I do." She held up a hand mirror for the woman whose hair she'd just finished styling. She spun the girl around so that she could see the back.

Not picking up on the shift in the atmosphere, she motioned for her next client to come sit in her chair.

"So you take our money to do our hair every weekend, but you think you're better than us because we party instead of sitting up under our kids?" the girl in the chair interrogated her.

There was a silence in which the girls stared at her in anticipation of her answer while Shatima tried to figure out how they got to such a negative space. Often people called her on her snobbish ways. Though she denied having any, she tried to consider how other people viewed her. She wasn't much of a talker. Whenever she spoke, she left people with the impression that she was arrogant. Was it the words that she said or the people to whom she said them?

"I don't have a feeling about what you do with your weekends or your kids," was the best answer she could give. It was a lie.

She frowned on them for leaving their kids with their parents every weekend. Another part of her felt jealous that they didn't feel the anxiety she did when she left Jabez. They didn't let the news of kidnappings get in the way of having a good time.

"You know what? I don't like my hair. Let me call Ayana. She does it better than this. This looks like a bad wig."

The other girls agreed.

"It looks exactly like the picture you brought me," Shatima protested, visibly offended that they had anything bad to say about her sculptured and molded ponytail.

"Let's go y'all."

"Where you going? I gotta get paid for doing your hair. You and me both know you owe me some money." She watched their body language. One of them reached in her purse. Shatima reached in her comb drawer quicker and drew her gun. She hoped she didn't have to use the tiny Dillinger, but she knew the day would come. Sooner or later, she knew someone was going to try to hustle her. She wasn't going to let anyone push her back into job searching or being broke. Never working for another Loretta again was something for which she was willing to risk it all.

Jabez was in his room with the door closed, watching a Disney movie. With the gun pointed to the girl's abdomen, Shatima stared at her intended target and prayed that she didn't have to break her child's innocence. The showdown was brief. They had razors and knives. She had a gun. She was paid.

"That's okay. You can take this money, because once we tell Banger that you out here getting money on his block and he ain't getting his cut, you gonna feel real stupid...*if he* don't kill your ass," the girl with the sculptured and molded ponytail said as Shatima backed them out of her apartment. She locked the door behind them and then locked the gun in the drawer with her combs.

After performing her first shakedown, she sat and worried for the rest of the night into the morning. Hopefully, the code of the streets would protect her from being snitched on to Housing Authority. No one wanted to be the cause of an impromptu, complex wide inspection for weapons. Her real worry was Rahshaan. Suddenly she wished she'd listened to the rumors about him being a murderer and an extortionist. Her hands shook while she cooked, wondering when he'd catch her and what he'd do when he did.

When all of Thursday night and Friday passed without incident, Shatima tried to convince herself that the street tax was just another rumor. Still, she needed to do something to bring down her anxiety. There was one method that she hadn't tried in years. After judging the women for going out to the club, she hated what she was about to do, but she needed to do something to cease her shaking body and her trembling heart. She took Jabez upstairs to G-Ma's house. She fibbed and whispered that she was going to the liquor store to get some wine and didn't want him in there. G-Ma told her that she owed no explanations and told her to take her time coming back. Her presence in the evening darkness surprised the boys on the stoop. They spoke to her and out of concern asked her if she needed anything. She whispered her request. They told her that they couldn't sell her anything without Rahshaan's permission. She looked at them like they were either crazy or liars. Who ever heard of a hustler needing permission to push drugs, especially something as petty as weed?

"Thanks for nothing, y'all," she grumbled.

The smallest one in the bunch, Meechie, spoke up. "Don't be mad at us, Miss Tima. We love you. It's just rules to this shit, you know?"

Meechie was about eleven but had the mouth of a forty year old sailor. Something about him also tugged at Shatima's heart. "What did I tell you about the way you speak to adults, Meechie?" she asked.

"My bad, Miss Tima." He covered his mouth.

"Come up to my apartment before the weekend is over so

that I can cut your hair before you go to school on Monday. I bought you a heavier coat, too. Come and get it if you're gonna be standing out here all weekend." Shatima gave the preteen a slight smile and patted his back before going down the street to get a Dutch anyway. Somebody was going to sell her something.

Despite the cold, she stopped to admire the mural on the side of the store as always. It was too beautiful. Someone put his or her heart and soul into it, and she didn't want the work to be in vain.

"Yo why you always be so fascinated with that picture every time you walk by it?"

Shatima turned to see Rahshaan and Squeak behind her. She bristled and then muttered a dry hello.

"Who that Dutch you just bought for? Your little pretty-boy boyfriend?" Squeak questioned her.

"Not that it's your business, but, number one, I do not have a boyfriend, and, number two, I was tryna cop something from the stoop, but everybody said I needed a permission slip signed," she snapped, sizing up Rahshaan. She turned her attention back to the mural.

"You smoke?" Rahshaan asked in a low voice, surprised.

"I haven't since my brother was alive, but tonight, I'm stressed about some things, so I needed to do something to clear my mind." She stared right into the eyes of the younger man the mural featured.

Rahshaan followed her line of vision and spoke over a lump that was forming in his drying throat. "Yo. Who is your brother?"

Just as he feared, she pointed toward the younger man in the mural. "That man right there. Second greatest man to ever live, only following that one." She pointed to the older one. "My daddy."

Rahshaan and Squeak looked at each other and then back at the back of her head.

"She lying," Squeak accused her, sucking his teeth.

She spun around and glared at him. "You've said a lot of fucked up things to me since I've lived down here, but don't ever say no shit like that to me again. I'll kill you and won't give two fucks about it."

"Yo who the fuck you talking to?" Squeak demanded, starting to lunge toward her. She rocked backward and threw her clenched fists into a fighting stance.

Before she swung, Rahshaan stepped between them and told them both to chill. He told Squeak to go home and that he would get up with him later. Squeak stormed away. Rahshaan stepped beside her.

"Was your bedroom turquoise when you were little?" he asked.

Her eyes widened as far as her tight, tiny lids would allow. "At my daddy's house, yes. How did you know?"

"You're the pretty girl from the pictures," he concluded.

"What are you talking about?" she asked.

He looked from the mural to her. "I've been wondering why you always stop and stare at this every time you pass it."

People passed by him and spoke, but he ignored them. He was still wrapped up in her.

"I used to live with your pops sometimes. Rize was like my brother. All of his brothers really, but Rize was my best friend." He stepped closer to her. "I helped paint your room that color. It was on the top floor, right next to Chillz's and Selena's. I had a bedroom in the basement, right next to Rize's."

She stared at him but couldn't remember his face having a place in her past. Thoughts of her brother came to her. "Wait. You were locked up. My brother was very sad about one of his friends going to jail on false charges and used to talk about it all the time. Your nickname is Banger, but Rize used to call you something else..." She looked toward the sky as though the answer was written in the stars. After several seconds, it came to her. She gasped. "*You're 'Sh*aan'? Wow!"

Over and over again, Rahshaan shook his head. "Yo, Shorty,

you like the princess of this hood or some shit. You're ghetto royalty. How did I not recognize you?"

"How would you recognize me? I only went over there, like, three times the whole time he was alive, and the last time was when he got killed. Outside of my immediate family, I don't remember anyone who was there that day," she said sadly.

"Chillz had your pictures all over the place. He used to keep one on his desk in his furniture store and show it off to everybody who came in." He looked at the mural again and looked at her smiling. He never noticed that she had their dimples, but it was glaringly obvious once he did see it. "Where you was going after you got your bag?" he asked her.

"Back to your grandmother's house to get my son. Oh and the liquor store. I lied and told her I was getting some wine because I didn't want her to think I was a hoodrat for what I was really going to get. I don't know what I'm gonna buy. I don't even drink."

Rahshaan chuckled at that. His eyes sparkled when he looked at her. Finally his fascination with her made more sense. She was gorgeous, but he always wondered what it was about her that made him interested beyond the surface.

"Can I chill with you?" he asked.

For once she smiled and said, "Okay." Then she added, "But only if I can call you Shaan."

He smiled back at her. "Of course."

The boys on the stoop all held bewildered expressions when the two of them walked through the door together, close, hands almost touching. Together they walked upstairs to get Jabez, but he told her he would be down later. About half an hour later after Jabez went to sleep, he returned. Upon entering he smelled the food she had cooking and complimented her on it.

"You selling them tonight?" he asked.

Her insides were jolted by his question. She forgot about the street tax rumors. They were the reason why she wanted to smoke in the first place.

"Nah," she said slowly.

"Why you lying?" he asked. "I saw you taking them out earlier. It's cool. Get money."

Cautiously she looked at him. "You ain't come over here to take your cut?"

"Take my cut?" he let out an obnoxious laugh. "What you talking about?"

"Streets talk. I don't normally listen unless it comes to my money," she said. "I got a son to take care of. Ain't nobody taking nothing out of his mouth."

He nodded. "I agree. That shit you talking about is for something else, not you. I like what you're doing." He reached his hand out. "Lemme get that Dutch."

She took it out of the bag and handed it to him. She watched him take a pound of weed from his pocket. He took some from the bag and put the rest on the table. "You didn't have to-"

"Shit. For Chillz's daughter? Yes in the fuck I did. This is the least of what you're owed," he said.

"What I'm owed?" she repeated, confused.

"You're supposed to be set for life," he told her.

She shrugged. "Life don't always work out the way it's supposed to. Nobody knows that better than I do. Trust me." She looked at his head and frowned. "Rahshaan, why do you always walk around looking like that? Can I please braid your hair?"

He felt the top of his head where an afro struggled to form.

"You look unloved," she told him. She'd been wanting to get her hands in his head for years but was too shy to offer.

"Yeah. You could twist my shit up."

She led him over to her styling chair. His hair smelled of the same Brazilian nut shampoo that his grandmother used. Despite being so tangled, it was surprisingly soft. She bent his head forward and noticed a scar on the back of his neck. Not realizing how invasive her action was, she traced it with her finger. She wasn't even sure why she did it. He tensed, turned around, and grabbed her finger. She apologized.

"Why would someone do that to you?" she wondered, even though she had an idea in her head about some scorned woman.

"My baby mama got mad at me and threw a pot of spaghetti at the back of my head," he explained.

Shatima poked out her lip. "I'm sorry I asked." She was more sorry about bringing up the mother of a child he didn't get to see, but she didn't let on that she knew about that.

Within twenty minutes, she had his long, thick hair braided into a complicated style. When she handed him the mirror, he was impressed with his reflection.

"You know who you braid like? Chillz's sister Lynn." He continued to admire her work on his head.

"That's who taught me. You really do know my whole family," she remarked.

He handed the mirror back to her. "Yeah. I used to have a room at Lynn's crib too. A whole bunch of your family took me in when my mom..."

She didn't want him to know that his grandmother told her a little bit of his business, so she just let his voice trail off. "So you and me? We're related or something?" she asked.

"Hell nah!" he said, quicker than he intended. "Not by blood. Chillz's best friend was my uncle, and we just always called each other family."

Shatima opened the drawer and replaced the comb, eyeing him, trying to remember, "Uncle...Mont? My godfather?"

"Yup."

"Small world," she remarked.

Rahshaan glanced inside of the drawer she was closing and took note of the cold steel hidden among the combs and brushes. Quickly she slammed it shut and locked it.

"Mind your business," she told him.

He reclined in the chair. "Yeah. You're definitely Chillz's daughter."

While she tended to the food on the stove, he wandered into her living room and looked at the pictures. Most were of her and Jabez, but there were two placed between the glass panels of her coffee table that caught his attention. One was the program from Chillz's and her godfather's funerals that she had blown up to portrait size. The other was a picture of her and Rize. Instinctively he reached out to touch them but caught himself before getting fingerprints on her glass. Everything in her apartment was so pristine and arranged as though she had a television show on the Style Network. Her hardwood floors looked as new as the day she moved in, and her cream microfiber furniture had no stains. Jabez's books, toys, and educational games were woven in with her movie collection and books in a way that declared that was their family, and you couldn't take one without the other. He loved it.

Citing that she was breaking two of her cardinal rules, she told him to bring the blunt into her bedroom. No food was to be eaten in the bedroom, and no men were to cross her bedroom threshold. From a shelf in her closet, she got towels and started stuffing the crack under the door with them. He eyed her strangely and asked what she was doing.

"I don't want my son to smell the smoke. He thinks I'm an angel. I want to keep it that way."

Briefly, they debated over whether or not she could prevent the smell from escaping her room. After the towels stuffed the space between the door and the floor, she invited him to sit next to her on her bed.

They started the routine of puffing and passing. During Rahshaan's turn to pass he went on and on about Shatima's status in the hood. She never should have been working at the medical complex, selling dinners, or doing hair. Although she insisted that she loved cooking and doing hair, Rahshaan constantly reminded her that anything she wanted to do should have been on a larger scale. She admitted that the only reason she lived in the Nat Turner projects was because she knew that she would be able to reconnect with the father she barely had the chance to know. Rahshaan looked around the room and remarked that her paintings were supposed to be originals, not prints.

As the weed took over, they set aside the conversation about what was supposed to be. The anxiety that plagued Shatima over the last two days went away. She forgot about her rules and instead gave into the feeling of enjoying sharing space with a man. Rahshaan was fun to talk to. The mixture of his skin and whatever soap he used crept up her nostrils and made them never want anything but that scent in them again. She inched closer to him. Somehow the moving closer to him landed her head on his chest with her body resting in the crook of his arm. It was everything she longed for a few weeks prior.

Suddenly, Rahshaan rolled away from her and yanked his arm from under her body. The softness of her skin under her t-shirt, the smell of essential oils in her hair and cocoa butter on her skin put him under a trance. His fingers got way too comfortable running through her hair that was in a mass of kinks and coils on top of her head. She reached for him, grabbing a large, veiny forearm. With all the strength she had, she locked her arms into his.

"Please stay with me."

Her voice crooned a ballad, luring him back. It scared him that she held his attention without disrobing. He wanted to learn everything there was to know about her. Reluctantly, he slid out of his Timbs and climbed back into the bed.

"Why haven't you been going to work?" he asked out of nowhere.

She shrugged her shoulders. "Got fired. It's all good though. I didn't feel like working for anyone anymore anyway." She took a long puff of the L and exhaled for twice as long. She stared at the ceiling and willed away visions of Loretta and her awful last day.

"G-Ma showed me a story in the newspaper and a story on the news. You were in both of them."

"One thing I can't stand is for people to ask questions they already know the answer to." She positioned herself to make eye contact with him once again. His face held no judgment, no amusement. Slight curiosity lived there. "I draw the line at being sexually inappropriate," she muttered quickly. It wasn't a complete lie, but she didn't want to get too deep and blow their highs.

Rahshaan took the blunt from her. The room was filled with smoke. They both were coughing violently. "What's gonna happen after tonight? You gonna go back to acting like you don't know me?"

"I need to," she confessed. "The police have been watching you and trying to use me to get to you. I don't want to, though. I want you to get me back in touch with whoever you can from my family. Do you know if any of my aunts are still here?"

"Your Aunt Lynn is. She has a beauty shop. I'm gonna take you to see Unc first."

"Uncle Mont?" she guessed. "My godfather? He's still here? I thought he was-"

"A lot of your fam is still around. Chillz's death made them clear out for a little bit, but most of them couldn't stay away." Over and over he marveled about her being the "princess of the hood."

All her life, Shatima wondered what her father did so wrong to make her mother keep him away. Hope didn't do a good job of hiding Chillz's financial efforts. She left stubs from his money orders lying around. On birthdays and at Christmas, the boxes that held his gifts were always in the trash with the return address labels showing. In Shatima's older years, she wondered if her mother left those things lying around to taunt her. She could count on one hand the times she was able to spend with him. The weekends with him were her fondest childhood memories.

Thanksgiving when she was 9 was the last time Hope let Shatima visit her father. He pressed his luck by requesting to have her for the entire school break. If Hope agreed, then he was going to negotiate regular visits with his daughter. Gradually, he planned to work his way to shared custody. He knew that Hope would cooperate if he agreed to fuck her every time he took his daughter, but sex in exchange for visitation was asinine to him. He was in a serious relationship for the first time since he and Hope split, and he wasn't willing to compromise it for his ex. When he dropped Shatima off, he tried to level with Hope. In response to his request for a serious conversation with her, she made him speak to her through the screen door. Reminiscent of his time in jail, the barrier between the two of them incensed him.

Nevertheless, he played her game. Chillz presented his case through the door. He wanted their child to have both of her parents in her life. Shatima chimed in, begging to be able to go to her daddy's house on the weekends. He had a large family, whereas she was the only child on Hope's side. With Chillz, Shatima got to enjoy herself more. She had brothers and cousins to play with. Hope's mani-pedi and shopping weekends were a treat, but Hope simply did not know what to do with a child.

Hope tossed her head full of huge, wavy curls from one side of her head to the other, a sign that she was trying to seduce someone. For the first time, she noticed there was a woman sitting in the car, a beautiful woman with cinnamon skin who sat staring eagerly. Hope snarled. Her body stiffened. Chillz didn't fumble his words when he explained that he was in a serious relationship with the woman sitting in the car. Her name was Selena, and Shatima took a liking to her.

At first, Hope declined his request, citing that she didn't think he could be a good father to their daughter if he wasn't good to the mother. Chillz refused to discuss or argue about why they weren't together. The only thing he wanted out of this discussion was to be in his daughter's life full time. Shatima emphasized how much she wanted to be with Daddy and Selena, which sent Hope into a rage. The third time Shatima said something about "Daddy and Selena," Hope lost it. Her backhand flew into the child's mouth, causing her to fall backward and scream in agony. Hope didn't stop hitting the child on the cold porch floor. Chillz ripped the screen door off the hinges to rescue his daughter. Selena flew from the car to the door to help.

A neighbor called the police and reported a break in. When they arrived, they wouldn't even listen to Chillz's and Selena's side of the story. They recognized Hope Thomas from the news. Shatima was wailing too hard for her side to be understood.

After that, Chillz backed off. Selena told him a thousand times that she would disappear from the picture if it meant that he could have his daughter in his life. He refused to let Hope manipulate him any further. Shatima saw the court petitions where he asked for custody, but after the confusion from that horrible night, no judge in the world would grant him visitation. Hope placed a restraining order against him. When it expired, she threatened Chillz's family's lives with her police connections. He never stopped trying to be a part of his daughter's life, and Hope never stopped using her daughter to torture Chillz. She wanted every single day that he woke up to serve as a reminder that he chose someone else.

Selena met with Hope "as a woman," and told her that she would remove herself from the picture if it meant Chillz could be in Shatima's life. Hope in turn filed a restraining order against Selena. That didn't stop Selena. She took risks by riding around the neighborhood and catching glimpses of Shatima when she was walking home from school. When she figured out that Shatima was a latchkey kid, she took little gifts to her and let her know that her father loved her very much and wouldn't give up trying to see her. This went on well into Shatima's high school years.

As Shatima got older, it became easier to hide the gifts. After a while, she got wise enough to use Hope's vanity against her. She told Hope she was just like her and had a couple of boyfriends with some money who were tricking off to her. Hope beamed with pride that her daughter picked up her ways. Curiosity got the best of her, though. She hoped her daughter wasn't spending time with ugly boys. One day she drove along the route that Shatima walked home to spy on her. A red Q45 stopped at the corner. A brown skinned boy got out of the car and gave her a hug. Hope noted how tall and cute he was and wondered if his daddy was single. When he smiled, she realized she knew his daddy already. That was Chillz's youngest son, Rize. All of Chillz's children had the same dimple-filled smile.

It took all of three seconds for Hope to leap from her car to in between

Rize and Shatima, destroying their embrace. Selena leapt out of the car and got ready to knock Hope out the way she wanted to for years, but Rize turned around and pulled her away. He wanted nothing more than his mother to lay Hope out in the middle of the street, but Hope had police connections that could get Selena put away for a very long time. Shatima waved them off, giving them a look that said, "I got this."

"Get in the car, Shatima!" Hope barked. Shatima refused. Hope commanded her again. Shatima ignored her and ran to the house to start packing her things. Hope sped in her car to the house and locked Shatima out.

"You can keep everything in that house. I'm never coming back here again. My daddy and Selena will buy me more stuff, better stuff!"

Hearing "my daddy and Selena" triggered Hope just like it did back when Shatima was 9. Hearing that again, six years later, brought back that same blood boiling rage. She ran outside and charged her daughter in the front yard. This time, Shatima was ready for her abuser. They tussled until Shatima got the better of Hope. She remembered Hope's slap from six years ago and was waiting for the right time for her revenge. The time came at that moment, and she promised this time Hope would be the one left wailing. Hope was too prissy to be a fighter. Her daughter seemed to have inherited her father's strength. Hope was left on the grass wailing after her daughter. Her daughter, though, was off to the bus stop. She was going to be where her heart belonged.

Rize and Selena were pacing around on the living room carpet, explaining to Chillz what transpired. Chillz was angry with both of them. His concern was Shatima's safety. He was convinced Hope was going to beat her again. For several hours, he paced around the house to psych himself up to spend another night in jail. He got ready to drive from South Sanford to East Sanford to save his daughter. The surprise of his life was received when the doorbell rang, and his daughter was standing in the doorway. Every prayer he ever prayed was answered. They embraced long enough to compensate for all the years they missed.

"Can I stay here with you?" she asked. She gave them the rundown of what happened after Selena and Rize left.

"Y'all could've at least doubled back for me instead of me having to catch the bus," she half-joked.

They quickly showed her to the room they set up for her. Chillz always knew the day would come when his daughter would be with him, so he made sure she had a place in his home. She was delighted that he remembered her favorite color was turquoise. Her bedroom at Hope's house was pink, and she hated it. Everything in the room was either turquoise or silver, and her closets and drawers were full of clothes and shoes. Selena promised her they would get whatever else she needed or wanted the next day. Selena quickly told her to pick something out and get dressed. They were going to a fish fry.

Before the fish fry, they stopped at a beauty shop on Sundown Blvd. Four women with dimple-laced smiles manned styling chairs. The heavier of the four was the first to speak.

"Selena, don't come in here nagging us. We on our last clients, and we ain't gonna leave you shopping for the fish fry by yourself this week."

"That's a lie, and the truth ain't in it, Lynn," Selena shot back. "I didn't come here to stress you out. Look who I have with me."

All four heads turned toward the door. Immediately, they abandoned their posts and their curling irons and ran to their niece. Lynn was the first to reach Shatima, and held her against her bosom. Next was Adrianne, then Lisa, then Renee. To Shatima, the four of them looked like a glamorous R&B group. Even dressed in boot cut jeans and smocks, they were stunning to her. The sisters were overjoyed at the news that their niece broke free from her mother. They wanted to take care of her mother the street way, but they respected their brother's wishes. For the next hour or so, Shatima busied herself in the shop, watching her aunts style hair, sweeping floors, and helping out wherever she was needed. The whole time that she worked and got her hair done, Lynn told her that the shop would one day be hers.

They rode to the huge house belonging to a woman named Big Grams. That she knew of, the woman was of no real relation to Shatima; she was her godfather's grandmother. It was strange that she felt more comfortable in this woman's house than in her own. The feelings of belonging, family, community, and home all returned to Shatima that night at the fish fry.

She stood in the kitchen and helped dredge catfish and haddock. Rize taught her how to play Spades at one of the many card tables set up in the living room. The DJ played all of her jams. She was the life of the party, popping to Luke and wining to reggae.

Eventually, Rize pulled her away to get reconnected with her brothers. He led her up to the attic where Shameik, the oldest, was breaking down weed. Rico was emptying the guts of a Dutch. Nyir wordlessly patted the seat next to him, inviting her to sit next to him. Rize told her they were going to have a cipher. Everything after she took her first toke was a blur.

In the morning, she woke up in her room in Chillz's house. The turquoise room embraced her, made her feel more welcome than the pink one she normally woke up in. She was starving. Selena was downstairs pouring cereal. She gave a half-smile when Shatima came downstairs. The phone rang. Selena seemed reluctant to answer. She picked up the phone, screamed something in Spanish into the receiver, and then slammed the phone onto its cradle. The cereal went soggy as she paced around the house. Shatima urged Selena to sit.

"Chillz got up very early this morning to see if he could find a certain preacher so that he and I could get married today," she explained. "We didn't want to do it unless you were here, so now that we're here we want to do it immediately. Just in case..."

"Just in case what? I'll go to the court to get emancipated or whatever I have to do to make sure I can stay here. I'm not going back to Hope's house. I want to find a way to tell a judge or somebody what really happened that day, when...you know." Shatima visibly shook at the idea of having to be away from her family again.

Selena patted Shatima's hand, told her that they could worry about that on Monday. The current dilemma was finding where Chillz went and finding dresses for their day.

"If you know where he went, then why do you seem so worried?" Shatima wondered.

"Because your mother called this morning. I don't even know how she got our number; it's private. She made some threats."

Shatima hooked her arm in Selena's. "We're not going to worry about her today. Today, we're gonna get you and my daddy married." She beamed at the beautiful woman and asked her how she wanted to wear her hair.

The phone rang. They contemplated answering it. The machine picked it up.

"Selena, I found the preacher. He's gonna be at the house around 6 so that I can finally call you my Mrs. My sisters are on the way to help decorate. We're gonna get married right in front of the fireplace. And I know it's bad luck for the groom to see the bride before the wedding, so I'm gonna stay away until then. I can't wait! The next time I see you, you're gonna be my wife. I love you."

Shatima gushed harder than Selena at her dad's affectionate message. The way he almost sang "I love you," at the end made her smile. She and Selena laughed at the ridiculousness of having an impromptu wedding in the living room, but they went to the fireplace and looked at how beautifully crafted it was. Chillz was a man with many talents. If it went on or in a building, he could make it. The stone mantle with the granite framing for the fireplace promised a stunning background for pictures.

At 5:30, a man with brown skin and a commanding presence came into the house dressed in a black tux. Shatima was the one who let him in. He hugged her before she got a good look at his face. He was her godfather, her father's best friend, Uncle Mont. She took in his twinkling eyes, big lips that seemed to always be smiling, and his stature. The man was easily 6'10". He was the kind of man that she would want to be in charge of looking after her. He gushed over how big she'd gotten and handed her the biggest roll of money she ever laid hands on. Whatever she needed, he told her, go to her father first and then come to him if Chillz said no. She giggled at the thought as his long legs took him up the stairs two by two.

"Why y'all ain't answering the phone?" Uncle Mont asked Selena as Lynn applied lip liner to her. "You look nice, by the way."

Adrianne hissed at him. "Don't tell a woman she looks 'nice' on her wedding day. She looks like a cover model."

"She's been a cover model, though. Why do I have to tell her she looks like what she's already been?" Uncle Mont asked with a furrowed brow.

"Thank you, Mont," Selena giggled. "The phone has been...a nuisance today."

"Well, where Chillz at?" he pressed.

"He said he was staying away because it's bad luck for a bride and groom to see each other before the wedding," she explained.

Mont's brow furrowed again. "But y'all saw each other this morning. Anyway. Where he at? He ain't answering his phone or my pages, and there's people outside tryna get in. You want me to let them in or what?"

The ceremony was to be intimate. Selena gave Mont stern instructions on making sure he knew everyone who came through the door. She let him know Hope was up to something. He started fidgeting and excused himself from the room.

An hour later, the furniture was pushed to the back of the room to make way for the wooden folding chairs decorated in fragrant jasmine and orchids. Shatima and her aunts stood across from Chillz's sons and Uncle Mont. Until that point, Shatima never understood why people cried at weddings. She was doing everything she could to hold back sobs. She was grateful that her father held off until she could be a part of this. Internally, she urged the photographer to hurry up and take pictures before she started crying.

The whispers of "Where's Chillz?" ceased when bass dropped from around the corner. Case's Happily Ever After blared from the crystal clear Bose system of a brand new, 1998 BMW. Everyone went to the window and marveled at the car. Selena couldn't wait any longer. She rushed down the stairs to become his Mrs.

As soon as his hand reached the doorknob, a herd of cops yelled for Chillz to put his hands up. He did as he was instructed. That's when the bullets started flying. Everyone inside dropped and screamed. Windows were shattered. Glass sliced through the skin of Chillz's family members. The police pulled people from the house. Shatima felt someone grab her hair and drag her by it. She tried to fight, but her arms were pinned behind her. It was difficult to tell just how many people had her held hostage. All four of her limbs were being pulled in different directions as she was taken from the house in a whir. She was tossed in the back seat of *a car that sped off before she could get a last look at her daddy. Her mother was there, a smug grin on her face.*

"That was when Chillz got bodied. I would have been there too if I wasn't locked up for some bullshit. That's crazy."

"Yeah. Crazy," Shatima said with a sniffle and tried not to cry. She declined to smoke anymore. A sadness that not even THC could cure injected itself into each of her cells. Her body quaked. Recalling her worst childhood memory made her think about recent events. Every time something horrible happened, Hope was there. Her mind didn't doubt that Hope orchestrated both her father's death as well as what happened at the medical complex. She voiced this to Rahshaan, but he was tight lipped.

Regrets for moving to Nat Turner churned in her stomach. Worries about her son rose from her stomach into her throat. What was going to happen next? Would Jabez ever be one of Hope's targets in this perpetual quest for revenge? She buried her head in Rahshaan's chest.

"Why didn't anyone come back for me?" she wondered. "I didn't even stay with my mother. I was basically homeless."

"None of that was supposed to happen. There were a lot of things that you don't understand happening. Soon as I get in touch with Unc, everything is about to change for you, Ma. I promise."

She was sullen for several moments. Finally, she stared at the ceiling and muttered, "I was born so my mother could keep one hand in Chillz's pocket. She never even cared about me."

Rahshaan rubbed Shatima's back and played in her hair. She buried her face deep into his chest. His arms felt dangerously comfortable, as if their sole purpose was to shield her from every bad thing that was going to happen. It made no sense. Rahshaan wasn't the type of man who cared about women. Why did he feel so perfect to her? She wanted to chalk it up to never allowing herself to letting her guard down around a man. Then Rahshaan took things a step further: he lay her on her back, and he kissed her. She was confused how someone who treated women like they were disposable could make her feel like she was the only woman who mattered to him just by pressing his lips against hers. She made herself stop thinking and enjoyed her first adult kiss.

They lay in her bed, his tongue getting acquainted with hers. He caressed her curves, worked his kisses down her neck to her clavicle. He couldn't believe she was actually allowing him to do this. So many tried. Rahshaan had a crush on Shatima for years, but he didn't think he would ever share this close of a space with her. She seemed so guarded, but that night she told him all of her business and then let him be intimate with her. Touching her confirmed something he always suspected: she was special, more than just another faceless conquest. Something about her latched onto something inside of him and promised to never let go. His mind told himself he couldn't do anything to ruin this moment.

An outer force ruined the moment anyway when his phone sing Tupac's *Hail Mary*. Calls with that ringtone could never be ignored. He reluctantly pulled himself away from her and was pulled back to the surface level.

Marcus, Rahshaan's younger brother, was already talking when Rahshaan answered the phone. "Squeak said I gotta do a cleanup job for some chick?" He rambled on and on about how he'd rather be at the club than cleaning blood. His brother knew better than to say anything crazy like that on the phone. Rahshaan barked at him. When he glanced back over at Shatima, she was busy removing comforters from the bed, opening windows, and cleaning up like nothing happened. Part of him wanted her to feel anchored to that bed like he did, like that was their spot, and she could never move from it. Marcus's reckless speaking and her not laying there like she'd be waiting made him angry. He stormed out the apartment without a word.

The snow that fell earlier tapered off into a light freezing drizzle.

Rahshaan didn't usually care about his appearance, but he pulled his hood over his head until he was in the back of the white Dodge Stratus.

"What up, baby?"Mont greeted him from the front passenger's seat. The two men slapped hands, and then Rahshaan and Marcus did the same thing.

Mont's actual appearance contradicted Shatima's earlier recollection of him. He was only 6'2". He kept his face free of any hair and his body free of tattoos. The less distinguishing marks he had, the harder it was for the police to identify him. A black hoody with the hood pulled tight around his face and jeans were his camouflage. Riding as a passenger in his sister's car was a risky move. He thirsted for the ride down to his old stomping grounds for nostalgia's sake, even if he couldn't stay down there for longer than a minute or speak to anyone for fear of the police seeing him.

"Everything go okay up there? You look kinda stuck," Mont remarked.

Rahshaan didn't answer. It had been a long time since he was intimate with a girl he liked beyond the bedroom. He hung his head down in case his face held a goofy expression. The aroma of his ganja danced with the scent of Shatima's perfume and filled the car. Marcus made a remark about the smell and his hair. Kassidy, the driver, who was also Mont's 19-year-old sister, whipped her head around.

"Oooh, Banger. Who braided your hair like that? I know it wasn't G-Ma. Gimme her number." All of her sentences seemed to come out as one word.

Rahshaan didn't say anything. No one else pressed him. They knew he wouldn't say a single word until the car stopped, and he was out of it.

The drive to Big Grams's house was long. While everyone else laughed and chatted, Rahshaan sulked and recounted the night's events in his head. The crush he had was wrong. He thought he liked her because he couldn't have her, but her finally returning interest in him made him want her even more. The problem was that she was his deceased best friend's sister. Kissing her violated every code and stomped on Rize's and Chillz's graves. He didn't know how to tell Mont what happened that night.

Kassidy stopped at the bridge and rolled down the window. She flashed a smile at the sheriff and gave him flirty bedroom eyes.

"Good evening, Sheriff..." She peered into the dark at the name on his badge. "Kevin Grungy." She batted her lashes at him and deepened her smile.

"Oh I can tell you ain't from that trash pile back there. You got manners. Go on through, beautiful," the sheriff said without questioning her further.

When they crossed the bridge, everyone looked behind them and sneered.

"That's what they do to us down there now?" Mont remarked. "Cage us like animals and then take our babies?"

"I hate when y'all make me drive down there," Kassidy grumbled.

After what seemed like forever, the trek up the dark road to Big Grams's estate came to an end. Kassidy pestered Rahshaan until he agreed to take her to get her hair done. Marcus followed Kassidy to spend his night annoying her. Rahshaan and Mont traveled through the house to the back yard. In the kitchen, they each swiped a freshly fried chicken wing. Big Grams was always cooking. The two of them ventured through the back door to a sprawling set of pine trees that separated Big Grams' land from camping grounds. Mont sat atop a picnic table while Rahshaan gazed out into the night.

"So what's up? What's this shit I'm hearing about you?" Mont prompted Rahshaan to talk.

"I fucked up tonight, but what the fuck you mean you hearing shit about me?" He made eye contact. Only a few people's perception of him mattered to Rahshaan. Among them were Uncle Mont. Part of Rahshaan held on to the day his mother abandoned him and thought that eventually one day everyone would. In some ways, he walked on eggshells with "Unc" - who really was his cousin, but everyone called him Uncle, so Rahshaan did too - to keep him happy. Normally, he did whatever Unc told him without hesitation.

Mont looked up from the chicken wing as he bit it. "Squeak just called me and said you went to go collect taxes from Shorty y'all be sweatin all the time. Said you been wildin ever since she turned you down and went out with some college pretty boy. I ain't wanna believe him, but he ain't the first one to say that second part."

"That's where that stupid shit came from? What the fuck is up with your man?" Rahshaan asked. "She was just selling dinners and doing hair. She wasn't catching no licks or no bold shit like that."

Mont cut him off. "So what that gotta do with us?"

"Nothing," Rahshaan said. "Unc, I don't know what the fuck Squeak talking about, but he was just with me and Shorty until him and her got into it, so I sent him to the crib."

"And then what did you do?" Mont asked with a grin.

Rahshaan avoided the question. Instead, he recalled what he learned that night. He watched as Mont's face dropped the same way his did upon being told about Chillz's long lost daughter. Both of their eyes moistened. If either of them shed a tear, the drizzle and the night sky masked it. Very little moonlight peeked through the clouds.

"You mean to tell me," Mont cleared his throat after hearing his voice crack. He paused and made sure he could speak in an even tone before continuing. "That all this time I heard y'all talking about 'the dime from 4F' that y'all was talking about my goddaughter? She's been living right under my nose all this time, and I ain't even know about it? When I saw her on the news, it fucked me up that she even had to work, let alone at that place, in the same space as Loretta. And Andrew was around her, and I couldn't even do shit about it?"

Rahshaan looked at him like he was crazy. "Why you ain't come down there sooner if you knew all that? What if I woulda murked her?"

Mont waved him off. "I knew you wasn't gonna do shit. Your ass in love with that girl. I see how you talk about her. Same way Chillz used to talk about Hope's triflin ass and then how he used to talk about Selena."

That comment went without response. Rahshaan still hadn't processed what happened. Instead he said, "Why the fuck would Squeak call you and tell you some dumb shit like that? I'm putting my foot in his ass soon as I get back down to Nat."

They discussed how to proceed with the news. Mont admonished Rahshaan for his attitude since seeing Shatima with Tommy. Acting on anger rather than logic was going to be the end of him. That was their relationship - Rahshaan messed up, and Mont redirected him. Since the day Darlene abandoned Rahshaan, Mont assumed responsibility for him. The most difficult part of raising him was keeping Rahshaan out of Rahshaan's own way. Fury was always Rahshaan's fuel. He never acknowledged or dealt with any emotion other than anger. It made for a supreme trigger man, but a horrible everything else.

"You know I gotta fuck you up if you hurt my goddaughter, right?" Mont concluded at the end of their discussion.

Rahshaan looked away. "I ain't fuckin with that. That's Rize's sister. That's disrespectful as fuck."

"Then whose lipstick is that smeared on your face?" Mont wondered with a laugh.

Rahshaan laughed about it too, grumbled about them letting him ride all the way from the South Side to the North Side with lipstick on his face, and then wiped it off. He didn't acknowledge it any further.

When he was back in the projects that night, though, lying on the floor in his room in G-Ma's house, he did something he'd never done in his life: he went over his options. At first he told himself that the only reason why he kissed her was because he never thought he'd get a chance to do it again. Then he mulled his feelings and made a pro/con list. He knew he wasn't relationship material, but even as he closed his eyes, all that he could see was Shatima.

———

Squeak was surprised when Rahshaan sent him away. They both lusted over her for years. Both of them could have used Chillz and Rize as a conversation piece, but as usual, Rahshaan muscled his way in before Squeak could say a word.

After being sent away like a little kid, Squeak went to the stoop. His fat face dropped when he saw his friend walking with the girl who rejected them both for the past four years. Squeak waited awhile and then crept up the stairs. He put his ear to Shatima's door. Just as he suspected, Rahshaan was in there getting yet another girl who wouldn't give Squeak a second look. He thudded down the stairs and went back to his normal post on the stoop. When he was the only one left out there, he took out his phone and made a call.

"You busy? Can we meet up? I'll tell you everything you need to know. I'm sick of getting kicked around."

SATURDAY MORNING CLEANING, FAMILY REUNIONS, AND THE SOFTEST PLACE ON EARTH

Saturday mornings had an unbroken ritual. It was the day that Shatima and Jabez cleaned the apartment from the floor to the ceiling. With her windows opened, she blasted music and danced around as she swept, scrubbed, washed, and mopped. That morning, Total's *Kissing You* was her soundtrack as she scrubbed her bedroom walls with tea tree oil. She wanted to make sure to have her bedroom clean and aired out before Jabez woke up and asked any questions about Mommy's activities from the night before. Her comforter was in the wash before he even brought his smiling face out of his room.

"*I been thinkin' 'bout ya dreamin' 'bout ya thinkin' 'bout youuu -* Good morning, baby."

"Keep singing, Mommy. I like this song," he said as Shatima scooped him up into a big hug. "How come you're not watching the news lady who looks like you today?"

The thought of her mother made her heart sink. She still thought of the smug look Hope had on her face as she watched Shatima being dragged out of her job. "We don't watch the news in this house anymore. It's all lies," was the response that she gave him. She deflected any further questions about why the lady wasn't on their TV for the past two weeks. Instead, she gave him his tiny broom and told him to go take care of the floor in his room. By eleven, the two of them were done and deciding whether they wanted to eat a big breakfast at home or wanted to go to IHOP.

The phone rang. Assuming it was someone calling to book an appointment, Shatima didn't bother to look at the Caller ID. "Hello?"

"Tima! Hey girl!" a voice screamed into the phone.

Shatima snarled at the excitement of the voice on the other end. "Hi, April," she said dryly to her childhood friend. Once upon a time, the two of them were part of an inseparable trio.

"Aw, don't be all salty towards me. I ain't choose no sides with what happened between you and Nicolette," April admonished her.

"How did you even get my number?" Shatima wanted to know.

April paused. "Dang. You really are mad at me. Look, Tima. I'm sorry I haven't come to visit you. It was just that thing between you and Nicolette was some drama that I couldn't be part of. I didn't understand it. Y'all left me and had kids, and I couldn't even get a date."

"Poor you. Nobody wanted to make you a teen mom," Shatima quipped. She lay on her loveseat and let her legs dangle over the arm. "You still didn't tell me where you got my number."

April sighed. "By accident. I saw a girl in the store with her hair looking really nice, so I asked her who did it, and she said your name. I figured there couldn't be too many 'Timas' in the world, so I described you, and when she said something about dark skinned with chinky eyes and dimples, I knew it had to be you."

Shatima rolled her eyes at April's racist tinged description of her. She looked over at Jabez, who busied himself reading a book while she was on the phone. It brought a smile to her face. "So what? You called to get your hair done? Why are you here anyway? Didn't you go away to college?"

"Yeah, girl! I go to the *real HU*, just like we always used to talk about!" April proudly announced. When Shatima didn't congratulate her, she continued, "But I'm home just for a little weekend visit. I ran into Nicolette, and she wants to get the kids together."

Shatima sat up. "What kids?"

"Your kids. Yours and hers. She wants her daughter to know her brother." April paused. "I know I'm wrong for even coming to you about it, but she looked so sad. She just wants to talk to you about what happened."

"I don't have anything to say." Shatima felt her heart breaking all over again from the betrayal.

April's husky laugh was so loud that Shatima had to hold the phone away from her ear. "Word to Chillz, your foot said everything it had to say to her ass that day."

Inside, Shatima seethed. How dare April bring up her father's name? That she knew of, April only met her father once. He had a party for her at a skating rink and bought jackets and had dolls made as party favors. April also gifted Shatima a program from her father's funeral when Shatima wasn't able to attend. That in no way gave her the right to use his name in vain.

"It was nice talking to you, April, but-"

"Okay. Okay. I'm sorry. I'm sorry I turned my back on you, and in a way, I did take Nicolette's side. But, Tima, we promised each other we would never fight over a boy. She was in the hospital, and now with everything she's going through... And with you just cutting everybody off like that. I can't believe you still haven't gone to your mother for forgiveness. That's the only parent that you have."

Shatima jumped in. "April, I hope everything goes well for you at school. I have to go."

With that, she simply hung up the phone. That part wasn't personal. Shatima never said goodbye before ending a call or a conversation. Since she didn't get to say goodbye to her father or her deceased brother, she didn't say it to anyone.

After the phone call, Shatima was too consumed by anger to leave the house. April's lips were looser than ever. Rather than taking her negativity into the world, she elected to cook breakfast at home. Just when they finished eating the last of their pancakes, someone rang the doorbell. Jabez ran to answer it.

"Red light!" Shatima called out to him, prompting him to stop. "What's the first thing you do when someone rings the doorbell?"

"Who is it?" Jabez bellowed in the most manly voice he could muster.

"It's your mommy's best friend. Now open the door."

Shatima froze. Regret started to hit her. She hoped that Rahshaan didn't think their kiss meant he could pop up whenever he felt like it. Then again, she kind of wanted him to pop up at her house as often as he felt like it. There were a lot of complicated feelings going on inside of her, and she didn't want to deal with them at the moment.

"I'm busy," she responded. "I'll see you later."

There was a pause and then a girlish giggle followed by an "Oop." Shatima frowned. Curiosity got the best of her. She had to know what woman he would dare bring to her house, so she opened the door.

"This is Unc's sister Kassidy. She wants her hair braided," Rahshaan explained.

"Then you should've had her make an appointment. I'm busy." She hoped no one heard her exhale her relief.

Kassidy laughed. "Thought you said this was your wifey. You lied." She looked to Shatima. "You look like Rize. Could I get your number please, because I ain't never seen Banger's hair look that good, and I promise to tip." Her sentences came out in one long string once again.

Shatima looked into the girl's hazel eyes and wondered if they were contacts. She didn't remember anyone else in Uncle

Mont's family having light eyes, but this girl seemed too young for her to remember. She decided to take the girl then. She handed her the book she constructed with all the hairstyles she did and advised Kassidy to choose one. As Kassidy flipped through the book "ooohing" and "aaahing," Rahshaan and Shatima exchanged awkward glances. He wanted to scoop her up, pin her against the wall, and kiss her just like they kissed the night before.

Their staring was interrupted by Jabez tugging on Rahshaan's sleeve. "How come you don't walk with us to the bus stop in the morning no more?" Rahshaan was tongue tied until Jabez gave up waiting for an answer and took him into his room. He made Rahshaan play basketball on his Little Tikes basketball hoop until Shatima finished Kassidy's hair.

Within ninety minutes, Kassidy was a new permanent client of Shatima's.

"Unc wants me to bring you and Jabez out there to come see him today," Rahshaan announced.

A jolt passed through Shatima, but she didn't understand the reaction. This was the moment she had been waiting for since she moved down to Nat Turner. Rather than scared, she was supposed to feel joyous about it. Apprehensively, she showered and then bathed Jabez. Then she carefully selected outfits for them to wear. They climbed into Rahshaan's Jeep. It was the single luxury he afforded himself.

"This is the fish fry house," Shatima said under her breath when they pulled into Big Grams's driveway. Though it seemed much larger than the last time she was there, she remembered the white colonial style mansion with black shutters. The shutters were always her favorite part of the decor. For some reason, they made that house feel...homier than other homes. Her insides were jelly as she made her way up the brick driveway.

In the doorway stood her godfather. She realized she exaggerated his height when she told the story about him, but his presence still made him seem like a giant. He scooped her up and lifted her off her feet, squeezing her. The faintest whisper of apology came from him. When he looked at her standing there smiling, he saw Chillz, Rize, and a failed mission. When he caught a glimpse of Jabez, though, he had to excuse himself. Jabez's face was a cookie cutter cutout of his late friend's. It hurt Mont that Chillz wasn't here to see this.

When Uncle Mont composed himself, he linked one hand with Shatima's, the other with one of Jabez's, and he led them to the basement. Kassidy disappeared to look at herself in a mirror. Rahshaan tailed them, giving them their space while they got acquainted. Mont rattled off everything Rahshaan told him about them. Shatima corrected the parts about them being "lonely," "weird," and "holed up in that tiny ass apartment." She explained that she only moved to those projects for two reasons: they paid for school, and she knew that somehow being down there would reconnect her with him. In return, he apologized for the time she had to work under "evil ass Loretta."

Part of the basement was repurposed into a library of sorts. Books covered the room from floor to ceiling. They wound through the rows of shelves and end caps. There was a section of biographies and autobiographies by black female activists. Mont pulled out a copy of Elaine Brown's *A Taste of Power,* Maya Angelou's *I Know Why the Caged Bird Sings,* and Audre Lorde's *Sister Outsider a*nd handed them to her, telling her that her father said they were required reading. Then he pulled out one of the wall panels and handed her three cookie tins.

He pointed her to a fabric covered bench and then led Jabez away from her so that she could study the contents. Her hands quivered as she tried to take the top off the first one. It was full of money, rolled tightly so that he could fit as much in it as possible. A shriek almost escaped her mouth. She silenced herself and put it to the side for later. The second was filled with some more money and letters. Most of them were just things he wanted to tell her during his days. Some of them were supposed to accompany the Christmas gifts he sent her every year. One was a manifesto of sorts. Not wanting to bring herself down from the high of being reunited with her family, she put it away for later.

The last one had the word "proof" written across the lid in permanent marker. In it were pictures of every time they were together. Finally she had pictures from her childhood to put in her house. She thought the most cherished parts of her life were only etched into her mind. That he thought she would forget any of those times made her break down and cry.

At the sound of her sniffles, Mont prompted Rahshaan to go to her, comfort her. Rahshaan had no idea what to do, so he awkwardly patted her on the back. Mont crumpled his face into a disapproving expression. He sat on the other side of Shatima and allowed her to sob onto his shoulder. She thanked them both for saving her father's memories for her. Then she asked to be alone so that she could cry over her father. She never got to go to his funeral. She didn't know whether he was buried or cremated. This was the closest thing to a memorial service that she would get. The two men gave her peace and something to lean on as she cleansed her soul. She finally found what she was looking for.

Later that day, Shatima decided to take G-Ma out to lunch before curling her hair for church the next morning. It took a lot to get G-Ma to descend the fourteen flights of stairs for anything other than going to church and going to the grocery store. G-Ma loved crab legs, though, and was coaxed out of her apartment for her favorite indulgence.

"I'm glad you gave my grandson a chance. It feels like he hasn't smiled in years," G-Ma remarked while they waited for their salads. Around them, conversation buzzed. Hands and utensils split crab shells. A couple of champagne bottles popped. It surprised Shatima when G-Ma ordered a glass of Chablis, remarking that Jesus' first miracle was changing water to wine, so they should have some too.

"I'm very glad to hear that Rahshaan is happy, but I doubt it has anything to do with me." She took a sip of water to keep her from having to say anything else.

A waiter carried a plate of lobster tails by them. They caught a whiff of broiled seafood and butter. Jabez asked them if their food was coming next. A couple sat next to them and complained about sitting next to a table that had a child. They ignored the couple who made more noise with their complaints than the child they complained about. Jabez asked for his bread to be buttered and busied himself eating it. The restaurant was too full for the couple to be seated elsewhere.

"I wish you'd stop being so prissy for once and just enjoy your life," G-Ma said. "I ain't calling you uptight or nothing, but, baby, you is uptight. I know you and my grandson spent time together."

Shatima's eyes darted toward Jabez. G-Ma clasped her hands over her mouth and was apologetic for being so open in the presence of a child.

Throughout dinner the couple kept complaining about Jabez, even though he barely said two words and didn't move from his chair. It was all Shatima could take when she turned toward them and snapped, "If being near children in a restaurant is such a problem for you, then why don't you go to a restaurant that doesn't have children's menus?"

The moment she locked her eyes with a smirking Hope, Shatima wished that she'd just continued to ignore them. The relief she felt after purging the sadness from her system earlier was foolish. It was no coincidence that on the same day that she was reunited with her father's side of her family and received a large sum of money that she bumped into Hope. Her life was just one huge game. The dark cloud that moved away just hours ago zoomed right back over her head.

"What are the chances of us bumping into each other twice in the same year after not seeing each other for so long?" Hope gushed in a voice that was an octave higher than her regular pitch.

Jabez's eyes grew wide. He bounced in his chair. "Mommy! It's the lady from the news that looks like you! She wasn't on the news this morning because she was here!"

That got a giggle out of G-Ma and the man who accompanied Hope.

"So how have you been? The last time we saw each other ended in less than favorable circumstances. You must be doing well if you're eating here," Hope pried.

"They have a two for twenty menu," Shatima grumbled. "Why are you here? Why are you following me? Why are you with the police?" She gestured toward the tan skinned, curly haired detective sitting across from Hope. Even dressed in plain clothes, those brown puppy dog eyes were easy to recognize. He was the partner of the redhead who approached Shatima in the park weeks ago.

Hope stood and clasped her hands together. "Well, Shatima, it just so happens that I have missed you. I wanted to work toward a reconciliation, but I couldn't find you. Officer Santarez moonlights as a private detective. I hired him to track you down."

Shatima glared and shook her head. She took in Hope's perfect posture and the voice she used. This wasn't a conversation between a mother and daughter. This was an interaction between a reporter and her audience. This was the story she had to spin, like making a mass of people believe there was no money for schools while also reporting that the county's officials just got a million dollar raise. Only a fool would believe Hope.

"You wanna know how I know you're lying?" Shatima called her out. "You've never laid eyes on your grandson, yet you're in the same room as him and haven't so much as glanced at him."

Hope didn't miss a beat. "I'm not interested in dealing with the fact that you made me a grandmother while I'm still in my prime."

"Well, then you don't want to know me either."

On the ride home, Shatima apologized over and over again for dragging G-Ma out just to cut the dinner short. She understood that takeout crab legs weren't as good as being able to sit at a table and savor them. She apologized to Jabez for not letting him pick out a dessert. A fresh wound opened, and she was trying to talk herself out of giving into the pain it left. She knew her story wouldn't end at "She got money from her dead daddy, and they all lived happily ever after. The end."

What she wasn't prepared for was the callous way Hope dealt with her first encounter with her grandson. Part of Shatima hoped that she would see how well she did with him, how happy he was, and be proud. Or envious. Or angry that she missed so much of his life. It was the indifference that sliced her open with a jagged edge. How could she know a part of her was sitting in the room with her and just not care?

This thought consumed her until she pulled into her assigned parking spot behind her high rise. Rahshaan and Squeak stood against a light pole waiting for them.

"Unc's having a party tonight," Rahshaan told her.

"So?"

"So quit acting stuck up and get dressed so I can take you. Why you so difficult?"

"Rahshaan, don't you raise your voice at her!" G-Ma snapped.

"But, G-Ma, she..."

"I said don't you raise your voice at her." She turned to Shatima. "And you stop being so difficult. After the day you had, you deserve to wind down. Now leave Jabez with me for the night. We'll get a ride to church in the morning." She saw Shatima open her mouth to protest. "I said go! Bring me some clothes for this boy tonight, and go have you some fun!" On her way inside, she grumbled, "I ain't never seen two more stubborn people in my life."

After making sure Jabez had clothes and was okay with

spending the night at G-Ma's house, Shatima stood in front of her closet and just stared. Nothing seemed good enough. She didn't have very many revealing outfits that girls who went out on Saturday nights wore, but she did have form fitting. A grey sweater dress, wide belt, and snakeskin stiletto boots made the perfect ensemble. Her fragrance of the night was Allure by Chanel. A little light makeup and jewelry took her from gorgeous to goddess. Heads turned when she stepped out into the cold night air. The promise of snow made her regret the boots. They had no traction on them. Rahshaan took her hand and walked her to the passenger's side of his car. Squeak was already sitting in the front seat.

Rahshaan tapped on the glass. Squeak rolled the window down, bobbing his head to Three-Six Mafia's *Stay Fly*.

"Get in the back. My shorty riding with us."

Squeak bucked his eyes at Shatima and Rahshaan's joined hands. "I ain't getting in the back for no bitch."

It was like someone flicked a switch in Rahshaan's back. "Nigga, do you know who the fuck this is? Nigga, this is royalty! You supposed to bow down when you see her! Don't ever call her out her name!"

Squeak's fat face contorted into a ball of confusion. "Nigga, you buggin' out over some pussy you ain't gonna get. You know her stuck up ass ain't gonna give you none, but you out here doing the most anyway. And you been a real sucka for love ass nigga ever since you seen her out with that pretty boy. You about to end your night mad as fuck when she disses you again."

Rage pumped through Rahshaan's bloodstream as he listened to someone who was supposed to be his friend air out all of his dirty laundry. It was one thing coming from Mont. To hear it coming from someone who wanted Shatima just as badly as he did, however, incensed Rahshaan. They never competed for women. It angered Rahshaan that Squeak even thought he had a chance with Shatima. In Rahshaan's mind, Squeak should have just accepted that he was never on her radar. Hell, he barely thought he had a chance. That there seemed to be jealousy brewing was almost funny enough to make Rahshaan laugh. Except, Squeak disrespected her. That was an offense that couldn't go unpunished.

The two of them stared at each other, waiting to see who would challenge whom first. Squeak spat on the ground by Rahshaan's feet. The saliva barely missed Rahshaan's shoe.

In a voice usually reserved for his murder victims, Rahshaan commanded, "Get down on your knees and apologize. You just disrespected the fuck out of Rize and Chillz." Each syllable was slow and deliberate. His eyes never left Squeak's.

Squeak held up his hands and uttered a quick "Sorry."

"Nigga, what the fuck did I say? Get down on your knees and apologize!" Rahshaan pressed.

"Oh my God, Rahshaan. It's not that serious. He said he was sorry." Although being referred to as a bitch made her want to dig all seven inches of one of her heels between Squeak's eyes, the scene Rahshaan made was too much for her. She just wanted to go home and forego the night.

"You serious, nigga?" Squeak wanted to know. "Fuck that."

"Then walk your ass to the party. Matter of fact, don't come to the party at all. And don't think you won't get dealt with later on. Fuck away from my ride."

"You know that wasn't even necessary," Shatima said when they were en route.

Rahshaan's jaw tightened. "I don't talk in my car," he told her. "Niggas get locked up behind conversations in vehicles."

"Well, you ain't the one talking. I am. Why would you make a scene like that?"

"He called you a bitch."

"I'm sure you've called me a bitch too before you knew who my brother and my father were," she tried to reason.

Rahshaan gripped the steering wheel with one hand and banged on the dashboard with the other. His eyes darkened. "I have *never* called you anything but your name. Don't ever assume the worst about me."

Dumbfounded, Shatima sat back. He had a temper, but he had her best interests at heart. She wondered what the combination of that was like on a permanent basis. Would there be a time where she didn't do what he liked, and he hit her? Would he make her get on her knees out of anger? Part of her wanted to jump out the car while it was moving and just disappear.

There was still tension between them when they made it back to Big Grams's house. He reached for her hand. She declined, saying she wasn't really the hand holding type. He paused, cut his eyes at her, and then shrugged and watched her stroll ahead of him. As they got closer to the house, Mary J. Blige's *Real Love* could be heard blaring from a home's speakers. Her hips began to sway to the beat as she walked. Her heels clicked in tune with the drums. Even in the darkness, the black shutters were like arms extending themselves for an embrace, welcoming her home. The kitchen was full of women frying fish on one side and chicken on the other. Shatima's eyes fell on a woman who danced as she dredged fish. Her svelte frame bent in perfect time with the song, boasting of years of training. Shatima's heart skipped a beat as she watched the woman's long, dark hair swing from side to side. The woman spun around and met eye-to-eye with Shatima.

"My baby?" she whispered. Then she ran over to Shatima, and they locked onto each other. "Oh my God! You're the same height as me!" she gushed.

Shatima had to thank God for waterproof makeup and setting spray. Otherwise, she was sure to cry and ruin Selena's white blouse. She didn't want to let go.

"I'm so sorry I left you behind," Selena cried. Again they hugged. "Shaan told me you had a baby. I want you to bring him by as soon as I get my house unpacked, do you hear me? I want to meet my grandbaby."

Hearing that made Shatima hug her even harder.

"Can y'all cut that shit out so I can hug my niece?" Lynn pushed between them and latched onto Shatima. "That nigga Mont fucked around and found you like he said he would, and just in time. I got an empty chair in my shop with your name on it."

"How did you know I did hair?" Shatima wanted to know.

"Bitch, please. You been watching me since you was nine. Plus your little ugly ass boyfriend came by earlier. I ain't never seen his head look that good."

"He's not my-"

Rahshaan grabbed her hand and led her through the kitchen into the open living/dining room area. The DJ spun mostly '90's Hip Hop and R&B jams. Jodeci & WuTang Clan's *Freek'n U Remix* was on when they joined the others dancing the night away. He watched her move and wasn't disappointed. Aggressively, she pushed him against the wall and gyrated her body in front of him then ground against him. He held her hips and fell into an even deeper trance than she had him under when they kissed the night before. People watched them from the corners of their eyes with raised eyebrows. Normally, Rahshaan was low key at these parties. He smoked blunts and ate. Never did he dance. Instead, he stayed against the brown wall and let some faceless chick dip, pop, and roll for her life in front of him. With Shatima he really danced, and he was good at it. When the DJ switched to Reggae he caught a wine. She had supreme control over her wide hips and high-sitting ass. Her body flowed like water.

The DJ put on a series of slow jams, starting with Joe's *I Wanna Know*. The two faced each other and really looked at one another for the first time since the night before. Shatima thanked him for everything he did that day. She was exactly where she longed to be since that fateful day back in 1998. It wasn't until that moment that she realized that the two of them had been pressed against each other for the better part of two hours. She wondered if her Friday and Saturday night clients went out every night in search of what she felt right then. Because, although the room was filled with people from wall to wall, the only face she saw was Rahshaan's. Her feet hurt, but her heart fluttered. She didn't want to let go of him. G-Ma's words kept creeping into her mind. She really wanted to let go of her inhibitions if only for that night.

"You know Jabez is spending the night at your grandmother's house, right?" she whispered in his ear as Xscape's *Softest Place on Earth* crooned from the overhead speakers.

"So what that mean?" he asked her. "You ready to go home?"

She nodded. "And I want you to stay with me...if you can and you want to."

While Rahshaan pulled his Jeep to the front of the house, Shatima exchanged contact information and addresses from her long lost family. He came inside and walked her to the car, opened the door for her, and made sure she was in secure before getting in on the driver's side and turning on 112's *Cupid*. In response Shatima's eyes rolled to the back of her head. She threw her head back against the upholstered seat and squealed about how that was her jam back in the day.

"You know that was all for you, right? All them old ass songs the DJ was spinning? You stay listening to some old shit every time I pass by your crib."

A smile spread across her face. "You really be checkin' for me like that?"

Rahshaan shrugged his shoulders as he drove down the icy roads. "I thought it was obvious."

"May I ask why?" Shatima queried.

It felt good to be off her feet. At the same time, she still wanted to be dancing with him. She hoped the parties were a regular thing and not just some *Antoine Fischer* mockery they put together in honor of their reunion.

He shook his head. "I don't talk in cars or in houses. That's one thing you gotta understand about me."

She sucked her teeth. "Well can I talk, or is that not allowed?"

He didn't respond.

She took that as permission to keep going. As Janet Jackson whispered *Let's Wait Awhile,* she told Rahshaan about how cute she always thought he was and how much she appreciated him looking out for her over the years. Even before he knew who she was, he treated her like royalty by making sure someone always helped her take her groceries up the four flights of stairs it took to get to her apartment and calling off his peers when they catcalled her. She didn't realize until he showed up at her apartment last night how much she looked forward to seeing him every day. Walking from Jabez's bus stop without him was lonely. Staying away from him for that amount of time was irritating. Finally, she told him that she was eternally grateful for everything he did, except that scene at the gas station.

By the time 12 more 90's slow jams played, they were back in Nat Turner. Squeak was standing on the stoop. Anger pulled down his face. For a second, Shatima felt bad for him. Then she remembered she couldn't stand him. Rahshaan led her past him up the stairs to her apartment. The two men didn't even make eye contact.

It wasn't until they crossed the threshold of Apartment 4F that she noticed her legs wobbling. The previous night was different. She didn't know if she could stop being uptight long enough to lead him back into her bedroom. At first, it was easy to busy herself. She turned on slow jams and offered him something to drink. Then she changed her sheets, even though that task was completed during her Saturday morning routine.

Rahshaan appeared in the doorway. His stature and the concerned expression on his face startled her. With a sober mind, he was able to comment the artwork on her walls and the collages of pictures of her from over the years. He asked her why she was stalling, told her that they didn't have to do anything she didn't want to do. He heard everything she said in the car, and he assured her that he was there to do whatever she wanted to do.

"I know how you normally do on the weekends, Rahshaan," she warned him, her voice wobbling like her legs.

"What you mean?" a slightly amused smile danced on his face.

He walked over to the bed to help her with the sheets she was so committed to changing. The music was still coming from the speakers in her computer in her living room. He didn't mind just lying in bed with her until they fell asleep, but that sexually suggestive music needed to stop if that was the plan. Janet Jackson's *Anytime, Anyplace* wasn't the soundtrack to a night of conversation and cuddling.

"The girls who hang out by my car every morning waiting for you, mad because you don't pay them any attention anymore?" She raised her eyebrows and stared straight at him. "After tonight, am I gonna be like them and standing by some other woman's car, asking why you don't call me no more?"

Sam Salter's *After 12, Before 6* came on, and Rahshaan wondered if they'd be done talking about a bunch of women who didn't matter to him before 6. He wondered what he had to do to let her know that the other women were canceled. He inched closer to her and touched her for the first time since they walked through the door.

"What's really good, Ma? Why you shaking?" He ran his hands down her torso. "You want me to leave? I will if I'm making you this nervous."

She hesitated. It took her so long to get to this point with a man. Did she want to back out now and try again in another 5 years? The thought of him leaving made her feel lonely.

"It's not you. Not really." She looked at the floor. "It's... The last time I did this was when I got pregnant. I don't want you to be disappointed. I don't really know what I'm doing."

Inside of Rahshaan's mind fireworks and jackpot sirens went off. His heart raced. He hoped he didn't have a stupid grin on his face. Finally, he lucked out and found someone different from the ran through birds in the projects who were leaving their kids' fathers for a night with him. He realized he was complicit in helping them cheat, but he thought less of them for doing it. At the end of the night, he went home to no one. They went home to men who were powerless against him and kissed them in the mouths. To him, the night prior signified the end of that disgusting cycle.

As he turned her so that she was facing him, he kissed her slender neck, her earlobes, her cheeks, and her forehead. His lips grazed the tip of her nose and met her lips. Her trembling subsided. *Always by* Pebbles came on, beckoning him to never leave her. Never one to rely on cryptic messages, he sought her permission to go further and begged her to let him know if he did anything out of pocket.

"Tell me to stop if I go too far."

She allowed him to lay her on the bed and remove her dress. Her skin was still cold from being outside in nothing more than thigh high pantyhose. She reached down to take her boots off, but he stopped her.

"Keep them 'fuck me boots' on," he told her.

She giggled at the name he gave her stiletto over-the-knee footwear.

He undressed them both, leaving kisses everywhere on her body where there was once clothing. She cringed when his lips ventured below her navel, expecting him to be repulsed by her c-section scar. Instead, he used his tongue to trace over the tattoo that served to conceal it. His lips on her body sent a seismic wave through it. With the pillows out of her reach, she clung to the sheets. Somewhere between his hands, tongue, and stroke he stirred something within her. The tempo Rahshaan created compelled her to move in sync with him. She let go of the sheets and instead put her arms around his back. Her hands rested on his shoulder blades. The heels of her boots clinked together when she locked her legs around him and exhaled into his ear. In turn he responded by touching a spot inside of her that made her shriek.

This was nothing like the awkward rigidness that she remembered sex being. She wished she saved her first time for him. His grunts and groans harmonized with her moans when he moved a certain way. Him stopping to kiss her and ask her how she felt and if she liked what he was doing showed her this was something they were supposed to mutually enjoy. He moved in such a way that caused her back to arch. She tilted her head backward and squeal-screamed until she was out of breath. Every part of her body from her scalp to her toenails felt too sensitive to touch. His speed increased. She thought she was going to lose her mind. Not much longer after, he let out what sounded like a growl and pulled away from her. He went to dispose of the condom and the wrapper before climbing in the bed with her and wrapping his arms around her.

Even with the sedative she had to urge her to sleep, she was still jarred awake by the nightmares about her brother and father. Rahshaan woke just enough to hold her tighter, and she was able to get back to sleep without incident. The second time it happened, though, she was embarrassed. She showered, dressed in pajamas, and went to the kitchen to fry bacon and scramble eggs. She served him breakfast in bed. He earned it.

"Can I ask you a question now?" she asked. "I know you don't like to talk inside buildings - whatever that means - but I'm just curious about something."

"Go ahead," he agreed with a flat voice.

"Last night and yesterday you kept calling me wifey and telling people you were my boyfriend. What was that about? Do I get a say?"

"You could say no, but then I'd just be putting that arch in your back every weekend until you said yes," he told her. His face dropped. "You ain't tryna say you wanna be wack ass friends with benefits or some corny shit like that?"

She giggled and shook her head.

"Oh good. Because I put my mouth on you. I don't do that shit in the friend zone."

She giggled again.

Eating in bed made her uneasy, but she tried to relax. Their time together was so perfect after their spat in the car. She wanted to thank him for making it happen.

After taking a bite of the cheesy eggs, Rahshaan's eyes twinkled. "Girl, you cook just like your pops!"

"Really?" Her eyes danced with delight. It was a compliment of the highest order.

"Hell yeah! Your pops used to cook for us late night after we came home from-" He stopped talking.

"Please continue, Rahshaan. I want to hear about my father."

"I know you do, but I can't. I just know those eggs taste just like the ones he used to cook when me and Rize were little." He went back to eating.

Shatima let him eat before she asked a more important question. "Where were my brothers last night? Are they still...alive?"

"They're around. Rize's death hit them kind of hard, so they disappeared. I heard Shameik was locked up, but might come home soon. That's all I know."

The way he said that last sentence let her know that the subject was closed.

She snickered. "Is he still mean?" she wondered, realizing that every memory she had of her oldest brother featured him with a scowl.

Rahshaan laughed. That was all she needed to know.

Their breakfast date was cut short when Rahshaan's phone sang *Hail Mary*. He peeled back the turquoise and silver bed spread and climbed out of the bed to find where his pants landed after he tossed them the night before.

"No call, no show?" Mont said.

"Fuck is you talking about? Rahshaan asked.

"Squeak keep calling my phone talking about you ain't show

up for work. Last thing I remember was seeing you leave with my goddaughter."

"Unc, I'll be at work in a minute. I forgot what day it was," Rahshaan lied, trying to dodge the conversation Mont attempted to start.

Mont snickered. "Don't make me fuck you up behind my goddaughter."

"Nigga, I know that's your goddaughter, damn. Why you keep saying that shit? You ain't never had a position in nobody's life before? Damn."

Mont's tone switched to a serious one. "When anybody but you calls, you know I think the worst. Fuck that nigga calling snitching on you for anyway?"

"I don't know. That nigga been acting real funny lately. I'll talk to him. I'll be at work in a minute." Rahshaan hung up the phone before the conversation went any further. He dreaded having any conversation with Squeak that would be a reminder that he was his superior. It would be taken personally, just like everything else that happened lately.

Rahshaan dragged Shatima into the shower with him and made love to her under the project's terrible water pressure. In a backward move, he asked for her phone number and told her he'd be back to chill with her later. She kissed him goodbye.

By the time G-Ma dropped Jabez off after church, Shatima had her kitchen spotless and overnight bags packed for the both of them. She took him to Lynn's house to spend a few days with her and Selena. When she got to her car, there was a note on the windshield:

"We gave you a chance.
Now you're a target too.
You're dead, bitch."

"You don't think that note was a little much?" Santarez asked Hope. "Calling your daughter a bitch wasn't going too far?"

Hope shrugged. "She chose those people over me for the

third time in her life. As far as I'm concerned, bitch is too nice of a word."

"Baby, you are ice cold," Santarez remarked, wrapping his arms around Hope and grabbing her ass with both of his hands. "Remind me never to get on your bad side."

"Well, bring me to Montell, and you'll never have to know what being on my bad side is like," she told him.

CHAPTER
Six

After years of working under evil ass Loretta, working in Hair Revolution was like waking up and going to Heaven every morning. Lynn immediately brought her in as a business partner. Combined with her talent, entrepreneurial mind, and drive for success, Shatima was a welcomed asset. Initially, Lynn had Shatima washing clients' hair and braiding them in preparation for getting sew-ins. When she saw her niece's style book and how many clients Shatima brought in, Lynn was happy to give her niece her own chair. It was Lynn's dream to make that salon a family business. Her sisters were long gone, doing their own things. Her dream continued through her brother's only daughter.

The social aspect of working in a beauty shop was difficult for Shatima. It was obvious that the staff only tolerated her because she was Lynn's niece, and because she brought them breakfast every morning. Other than that, they found her distant and cold. Working in the beauty shop really tested Shatima's tolerance for gossip. The clients in Hair Revolution knew and told everything. They brought stories from every side of town and every walk of life. Most of them sat in Lynn's chair to volunteer the details of their own lives. Shatima would never share the things they shared, especially knowing how the staff was going to remix it after they left. The staff found it odd that she was so repulsed by gossip.

On the first Friday that she worked there, Shatima came rushing into the shop. In five minutes she had an appointment. Lynn rolled her eyes. Like father, like daughter. Chillz always considered himself late if he weren't fifteen minutes early. Her niece had adopted the same policy.

"Someone's been calling about getting his hair braided all morning!" Lynn called to Shatima from the black receptionist's desk. It was no surprise when Shatima learned that her father constructed it. The desk was painted with black lacquer and had cracked onyx tiling on the front that matched the floor tiles. It was an elegant sight, the perfect aesthetic for when people first walked in. "You need to get a cellphone or a pager or something. Erica ain't here in the mornings, and I ain't about to play secretary in my shop." The phone rang again. "How this bitch in higher demand than me in my own shop?" she grumbled before snatching it off the hook. "Hello? Look, I ain't gonna tell your little ugly self to stop calling here again! I told you she would return your call when she got a moment!"

Giggling and shaking her head, Shatima continued to set up the soufflés she picked up for breakfast. Her aunt only called people "ugly" or "bitch" if she really loved them. It was an odd way to display affection, but she found it hilarious. She took a soufflé and a glass of orange juice to the desk and sat it off to the side so that her animated aunt wouldn't knock it over.

"Bitch, quit serving me every morning like I'm the Queen of England or some shit," she scolded. "I get it. You're glad to be employed. You own this shop too, bitch. Start acting like it." Into the phone she said, "I don't even know if I want you to have a standing appointment with my niece the way you sweating her. You might be some kind of serial killer or something. Priority? What kind of priority do you have over my niece?"

Realizing who was on the other end of the phone, Shatima

tried to slink away. She'd successfully dodged him all week by staying at Lynn's house. Obviously, she couldn't avoid her apartment forever, but she thought she'd have a little more time.

"Where you going? Get over here and talk on this phone. I don't have time to be bothered with y'all. This ain't *Love Connection,* and I ain't Alex Trebec." Into the phone she yelled, "What? Who gives a damn if Chuck Woolery was the host? Dick Clark was my muthafucka anyway. Shatima, take this phone. Ain't nobody gonna call my shop, correcting me."

Shatima tried to laugh her nervousness away. All eyes in the shop were on her. With a shaky hand, she took the phone from Lynn. "Hello?" The only response was the dial tone. She shrugged, hung up the phone, and turned to her first client. Just as she got her seated at the shampoo bowl, the door flung open. It hit the wall so hard that it shook the pictures on the wall.

Lynn hopped out of the high backed receptionist chair and ran to the door way. "Nigga, I don't know where the fuck your mean ass got feelings from, but this ain't the time or the place to start expressing them."

The seven or so clients in the waiting area paled in the face. Dressed in coveralls, construction Timbs, and a scowl, Rahshaan's reputation preceded him. Things never ended well when his temper flared. He locked eyes with Shatima.

She turned away from him.

"So that's how it is? You just fuck me and leave?" he bellowed. It wasn't his intent to carry on in such a way. She did something to him that made him change his approach to everything.

With a frown, she asked him to lower his voice and not scream out her personal business. It was too late. They had a full audience.

He stalked over to her and followed her into the supply cabinet. Since he already made a fool out of himself, he decided to fully commit to the role. "I thought we agreed that we were together? Where you been? I been calling you all week. You ain't been at the crib."

"I was at my auntie's house," she replied nonchalantly as she mixed a conditioning concoction in a bowl.

"Well, how you just gonna fuck me and not return my calls? You made me bacon and eggs and catfish and grits and shit. How you gonna treat me like a lame after that?"

"Because you are lame," she shot back with a raised index finger. "According to you, I'm the princess of the hood, so I do what I want. That means I don't have to call you after we do what we do, unless I want to. The way you're in here yelling my business, I'm glad I didn't call you after. I thought you were the quiet type."

For a second, Rahshaan's world froze. She was treating him the way he normally treated women, and he hated it. He shook off the shock and stepped closer to her. He reached for her wrist and pulled her so that they were almost touching noses. She exhaled. All week she wanted to be that close to him. "Why you been avoiding me? I ain't never wanted to be with nobody like I want to be with you."

"Ah shit now! My niece out here pussy whipping niggaz. That's right, Tima!" Lynn called from the sidelines.

"I can't do this." She whispered in his ear about the note that was on her windshield.

He stopped and considered this news. "Fuck the police," he whispered. "You trying to be with me or not?" From his pocket, he produced a rectangular jewelry box made of a dark blue velvety material. In it was a gold XO necklace. He tried to put it on her neck, but she recoiled.

"So what? You think you just put a collar on me, and I'm your bitch now?" she snapped, pushing herself away from him.

Lynn pounded her fist on her desk. "Tima, quit being so fucking analytical and just tell the boy he can be your boyfriend. Damn. Y'all are like a ghetto soap opera."

Shatima rolled her eyes. She was tired of people pushing

this man on her. Not that she didn't want him, but she wanted it to be of her own volition rather than being told she needed a man.

"This is only a collar if you're into that type of shit," Rahshaan told her. "Otherwise, this is just something I picked up for you. I was gonna give it to you before, but you dipped on me. How did you do this to me?"

Shatima thought about it, but came up empty. She thought someone pursuing her so heavily should know why he was chasing her. "With what I just told you, why aren't you backing down?"

Rahshaan shrugged. "Because I gave the state some years I ain't owe them already. I don't owe them shit, and the fucking pigs ain't about to dictate my life. And I know I can keep you and your seed safe, so ain't shit for me to worry about."

It was his inclusion of her soft spot, Jabez, that won her over. His understanding that they were a package deal opened her up to the possibility of them being together. She listened to him tell her how badly he wanted to be with her and how much he thought about her. Truth be told, he had stayed on her mind all week. His promise of protection convinced her to stop living in fear and do what she wanted.

After he kissed her and left, she floated over to her client and began washing her hair, hoping everyone would go back to what they were doing. There was no such luck.

"I don't know why you fronted on him so hard anyway. You've been walking around my house singing Ralph Tresvant songs all week," Lynn further embarrassed her.

Haddus, the self proclaimed king of sew-ins, rolled his eyes to the back of his head and sang, "Any dick that takes you back two decades must have been a spiritual experience!"

"Hallelujah!" Antoinette chorused, waving her nail buffer in the air like a church fan.

"Y'all heard that menu that boy rattled off. That boy put that thang on her!" Lynn teased.

Shatima put her head down and laughed. She couldn't wait for him to put it on her again.

In his twenty-five years of life, Rahshaan only had one committed relationship. It started with him being scammed and ended with him being incarcerated. He figured that starting this one in a more positive manner would bring better results. Mont suggested that since Rahshaan already knew Shatima's family, that he should introduce her to all of his. Rahshaan was reluctant. He'd just gotten on speaking terms with his mother after decades of being repulsed by her existence. After considering Mont's point of view, he took Shatima and Jabez to dinner with his immediate family.

G-Ma was staunchly opposed to this. She didn't feel her daughter deserved to know this part of Rahshaan's life. She hated the way Darlene conspicuously favored Marcus over Rahshaan. If it weren't for Rahshaan, Marcus wouldn't be here for her to play favorites with. Only after some intense begging did G-Ma agree to the dinner. She made no promises to behave.

Darlene Bailey was newly clean and newly saved. She had a close relationship with God that gave her license to judge everyone. She went over Shatima with a fine toothed comb as they sat in the restaurant.

"You must've picked this place," she said of the seafood restaurant where G-Ma's lunch was cut short the Saturday prior. "It seems too stuffy and expensive for my son. He's more of a McDonald's man. Can you accept that?" She fingered the white tablecloth and looked at the chandeliers dangling from the ceiling.

Shatima snarled at the woman's erroneous assessment of her own son. As long as she knew Rahshaan, she never saw him eat McDonald's. She concentrated on Jabez, who was tired after a long day in school. If he showed the slightest sign of crankiness, she was taking him home. She thought the dinner was unnecessary, especially at such an early point in their relationship. Every time he went to put his mother in her place, Shatima squeezed his hand. The unending stack of questions Darlene rolled at her made Shatima uncomfortable. She endured them in appreciation of what Rahshaan was doing. As soon as Darlene asked about Jabez's father, though, Shatima stopped playing nice.

"Does me asking who he is offend you?" Darlene asked. "You can't be ashamed of him. After all, you chose him."

"You don't know that," Shatima snapped. "You don't really know anything about me."

"That's because you won't answer any questions," the brown woman with thin hair responded as she buttered her roll. "I'll ask you an easy question: Who are your parents? Are you ashamed of them?"

Shatima smirked, glad Darlene gave her the upper hand without knowing. "You might know my daddy. His name is William Revolution. You might know him as Chill Will or Chillz."

Darlene's big eyes bucked out of her face. "I didn't know Chillz had a daughter." She looked to Marcus, who was supposed to keep her abreast of all of Rahshaan's gossip. He shrugged his shoulders as he buttered his own bread.

G-Ma cocked her head to the side. "Tima, you never told me that. All this time I been trying to figure out who Jabez looks like. He looks just like your daddy."

The mood shifted. Darlene was suddenly very warm toward Shatima and Jabez. All of the judgment and questions went out the door. Over their salads, Darlene praised Chillz and shared stories about him. Everyone was sure they were made up. Darlene was too high most of her life to remember such vivid details. By the time their entrees came, Darlene had told enough stories to make a comic book series about Chillz. G-Ma rolled her eyes at her daughter.

As they enjoyed their dinner, an obnoxious group of young women were seated next to them. Marcus and G-Ma's faces contorted into confused expressions. They had the best view of the party due to where they were seated. Refusing to be left out, Darlene craned her neck. When she saw who had their attention, she whipped her head back around. She looked to Marcus and G-Ma for confirmation before looking back at the girls. Her focus was on the little boy with them. He wore a thin hoody despite the snowy weather. His hands clutched the fly of his pants. He danced and whined for his mother to take him to the bathroom. She ignored him, chatting a mile away on her phone and swinging her parentheses shaped hips and round ass as she sat down.

"Sit down and hold it, and you better not piss on yourself!" she barked when he tugged her sleeve to urge her to take him to the bathroom.

The harshness of her hoarse voice, which faded in and out every few syllables, caught Rahshaan's attention. His head snapped up, and he poised himself for attack. His body language made Shatima look at the women seated at the next table. One look at the little boy, and she knew it had to be Rahshaan's son. He was tall for his age and had that same mean look on his face his father's always did. His mother was a caramel colored woman with green eyes that had flecks of gold. Her long hair was dark and wavy. She had what could only be described as a rack of breasts, wide hips, thick thighs, and almost no waist. Her skin was so smooth that she looked like an oil painting. She was so pretty that she almost didn't look real.

Rahshaan leaned back in his chair. "I should have somebody fuck you up just for bringing your ass back here after all this damn time," he said to her.

She stiffened and then looked at him and rolled her eyes. "Fuck outta here, deadbeat."

Rahshaan ignored the label. "I'm gonna have my brother take my son to the bathroom, and you and me are gonna have a little talk."

"I ain't got nothing to say."

"It's okay. I'll talk for the both of us." Continuing to ignore the game she played, Rahshaan instructed Marcus to take his son to the bathroom. Marcus took NyQuest's hand and extended his hand for Jabez to join as well.

"Rahshaan, stay calm. Don't do anything that's gonna make me have to fuck that little bitch up," G-Ma cautioned him.

That made Rahshaan laugh. His grandmother was his favorite holy roller. "I got this, G-Ma." He stood up and positioned his chair so that he was facing Monaysia's table. "Your phone must be broke. I've been calling you for eight years. Every time I think I found you, though, the number gets disconnected."

"You ain't been calling me," she lied.

"Monaysia, I take five hundred dollars from my check every week and have Marcus take it to your mother's house. Then I have him take her to wire it to wherever you are," he said in an even tone. "Your mother likes to play both sides, because as soon as she gives me your new number, I know she calls you and tells you to change it.

Monaysia turned off her cellphone and stuffed it into her purse. Her friends became the audience instead of offering support. "So if you knew how to get money to me, then you knew how to get your son."

Rahshaan watched how uneasily she looked around. He wanted to smack her head off of her neck. Instead he invited Shatima to turn her chair around and be a part of the conversation. She silently catered to his request with a straight face.

Marcus returned with the children and turned his chair to the table as well. He stared at Monaysia and listened as she continued to lie.

"Shouldn't've chose hoes over your family." She shrugged and then shifted in her seat. "You know what you did."

Marcus spoke up. "Whatever he did ain't shit compared to you testifying against him in court on some bullshit lies and then taking his son away from him to run behind a nigga he had to pistol whip for beating your ass!"

Monaysia's group of friends exchanged surprised looks. This was a different story from the one they heard. Rahshaan passed on admonishing his brother for screaming out his personal business. He knew Marcus's heart was in the right place. Instead, he pulled his chair closer to Monaysia. The wood scraping against the floor caught the attention of people seated near them. It was only a matter of time before their scene got out of hand. He wanted to make sure he made his intentions clear.

"I'm taking my son with me tonight. I'm going to be in his life for the rest of my life," Rahshaan declared.

Monaysia sucked her teeth. "You ain't taking my son nowhere. My son don't know you, and I don't know that ho you're with. I see she got you taking care of her son, though."

Before Shatima could respond, Rahshaan shut Monaysia down. He took the time to rub in her face that his new woman was an independent queen who never used men for personal gain, and who didn't treat her child like a joystick to control the game lesser women liked to play. Before the mother of his child could feel the full impact of his insults, he drove back to the original issue. "Like I said, I'm taking my son with me tonight. I'll have him back to you on Sunday. This ain't up for debate. Now that I can get to you, I'm gonna make sure my son knows me and knows that I love him."

"Nigga please. You left us for dead. Ain't no court gonna let you have visitation after how long you was in jail for." Even worse than Monaysia's voice was the way her evil laugh came through her nose two seconds before it escaped her mouth.

A waiter came and poured water for Monaysia's table while asking them to quiet themselves. They had the surrounding tables as an audience.

Darlene wasn't sure if she should speak up. She wanted to be back in her son's life and felt she had the Big Joker that would help her secure a spot. When she looked at him and Shatima, though, she wondered if his heart was big enough for the both of them. She decided to take a risk. "Monaysia, I saw your name in an online police blotter from that city you ran to after you had my son sent to jail. What is this child endangerment charge about? There's an article that says you left him in the car while you went to some club. Care to explain?"

"I don't have to explain nothing to your crackhead ass," Monaysia defended herself. "Everybody at this table knows you abandoned your kids for way longer than a few hours."

"It says your son was almost hit in a shootout, and you didn't even check on him," Darlene read from the printout she kept in her purse.

Monaysia ignored the accusation. "You left your kids in the house with nothing to eat but raw spaghetti noodles." Her friends laughed.

"I heard you lost your job at that nursing home for having dirty piss," Darlene said. "Did you come back here to move in with your mama? Does she still live with that unemployed nigga?"

As he listened to the two women compete for mother of the year, Rahshaan's jaw tightened. He gripped the sides of the wooden chair in which he sat. He couldn't believe he served time for physically defending a woman who neglected his child. NyQuest came to his side, tugged his sleeve, and asked, "Why do you look so angry, Daddy?"

It shocked Rahshaan that the little boy already knew who he was. Not having to reintroduce himself to someone who shouldn't have been a stranger made his heart a little bit lighter. He crouched and opened his arms. The little boy leapt into his arms and kissed him on his forehead. Monaysia sneered, but withheld any comment. She stood off to the side with her arms folded. Rahshaan excitedly turned to Jabez and introduced the two little boys. Immediately, the boys formed a bond over their Power Rangers clothing. Monaysia hissed for NyQuest to come back.

"Let him sit here. He ain't doing nothing but playing. It's

better than him being up under grown women," Rahshaan protested.

"You don't get a say in what goes on with him. You left us, remember?"

The way she kept saying "You left us," reminded Shatima too much of her own mother's accusations of her father. It got under her skin. She turned back to her plate and tried to eat some of her food. Her patience, though, was wearing thin.

"You out here looking mighty nice with all that jewelry. Is that from the five hundred my brother makes me take to your mom's crib every week?"

Since Marcus' intentions were pure, Rahshaan still did not admonish his younger brother's loose lips. Another waiter came and asked them to keep their voices down.

"Tonight, I'm taking my son. On Sunday, I will bring him back to you. We'll do this every week. After a while, he'll be with me more. I ain't arguing with you about this either." Rahshaan's voice was firm. He leaned on the two back chair legs.

Monaysia's eyes focused on the XO chain around Shatima's neck. Jealousy pulled at her stomach. Once upon a time, she didn't have to use Rahshaan's child support to buy jewelry. He brought home gifts for her as well as their baby. "So I'm just supposed to let you take my son around your little hoes that you be having on the weekends?"

"Ain't no more hoes. This is my wife." Rahshaan put his arm around Shatima.

Shatima kept her eyes on Monaysia and studied her reaction.

A pain ripped through Monaysia's heart. When they were together, he never looked so proud to be with her. "I don't know her."

"She here. Get to know her. She's gonna be around our son a lot."

Seconds passed while Monaysia stared at the two of them. The XO necklace was really getting to her. "She ain't gonna be around my son. I don't like him around all these different people."

Marcus guffawed. "As I recall, the reason why we're sitting here like this right now is because while my brother was out there on his grind, you had niggaz running in and out of the house you shared. I can't believe you're sitting here acting like this over someone who went to jail for you."

The memory of being locked away caused Rahshaan to disassociate. A cold room and a set of bunk beds flashed before his eyes. Shatima felt him go cold and lightly raked her acrylic nails up and down his arm. The action was soothing to him, and he came back to the present.

Looking like a fool, Monaysia grasped for straws. "Why you wanna take him? You feeling guilty because you taking better care of your girlfriend's son than your own?"

No longer able to keep quiet, Shatima pushed her plate away and stood in Monaysia's face. "I take care of my child on my own. Don't bring my son into your petty drama again." She glared at the Amazon to let her know that she wasn't playing.

G-Ma got up and stepped between the two of them. Her eyes darted to the waiter who was coming back to them. Everyone within earshot had their full attention on them. "This gotta end before I don't get to eat my crab legs again. Monaysia, it's time to grow up. Rahshaan's either gonna be a father to NyQuest, or I'm gonna snatch a bone out your head, and then Rahshaan's gonna be a father to NyQuest. Which do you want it to be?"

Darlene looked at the two women standing up for her son and was instantly jealous. These women had his heart. There was no room for her.

Most days, Rahshaan looked at life as something to do before he died. That day, however, with his son back in his life and his girlfriend by his side, he felt like life was worth the effort. With them were two little boys getting the love that little black boys deserved. He hadn't felt that way since his grandmother took him in. This was the vision he had when he found out Monaysia was pregnant. After seeing how she was as a mother juxtaposed with Shatima and his grandmother, he was glad that things didn't work out between them.

Rahshaan took his newly formed family to the mall. It was an out of character move for him, but he splurged. He bought clothes, toys, and games for NyQuest and Jabez. It reminded Shatima of her own father and how he spared no expenses when they got to spend time together. In that moment, watching him get to know his son, watching him include her son in everything, she was certain that she fell for him.

"NyQuest, what's your favorite color? We can get you a coat that color," Shatima told the little boy in the clothing store.

She couldn't get over how much he looked like Rahshaan and Monaysia's gene pool split right down the middle. His skin color fell exactly halfway between Monaysia's caramel and Rahshaan's dark brown. He had Monaysia's eye color but Rahshaan's eye shape. Rahshaan's face structure with Monaysia's lips and nose. Monaysia's generous forehead with Rahshaan's hairline.

"I don't need a coat," the little boy replied. "I'm just going from the house to the car."

Shatima stopped looking through the rack of coats and eyed the little boy strangely. "What does that even mean? Won't you get cold while walking to the car?"

NyQuest shrugged. "If I get cold, then that just means I'm not walking fast enough."

Rahshaan stood off to the side, clenching and unclenching his fist. That was just the type of bird logic Monaysia was famous for. He was glad that he didn't mention his son's lack of a coat in the restaurant. Had he heard that, he knew for sure his clenched fist would have went right through Monaysia's jaw and shattered it. He'd be in jail instead of in this space, enjoying his family. He watched Shatima squat so that she was eye level with NyQuest.

"When you are with me, you dress for the season that you are in, okay?" she said to him.

He nodded his head and kissed her on her forehead. She was

surprised by the action, and she knew then that she would love that little boy forever.

They stayed out with the kids much later than they should have. By the time they got back to Nat Turner, only the boys who kept watch over the stoop were out. When they saw Shatima's car pull up, they dutifully ran to it to help with the bags. Squeak avoided eye contact with the little boy while NyQuest moved closer to Shatima. She quickened her pace. Ever since the scene in the parking lot, she had less to say to him. She was embarrassed for him, but still couldn't stand to be around him.

Once they reached the fourth floor, there was an awkward pause. Rahshaan usually came by in the middle of the night after Jabez went to sleep, and he left before Jabez woke up. It was a rule that she held firm to. But that night was different. G-Ma's house was so crowded with children. Where would NyQuest sleep? On the floor? Squeezed on whatever bed Rahshaan slept on? Shatima had a pull out couch. She, as much as the rest of them, didn't want their night to end. For the sake of comfort and a sense of family, she bent the rules.

The last time that Shatima spent Thanksgiving with a big family was when she was nine. Not even that prepared her for what she walked into the year she was reunited with her family. Big Grams called her with strict instructions to be at the banquet hall at 4 am. She heard all about Shatima cooking just like her father and needed her to make the macaroni and cheese and the collard greens. Shatima and G-Ma rode there together and worked to help make enough food to feed every borough in New York City. Since Shatima's childhood, Thanksgiving had evolved from a family affair to a community wide affair. Anyone in need of a meal was welcome to come down there, get a plate of food, take some home, and possibly make a friend so that their holiday wasn't lonely.

"You just make sure that macaroni and cheese is as good as everyone keeps telling me it is," Big Grams warned Shatima, pointing a finger in her face. "The macaroni and cheese can make or break any meal. Now these people are too nice to say it, but it ain't been the same since your daddy was taken from us. Show me you can help us get that old thing back." She pointed her finger again and walked away to oversee the other dishes being prepared.

G-Ma sucked her teeth. She mumbled something about bossy little sisters and kept peeling the sweet potatoes. Their relationship was strange to Shatima. How did G-Ma get stuck down in the projects when her sister lived in a mansion? Big Grams made it sound like she wanted her sister to live with her. G-Ma said it was fake. The only reason she even bothered to show up at the dinner that year was because the people she normally spent Thanksgiving with - Shatima and Jabez - were there. She would have been fine with them coming upstairs the same way they did for the past four years, but she understood Shatima's need to be with her family. Her sister was pleasantly surprised when G-Ma volunteered her services for the festivities. That was eclipsed by her dictator attitude in the kitchen.

Later on that evening, when her feet ached and her hands never wanted to see another wooden spoon again, Shatima found Rahshaan with Jabez and NyQuest. He made a point to tell everyone that his wifey was responsible for the macaroni and cheese and collard greens. All she wanted to do was sit down and get a taste of what she worked so hard to cook. Rahshaan insisted that they sit at a special table. She made sure that he got one that had a seat for Selena. Since Selena was an awful cook, she was stuck serving. Even wearing a hairnet and gloves, Selena was still absolutely stunning. They smiled and waved at each other while Rahshaan led them to their special table.

There was already a man sitting there when they arrived. At the first glance, the dark, fat face looked like Squeak, but his features were more chiseled. His eyes were gray. A thick, freshly groomed beard framed his face. Though there seemed to be a dark cloud looming over the tall man, he was handsome. Shatima peered at him until being stared at bothered him. He looked up from the food that he was shoveling in his mouth.

"Shameik?" she said slowly.

He looked from Shatima to Rahshaan then at their children. He crumpled his round face while he tried to place hers. "Tima?"

Her grin was a mile wide as she waited for him to get up and hug her.

Instead he demanded, "What the fuck y'all doing here together?"

Shameik had been released from jail that week and was staying with Selena. It was supposed to be a pleasant surprise. For NyQuest and Jabez, it was. He was warm to them. He squeezed NyQuest and commented on how much Jabez looked like their father and Rize. When she reunited with her brothers, Shatima expected to be hoisted onto shoulders and told how much she was missed. She remembered Shameik scowling and grunting a lot when she was younger, but she also remembered him sharing minor tender moments where he placed her head on his shoulder and told her he missed her. She at least expected a hug. Instead, she and Rahshaan sat at the table and explained to Shameik that their being together was a good thing.

G-Ma didn't feel they should have to explain anything to anyone, but did chime in with, "My grandson's been so much better since they got together," a few times.

"You eating like you missed a few meals," Rahshaan joked when Shameik was on his third plate. "You ain't like the cuisine up North?"

"Nigga, fuck you. You just make sure I don't gotta fuck you up over my sister." He looked up and saw G-Ma glaring at him. "My bad, G-Ma. I gotta watch my language around you. I know you and Jesus roll tight."

G-Ma cut her eyes at him.

After dinner, the adults went to party while the children stayed for a lock-in at the hall. All of the top employees at Malachi James' factories were treated to VIP. The section was blocked off by frosted windows, making it a party inside of a party. Rahshaan, Selena, and Shatima sat at a table with a bottle of Krug Grand Cuvée sitting in the middle. Waitresses wearing next to nothing served appetizers, although no one could eat after the feast they just had. They took advantage of the open bar. Never a drinker, Shatima didn't know that champagne followed by glasses of Crown Royal was a recipe for disaster.

It started with dense air looming over their table. Shameik kept making rude comments about Rahshaan and Shatima's relationship. Not even the thudding of the music, the cheering from the people surrounding them, or the liquor could dispel the tension. This was what Rahshaan feared from the first time they kissed. He wasn't supposed to be with this woman. Her life of solitude meant Shatima never had to answer for the decisions that she made. She didn't understand why Shameik's ten years of absence failed to curb his insistence on gatekeeping her love life.

"I'm just saying, Tima. You could open your legs for this mafucka all you want, but you better know what the fuck you're getting yourself into. I've run with this nigga all my life. He's a whore. You want a boyfriend. He ain't that." Shameik tossed back a shot of Hennessy without taking his eyes off of the couple.

Sensing how heated the discussion was getting, Selena moved the bucket holding the champagne bottle from between the siblings.

Rahshaan listened to the two of them go back and forth, but spoke up when his intentions were questioned. "It ain't even like that. I could never disrespect your sister. You know that."

"You fucked her yet?" Shameik asked, cutting his eyes in Rahshaan's direction, but keeping his body turned toward his sister.

The VIP crowd cheered, "Aaayyye!" at the opening riff of Jay-Z's *Give It To Me* being played. When Rahshaan didn't answer, Shameik said, "So you disrespected me, Rize, Nyir, Rico, and my pops."

Shatima rose to her feet, "My pussy ain't got nothing to do with nobody but me. I'm a grown woman. Y'all don't own me or what's in between my legs. I've been on my own since the day Rize was killed, so don't come here now acting like you care. Rize was the only one who looked out for me and made sure I had somewhere to stay. You couldn't keep yourself out of jail long enough to care, and who even knows where Rico and Nyir went? As soon as I got myself established, I went looking for you, and surprise, surprise. You were locked up yet again. I couldn't even find which jail you were in to put money on your books. It took getting with Shaan for me to get linked up with my family. He sat *in my house a*nd told me about y'all, and you know he don't hardly talk. So instead of worrying about what I do in my bedroom and who I do it with, how about you explain where you were when I really needed you?"

Selena stood between the two of them and stretched her arms as though they were enough to keep the brother and sister away from each other. "Just stop! This is the first time I get to see any of my children together since you-know-when, and you're gonna spend this time arguing? Are you serious? Shameik, your sister is grown. You're gonna have to deal with that. Shatima, you can't hold your brother's jail time over his head. You don't even know what he was there for. There's a lot that you two need to hash out, but that's not gonna happen right now. Tonight, we celebrate this little reunion. I never thought this day would come." Her lips forced a smile, but the rest of her face was taut. The two of them thought it to call a truce or get a whooping with the wide leather belt around her waist.

Shatima narrowed her eyes at her brother and then turned to walk away.

"Baby, don't leave," Rahshaan called out to her.

Shameik started to protest, but Selena gave him a stern look. He slumped back on the crushed velvet covered chair and glared out into the crowd.

Shatima blew him a kiss. "I'll be right back. I just need to walk around. I'm gonna go to the bar and get another glass of Crown."

Rahshaan watched her, but didn't say anything. He was apprehensive about her drinking so much. Her chasing glasses of champagne with shots of brown liquor wasn't smart. Selena put the champagne Bucket back on the table. Giving them both a wry smile, she sat back down.

"And where the fuck is Squeak at? That nigga still owes me $20 from before I got locked up. I told him I was coming for my money as soon as I came home." Shameik took a swig of the champagne directly from the bottle.

Barely listening, Rahshaan watched Shatima. The way she looked in the turquoise dress and silver heels she wore let him know he may have to bust a head or two open over his woman. As it was, she was commanding the attention of everyone in the VIP section with the way she threw her ass from side to side as she strutted to the bar. "I don't know. That nigga been acting like a bitch since me and your sister got together," Rahshaan absently replied, his eyes still on Shatima.

Shameik narrowed his eyes. "Why? He like her or something?"

"Everybody wanted your sister when she first moved to Nat Turner," Rahshaan said with a shrug. "She's a dime."

"Yeah, yeah, yeah. She cute. Whatever. But *Squeak* wanted her? Fat ass, ugly ass Squeak thought he had a chance with my sister? Banger, quit playing with me." Shameik let out a loud, obnoxious laugh.

Rahshaan tried not to join in. Squeak had been their friend since childhood. He hated when people picked on him for being facially unfortunate. Because of recent events, he couldn't bring himself to defend Squeak the way he normally would.

Shameik kept ranting. "I got a problem with you fuckin' with my sister because you're a slut, and I know I'm gonna have to fuck you up for breaking her heart. *Squeak,* though? Tell me he ain't serious? How many kids he got now? Ain't he still with that stripper that looks like a Cabbage Patch?"

Rahshaan and Selena had to join in laughing that time. Rahshaan's eyes stayed on Shatima, who seemed to be trying to blend in with the crowd. He could tell by the way her shoulders drooped that she needed him. "I'm about to go check on wifey."

"Wifey?" Shameik repeated. "Nigga, you got my sister pregnant?"

Selena doubled over with laughter at the accusation.

When Rahshaan made his way through the crowd to Shatima, she was drinking an Incredible Hulk and singing and dancing along with the song the DJ played. He put his arms around her.

"You aight?" he asked her.

"I told you I'm good," she said, her words slightly slurred. She didn't sink into his embrace. Her eyes stayed closed as she spoke. Not until he pulled her close to him and started dancing with her did she respond positively. The wall she built around her emotions annoyed him. It was like dating the female version of himself.

A couple of songs later, Shameik broke them up and advised Rahshaan that they were being summoned to the DJ booth. A quick kiss on her lips hinted to Shameik that their relationship might be real. Rahshaan never showed signs of affection publicly. Reluctantly, Rahshaan left Shatima in Selena's care.

As they made their way to the booth, a thick pair of hips stepped in their path. It would be a lie to say Monaysia didn't look good in the tiny metallic halter dress she wore with its neckline plunging down to her navel and giving a peek at her belly ring. If they were still together, Rahshaan would have hoisted her onto something and given her something she could feel in her gut. But he learned the hard way years ago that she was nothing more than something to look at.

"Where's my son?" she demanded.

"With Big Grams just like the rest of the kids, enjoying

himself. Fuck out of my way." Rahshaan put his arm out to move her, but she stepped even closer to him. "What the fuck do you want?"

"Another chance," she said, posing in such a way that her breasts were pushed out. He tried not to pay attention to the way the dress just barely covered her vagina. She couldn't help but admire how good he looked even in a plain white t-shirt and jeans. Much like his attire, life was simpler when she was with him.

He guffawed. "I got a wife now. I told you that already."

"Banger, you never gave me a chance to apologize for what happened. I was stupid and young. I never should have kept NyQuest from you." She grabbed his hand. He recoiled. "Banger, please. I want our family back."

"After you lied on me in court?" he asked. "I lost three years of my life getting caught up with you, and you neglected my son the whole time. You're lucky I don't send some bitches to stomp your ass out, but I'm trying to make sure I have a fair shot at custody."

Monaysia shook her head. "Ain't no fair shot. The only way you'll be a permanent part of my son's life is if *I say*. You still live in them raggedy ass projects, and you probably still sleep on the floor when your grandmother can't say no to people dropping those kids off over there. Meanwhile, I've moved up in life. I just got a townhouse in Midtown. I know you're not gonna go to court and explain how you're able to send me five hundred dollars every week, not living in them raggedy ass Nat Turner buildings."

The way she bounced around while she spoke attracted several passersby. Rahshaan's folded arm and flexed jaw told them to keep going.

"Don't forget you used to live in them same raggedy ass projects and sleep on that same floor with me before I moved you out of there and into a nice apartment," Rahshaan grumbled. The more she spoke, the harder it was for him to believe that he had dealings with this woman that amounted to more than just sex. He watched the men gazing at her as they passed and wondered why she wouldn't just go be one of their headache. After taking the first eight years of fatherhood away from her, he didn't understand why she was so bold.

Monaysia sighed. She knew she was taking a big chance, but she just couldn't stand to see the father of her child happy with someone else. She'd been watching them since the minute they walked in, holding hands, laughing, sitting in VIP, and drinking champagne. That was supposed to be her. "Banger, just let me make it up to you."

"It's all good," Rahshaan said, snatching his arm away from her once again. "Stop using my son to manipulate me, and I'll let you live."

"And what about us?" she pleaded. "I came back for us."

"Ain't no us. I got a wife. When our son is with me, he'll know what it's like to have a complete family. You like them dope boys and fast money. Go pull another one. I'm done with you."

He and Shameik pushed past her. They left her standing there, looking stupid.

Uncle Mont stood to greet Shameik and Rahshaan once they reached the DJ booth. It was a safe space for them to talk about business. The DJ was a husky man named Shondell. He was a part of the extended family and had worked for Mont for years. From that spot above the crowd, they could watch everything that was going on. Mont shuffled through Shondell's selection of records. He looked out at the party longingly. One day, staying low-key would pay off. Then he'd be able to join the party.

"Welcome home," he said to Shameik. The two of them slapped hands and then gave each other a quick half-hug.

"Yo, Unc. You knew this nigga was fuckin my sister and didn't tell me?" Shameik demanded.

Mont shrugged. "It wasn't my business to tell. They're adults. Personally, I think she's a good look for him. Since he got with her, he's been thinking before he reacts. You saw he was within six inches of Monaysia and didn't end her life."

Shameik considered this.

"But y'all hash that out on your own time. Right now, I wanna know what's up with all this spending," Mont switched gears.

Immediately, Rahshaan jumped to defense. "Unc, that was my first time seeing my seed in years. I had to do something for him. Monaysia don't even put a coat on him before taking him outside."

Mont cut him off. "Nigga, you bought some clothes for your son. You was supposed to do that. I peeped you bought Shorty some jewels too. That should've been run by me, but I could let that slide too. I'm talking about this nigga Squeak. The rule is that we never floss, never get flashy. That's how them niggas in the dope game get caught up. We moving something a lot more risky than product. One wrong move, and we could get linked to some shit that will get all of us put away for a very long time. So we keep eyes off of us. This nigga bought two cars and a waterbed in the past two weeks. Who the fuck still buys waterbeds? Where the fuck would he even put a waterbed in the projects?"

Rahshaan and Shameik both shrugged their shoulders.

"This nigga Squeak calls me every five minutes and tells me what you're doing. Meanwhile, he's spending money like crazy. Lynn said he dropped a girl off at a job and left her there. Ain't nobody seen him since. You losing control of your team, son."

The thought of letting down his mentor bothered Rahshaan. "Yo, Unc, I ain't slippin'. He must have somebody else buying that shit for him, because his baby mama still catches the bus with all seven of their seeds, and he's been where he's supposed to be at all times."

"Where he at tonight then?" Mont wondered. "Until up about a month ago, I couldn't see you without him. What happened?"

He didn't get an answer to his question, because a commotion broke out on the dance floor. The looked down to see people surrounding four people. Security was making its way through the crowd to get to flying tracks of hair and fabric.

"Oh shit! That's Shatima and Selena out there fighting!" Mont announced. Rahshaan and Shameik thudded down the stairs. They couldn't make their way through the wall of people who were pushing their way toward a better view of the fight. The security guards were trying their hardest to give the police access without letting the people who were lined up outside in with them. Shondell stopped the music when the lights came on. The police burrowed their way through and pepper sprayed in the general direction of the brawl. With burning eyes, Shatima was dragged and dropped in the back seat of a police car with Selena. Her hands tied behind her back by silver bracelets that were cutting into her skin, she gripped the fabric she ripped from Monaysia's dress and wondered how she got there.

It was a combination of the glasses of Crown Royal, the argument with Shameik, Lil Jon and the East Side Boys screaming *"If you don't give a damn, we don't give a fuck!"* and a decade's worth of anger that got her there. After kissing Rahshaan, she and Selena walked back to the bar. Shatima finished her Incredible Hulk and went back to ordering back to back shots of Crown Royal. After the fifth shot, Selena became concerned. She suggested they leave the open bar area and go see what the party outside of the VIP was like. They made their way to the dance floor. Just like when she was younger, Shatima marveled at Selena's command over her body against the beat. The two of them bent over had the attention of everyone around them who liked to see nice asses gyrating in tight dresses. The loud music, the flashing lights, and the alcohol gave Shatima a headache. Selena led her back to VIP with the intention of hydrating her immediately. They pushed their way through the line of people hoping to get in and flashed their bands. Monaysia started the fight before they could get through the door.

"Didn't I tell you I was gonna fuck you up the next time I saw you?" she called out with close to ten people separating them. "Drunk ass bitch think she cute because she think she got my position. You could never be me."

"Girl, get back," Shatima dismissed Monaysia as Selena pulled her arm.

Monaysia stepped out of her shoes. With delayed reaction time and double vision, Shatima didn't see one of the heels come flying at her face until it connected with her jaw. Before she could swing, Selena was out of her shoes and flying toward the girl. One of Monaysia's friends tried to stop her. Monaysia had tunnel vision as she charged at Shatima.

By the time Monaysia reached her, Shatima had one of her shoes off and smacked her opponent in the face with it. Shatima got her into a headlock and repeatedly beat her in the head with the shoe. Monaysia managed to get free and jabbed Shatima. They boxed. Shatima was at a disadvantage since she only had on one shoe. She managed to get it off her foot, and then she was able to get into a proper stance and footing. The two girls continued to box. Shatima reached for Monaysia's neck to choke her. Monaysia weaved out of Shatima's path. Instead of her neck, Shatima was able to get her dress. The shiny fabric tore. Bare breasted Monaysia charged Shatima once again.

The women turned into a tornado of hair and fabric as they pounded into each other. This was a moment Shatima longed for since she heard about the woman who kept a father from his child. She tried to beat the life out of Monaysia. What she failed to take into account was that for the past month she lived the life Monaysia left behind. With her in the picture, there seemed to be no chance of reconciliation between Monaysia and Rahshaan. She fought as though winning would change the fact that at the end of the night Shatima would be going home with the father of her child.

Her jealousy wasn't enough. Monaysia didn't realize that Shatima had been the victim of a mother like Monaysia. She wasn't going to let that child's relationship be destroyed the same way. In the end, Shatima was the one being pulled off of Monaysia, trying to break a bone in her nearly naked body.

In the back of the car, Shatima struggled to find a comfortable position. The alcohol and bumpy ride had her ready to toss her Thanksgiving dinner. Somehow seated both next to and on top of her was Selena. Throughout the fight, people yelled that she was too pretty to be carrying on like that, but she had no regrets about defending a daughter she'd been separated from for ten years.

When they got to the jail, they had to face the harsh reality that they both were shoeless. The ground was cold, and the floor was filthy. Police officers with bad attitudes and tight grips on their arms dragged them down a corridor to have their mugshots taken. They were thrown into a holding cell together and released from the handcuffs. Into a metal toilet, Shatima discarded every shot of Remy she drank along with all of the food she ate earlier. When she thought she was done, she looked up at the wall and realized someone drew a heart on it with feces. That made her vomit all over again. When she had nothing else to throw up, she stumbled back over to Selena and collapsed beside her on the bench that was to be their bed for the night. She leaned on Selena's shoulder and wept. Selena was mindful that her daughter was sore from the fight as she stroked her head.

"I'm so stupid! Rahshaan is gonna leave me!" she sobbed.

"No, he's not. If anything, he's going to appreciate that you were defending him. He knows why you were out there fighting."

An officer came in and bellowed for Shatima to follow her. She gave Shatima a pair of what equated to wooden flip flops and cuffed her hands. She and another officer led her to a frigid room that looked like it once held a guillotine. The woman left her there without a word. Just as the alcohol started to pull her into a drunken sleep, the door swung open. A female police officer with red hair came in followed by a tall, tan-skinned man with curly hair. She recognized them both, but was confused by their presence.

"Don't worry. We've already called your mother, and she's here to pick you up. We just wanted to talk to you a little bit before she takes you home. Now, do you remember me? I'm Officer Kimborough. We had a little chat in the park where you tried to act like you didn't know who Banger was or what he does. Tonight, seeing you fighting with the mother of his child, it's a little obvious that you lied to me. Do you want to clear that up?"

Shatima started screaming the word "lawyer." She refused to say any more than that one word with its two syllables. When they refused to comply, she screamed louder. The cops taunted her with cackles while Hope made a grand entrance.

"What are you doing with your life?" Hope asked. "You're publicly intoxicated. You're fighting in clubs. You're a single mother. Your hair looks a mess. You're a disappointment."

Hope seemed to be spinning. In her least proud moment, Shatima started sobbing all over again. She never wanted her mother to see her cry.

"You're very violent," Hope continued to berate her. "This is the second time I've seen you in over five years, and both times ended in a fight. I thought that you'd get some help for those issues when you left my house." She sat down and stared at her daughter. A cup of something that smelled like cinnamon and vanilla was in one of her manicured hands. When she leaned over the table, her Angel parfum invaded Shatima's nostrils. "What have you gotten yourself into? Are you in a gang? Are you a hustler's wife? Tell me something. I can help you get out."

"You can't help me," Shatima said with a laugh. "You wouldn't help me when I had nowhere to go and a child to feed. Why would you help me now?"

"Let me ask you this," Hope said, ignoring her daughter's

accusation. "Does any of this have to do with you reconnecting with your father's people?"

"You don't get to ask me about my father!" Forgetting that she was cuffed, Shatima tried to charge for Hope. Officer Kimborough hopped up to protect Hope, but Officer Santarez reached her first. He held her and caressed her like a wounded child. She buried her head in his chest. It was enough to make Shatima vomit again.

"This is getting out of control," Kimborough remarked. She locked eyes with Shatima and said, "I'm gonna give you one last chance. You can be our informant. You can tell us all about what really goes on in those factories. We still have a bench warrant out on you for assaulting a woman named Nicolette Townsend five years ago. We have every reason to lock you up for missing your court date."

"Don't say a word!" a man in an expensive suit bellowed as he burst into the room with two cops. The two cops were Black men with warm smiles and soft eyes for Shatima. She bent her head and stared at the concrete table in front of her. Kimborough and Santarez leapt backward, their skin turning red. Hope sashayed out of the room. The man in the suit called an ambulance to take Shatima to the hospital. He warned the cops who escorted him in of the hell there would be to pay if she had any serious injuries.

Santarez and Kimborough glared after Shatima.

On the way to the hospital, she heard something about not being able to distinguish between the bruises sustained from the fight and the ones given to her by the police's rough handling of her. In the hospital bed, she fell into a deep sleep. Selena took her home as soon as she opened her eyes. When she flipped down the visor in Selena's car, she saw the total opposite from what she looked like when she left the house before the last sunrise. Mascara and black eyeliner streaked down her face. Her hair was straggly. Her dress was torn. She cried the whole way home.

Selena climbed into her bed with Shatima. She wanted to comfort the truest maternal figure she had, but she was still useless under the influence of the morphine they gave her in the hospital. Selena's sniffles and cries were like a bad lullaby, sending Shatima into a restless sleep.

"Those bastards killed my husband. They won't kill me," were the last words Shatima heard.

The next time Shatima awoke, Selena was asleep and Rahshaan was standing over her. She looked around the messy room. Across from her was an 11" x 13" picture of Selena and Chillz, whose frame was in bad need of cleaning. She stared at Rahshaan and tried to remember how she had gotten into Selena's bed. Before Rahshaan could say anything, she panicked.

"Where are Jabez and NyQuest?" she demanded, leaping out of the bed.

Rahshaan grabbed her and hugged her shaking body. "I went and picked them up early this morning. I left them at G-Ma's house so that I could come get you."

During the ride home, she cried about what a horrible mother she was. Rahshaan grew irritated with all of the emotion she displayed. Part of him was grateful that she wasn't upset with him for not being there to pick her up from the jail. Still, the whimpering was annoying.

"Quit babying that little nigga, Tima. Damn. He aight!" Rahshaan scolded her, forcing a laugh to hide his aggravation.

"There's a big difference between babying my son and worrying about what happened to him while I was in jail for fighting in the club like some drunk bird," Shatima snapped.

The thought of her being drunk brought a smile to Rahshaan's face. He saw why she was so uptight all of the time. When she let loose, she went off the chain. By the time he finally made it to the front of the crowd, she was being carried away by police officers.

Shameik had to hold him back. He was going to risk it all with the way they were dragging her, but she was still fighting. Her kicks landed on nothing but air, but she went down swinging. Monaysia, on the other hand, was just down and naked. She and the friend whom Selena beat up were both being escorted to an ambulance looking pretty embarrassed. It took Rahshaan back to the day when Shatima told him not to jump into her affairs because she could handle herself. He felt silly for ever doubting her.

"How you feeling though?" he asked, changing the subject. He figured she would consider it tacky to talk about how well she handled herself.

"I'm sore," she admitted. "I'm worried about Selena, though. She wasn't doing too well when I left."

"Trigga's there," Rahshaan told her, referring to Shameik by his nickname. "That's a mama's boy if ever there was one. He'll make sure she's okay."

It touched Shatima that, even though she was very young and none of their biological mother, Selena was everything Chillz's children ever needed in a mother and more. Shatima wasn't sure what happened to her older brothers' mothers. She didn't even know if they had the same mother. It had never dawned on her to ask.

Once they got back to her apartment, Shatima was able to see just how big of a fool she was. The police ripped the pins out of her hair before throwing her in the holding cell the night before, so all she had left was a ponytail that was hanging onto her head for dear life. A patch of hair was missing from the front of her head. She had no problem covering that with a swing bang or a wig until it grew back. It was the bruises on her face that upset her. A white bandage was taped to her chin where Monaysia's heel had hit her. She wondered how much Dermablend it would take to make herself presentable for her next work week. At least she had the rest of Friday, Saturday, Sunday, and Monday for the swelling to go down.

"Happy birthday weekend to me," she sighed to her reflection in the mirror.

After taking a long bath and icing her sore knuckles, she climbed in the bed. Rahshaan brought her a plate of leftovers from Thanksgiving. Over and over, she apologized to him for messing things up with his son. He told her that everything was going to be all right. Monaysia was the aggressor. There were hundreds of people there to witness her throwing the shoe at Shatima's face. If anything, the fight only made her case stronger. Since Monaysia had attacked Shatima, Rahshaan didn't plan on the case making it to court.

Eventually, Shatima fell back asleep. Rahshaan had made plans for her birthday, but canceled them. He knew she wasn't going to go out with her face bruised. So he lay in bed with her and watched her sleep. When she started calling for her father and her brother, it pained him, but he held her until she screamed herself out of her sleep. She was embarrassed, but he told her everything was okay. Then he kissed her and held her until she fell asleep again.

———

"Who's the girl?" Hope whispered to Santarez as they watched Kimborough through a window. The little woman stood in another interrogation room, red and seething.

"Let's see." Santarez's smile showed how amused he was. "That would be your daughter's step-son's mother, which would make her Banger's baby mama. She's also Squeak's new girlfriend or something."

"Oooh!" Hope drawled, nodding her head. "That's why Shannon's over there fingering her gun. She's jealous. Sloppy. Sloppy. What a pretty girl, though. She's either really desperate or really manipulative."

"Add really hurt to that list," Santarez told her. "Your daughter just beat her up in a club."

Kimborough stomped over to Monaysia and slammed a stack of papers in front of her. "Sign this, or else I'm shipping you back to Syracuse."

Monaysia looked stunned. "What is it?"

"The lease for your apartment." Kimborough stared at her, trying to intimidate her.

"Why do I need to sign it if it's already in Squeak's name?" Monaysia asked.

"You're in no position to question me. It's been a month, and neither of you have been able to get us any closer to Montell Drayton. Now sign this lease, and from this moment on, the basement is off limits to you and your son!"

Hope and Santarez looked on, amused by Shannon's rage.

As soon as she had the signature, Kimborough stormed out of the room, purposely bumping Monaysia on her way out. Squeak dashed behind her and then put his arms around her.

"Let's go for a ride," he suggested.

They got into his Escalade and drove around while Kimborough whimpered about him treating Monaysia better.

"Fuck her," Squeak said. "I told you she ain't shit to me."

"Then why have you moved in with her?" Kimborough demanded.

Squeak looked at her like she lost her mind. "I can't live with you, can I?"

"Well, no, but it was different when you were just living with your children's mother. That I could understand. Why are you with this one?"

Squeak pulled over by a set of townhouses. In the distance, he saw an old friend. He knew the friend saw him, so he shot him a cocky look.

"She's an aesthetic," he told her.

"What do you mean by that?"

Squeak unzipped his pants. "It means I want them niggas to see me shining. They can't kick me around when I flip it on them. Now stop asking questions, and suck my dick."

WHY YOU SHOULD NEVER LEAVE YOUR KIDS AT DARLENE BAILEY'S HOUSE

Selena was a terrible cook. It was a wonder that she could pour a bowl of cereal without error. For that reason, Lynn, Shatima, and Shameik rotated cooking duties every night. On nights when dinner was at Shatima's house, G-Ma joined them. On other nights, they made enough for G-Ma, and either Rahshaan or Shatima took a plate up to her when they got home. That was their family.

It was lovely for them to be together at seven o'clock, no matter what. Even if Lynn and Shatima had to rush back to the shop to do more heads, or if Rahshaan and Shameik had to run back to the factory, or if Selena had to teach a dance class, from 7 pm to 8 pm, they sat around the table for dinner.

Shatima thought this was especially important for Jabez and NyQuest, who was there a lot more after Shatima and Monaysia's fight. Her intent was to give them everything she missed during her childhood. Until she learned how to cook for herself, dinner was usually some microwavable meal during the week while Hope was out covering a news story. On the weekends, she ate takeout while Hope went on dates. On those nights, she was thankful for the primetime TV lineups. Otherwise, she would have gone crazy from the sound of hearing herself chew. Sometimes she ate with either Nicolette's or April's families, but she only went when an invitation was extended, and she made sure to help with cleanup afterward so as not to seem like a moocher. She wanted the boys to feel the love that she only got in small doses.

Dinner was the only time Shatima saw Rahshaan after her fight. She couldn't tell if it was because he was concealing the fact that he was truly angry about her fighting, or if he simply was busy. They communicated through brief phone calls and text messages throughout the day. He was so sullen that it was hard to gauge what was going through his head. Sometimes, he stopped by for sex in the middle of the night. She guessed she was supposed to feel used, but she felt a lopsided satisfaction. If it turned out that he was just busy, then it was fine that he at least cut out a portion of his day to give her one part of him that she was becoming addicted to. Though she longed for the quality time he gave her just a few weeks ago, she wasn't about to beg him for something he barely had for himself.

There was nothing Rahshaan wanted more than to take Shatima out every night and spend the whole night with her, but things were getting rocky for him. Squeak's purchases were getting more and more reckless. People reported to him that Squeak was telling anyone who would listen that he was tired of Rahshaan being Mont's right hand man. Some people said Squeak was jealous of Rahshaan getting Shatima. Squeak's relationship status and the seven children made that stupid to him. Add that to the fact that Shatima pretty much hated Squeak, and there was no point in Squeak being mad.

To Rahshaan, jealousy was the ugliest trait one could show a friend. Many said that it was an emotion reserved for women, but Rahshaan disagreed. Jealousy in men was dangerous. It could cost a life. With Squeak letting this get to him to the point where he was going to the police with lies, this could either end in death or prison. Rahshaan wanted neither. He finally had a reason to live.

"Yo, Banger, was Squeak a bitch before I got locked up?" Shameik asked as they sat at the table, waiting for Shatima to finish cooking dinner.

Shatima turned to him and frowned. "Shameik, I've told you not to talk like that in my house or around my child."

Shameik frowned back at her. "Quit babying my nephew. It's some shit that he's gonna hear in life. Long as he ain't saying the shit, we good. I can't stand no little cussin' ass, bad ass mutha-fuckas." He turned to Jabez. "Nephew, don't say shit, damn, bitch, muthafucka, cock sucker, muthafuckin' cock sucker, hell, damn, fuck, ho, pussy, dirty pussy eatin' bitch, or nigga until you earn the right to say it. Uncle Shameik earned the right to say some fucked up shit, so he says fucked up shit. Aight?"

While the adults at the table cracked up, Jabez clasped his hand over his mouth and tried not to let his mother see him laughing. Shatima was only slightly amused.

Shameik's phone sang out Beanie Siegel's *Think It's a Game*. He told Shatima to answer it. When she did, someone took a puff off of a joint before responding.

"Who the fuck is this? Trigga got a chick answering his phone?" the voice on the other end said.

A smile spread across her face. "Rico, it's Shatima!" she announced, her voice the cheeriest it had been in weeks.

Rico blew smoke into the phone. "Who?"

"Your sister. I know we haven't seen each other in some years, but-"

"I know who the fuck you is," Rico cut her off. "You're that little shit Hope pushed out of her pussy. You the reason my daddy dead and my brother dead. I ain't got shit to say to you. Get the fuck off my brother's phone." The announcement that their call ended sounded in her ear. She shut the clamshell and tossed it back to Shameik. Everyone looked at her for an explanation.

The area code on the phone said 757, but it felt like Rico was in the room with her, punching her in her face repeatedly with his words. Tears streamed from her eyes without her permission. She knew these reunions would be difficult. She didn't know that they would cut this deep. For the first time, she regretted keeping her story to herself.

Shameik dialed Rico's number again and turned on the speakerphone.

"Nigga, fuck you for even being around Hope's daughter. She ain't shit but her mama's puppet. Every time she comes around, somebody gets murked. Life is way too good for me right now." Rico was relieved to finally get to let his sister know how he felt about her.

Shatima gripped the edge of her table. Through clenched teeth she said, "Jabez, go get your Power Rangers tray, set it up in your room, close the door, and eat in front of the TV."

With a grin on his face, Jabez did as he was told. Very rarely was he allowed to eat in front of the TV.

"How you gonna hold it against her that her mother's a snake?" Shameik demanded.

"Come on, Trig," Rico urged his oldest brother. "She comes over one day, and the next day Daddy gets murked, and then she just disappears? That don't sound suspect to you?"

"You don't even know what happened to her when she disappeared," Rahshaan spoke up.

Rico paused. "*Banger* over there too? What the fuck? You tryna get caught up like my pops did with that snake bitch, Hope? All of y'all some suckas."

"Nigga, get the fuck outta here with that bullshit. She don't even know what went down, and watch who you calling a bitch. That's your damn sister." Knowing how stubborn Rico was, Rahshaan prepared himself to go back and forth for several rounds with his friend.

"Oh that's the shit she gassed you with?" Rico laughed, coughed, sputtered, and laughed again. "I thought you was done getting gassed by bitches after Monaysia."

Rahshaan clenched his fist and had to restrain himself from punching a hole through the glass table.

Shatima finally suppressed her sadness and found her voice. Knocking her plate to the floor, she stood up and grabbed Shameik's phone the way she wanted to grab Rico's neck. "Look. You don't have to like me or love me, but don't get it twisted. Hope wants me dead just like *my father* and *my brother*. She got police surveillance on *me*, and *I'm next* to die. Learn what you're talking about before you run your mouth."

"You should've died that night she fucked your ass up," Rico shot back. "Then I don't know about Daddy, but I know Rize would still be here. You was the last person he was seen with. Next thing we know, we're getting video tapes of him getting raped and killed."

"Rico!" Selena's voice was sharp. Her eyes were squeezed shut, and she rubbed her temples as she spoke. "Apologize to your sister."

Rico paused. "Y'all got Mommy over there too?"

"Apologize to your sister *now*, Rico." Lynn's voice was firm, but Rico didn't say anything. Selena picked up the phone and took it outside to finish the conversation with her second oldest, and most stubborn, son. Lynn followed, cussing Rico out the whole time.

Shatima retreated to her bedroom. Rahshaan followed her and tried to talk to her, but didn't know what to say. Her thinking that she was about to die rattled him. He wanted to ask her why she thought that, but didn't know what to say about that either. So he just sat there and watched her retreat to that place she went when she didn't want to be reached. There was no time for him to try to bring her back. He had to return to work. He kissed the side of her face before leaving, but she never responded.

Rahshaan and Shameik went into the basement level of the

factory where they worked. They went into a room made of concrete floors and walls where Shondell, and three other members of their family - Moosie, Ken-Ken and PeeWee - sat with Mont. Shondell, Ken-Ken, and PeeWee were sitting in folding chairs at a metal table, furiously counting money and rattling off totals to Moosie. Every time they gave her a total, she looked at a ledger book and frowned. Then she told them to count it again.

"Where the fuck is Squeak at?" Rahshaan wanted to know after mentally taking attendance. "I ain't seen that nigga since Shameik got home."

"I was about to ask you that question," Mont said. "Because he's missing, and so is some money."

Shameik sat down. "His baby mama asked me about him too when I was going into their building earlier. What the fuck is going on?"

"That's what the fuck I called you in here to ask you!" Mont's voice thundered across the room. "I got a whole room full of girls saying he ain't escorting them to jobs, and if he escorts them to the spot, then he ain't there when they come out. Now, I wanna know what the fuck is going on?"

Shondell finished counting money and wrapped a rubber band around it. "I know where that nigga at: the police station. He down there snitching on all of us, got them thinking we dealing dope. That's the only thing that's keeping them from arresting any of us: they can't prove what we doing. I seen him around my way the other day. I peeped him getting head from that redheaded cop."

"He see you?" Mont asked him.

"He wanted me to. Why else would he come over to Frederick Douglass to do some shit he could've done at the telly?"

"Red hair? Banger, didn't Tima say the pig that keeps approaching her has red hair?" Shameik questioned.

Rahshaan stood against the concrete wall with his arms folded across his chest and nodded, but didn't verbalize anything. He rested one steel-toed boot against the wall and paid attention to everything that was being discussed in that room.

"How is it that everybody in this room can work for me and be happy with what they have, but that nigga is about to destroy a three generation empire behind his jealousy?" Mont asked. "How is it that y'all niggas are happy with living regular ass lives while one nigga got to be flashy? Y'all tell me where shit went wrong, cuz I'm lost."

"Unc, we don't know nothing more than you," Shondell said.

Ken-Ken stopped counting money so that he could make eye contact with Mont. "Keep it thoro. We know what the streets are saying. He's tired of staying in the PJs and having to live low-key. He's tired of the dope boys who are supposed to be answering to him living flashier than him, and he's tired of not being 'that nigga.' He wants status like Banger, but nobody fears him unless Banger's around."

Mont squinted at Rahshaan and tried not to laugh. "You hear this middle school ass shit. How you with a nigga every day and don't know he feel this way?"

Rahshaan didn't say anything. It all sounded stupid to him.

PeeWee added, "He said he came to you about moving up, and you played him."

Mont leaned on the back legs of the metal folding chair in which he sat and tried not to be amused by the report. "Move up to what? That nigga don't work the fryer at McDonald's."

PeeWee put his hands up. "I don't know what the fuck the nigga talking about. I just remember one day he was bitchin about having all them kids in a three bedroom apartment, and he felt like you should have given him a bigger crib on the strength of it. Shit sounded stupid to me, so I asked him why he ain't put in more work for you than he put in making babies, and the nigga got mad. I ain't think nothing of it, because you know Squeak. He always mad about something."

That time Mont did let out a long laugh. "Nigga said I should have *given h*im a bigger crib. Like 'Congratulations on knocking up your girl for the seventh time. Here's a house even though you don't do shit but stand on that stoop with a bunch of little niggas unless Banger tells you you're needed somewhere'? Fuck outta here, PeeWee."

"I'm just tryna help make sense out of all this shit, Unc," PeeWee told him.

Mont became serious as he addressed the room. "Do you niggas know what we're facing? Every woman that we employ consents to this shit. She does it because this is what the fuck she decided to do to pay bills. We provide a safe environment for them to make money, and we take that money and give it back to the hood. We provide jobs and food for those in need since that shit is so scarce everywhere else. What we do shouldn't be considered illegal. We have adult fucking women fucking for money and dancing naked for it. Some do it to pay for school. Some do it because they can't support a family on the little bull-shit they bust their asses for at their full time jobs. Some do it because they like to fuck. And fuck it; why not get paid to do something you enjoy? I don't know their individual stories unless they tell me. I just promise them that they won't get caught or killed doing something that shouldn't be illegal in the first place.

"We don't get to be flashy and floss, but so the fuck what? We ain't rappers. We grown ass men who understand what it means to sacrifice so that our families can eat. I can't show my face in public, but my grandmother has a house, a restaurant, and a catering business. I put my mama through nursing school, and now she's a nurse practitioner. It's not a nigga in here who can say his family ain't being taken care of. Maybe not on the same scale as mine, but y'all ain't put in the work that I have. You'll all get there one day soon, if you choose. I look at all of y'all niggas as my kids. So what the fuck is there to be jealous of?"

Mont's small audience mumbled that they agreed with every-thing he said, and no one had an answer. The frown on his normally smiling face concerned them.

"This nigga is potentially fucking with niggas who can somehow have those kidnappings going on around town tied to us. They tried to tie them to my pops and to Chillz's pops, and both of them niggas is dead. The fuckin' pigs have a human trafficking ring going on. They're moving *children,* and selling them as sex slaves, and they're trying to pin that on me. And this nigga Squeak is trying to help them."

Mont continued his rant. Rahshaan only half listened. When Mont got going, there was no telling when he'd be finished. The important things to take away from the rant were that Squeak was a snake, and Squeak had to die. In Rahshaan's opinion, nothing else needed to be said.

"So, Unc, we about to go find this nigga and smoke his ass," Ken-Ken said, rising from his chair to leave.

"Nigga, sit your trigger happy ass down!" Mont barked. Sometimes having the shoot first, ask questions last mentality that his squad operated on was more of a curse than a gift. Within the crew were a couple of hotheads. "Think about this shit logically. If he's working with the pigs, then he's got the pigs protecting him. We can't just go blasting. We don't even know where he's at."

"Then let's go visit his baby mom. She should know where that nigga at," Shameik suggested.

Moosie, who was the only woman in their crew, spoke up. "Keep loud mouth Shanae out of it. If she knew what he was doing, it would be the buzz around the club. I ain't heard nothing. Matter of fact, she's been going around to a couple of girls in the club asking if they know where he is. So if she knows anything, then she's doing a good job of hiding it."

They sat in the room, hypothesizing on what Squeak was doing and how they were going to catch him in the act. Mont was still stuck on the jealousy thing. He knew he treated Rahshaan better than them, but that was because Rahshaan was his personal responsibility. Everyone else in the room grew up with parents and a steady address. Rahshaan lived as a nomad, trying his hardest not to be a burden to anyone. Mont always went out of his way to let Rahshaan know he wasn't a burden, that he was welcome and loved, but he knew his parents' abandonment did something to Rahshaan's psyche. In turn, Rahshaan put in twice the work that was asked of him. He took for granted that everyone else understood that.

Just as they were getting ready to call it a night, Rahshaan's phone sang out Amerie's *Why Don't We Fall In Love?* Eyebrows raised all around the room. Jokes were cracked. He ignored them and tried to conceal how nervous he was. Shatima calling him at that time of night couldn't be good news.

"Yo?" he said into the phone as in as nonchalant a voice as he could muster.

"Um...Could you check your homies please? They should know by now that you don't stay here, and I don't appreciate a lame coming here at 3 am disrespecting me and my son." Shatima's voice sounded like she was ready to murder someone for interrupting her sleep.

Rahshaan motioned for everyone in the room to quiet down. "Who came by your crib?"

"Squeak!" she snapped. "He was bragging about how he was next up or something and flashing some cash in my face. "Then he called me a 'B' and said eff my son when I told him that you weren't here."

Rahshaan let that go without comment and added that to the list of rounds he was going to fire into Squeak. "What else he say?"

"I don't know. He was talking a lot of nonsense," Shatima replied. "He started talking about moving to Midtown. Then his kids' mother came running up the stairs and screaming on him, so I just slammed the door in his face and called you."

Rahshaan inhaled, exhaled, and tried not to tear out of the room and find Squeak by himself. He concealed his anger. "Yo, Ma, I might not be around for a few days, but I'm gonna get up with you as soon as I can." He paused before saying the next sentence. "I love you, aight?"

Taken aback, Shatima didn't know what to say. Instinctively, she responded with bitchiness to conceal the butterflies and delight she felt. "Whatever, Rahshaan. Just make sure your homies know that you don't pay a single bill here, so they don't have a reason to look for you over here at 3 am. Get that under control. My son is asleep, and I have a job to go to in the morning." She hung up the phone without another word.

Being handled in such a way after being so vulnerable put Rahshaan in an even worse state. He ignored the teasing coming from his friends. He relayed everything that Shatima told him. They ventured back to Nat Turner in hopes of finding Squeak.

Instead of finding Squeak, they ran into the mother of his children and the aunt with whom they stayed. The hallway's acoustics carried their argument to the doors of every apartment under and over them.

"You do know where he at, Mavis!" Shanae screamed. "You just said he came through here earlier and told you where he was staying at. I heard you on the phone. How come you can tell everybody about my nigga but me?"

"Bitch, I ain't got shit to do with what y'all got going on. If you don't know where the fuck your man is at, then maybe that nigga ain't your man no more. It would do you some good to calm the fuck down anyway. How many fucking babies do y'all muthafuckas think we can fit in a three bedroom apartment with one damn bathroom? Got my house smelling like cum, gonorrhea, and Enfamil." She lit a cigarette and started smoking it.

"But, Auntie Mavis, we supposed to stick together. You supposed to tell me if he cheating on me!" Shanae whined.

Mavis looked at Shanae as if she lost her mind. "Bitch, if you out here arguing with me about whether or not he's cheating, then you know he's cheating. What the fuck you gonna do? Move out and get an apartment and take care of your own damn kids? Or you just gonna sit in my house and hope he comes back to let you drive one of the cars that he bought?" She looked at the audience they had and locked in on Rahshaan. "Yeah, I'm snitchin. I'm telling it all, because when whatever this nigga got going on blows up in his ugl'ass face, I want y'all to know that I ain't have shit to do with it." She took a drag of her cigarette and damaged her already rough voice even further. "The pigs been calling here looking for him, threatening to lock me up if I don't tell them where he's at. I don't like that shit. Police make me itch."

Irritated with the cigarettes and the arguing between Mavis and Shanae, Shameik interrupted them. "Shanae, go inside. I hear your baby crying." Shanae got the hint and went inside. He then asked Mavis for any other information she could give on Squeak's whereabouts.

Mavis's information led them to her niece's barbershop in Midtown. In the morning, she was waiting for them. She set them up in her office in the back where there was a window facing a row of townhouses. They piled in the dark room with the window cracked and watched as a silver Cadillac Escalade pulled in front of the house. Squeak laid on the horn. His body language said that he was frustrated as he got out. When he was halfway up the walkway to the townhouse, Monaysia and NyQuest came out. Monaysia was texting on her cellphone and not paying attention to NyQuest, who trailed behind him.

"Mommy, it's cold," NyQuest complained.

"Then that means that you not walking fast enough!" she called back. "Now come on. The seats in Mr. Squeak's car are heated. The faster you walk, the faster you'll get to them."

Smoke came from Rahshaan's head. The years that he was apart from his son weighed down on his mind. To know that this was the care NyQuest was under while he had a parent willing to love him ripped Rahshaan's heart in half and turned his stomach.

They looked on as Monaysia continued to ignore NyQuest. She and Squeak kissed. Squeak grabbed two handfuls of her ass.

NyQuest groaned and complained for them to open the SUV's door for him. Instead, Squeak mushed the little boy's face with his large hand. NyQuest stumbled and fell backward into a slushy puddle. When he started to cry, Monaysia screamed for him to man up.

"Unh-uh. My cousin is out of control," Cherise remarked. "He do that little boy dirty like that all the time."

"Cherise," Rahshaan's voice was a low growl. His eyes never left his son. "First chance you get, I want you to go out there and get my seed and bring him over here." His hand rested on his hip where his gun sat waiting for him to use it.

"Oh, I'll have a chance real soon. They'll take him down the street to the bus stop and then leave him there to get the bus by himself," she told him. She left the room to retrieve some towels to wrap around NyQuest. When she came back, she tossed a pile of them to Rahshaan. They landed around him. He left them there.

Behind the Escalade, a Crown Victoria pulled up. Kimborough and Santarez got out of the front of the car. They spoke with Squeak and Monaysia briefly and then pulled off. Whatever they said made Monaysia buck her eyes at them. She looked like she wanted to run away, but Squeak pulled her backward and commanded her to stay, as though he was talking to a dog. For several minutes, Squeak and Monaysia stood there arguing about whether or not she could go inside and change NyQuest. Squeak urged her to get him out of there. She continued to protest until Squeak drew back and slapped her. Holding her face, Monaysia hollered for NyQuest to get in the car.

Just as Cherise predicted, they dropped NyQuest off at the bus stop and sped off.

In Santarez's and Kimborough's places came a Lincoln Town Car. A light skinned man wearing a navy blue suit exited. He opened the back door. Four middle school aged boys were dragged out of the car in a line, their wrists cuffed. The man commanded them into the house.

Inside of the shop, the silence was thick and uncomfortable. Every man and Moosie reached for his and her gun. Cherise's focus remained on the little boy who was in wet clothing in an icy puddle.

"Somebody let Unc know the kid toucher is here," Rahshaan instructed, his voice dry.

Cherisse took off down the street in her car as soon as they left and told NyQuest to get in the front seat. He was reluctant at first, but as soon as the little boy heard that his daddy was waiting for him, he hopped into the car. Water and slush dripped behind Cherise as she carried the little boy into the room where Rahshaan was still staring at Monaysia's house. He held his son, and certain things that irritated him before became painfully clear.

The way Shatima treated Jabez came to mind. She wasn't babying him; she was protecting him. There was some sick shit in the world, and she wanted to make sure that none of it touched her son. He loved her more for the lessons she taught him through example.

Rahshaan called Marcus and instructed him to go buy a few outfits for NyQuest as quickly as possible and to meet him at the barbershop. Then he went to do something he never thought he'd do.

Darlene Bailey's house was the last place any child needed to be. Walking through the door was a reminder of the last time he was there, almost two decades ago. The same wallpaper that was there in the '80's peeled from the walls. One of the rooms still had shag carpeting. She didn't do anything to decorate such as hanging pictures on the wall or putting plants in it. It didn't smell like anything. It rarely did. Looking at how dreary the house appeared let Rahshaan know that whatever they were going to do had to be done quick.

What was supposed to be a fast drop off turned into a full-fledged interrogation. Darlene ripped the door open as soon as Marcus and Rahshaan pulled into the driveway.

"I have been calling your little girlfriend's house for the past hour looking for you. Monaysia's mama has been calling me trying to see if you knew where your son was. The school called and said that he didn't get to school today, but Monaysia claims she put him on the bus."

"Ma, shut the fuck up!" Rahshaan growled. He looked at NyQuest and calmed his voice, although he was angry about the half-truth that Monaysia told. "I need you and Marcus to watch Quest for me while I handle some business." He led his son into the house.

Darlene gushed, "Oh, I'm so glad that my grandbaby is okay!" She crouched down and hugged the little boy who was still a little cold.

"I found him outside in a puddle," was all the explanation Rahshaan gave while glowered past her at the peeling wallpaper with the brown flowers. He didn't understand why Marcus returned and chose to live there.

"Ma, you clean?" Rahshaan interrogated his mother.

"You know I just celebrated eighteen months of sobriety," she proudly declared, batting her lashes. She stood there and waited for a congratulations that never came.

Rahshaan turned to Marcus. "You and her take care of my son. Don't let nobody know he's here. I'll be back to get him as soon as I take care of this thing."

Marcus nodded solemnly.

"Take care of him," Rahshaan commanded firmly. "Don't leave the house with him. If Monaysia calls here looking for him, tell her you ain't seen him, but you been out looking for him. *Do not let* her know where my seed is."

"I know she did you wrong, but I wish that you and that girl would try to get along better for the sake of your son," Darlene commented.

Rahshaan hated when Darlene used the word "but".

Anything that she said before the "but" should have been the end of her statement.

"Yeah, and I wish more bitches would stop chasing dick and be mothers." He hadn't meant for the comment to be a shot at Darlene, but it certainly applied.

One set of dark, offended eyes locked with one set of judgmental, angry eyes. It was the first time either of them came close to mentioning the reason for the rift between them. Darlene looked at a hurt son who would never accept her apology and felt helpless. Rahshaan's mind stayed fixed on the moment that made him who he was forever, and he wondered if she was any different from she was back on that day.

Darlene was the black sheep of the family. Her life's plan included rejecting higher education, a higher power, and working. She married a local, small time hustler called Slick. Within their first month of marriage, she was pregnant with Rahshaan. Slick was incarcerated by the time Rahshaan was born.

Without Slick, Darlene turned to the streets to cure her loneliness. She was seen hanging out in all of the local bars. That's where she became friends with the drugs and liquor that took her until the next century to flush out of her system. When she ran out of money to pay her debt, she became close with the local bartender. He was a married man. When Darlene got pregnant with his baby, he begged her to go away quietly and get rid of it. She refused and gave birth to Marcus anyway. When Slick came home to see his wife had another man's baby, he was livid. He came and went as he pleased, never acknowledging the baby and seldom paying attention to Rahshaan.

When Slick stayed there, he and Darlene tried to make the best of things. Even though he couldn't forgive her for having another man's baby, he got her pregnant once again. Darlene couldn't tell him for certain that the baby was his, so he left again.

In her seventh month of pregnancy, Darlene went into labor on her bathroom floor. She tried to hold her foot against the door and muffle her screams. Rahshaan heard her anyway. The eight-year-old pushed his way into the bathroom to see if he could save his mother. Her screams pushed the fear of dying into his heart. The amount of blood that he saw when he opened the door almost made him faint. She screamed for him to get a trash bag. Dutifully, he retrieved one and handed it to her. Several minutes later, she screamed out in agony. She put something in the trash bag and then shoved it through the door with the instructions to take it outside. She grunted and screamed out her pain.

"But, Mommy, it's moving," he protested. "That thing in that bag is alive."

Never was there a colder, lonelier walk than the one he had to take from the house to the dumpster that night. He hoped that someone would hear the cries of the triplets and rescue them. No one ever did. He stayed watch through his window throughout the night. In the morning, he watched intently as the garbage collectors tossed each bag in the back of their dump truck. They were so careless about the contents of the black bags. Rahshaan didn't know if the babies were actually still crying or if he was going crazy.

Days later, Darlene handed baby Marcus to Rahshaan and told him to hold him until she came back. She declared that she was going to find Slick and make him do right by them. Even at the age of eight, it was an insult to his intelligence. Rahshaan watched her walking around the house, tremors plaguing her arms. The woman couldn't stand still. With her eyes sunken in and skin hanging from her bony frame, she looked like a zombie. Her departure was a relief.

For hours, Rahshaan did not move from that spot. He held onto his brother and waited for something to happen. The only thing that happened was that Marcus needed his diaper changed. The eight-year-old went through several diapers before he figured out what he was doing. Every time Marcus cried, he did whatever he could to make the infant shut up immediately. It was a torturous reminder of the babies in the garbage bag. Rarely did he acknowledge hunger. When he finally grew an appetite, it was days later. He found that all they had stocked in the house were raw spaghetti noodles and a box of stale cereal.

At the end of a week, it was clear that neither Darlene nor Slick planned to return. The quiet of the house slowly drove Rahshaan crazy.

He had to get out of there before he became a zombie like his mother. There were three diapers left and just a pinch of formula for Marcus. The baby's cries collided with Rahshaan's hunger pangs. He did what he could to make a bottle. Then he packed the last three of Marcus' diapers in a bag, dressed him the best that he could, and set off to find someone to help them.

As Rahshaan pushed Marcus' stroller down the street in the air that couldn't figure out if it wanted to be winter or spring, a car pulled beside them. Lynn was on her way to their house to check on them, because she hadn't heard from Darlene in weeks. Rahshaan just stared at Lynn when she rolled down the window and asked where his mother was. She knew Darlene had a problem, but didn't know it was that bad. Rahshaan and Marcus were packed into her car and taken to her house. A few phone calls were made. Lynn gladly would have taken Marcus and Rahshaan in as her own, but when Charlene Glover got the word that her daughter abandoned her children, she picked them up and would not hear of another person raising them. Lynn, Mont, and Chillz made room for him in their homes anyway. They knew how crowded Charlene's tiny apartment got, and they wanted him to have space of his own.

After that, the babies' voices faded to the back of Rahshaan's mind. Years later, when Darlene returned to them claiming to be clean, Marcus went right along with her. Rahshaan refused. From that day on, he looked at Marcus as a sellout. He felt no sympathy for his baby brother, who seemed to be raising his mother more than the other way around. While Rahshaan was being taken under Uncle Mont's wing, Marcus was bribing Darlene into one drug rehab after another. Rahshaan looked at their toxic relationship with much disdain. Rarely did he comment on it.

"You never blamed Slick for none of the shit he put us through," Darlene snapped, reading the judgment in Rahshaan's eyes. The only time she relived her biggest sin was when she was in his presence. She knew that act was the moment that defined their relationship. It was a personal goal of hers to get them both past that, but Darlene knew it wasn't a logical goal to set. Inside, she knew that what she made him an accomplice to hurt him.

She rationalized the act by telling herself that if her husband was around more, then the act never would have happened.

Rahshaan never wanted to discuss with her why she made him do what she made him do. "Whatever, Ma. You just make sure you don't tell anyone NyQuest is here until I come back to get him. Call into work if you can't keep it off the gossip circuit. Once anything gets talked about at that place you work at, it's all around town."

Darlene had to chuckle at that. The housekeeping staff where she worked was nicknamed "Channel 6 News."

Rahshaan went through the house to do a brief inspection. Something told him this was a bad idea, but this was the last place anyone would look for his son. He checked to make sure there was food in the refrigerator and pantry. The sight of spaghetti noodles made him shudder. A quick trip to Marcus' room, the only room in the house that was updated, made him feel a little more at ease. He held NyQuest to his chest.

"Be good for Grandma and Uncle Marcus, okay? Anything you need, Marcus will get for you. I'll be back to pick you up soon, okay?"

NyQuest nodded his head and kissed Rahshaan on his forehead. It touched Rahshaan. Before they were separated, he always kissed his son in that exact spot.

"Now why couldn't you just take your son to your girlfriend's house is what I want to know. What kind of relationship do you have if you have to keep your children separate?" Darlene asked Rahshaan as he was heading out the door.

Rahshaan almost was able to ignore the question, but something tugged at him. "Ma, shut the fuck up! Don't ask about Tima again. If I wanted to leave Quest there, then I would have."

"Well, I don't understand why NyQuest is here. You're obviously closer to that girl than you are to me. You obviously don't trust me, because you're making Marcus watch him in *my* house," Darlene went on.

Rahshaan tried not to pick up something off the counter and launch it at his mother's head. "Ma, I need you to shut the f- I just need you right now, okay? I need you, and your house."

A grin that irked Rahshaan started forming on Darlene's face. He left before she could say anything else to upset him.

Once Rahshaan got back to Nat Turner, Moosie was standing on the stoop in Squeak's usual place. Rahshaan looked toward the windows on the fourth floor. Soon, he and his son would be able to retreat there at the end of every day.

Moosie laughed. "Nigga, what the fuck is you, the dime whisperer? You only settle down with the baddest of chicks. With an ass like your wifey got, though, I would've stopped fucking around too."

"Quit talkin' about my girl's ass, and focus," Rahshaan snapped. "That nigga Squeak been through here yet?"

Moosie nodded. "Yeah. Him and Shanae got into it, and then he left. Shameik wants us to come pick him up from the barbershop."

Rahshaan nodded his head. His phone rang. He frowned at the display. He hadn't seen that phone number in years.

"Quest's school called and said that he never made it there. Did you take him?" Monaysia's voice came across the phone in breaks and waves.

"Nah, I wouldn't do that without letting you know. Fuck is you talking about?" Rahshaan asked and signaled for Moosie to be quiet by putting a finger to his lips. Moosie lit a cigarette and leaned against the snow covered railing. She strained to hear the other end of the conversation.

Snot preceded her words. "Banger, you have to help me look for our son. I'm scared that something bad has happened to him. I...I fucked up."

Hearing her say "our son" infuriated Rahshaan. It was the first time she did it since NyQuest was a baby. "What you mean you fucked up? Where's my son?"

"Banger, I got into a lot of trouble where I was, and I met this lawyer named Andrew Jones, and he said-"

"Andrew Jones?" Rahshaan barked. "Monaysia, get the fuck off of my phone. You better hope I find my son before I get to your ass."

"Banger, *please f*ind him. That man is creepy, and I-"

Rahshaan hung up the phone mid-sentence. The night of NyQuest's birth, he specifically told Monaysia to never have his child around that man. He wanted to do unspeakable things to the mother of his child for the danger that she put his son in. He wanted to hurt himself for letting it go on for so long. NyQuest deserved better parents.

Moosie motioned for Rahshaan to follow him. They climbed into a car that was unfamiliar to Rahshaan. He didn't ask who it belonged to. Moosie took care of the minor details they otherwise overlooked so that nothing got traced back to them. Rahshaan's phone sang out *Hail Mary.* Rahshaan answered and told Uncle Mont to speak quickly.

"I just called to make sure you were good. I spoke with Marcus earlier..." Mont's voice trailed off.

Rahshaan was distant for a second. He looked at his phone. Back to back, envelopes appeared on the screen. All were text messages from Shatima, asking him where NyQuest was. He hated having to ignore her. "I'm good."

Mont relayed a few things that Marcus wanted Rahshaan to know after a conversation with NyQuest. Squeak and Monaysia had been together for a while, for one. He visited her for months before she moved back to town. For another, Squeak physically abused Monaysia often. Finally, Squeak recently started abusing NyQuest as well.

Rahshaan hung up the phone. He couldn't stand to hear what he was being told. The phone's voicemail alert sounded. Checking his voicemail was a mistake, but he did it anyway. He wanted to hear Shatima's voice. He knew at least one of the messages was from her.

"Rahshaan, why do I have to keep calling you about Squeak? Check him, and I'm not gonna tell you again!" she screamed into the phone.

Another message from her had a desperate tone: "Why do people keep calling here about NyQuest? I've gotten calls from your mother, from your grandmother, and from your brother. What is going on? Please just pick up the phone. I need to know that NyQuest is alright. Please call me back or come by and let me know what is going on."

They rode silently back to the barbershop. Cherise let them in through the back door. She asked Rahshaan about NyQuest, but Rahshaan didn't answer. Shondell pointed to the window they left cracked open so that they could listen for the perfect opportunity to attack. They all watched and listened as an argument between Squeak and Monaysia intensified.

"You better go get up with Banger and find my son!" Monaysia warned him.

"You don't even give a fuck about the little nigga!" Squeak argued.

"Yes, I do!" Monaysia shot back, her fists balled up at her sides. "I'm tired of people telling me I don't give a fuck about my son!"

Squeak said nothing. He started walking away from her. She ran after him, pulling the sleeve of the waist length chinchilla jacket he wore. He turned and smacked her so hard that she flew backward and landed in the same puddle her son sat in earlier. At first she looked stunned, and then she grimaced in pain.

"He be beating the shit out of that girl. I can't stand that nigga," Cherise commented, gathering some books and a planner. "I'm just gonna be out front if y'all need anything." She switched out of the room and went to the front.

Watching the mother of his child being beaten by his friend since childhood didn't affect Rahshaan in the least. By the end of the night, they both would get what they deserved. He watched Monaysia get up. She squared up to fight Squeak the way she fought Shatima in the club. He slapped her again. She lit into him with punches that only got minor reactions from him. In the midst of their tussle, a police car pulled up. Kimborough and Santarez exited. Then several other cars pulled in behind them. Kimborough pointed Monaysia out to them and commanded them to arrest her.

She screamed at Squeak that he promised her he would keep her out of jail. Squeak looked away from her crying. Something he saw when he took his eyes off of her angered him.

"You snake bitch! You set me up!" He ripped a gun from his coat pocket and shot her between her eyes just before the police reached her to cuff her. Kimborough put her hands on her red head and screamed. Her eyes grew wider, screams grew louder when he turned the gun to his own face and shot himself. The police officers stopped moving toward them, unsure of what to do next. Even Kimborough and Santarez looked confused. Then Santarez led some of them into the house while others stayed and called an emergency response team.

For the next two hours, Rahshaan and crew watched from the barbershop window as boys and corpses were pulled from the basement. Neither one of them spoke or moved. They couldn't believe that they were so close to people who had a hand in that. Rahshaan hated himself even more for the last eight years of his life. What did he leave his son with? Once he was released from jail, he should have done more to find him and saved him from the woman who separated them. There were probably things that happened to NyQuest that Rahshaan would never know about.

The last boy was pulled from the basement and placed into an ambulance. Then the news crews came. It was dark outside before the scene was cleared, and Rahshaan and the rest of them were able to leave the barbershop. Before they left, Shameik picked up the phone and dialed Mont's number. "Yo, Unc. It's taken care of."

———

"We are fucked!" Santarez shouted at Kimborough as they pulled into Hope's driveway.

"No, we're not," Kimborough muttered. "This is perfect. Everyone thinks we've caught the culprits. Now they'll rest a little."

"Andrew was shipping those boys out tonight. No one is going to pay for dead boys. If they don't pay, then we don't get paid," Santarez insisted. "Besides, we never achieved our goal of catching Banger over there while the boys were there. We were supposed to pin this all on him. There was no way he was going to jail for a crime he didn't commit. He would've given up Mont to keep himself free. I know it! We wasted so much money and time that we don't have bringing Monaysia back here."

"I told you she was a liability," Kimborough gloated. "I worked with her for years, and she never proved to be of any use. Good riddance to the bitch."

CHRISTMAS JUST AIN'T CHRISTMAS, HIS EYE IS ON THE SPARROW, &OTHER SONGS YOU DON'T WANT TO HEAR DURING THE HOLIDAYS

Moosie drove the minivan back to Nat Turner with Rahshaan in the passenger's seat. Shameik, Shondell, Ken-Ken, and PeeWee all piled in the two passenger rows. They were silent for the ride. If anyone in the family felt anything about watching their life-long friend shoot himself in the head, then they didn't express it. Disappointment from not being able to shoot anyone seasoned the air. Rahshaan looked at his phone, waiting for Mont to tell him he had a plan for NyQuest. He couldn't think straight. His mind was wrapped up in the fact that Andrew and kidnapping victims were in the same house as his son. He tried to redirect his thoughts to his son being in his care for good. Now that he could breathe a little easier, he was ready to take things a step further with Shatima.

Shatima sat on her couch, praying to hear the thud of Rahshaan's Timberland boots on the hallway floors. In that short time, she had memorized everything about him. She even knew how the door creaked when he opened it and slammed when he closed it.

Just as Rahshaan was debating whether he should go straight to her or bypass her house until the morning, the door to apartment 4F swung open. Shatima stood there wearing flannel pajamas, her hair wrapped in a scarf, and her arms folded across her chest. She locked eyes with him, silently daring him to pass her house without speaking. Rahshaan looked at his crew and then went into her apartment without another word.

Immediately, she started hammering him with questions. "What is going on? Why have your mother and grandmother, and then Monaysia's mother, been calling me asking about him all day? Monaysia's mother even came down to the shop and accused me of withholding information. Rahshaan, what is going on?"

Rahshaan grabbed her wrists to get her arms to stop flailing as she rattled off her questions. They locked eyes. He guided her over to the couch to sit with her and calm her down. "Listen to me. Everything is straight."

"What does that mean?" Shatima asked through clenched teeth. "I have been calling and texting you all day. You haven't returned a call or replied to any of my texts. Meanwhile, I'm getting accused of things I know nothing about. How is this fair to me, Rahshaan?"

Rahshaan heaved a sigh. "It ain't fair to you, but that's the price you gotta pay fuckin with a nigga like me."

"No, I don't. Not when children are involved. Save that for somebody else."

The couch started vibrating. Rahshaan reached out to stop the shaking of Shatima's arm. "What's going on?"

"That's what I'm asking you," Shatima snapped. "Monaysia's mother came to the shop accusing me of I don't know what, and then she said some man named Andrew kept calling her house looking for Monaysia, and if it's the Andrew I know..." her voice trailed off.

"What Andrew? Tima, what's wrong?" Rahshaan shook her lightly to get an answer, but she shut down. "I'm trying to help you. I need you to talk to me."

"No, don't flip this on me! You got a lot of explaining to do.

If we need to step outside to do it, then we can." She glowered at Rahshaan. He glared back at her.

"Damn, Tima. I haven't been able to spend real time with you since Thanksgiving-"

"If my fight with Monaysia made you have to do something—"

"Shut up about that damn fight, Tima! Damn!" Rahshaan's voice thundered throughout the living room, bounced off the walls, and carried into Jabez's bedroom.

Jabez called out and asked if everything was alright. Shatima calmed him back to sleep and then came back to Rahshaan to continue the back and forth that was going nowhere.

"Look. I ain't come here to argue with you, Tima. I came here because I missed you, and I know I haven't been doing right by you for a while," Rahshaan said in a calmer voice.

She sat on the love seat opposite from him. "Including tonight. I think you should leave."

"Why?"

She counted out each reason on her fingers. "Because it's 2 am, and I don't know anything more than I knew at 2 pm yesterday. Because I have no idea where NyQuest is, and you think for some reason that I don't deserve to know. Because I've seen your disrespectful friend more in the past two days than I've seen you. Because one minute you tell me you love me, and the next minute you're keeping secrets. I knew better than to believe you when you said that." She shook her head at him and walked past him to the bedroom.

Feeling like he'd been smacked, Rahshaan got up and went in the opposite direction. He slammed the door behind him.

Shatima cried instead of slept.

Christmas Eve was spent at Selena's house. They were supposed to go to Big Grams' house for another extravaganza, but Shatima didn't want to run into Rahshaan. Avoiding him became part of her professional skill set. Spending the holiday without him was bittersweet. While she wanted to be with him, she needed a low-key holiday. She definitely didn't want to spend another one in jail. Selena laughed when she told her that and was glad to have Shatima and Jabez over for dinner.

There hadn't been much reason to celebrate Christmas in recent years, but it used to be Selena's favorite holiday before Chillz was murdered. When she and Shatima decided to have Christmas Eve at her house, she was glad to have a reason to get a tree and decorations. It had been so long since her house was filled with the spicy smell of pine, the shine of garland, the sight of fake snow. The pile of presents under the tree with its golden lights brought her to a level of joy she hadn't experienced in years. Watching Jabez with that smile filled a crack in her heart.

"I can't get over how much he looks like your father," Selena gushed. She said that every time she laid eyes on Jabez.

Shatima smiled. "Yeah. I'm relieved. I'm so glad he doesn't look like his own father."

"You really hate him, don't you?" Selena said, wrinkling her nose.

"Hate is too kind of a word," Shatima said.

For a minute, she pondered letting her secret out, but she decided it was too dark for Christmas. Mariah Carey was singing her favorite Christmas song, *All I Want For Christmas Is You,* and there was a train with Santa Claus and reindeer going around in a circle on the coffee table. Cookies sat on the kitchen counter waiting to be iced. *Merry Christmas, Charlie Brown* was on TV. This was a happy time.

They sat down in front of the fireplace while drinking hot chocolate with peppermint sticks in the mugs. Shatima gazed at a picture of her father and Selena. With their dazzling smiles, they looked like they belonged on the cover of a magazine.

"You guys were such a gorgeous couple," Shatima gushed over the picture the way she did every time she came to Selena's house and sat on her pink couch.

"If I believed in perfect men, your father was perfect," Selena said. "He thought I was gonna shy away from him with all that drama with your mother, but I wasn't letting him go." She sipped her hot chocolate.

"Have you had a boyfriend since him?" Shatima wondered.

Selena shook her head, her silky hair swinging. "No. I went on a couple of dates, but I'm still in love with your father, and men don't understand that they can't replace him. It gets weird and annoying. I don't have time for it."

It got quiet. Shatima listened to Jabez singing along with Charlie Brown, the music on the radio, and the chiming of the bells. Perhaps it was the residual sadness from not being with Rahshaan, but there was a question that was burning inside of her that was going to ruin their perfect holiday.

"How come nobody came back for me?" She didn't make eye contact with Selena when she asked the question. She stared at the fire in the fireplace and the stockings they'd decorated earlier hanging over it.

Selena looked at her. "I'm sorry."

"There's nothing to apologize for. I just want to know why it took so long for me to find you. Not just you, but everybody. Why did you all disappear? Aunt Lynn has a shop on Sundown. I have eaten at the restaurant in that same plaza at least once a month for the past five years and never knew the two places had anything to do with each other." She fingered the handle of her cup.

"That's because we just moved back here right before Banger brought you to us. I couldn't stay in our old house anymore. Your father practically built that house from the ground up. I was going crazy walking down those stairs every day. Lynn and I tried to live a few other places, but none of them were home. So when Lynn said she was coming back, I followed." Selena looked at Shatima. "When I found out that Rize found you, I told him to bring you to me. He told me he was, but then I found out he was dead, and you were nowhere to be found, and until Banger brought you back to us, I thought..."

"I'm sorry I even asked that question. I just thought that maybe there was a way for my life to not be as hard as it was. Guess there was no way around it. Now I know," Shatima said with a shrug.

She rested her head on the pink sofa and sipped more of her cocoa. The pink sofa made her laugh. Her father never would have agreed to it, and she knew that his absence was the only reason for its presence. The two of them sang along with the Christmas music coming from the radio. They were much better dancers than singers, but that was fine by them. The holidays felt a little more complete that year.

The doorbell rang, and Selena hopped up to answer it. Shatima continued to stare at Selena's collection of photographs. There were pictures of her and each of her brothers scattered throughout. She wondered about Rico and her other brother Nyir. Despite being a jerk to her on the phone that day, Rico sounded like he was enjoying life. No one talked about Nyir, though. Shatima realized that she remembered the least about him. If not for pictures, she would have forgotten his face. She tried to remember his voice, but came up with nothing. She forced herself to remember what the people around him said about him. When that didn't work, she tried to remember her father saying something to him. The only thing she remembered was when her father told Nyir to stop acting crazy. She couldn't remember what he did to make her father say such a thing. It felt terrible that she couldn't remember him, but after her encounter with Rico, she wasn't pressed for a reunion.

Shameik came in, threw his arms around Shatima, and kissed her on her forehead. He had gifts in his arms. She pointed to his under the tree. She watched him scoop Jabez up and play with him and smiled. At least she had one brother to spend the holiday with.

When Selena returned, there was a sheepish grin on her face. NyQuest ran out from behind her. Shatima's heart was full as the little boy ran to her. His thick hair was pulled into a ponytail. A small shiny diamond stud was in one of his ears. She crouched so that she was eye level with him. He talked a mile a minute about how happy he was to see her. As he spoke, Shatima took his coat off and inspected him for bruises and scrapes. If there was one sign that he was hurt, Shatima was going to go after whoever did it herself. Over and over she asked him if he was okay, and he confirmed that he was each time. Having someone dote on him like that was refreshing to the little boy.

She was so wrapped up in making sure NyQuest was okay that she didn't see his father walk in behind him. He had a stack of gifts with him as well. On top of them was a newspaper. Shatima rolled her eyes at him and continued to dote on NyQuest. She cut her eyes at Selena and her sheepish grin.

"I need to talk to you," Rahshaan said.

"Are we going to have an actual conversation, or are you going to talk in a circle and then leave?" Shatima snapped.

Selena looked at Rahshaan sympathetically before taking Shameik, Jabez, and NyQuest into the kitchen to start eating. Shatima had a mean streak that Rahshaan might not have been equipped to handle.

"Merry Christmas," Rahshaan said, just to have something to say. "I bought you a gift too."

"You didn't have to," Shatima said dryly.

The two of them stood there, saying nothing to each other. Shatima didn't even look in his direction. She folded her arms across her chest and stared at the fireplace.

"Look. I'm sorry about the other night," Rahshaan said. "There was a lot going on that I couldn't talk about."

"You still can't and won't talk about it now, so I don't understand why you're even here," Shatima snapped. She softened her voice and added, "But thank you for bringing NyQuest to see me. You don't know how crazy I've been going not knowing if he was okay or not."

"I told you he was okay," Rahshaan said, trying to hold back a grin. Seeing how much she cared about his son sent him to another level.

She cut his happiness short with her sharp tone. "No, that's not what you said. You told me he was straight. What does that even mean? I asked you pointed questions and got no answers. If you can't tell me anything, then what is the point in us even being together? I was supposed to be your woman, Rahshaan."

"What you mean 'was supposed to be'?" he demanded incredulously.

Shatima's voice lowered. "I mean, you really fronted on me. You let people believe that *I, of* all people, let something happen to that little boy. I love that little boy."

"It wasn't that," Rahshaan said.

He put the stack of presents down on the table. Shatima couldn't help but eye them. She hoped there was a bracelet to match her XO necklace in the pile. Rahshaan put the newspaper in his back pocket and took her hand. "Get your coat. I need you to come outside with me."

They trudged through the snow in Selena's back yard. A foot of heavy, wet snow had fallen overnight, and the sky promised to dump more on them. The temperature had dipped below twenty. It was too cold to be outside to appease Rahshaan's paranoia, but the newspaper he carried around had Shatima curious. He gave it to her and watched her as she read it.

"Monaysia was behind the kidnappings?" she asked when she was done skimming the first article. "Does that even make sense?"

"Keep reading," Rahshaan said. He busied himself by forming snowballs.

The more Shatima read, the wider her eyes grew and the deeper her frown formed. "*Squeak* was behind the kidnappings?"

Rahshaan didn't say anything, so she kept reading. She leaned against the trunk of a pine tree, not caring that it was getting her coat and freshly blown out hair wet. She crouched down beside Rahshaan as he rolled the snowballs in the snow to make them bigger. Her voice was a forced whisper when she finished reading the three articles that took up the front page of the paper. "Monaysia was messing around with Squeak, and he killed her and himself? Rahshaan, what the hell?"

Rahshaan explained how he went looking for Squeak and found him at Monaysia's house. He told her about how they left NyQuest in an icy puddle and then about seeing the boys being led into Monaysia's house. When he explained keeping NyQuest at Darlene's house until the coast was clear, she understood and apologized for being so cold to him. He in turn apologized for leaving her out of things and promised her that he was going to make a better effort to let her in, especially where the children were concerned.

"Does NyQuest know?" Her voice caught in her throat, Shatima couldn't get it to go above a whisper.

Rahshaan shook his head. "G-Ma keeps saying I have to be sensitive about it because she was his mama, but fuck that bitch for real. She wasn't no mother to my son, abusing him like that and putting him in harm's way."

"Yeah, but, Rahshaan, you don't know what kind of relationship they had before they came back here. She might have just been messed up from everything else she had going on. These articles say that she had a *lot* going on. Plus, he's only eight, and that's his mother." She thought about what she was saying and to whom it was said. Though she didn't know the specifics behind Rahshaan's eviscerated relationship with Darlene, she knew that it had to be bad if Darlene's own mother hated her for it. "This is the one time I'm going to tell you to put your feelings about her aside and be sensitive. If you want me to be there to help you, then I will. Just do right by him, please. Losing a parent is never easy."

For a little while, Rahshaan just stared at Shatima. She had an angelic glow. He felt terrible for the way he treated her and was ready to change. She deserved so much more than what he could give her, but he was going to keep improving until he was the best for her. That Christmas Eve, they stood in Selena's back yard, fingers tangled, making plans to take things to another level. As he kissed her, he told her how he desired to be a family. He loved her, loved her son, and was tired of not coming home to them every night. He'd felt relief before, but he never felt happy. Shatima made him happy.

"So you want to move into my apartment?" she summed up, just to be clear.

Rahshaan put an arm around her. "When you're ready."

"I think I'm ready now, but..." Shatima's voice trailed off. "That night I got arrested, that redheaded lady asked me about becoming a snitch again. I don't want them to jump over my head and start doing things to our children. I also have to let you know that my mom was with them. I guess the Puerto Rican pig is her boyfriend now."

Rahshaan frowned. "I'm not about to not be with you because of some pigs. Fuck the police, and I mean that." They walked a little bit further. Rahshaan took his arm from around Shatima and picked up a stick that had fallen from one of the trees. He seemed to be absently doodling until Shatima realized he was writing both of their names in the snow in fancy letters. "I want to move out of the projects too, but not just yet. Our kids deserve a yard like this to play in."

Shatima nodded. "May I ask you something?" Her voice took on a solemn tone.

"Of course," he said.

She considered how she wanted to frame her question before speaking. They took several steps before she spoke any words. She leaned against the wire fence that separated Selena's property from the next. "Do you think we'd be here if I wasn't Rize's sister and Chillz's daughter?"

Rahshaan considered asking her reason for that question. It seemed odd that she would pick that moment for this particular interrogation. He suspected it was coming, though. It was one he wrestled with often. "I don't think we would, but I don't think it would be because of me."

She wrinkled her brow. "Really? Why?"

He leaned against the fence next to her and brushed some snow off of it. "How long did you live in the buildings before you even spoke to me?"

"I spoke to you the first time you spoke to me, remember? I told you that I knew your mama didn't name you 'Banger,' so I wasn't gonna call you that." They both laughed.

"But for real. I tried to chill with you every day for years, and you didn't even check for me until you found out I knew your people. If I didn't, would you have ever given me a chance?"

Silence fell between them. They both knew the answer. Shatima felt foolish for bringing it up, but she had to know what he meant when he said he loved her. No one had ever told her that besides Chillz, Rize, and Selena. She wanted to know if his love was like theirs. They all departed from her at one point in time. Even though Selena returned, her reason for leaving Shatima behind didn't seem to make much sense. Shatima needed to know that Rahshaan wouldn't abandon her.

"But do you love *me*, or do you love me because I'm Rize's sister/Chillz's daughter? Are you gonna get bored and leave me when you get over the shock of that?" she pointedly asked him.

Though early in the evening, the sun was going down. Shatima had to rely on the moonlight reflecting off the snow to really see him. "I ain't going nowhere. I been trying to get at you too long. You had me the first time we spoke. I always thought there was somebody better for you - like a doctor or a lawyer or something - at your college, so I fell back a little. But when I saw you out with that pretty boy that one round, it fucked my head up. I ain't never been no jealous nigga, but I was jealous of that nigga. And I know you heard some shit, but I really was angry as fuck for a minute, even though you cracked him. It fucked with my head so bad that I had to talk to Unc about it, and he told me I was in love."

Shatima's eyes and smile glistened. Not that jealousy was a turn on, but the fact that he was so into her was refreshing.

The temperature dropped lower, so he held her close to him.

"Well, I'm glad you were checking for me so hard," she said. "Because I wasn't looking for a man, so I'm glad that you found me."

"I guess we'll enjoy Christmas, and then I'll find a way to tell Quest what happened," Rahshaan said. "These kids deserve to enjoy what they can while they're young."

Shatima agreed. "They also deserve the truth. I don't want them to be like me, not finding out who I was until I was twenty-three."

Rahshaan let that go without comment. He knew there were still things Shatima didn't tell him, but Christmas Eve wasn't the day to argue about it.

Christmas was a long day for Rahshaan. He spent the whole celebration at Big Grams' house avoiding Mont. He knew Mont wanted to counsel him about Squeak and Monaysia, and he just wanted to put them out of his head for a minute. He wanted his son to be able to enjoy this last day of peace and joy before he had to wreck the little boy's world. It felt like whatever room in Big Gram's house Rahshaan went in, no matter how full it was, Mont was there, staring at him. While the children opened their gifts, Mont caught up to Rahshaan and motioned with his head for him to follow him outside.

Under the trees, Rahshaan reported to Mont what happened and when the funerals were scheduled. Squeak's aunt just wanted to do something for Squeak's kids. Otherwise, she would have just left his parents to figure out what to do with his body. When he went to Monaysia's mother to report that he found NyQuest and offer fake condolences, he made the mistake of adding "Let me know if there's anything I can do for you." That turned into him paying for her funeral arrangements and headstone. She gave him a sob story about money being tight and never thinking she had to buy a burial plot for her daughter. Rahshaan wondered why the woman expected him to do anything at all considering his relationship with her daughter, but he was willing to do anything to make her happy and not interfere with his mission to get sole custody of his son. He didn't fully trust her when she said she had no interest in raising anymore children, since all of hers were grown.

"So Andrew went right back to doing that same old disgusting shit his people tried to pin on ours," Mont surmised after hearing the whole story. In the distance, two squirrels chased each other, shaking snow down from the pine trees. "I guess with his pops about to die, he's ready to cash out. He don't have nobody else to protect him."

Rahshaan sighed. "I hope this time we can end it for real. Them kidnappings fuck up my head every time. And with that shit happening so close to Quest..."

"I'm confident in our team. This time, we can end it," Mont promised him. "So how you feeling about your baby's mom getting offed?"

Rahshaan put some distance between himself and Mont. "Yo, Unc, I ain't come out here for no *Dr. Phil* shit. I don't give a fuck about that bitch, not when I got somebody like Tima."

The corners of Mont's mouth turned upward. "I told you before you was in love with my goddaughter. You ready to tell me I was right?"

Rahshaan paused before admitting that he was. Talking about it to the person he was in love with was one thing. Having the father/son moment that Mont wanted to have was a different story. He sometimes felt that Mont tried to live vicariously through his romantic experiences, since he had to sacrifice a love life because of the way he lived. Being who he was afforded very little trust. "That's why I'm ready for this shit to be done. I got a family to think about now. I don't want her to have to worry about me."

Mont nodded his head. "Then it shall be done. How much money did you spend on the funeral?"

"As far as anybody who's watching can see, I ain't spend shit. I put money in Monaysia's mom's hand and told her to handle everything," Rahshaan told him.

"Fuck you do that for?" Mont asked.

"So that when school starts again, Quest ain't getting looked at sideways. Anybody who knows who Quest's pops is knows he ain't gonna put up a penny for nobody who got shit to do with them kidnappings. When the streets start saying that I put in on Monaysia's funeral, they'll know she ain't do what the news is trying to say she did, and they won't be on my son's nuts, and the pigs won't be able to convince anybody that I had anything to do with that shit. I did a lot of stupid shit on account of that broad, but I ain't letting nobody think I laid up with somebody who stole children."

"You think the pigs are gonna try to convince people you did that shit?" Mont wondered.

"Unc, why the fuck else would they use her and a house that she lived in?" Rahshaan reasoned.

"You smart," Mont said. He spared telling Rahshaan how proud he was of him for his growth, because he knew Rahshaan didn't want to hear it. But just watching his evolution from his pre-prison years to that moment was enough to make Uncle Mont shed a tear, if he were an emotional man.

A brown skinned man wearing a peacoat and slacks approached them. Around his neck dangled a badge and police identification. Rahshaan tensed as the man stepped in front of him.

Mont greeted him. "D! I didn't think I'd see you today as busy as the news says you've been."

Detective Derrick Darnell shook hands with Mont and a reluctant Rahshaan. In his left hand was a bottle of Crown Royal. Bags dragged his droopy eyes down even further, and his usually clean face was full of stubble. Working kidnapping cases had earned him 20 hours of overtime that week alone. "Man, I've been working around the clock, but wifey would've had my hide if I didn't bring her and the kids out here for gifts and some of Big Grams' cooking."

Mont chuckled lightheartedly. Rahshaan didn't say anything.

Derrick looked directly at Rahshaan. "My condolences, man. I know you and your son's mother didn't have the best relationship, but that's still fucked up what happened to her."

Rahshaan nodded. Although Derrick was their cousin, his being part of the same police force that falsely charged him caused Rahshaan to withhold his trust. Derrick always tried to present himself as being on their side, but Rahshaan always had few words for him. "Yeah. Life's a bitch."

Children pushed each other down the hills of Big Grams' backyard on sleds. Derrick looked at his two cousins strangely and then looked around. "Let's go somewhere and talk."

When they were far enough into the woods, Derrick began speaking. "You received a box at your old address, Mont. The sender is anonymous, but based on recent events, timing, and the date stamp, I'm confident in saying it was from Monaysia. It makes Squeak killing her make even more sense."

Mont wondered, "What was in it?"

"Some things we've already received — the video of Rize's murder — but also some new things. There are pictures and videos of the days leading up to his death. Rize was alive a lot longer than we thought. There is enough evidence in there to bury Andrew, but nothing about his fuckin' father. You wanna know what the wildest part about all this is? *Squeak* was the one sending us the shit the whole time. That nigga sat with us in funerals crying, knowing he recorded and took pictures of the murders."

"So it's over now? They off my nuts?" Rahshaan wondered.

"Not even close," Derrick replied while shaking his head. "With Tennessee's health declining so rapidly, they're on a time clock. They're afraid of facing consequences from the false charges that landed you in jail. If you file a lawsuit against them, then you can turn the tables. They'll have to look into the abuse you suffered in prison. The people's eyes will open."

Mont and Rahshaan had their "Aha" moment at the same time.

"The townhouse Monaysia and Squeak lived in was paid for with funds that were supposed to go toward renovating Nat Turner. The boys were trapped in the basement there in hopes of them catching Rahshaan over there and pinning the kidnappings on him. Their plan was to get you to put pressure on you to confess that Mont faked his death. Tennessee knows that Mont is still alive and wants the last person he thinks can expose him and his acts of terror."

The three men looked at each other, trying to brainstorm their next moves.

When Rahshaan and Shatima made it home with the boys and G-Ma, Shanae was in the hallway with her children. Instantly, Shatima felt sorry for her. She hoped the freckle-faced girl would be able to move on from Squeak. He never treated her like anything anyway. Rahshaan gave each of the children twenty dollars and some of their gifts from Big Grams' house. The expression on Shanae's face said that she expected him to give her money as well. He passed her as though she didn't exist.

"Sorry for your loss," Shatima offered as she, NyQuest, and Jabez followed Rahshaan up the stairs. G-Ma gave Shanae a hug and a kiss on the cheek, offering to watch the children any time she needed a break.

Shanae sneered at Shatima the whole time she walked up the stairs.

In the morning, Rahshaan took NyQuest out for breakfast. He took Shatima up on her offer to help him relay the bad news. He wanted her to come, because she knew what it was like to lose a parent. The fact that he never had parents to lose, combined with his feelings toward the victim, suggested that he lacked the empathy needed for the conversation. His life changed when he was eight. To most, that was still a child, but he saw different. He knew he was going to say something stupid.

In a restaurant that was packed with people filled with residual Christmas cheer, Shatima, Rahshaan, Jabez, and NyQuest sat in a booth in a back corner. They offered for G-Ma to join them, but she sensed why they were going and declined. She felt no obligation to say anything nice about Monaysia, even if it was for NyQuest's sake. The family sat sipping cocoa and eating stacks of pancakes and bacon. It felt wrong to wreck a child's world in a place where the biggest concern for the people surrounding him was how to spend their Christmas gift certificates. Rahshaan chose that place so that NyQuest wouldn't have to visit the place where he learned his mother was dead very often, if at all.

NyQuest was the one to bring up the subject. "Daddy, when do I have to go back to Mommy's house?"

Rahshaan cleared his throat. NyQuest's voice was seasoned with a certain level of innocence that was foreign to him. "How would you like to stay with me from now on?"

"It's okay, but I don't wanna stay with you when you're around Mr. Squeak. I'm not supposed to tell you why," NyQuest replied with a mouthful of pancakes.

When NyQuest said Squeak's name, Rahshaan remembered Squeak smacking NyQuest into that icy puddle.

Shatima watched their exchange. She clenched her fork in anticipation of the way Rahshaan was going to drop his bomb. Jabez kept eating his pancakes.

Rahshaan leaned in closer to his son and put his arm around him. "You don't have to worry about Squeak anymore. He won't be around."

"So he can't hit me anymore? Good." NyQuest said. "I don't wanna be around Mommy either. She hits me too, and I didn't even do nothing. And we always gotta move somewhere new. And she ain't never home, cuz she's always looking for a new boyfriend with money. And she don't never got time to help me with my homework."

"Your daddy helps me with my math homework. You should ask him to help you too," Jabez spoke up.

Shatima leaned toward NyQuest. "Tell me something good about your mommy. What is your favorite thing that she makes you for dinner?"

"Chicken nuggets," he replied. "That's the only thing she can cook without messing up. Sometimes she gets the ones with the cheese in the middle. Those are my favorite. She can make spaghetti too, but me and Daddy hate spaghetti."

Shatima grinned at that. "Do you do anything fun with her?"

"Sometimes she reads to me, but a lot of times she's busy getting ready for her dates and to go to the club with her friends," he said. "I wish the club would burn down so she couldn't go anymore."

Shatima sat back in her chair and was sorry that she asked the questions. It sent NyQuest down a road of voicing his gripes with his Sunday night through Wednesday morning living situation. He didn't want to move anymore, and he didn't want her boyfriends coming into their house and hitting her. He also wanted to play football and basketball but never got the chance. Then he questioned how someone could have time to go to every party but no time to take him to baseball practice.

"Daddy, you don't hit Tima, right?" NyQuest's voice was a micro-version of its regular tone.

Unable to stifle his anger at the question, Rahshaan closed his eyes and shook his head.

"Good. Because Mommy's boyfriends hit her, and it was scary. I don't want to lock my door while I listen to Mr. Squeak hit her anymore."

"You ain't gotta worry about that shit no more, because your mommy is dead, and so is Squeak!" Rahshaan blurted out.

Neither the sharp look Shatima shot him nor the sadness on NyQuest's face made him regret the slippage. The whole conversation was a trigger for him. As he listened to his son's complaints, he was faced with years of failing him. There was nothing he could do to change who he had a child with or how she chose to parent him, but his own absence was something that he had to account for. He should have spent more time trying to find his son than fucking everything with a fat ass.

He remembered the defeat he felt the first time he sought partial custody of his son upon his released from prison. The judge told him that due to his incarceration, he was unfit. Never mind the fact that he lost three years of his life because of a lie his child's mother told. The judge told Rahshaan that his son was better off with his father not knowing where he was. He remembered asking Monaysia's mother for Monaysia's address and only receiving a phone number that got disconnected every time he called. Listening to his son, he should have done more to find his son and take care of him the way he did before he went to jail.

Shatima studied NyQuest to see how he took the news. Indifference flooded his facial expression at first. In that moment, he never looked more like Rahshaan. Then he transitioned from shock to sad the way the sky transitions from evening gray to pitch black during the winter months.

"I didn't hate Mommy," NyQuest said as though he had something to apologize for.

It was that statement that made Rahshaan get up and walk away from the table for a minute. The feeling of guilt for having negative emotions toward someone who treated him like dirt wasn't foreign. NyQuest shouldn't have to feel obligated to feel any way about a woman who did him wrong simply because she brought him into the world. He didn't ask to be born. He owed her nothing, especially not his remorse for telling his truth. She should have done better by her flesh and blood. Rahshaan felt that since she knew about Darlene abandoning him, Monaysia would have taken better care of their son. For the first time, he felt something other than indifference toward his child's mother's death. He felt regret. He should have pulled the trigger himself.

His walk took him outside. His chest was getting tight. The blustery wind forcing itself down his throat and into his lungs tried to overpower him. He leaned against the cold brick exterior of the building. Passersby scooted around him. Some even clutched their purses. He just needed to stand out there until he could get himself together and garner some sympathy for his son.

Inside, Shatima held NyQuest. She wasn't sure of the depth of his understanding of life and death, but she knew that he needed comfort. The situation was a trigger for her as well, but this wasn't about her. He lost a woman who never fulfilled her obligation to nurture and protect him. Where did that leave him emotionally? Did he only feel sad because he felt like he was supposed to, or did he really miss her? If he did miss her, was it who she was that he missed or who she was supposed to be? At the tender age of eight, she couldn't ask him those questions. However, she could help him work through his feelings and find the answers in his own time. She and Jabez swallowed him with hugs. He was big for his age and heavy, but Shatima let him crawl into her lap and rest his head on her. That's what she wished someone did for her when her father was murdered, but there was no one there. She just hoped Rahshaan didn't come back in scolding her for "babying" him. She would break every plate in the restaurant over his head if he did.

Instead of finding sympathy, Rahshaan felt selfishness. He dashed to his truck when he felt the tears coming and sat there until he could stop the waterworks. He had to tell himself that this wasn't about him. This was about a child who lost his mother. Then he went back inside to focus on the person who was really hurting at the moment. The picture of Shatima holding NyQuest like he was her own baby and Jabez rubbing his back was one that he needed to be a part of. He slid back into the booth and took NyQuest from Shatima and held his son against his chest. He let the little boy cry for as long as he needed. Then he took his family home.

Crying uncorked NyQuest's curiosity. He lay in bed in between Rahshaan and Shatima, asking questions about things that seemed trivial to them, but were important to him. Could he get his favorite sneakers from his mother's house? Was there a Mother's Day in Heaven? Was there a club in Heaven for Monaysia to go to on New Year's Eve? He wanted to make sure that she enjoyed the same things in the afterlife that she did in life.

"Daddy?" he asked in between sniffles.

"What up?" Rahshaan didn't know how many more questions he could take.

"I'm sorry I asked Mommy if I could live with you so much. If I didn't, then maybe Mommy wouldn't be dead."

Harder than comforting the little boy, Rahshaan realized, was convincing him that he was blameless. That the little boy felt the need to shoulder any of this hurt Rahshaan. He let his son cry himself to sleep on his chest, something that hadn't happened since he was a baby. Then he carried him gently into the room he shared with Jabez and put him on the top bunk.

When Rahshaan came back into the room, he climbed into the bed and told Shatima his whole coming of age tale at the tender age of eight. Before he knew it, the tears spilled down his face again. She reached out and wiped the first set away. A fresh set fell. He choked on his words as he told her about the babies. It had been so long since he heard them, but talking about them brought their cries back to the front of his mind. He heard them rustling around in the garbage bag, and his arms got heavy as though he was carrying them to the dumpster again. Shatima listened to his story with her mouth agape. She wanted her heart to be full of appreciation for him peeling back a layer that he never exposed to anyone else, but all she could really think of was kicking Darlene Bailey's ass.

Squeak was a snake who got what a snake deserved. There were heavy debates over whether or not they would have a funeral for him at all. In the end, they decided that they would do it for his children. It would be a short service where they'd let the children cry and ask questions. Then, there would be a repast that would serve as a start to letting them know that they'd always take care of them. They concluded that giving the children the chance to say goodbye would stifle any conflicting feelings about a man who barely took care of them in his last days.

The day of the funeral was gloomy, both physically and emotionally. Squeak's mother, step-father, and father coming to town for the service humanized him for the first time since his transition into a demon. His mother sobbed and wailed all over Mavis' apartment, screaming about how she should have done better by him. Mavis rolled her eyes at the woman every time then took a shot of liquor, a drag off a cigarette, sang along for a few bars with the Al Green record that played, and cried. Squeak's sisters sat around in designer dresses looking like they had better places to be. His father and step-father stayed on opposite sides of the house, avoiding eye contact with each other. Shanae stumbled around the house, fussing at her older children and trying to get the baby dressed. More than likely, she was still drunk from staying out all night and drinking her grief away.

Shatima tried to do the children's hair quickly and get out of the way, but the tiny apartment full of Squeak's and Shanae's relatives made it hard to move around. She stood in the middle of the kitchen floor with a flat iron, trying to convince the seven year old girl that she wasn't going to burn her. Shanae's brother parked himself on the chair behind her and stared at her ass the whole time she tried to work. Shatima tried to maneuver out of his eyesight, but there was nowhere she could go.

"Banger's girl or not, I'm gonna let you know you fine as fuck!" he marveled, sipping on a bottle of E&J that he and

Shanae were passing between each other. "I see why them niggas was fighting over you."

"Their fight had nothing to do with me," Shatima said quietly. "Please don't talk like that in front of your sister either."

She leaned toward the seven-year-old and pleaded with her eyes to let her put the flat iron to her head. Shanae glared at her without offering soothing words to her daughter that would make the hairstyling process go faster. She let it pass since the woman was grieving. Raising Jabez alone was tough enough. She was sure raising seven would have sent her to the nut house. She offered lots of smiles and assistance while she was down there, but Shanae gave her nothing but dirty looks. Shanae never even thanked her for coming downstairs to do her children's hair.

After hearing countless stories about Squeak's father siring one of the girls who came along during Squeak's mother's second marriage, Shatima finally filled the seven-year-old's head with ringlets. After seeing how pretty their sister's hair was, the other girls were anxious to sit in the chair. It seemed to take forever to get all those heads done. All of the adults in the house drank copious amounts of liquor while waiting for Shanae to get the kids ready, except for the three quiet sisters. They sat on the couch with their mouths sealed shut, hands clasped together, noses in the air, and staring straight ahead. Every now and again, Squeak's mother would scream out "My baby boy!" and collapse on her husband's shoulder. That would make Squeak's father snicker, and the muttering about which man fathered which child would start again.

Once all of the children looked like they belonged in a JC Penny catalog, Shatima took the baby and dressed him. Then she gave him to Mavis, since she seemed to have a better grasp on the present than Shanae. She was going to leave, but there was a pile of dirty dishes in the sink, and Shatima couldn't stand filth. The corners of Shanae's lips turned upward when she saw Shatima washing her dishes. It seemed as though she was going to have a mental breakdown, so Shatima left. Shanae's brother followed her up the stairs, but quickly retreated when Rahshaan opened the door.

After the funeral, people gathered in Mavis' apartment once again for the repast. Mavis seemed joyous among all of her family and the liquor supplied to her. They partied hard and well into the morning. By 2 am, both she and Shanae were drunk and had lost all sense of decorum. Mavis yelled out to Shanae and asked her where she was going to stay. Shanae turned to her mother.

"Oh you know you can stay with me until you get on your feet, but, honey, you've got way too many children. I live in a two-bedroom. You and Mavis have been making due all this time. You should just continue with your arrangement." That was the last thing Shanae's mother said before retreating to the makeshift bar that was a kitchen table by day.

Mavis turned to Shanae. "I've been telling you all week to find someone to stay with. It was cool when Squeak was here and giving me money, but I don't know where the fuck your money goes. You get paid at 11:30 and come home broke at 11:45. It's too many kids for you to be expecting me to just let you stay here for free. I don't give a fuck how many food stamps you get."

"Fuck you, Mavis! You never liked me no way!" Shanae screamed.

"I sure in the fuck didn't. I gotta admit I was glad when I read that all this shit was over a bitch that he liked better than you." She took a long chug straight from a bottle of Paul Masson. "Now I'll babysit for you if you pay me, which I know you ain't gonna pay me, but you gotta get your funky ass outta my house by the end of the month."

"And go where, Mavis? Where the fuck am I supposed to go? You know I'm on a waiting list for a four-bedroom!" Shanae started crying in the middle of the floor. No one offered her any support.

Moosie rose from the couch and stood between the two

women. She looked rather dapper in the finely tailored suit she wore, better than most of the men in the room. "Shanae," she hissed. "Come here."

Shanae put her bottle down on an end table and sashayed over to Moosie. The two of them briefly conversed in another room. When Shanae reentered the room, she had an overnight bag packed for each of the children. She told Mavis she would be back for the rest of their things in the morning.

"Just like that, Moosie?" Rahshaan remarked with a half-smile.

"Squeak would want it this way," Moosie replied with a wink and a grin.

Monaysia's death brought different conflicts. People protested it happening until a controversial news report aired. Two survivors found in her townhouse's basement told a reporter that they never saw Monaysia, only heard her through the vents screaming while being beaten constantly. The interview was cut off after that, but everyone in the county started to suspect that the news was manipulating the stories for personal gain. Shatima had stopped watching the news the day she was fired from her last job, and Rahshaan never watched it, but they heard about it wherever they went.

There was a squabble about whether or not Shatima would even attend Monaysia's funeral. She spent the night prior braiding NyQuest's hair and explaining to him what the funeral would entail. She told him she didn't think it was a good idea to attend, but he insisted that she come. Her presence got dirty looks from Monaysia's friends and family. When they should have been making comments like "she looks so good" or "it looks just like she's sleeping," they were catching glimpses of Shatima and whispering. Why was she there? Hadn't the family been through enough? This was one time when she felt the gossiping was warranted. She sat on the back row and tried not to be a distraction while Rahshaan sat in front with NyQuest, per his request. He didn't understand why Shatima couldn't sit with them and wanted answers. That caused a whole new set of rumblings. Shatima sat on the back row, wishing she could throw herself in the trash.

The funeral was a grandiose sea of people wearing white. Early reports on Monaysia's death made preachers all over Sanford County decline eulogizing her or letting her services be held in a church. Her family opted for a different type of service held in the gym of a community center close to her childhood home. A civil rights activist spoke on the dangers of domestic violence. They made Monaysia as big of a victim as the boys who had been stored in her basement.

Sitting there and listening to the woman who locked her child in a car while she went clubbing being made into a martyr was nauseating. No mention was made of the child's life she messed up. All she had to do was give him to his father while she ran around and did whatever she felt like doing. She cost a man three years in jail. She put herself in that position. Sitting there where a false picture of her was being memorialized drove Shatima insane. She wanted to kick the casket over, but she had to keep all of her feelings inside for NyQuest's sake.

Instead, she sat back and admired the work she'd done on the corpse's hair and makeup. At the time, she thought that would be her only act of kindness in regards to the service. She didn't expect to be sitting through it and being sneered at like the villain in Monaysia's story.

One of Monaysia's friends started singing *His Eye Is On the Sparrow*. By the time she asked *"Why should my heart feel lonely?"* NyQuest tore down the aisle and ran to Shatima. She cradled him in her arms while he sobbed. Rahshaan got up and joined them in the back, relieved to have a reason to no longer be a spectacle on the front row. His feelings toward the dead were cut and dry.

Chief Lyles checked the crack of his ass to make sure none of the mayors' or county executives' feet remained in it. For the past hour, he'd sat completely blindsided, stuttering over why there was money coming out of the police's budget for several apartments throughout the city rented in a dead person's name. An investigation revealed that every apartment harbored some of the city's missing boys.

"Darnell!" Chief Lyles bellowed.

Detective Derrick Darnell peeked his head outside his office. When he saw the smoke coming from the chief's ears, he silently followed Chief Lyles into his office and closed the door behind him.

"Have you ever had the pleasure of having County Executive Gilead ram her foot up your ass for two hours?"

Derrick pulled out the chair in front of Chief Lyles' desk and sat in it, concern all over his face. "I can't say I have."

Chief Lyles tossed Derrick a file whose thickness rivaled college textbooks. "She went over every single page with me and cussed me, my children, and my mother out over each and every one."

Derrick chuckled and opened the file to skim it. His eyes widened. "Whoa! All of these apartments were rented to Squeak, Monaysia, and co-signed by... But that's impossible. Chief, some of these apartment complexes weren't built until last year. What is going on here? Chief Jones' son murdered Mont Drayton the same time he murdered Jeremiah Revolution's son."

"And we're still catching hell for those two murders. Citizens are questioning the validity of Chief Jones' story regarding what happened that day." Chief Lyles rubbed his temples. "I need you to find out who is doing this. This looks just like 1998, right around the time that man was murdered outside of his own wedding." He shook his head and closed his eyes as though he was trying to force the memory out of his mind. "I still can't believe that I stood beside men who would do that. Now they're trying to pin crimes on a dead man."

"Chief, don't beat yourself up about that," Derrick told him. "You weren't in a position to do anything about that back then."

"Yeah, well, I am now, and I know Chief Jones has something to do with this. I won't let that man die without this whole city knowing every evil thing he's done."

SHIT YOU SHOULDN'T HAVE TO DEAL WITH AT WORK, & A GIRLS' TRIP GONE WRONG

Something wasn't right. In the pit of her stomach, Shatima felt it when she went to work the Wednesday after New Year's Day. It settled in her stomach and made her feel heavy as she washed her clients' hair. The gray sky didn't do anything to lift her spirits. Maybe it was the fact that the holidays were done. Perhaps she had the winter blues. Or maybe she was just worried about NyQuest on his return to school. She kept checking her phone to make sure he hadn't texted her to come pick him up, which she told him she would if it was too much for him. Whatever it was, she couldn't shake it.

"You got a walk-in," Erika announced, handing Shatima a pack of hair. "She wants a sew-in. I already split the tracks for you."

Shatima's heart sank. She was just draping her scarf around her neck but stopped and reluctantly removed her coat as well. She didn't know if she could muster up the energy to be friendly to anyone else.

"You want me to take her?" Haddus offered, sensing that something was wrong. Everyone in the shop knew about Monaysia's death by then, and they all tried to make her days easier.

"Unh-uh! I said I want Sha-*TEEEEEM-uh to* do my weave!" a voice called out, ending her demand with a point and a clap.

Shatima's heart dropped. "Oh. Hey, Shanae," Shatima said to the yellow-skinned, video vixen-bodied woman with freckles on her round, flat face. "I'm glad you decided to take me up on my offer. I'm sure you can use a break. Come on and sit at the shampoo bowl. I'll hook you up."

Shanae didn't move from the doorway, but scoffed. "I ain't come here for no handouts. Today is all on Banger."

The heads of everyone in the shop jerked in Shanae's direction. Standing there, Shanae looked like a villain. She leaned on her heels. A smug look was on her face. With her head cocked to the side, Shatima studied her. Maybe what she meant was that Rahshaan sent her down there to get her hair done to pick her spirits up. Next to him, she was the one hit hardest by Squeak's betrayal.

Or maybe Shanae had lost her rabbit-ass mind.

With a cocky step, Shanae strutted toward Shatima's station. "Oh, yes, *honey.* You heard me right. My nigga is treating me to a me day. He ever did that for you when y'all were together?"

For the first time ever, it was quiet in Hair Revolution. Customers in the waiting area sat with their mouths hanging open. The ones under the dryer closed their magazines and style books to watch the scene. Lynn, Haddus, Antoinette, and Erika poised themselves to pounce. Only the water running from the indoor waterfall could be heard. It was supposed to soothe, but to hell with that. This loony bitch was out of her mind.

Lynn reached for her cellphone and texted Rahshaan the numbers 9-1-1.

Shatima stared at the nearly six foot tall woman and wondered if she was having a nervous breakdown. Finding out that her man was cheating on her right before taking his life must have left her in shock. That was the only thing that explained why Shanae was in her shop shouting this nonsense. While she never heard of a mental breakdown taking someone four blocks away to an oddly specific location, she would allow it for the sake of the woman's grief. Just that morning, she and Rahshaan passed Shanae in the hallway while she took her children to the bus stop. Rahshaan gave each of them twenty dollars as he was in the habit of doing. Shanae probably told herself that the money was hers to get her hair done.

That made more sense to Shatima than the scene that was setting in front of her eyes.

"Oh don't get quiet now, bitch. Your nigga must not have told you about that night he came through and scooped me to fuck my face." She stood right in Shatima's face. "All you wanted to do was cry and worry, so he came through to see how a real ride or die bitch do, and I did him well. All nine and a half inches."

Shatima went deaf. Her eyes were only able to see Shanae standing in front of her. How did she know about the night she and Rahshaan argued?

"If you're wondering what night I'm talking about, it was a couple of nights before Christmas. I guess you could say the same night Squeak died." A smirk was on her face.

Then every person and thing the room except Shanae went black. While Shanae continued to taunt her, Shatima carefully draped her purse and outerwear over the back of her chair. Her purse was open, so she was able to easily retrieve the lock in a sock that she always carried with her. Shatima's right hook went flying into Shanae's neck. Shanae wasn't expecting Shatima to be able to throw her hands so quickly. She was so quiet and prissy that Shanae thought she'd be able to walk in and bully her, but she was wrong. Upon impact, the metal hitting her throat made her scream. She recovered from the shock and tried to hit Shatima with a right-left combo, but only her right landed. Shatima blocked the left and tried not to let on how much the right hurt as she tried to punch and kick through Shanae's bread basket.

Haddus reached for the first thing he could find to throw at

Shanae while Antoinette pinned Erika's hair up in anticipation of their attack, but Lynn commanded them to stay back.

"Let my niece get her fair one before we fuck this bitch up, because once I get on her ass, I ain't getting off her."

The customers in the shop prepared for attack as well. As soon as Lynn gave the okay, they were all coming out of their chairs. They sat poised, shocked by the ass kicking Shanae received from the quiet beautician.

Every time Shatima hit Shanae with her sock-covered right hand, Shanae hollered. Shatima was on a mission to make sure that bitch never ran her mouth again. The only thing that was on her mind was this whore coming to her job and telling her clients and staff how big her man's dick was. She'd never heard something so absurd in her life. Shanae was more talk than fight and found out that she chose the right one to mess with that day. That bad feeling Shatima woke up with manifested itself into an ass whooping. She didn't even see Rahshaan and Shameik come into the shop and pull them apart. It wasn't until she saw Lynn, Antoinette, and Erika chasing Shanae down the street with Haddus yelling threats that everything came back into focus.

She broke away from Rahshaan, stepped outside and yelled, "Uh-uh! That bitch still gotta get her hair done! I could've been home by now, but she came in here acting stupid. Tell her to get her ass to this bowl so I could wash the blood out her hair and fix her weave!"

Dinner was eaten at a restaurant that night. Shatima was sullen, but trying to cover her anger by being extra polite whenever someone asked her something. Selena was in the dark about what happened. Watching how Shatima glared at Rahshaan without taking her eyes off of him made Selena nervous. She asked Shameik for a clue about what was going on, but Shameik wasn't entirely sure. So they sat at dinner, not saying anything. Not even the children spoke.

Internally, Rahshaan quaked. The last thing he thought he'd

be doing that day was pulling his woman off a chick he didn't give a damn about. His life was coming to an end. He was sure of it.

"I can take you to replace the jewelry that you popped today after dinner," he offered. Her silence was killing him.

"No thank you," came her robotic response.

Rahshaan kept special attention on Shatima whenever she reached for her knife. He was sure that she was going to slit his throat. He glanced at their children. She elected to sit between them rather than next to him like she normally did when they went out. He was sure that they were his saving grace. The fire in her eyes could make Hell envious, but she wouldn't kill him in front of children...he hoped.

Selena couldn't stand not knowing what was going on. Lynn urged her to leave it alone, but she pressed, "Tima, I thought that mark on your face was healing better than that? It looks fresh now."

Shatima laughed at Selena's comment. "I had a jumpy client," she said without taking her eyes off Rahshaan.

After dinner, they went home and resumed their nightly routine of checking homework, making lunches for the next day, and reading. Rahshaan felt like an outsider as he watched all of this happen. He tried to lend a hand where he could, but she shut him out. Unwarranted anger consumed him, but he pushed it away. He faded into obscurity until the children were asleep. Then he waited to be acknowledged by her, because he didn't know what to say. For all he knew, Shatima and Shanae could have been fighting about something other than what he suspected. Shanae's mouth had earned her quite a few ass whippings over the years. The fire in Shatima's eyes, though, let him know that he shouldn't be naive.

Shatima came out of the bathroom, freshly showered, skin glistening, covered in a regular pair of fleece pajamas. She slid under the covers like she did every night. He watched her for a cue as to whether or not he should join. She sat up reading one of her textbooks from school and making notes. He went and showered. There was no way he was leaving the apartment that night. She might change the locks on him. When he came out, he cautiously slipped under the sheets with her. She moved to the desk that was in the corner of the room and turned on her lamp. It looked like she was taking notes, but she couldn't concentrate. She was trying not to kill him.

"Come to bed," he complained foolishly.

"For what? So you could fuck me with the same dick you did that bird?" She hadn't meant to respond to him at all, but the words came out fluidly. Her trembling hands picked up the book she was only pretending to read and hurled it at his head.

"I ain't fuck that broad!" Rahshaan argued while dodging the flying assault object. "If that's what that bitch came in there and told you, then she's lying, and you mad over nothing." He hopped out of the bed and made his way to her.

She ripped her desk lamp's cord from the wall and flung it at his head. "Ain't nobody come to my job, telling me exactly how many inches long your dick is for no reason, Rahshaan! And how did she know we were arguing? And where did you disappear to that night?"

He swerved out of the lamp's path just in time to miss getting hit by it. "You kicked me out, so why do you care?" Internally, he was kicking his own ass for being so flippant. He was wrong, but he still hated the accusations.

"Because wherever you went made me have to whoop somebody's ass at my job. At my job, Rahshaan? You couldn't even keep your ho in check?"

"She ain't my ho!" Rahshaan's voice bounced off the walls in the room.

"Then explain why I spent the last hour of my day at work fighting some bitch over the size of your dick? I'm pretty smart, Rahshaan. That sounds like she's your ho."

"It wasn't even like that," he said, sounding pitiful even to himself.

Shatima folded her arms across her chest. "Then what was it like? Because I need an explanation about how I spent the last hour of my work day."

Being asked to leave after the day he had aggravated Rahshaan even further. All he wanted was to climb in the bed and sleep away everything that happened. He knew sleep wouldn't come easily as long as NyQuest was with his mother, so he hoped Shatima would let him sex the trouble away. A mindless fuck would help him burn off some of his anxiety. Instead, he was met with a whole lot of questions and feelings. Women he usually dealt with after a day like this knew to spread their legs without speaking. Shatima had every right to question him. He refused to be burdened with responsibility. Slamming the door behind him, he had no idea where he was going. G-Ma's house wasn't an option. There was no telling how many children were over there, and he wasn't in the right frame of mind to share space with any of them.

He got into his truck, and was at the factory before he knew it. His feet carried him to the subbasement and into a smokey room. Music was playing, but he tuned out the song. Colorful lights were flashing. Moosie was sitting in a corner drinking. A naked woman was dancing on her lap. Rahshaan sat at the table with them. A girl approached him, but he shooed her away and told her to get someone to bring him a drink. If he couldn't sleep or fuck, then he could certainly drink his troubles away.

Shanae approached him carrying a tray of Crown Royal and two glasses. She wore nothing but pasties and a g-string. She set the bottle and glasses in front of him.

"I need a ride to a job, and Squeak ain't answering his phone," she grumbled from the side of her mouth.

Rahshaan poured one drink for himself and one for Moosie. "He got you doing jobs again?"

"We ain't got no choice," she snapped. "I'm pregnant again, and he keeps buying these cars and clothes while he got me walking. I can't catch the bus with all these kids if he ain't helping me."

Sorry that he gave the impression that the floor was open for a counseling session, he just grunted and said, "Oh."

"So you gonna take me?" Shanae pressed.

"Moosie here. Moosie can take you," Rahshaan said.

Moosie's eyes darted from him to the girl dancing on her lap. "Come on, Fam! Everybody ain't got fine ass Shatima to go home to. Help me out. What you doing here anyway?"

"Me and Shorty got into it. She put me out. Fuck it. I'll do it this time, but I'm taking your car." Rahshaan grumbled some more and downed his drink. He told Shanae to grab whatever she needed to so that they could leave.

"I mean, don't let me get in the way of you getting home to 'fine ass Shatima,'" Shanae quipped.

"Don't let my girl's name come out your mouth again," Rahshaan barked at her, standing and shoving a finger into her face.

Shanae switched her ass and went to the back to get changed. Rahshaan poured himself another drink while he waited. Two drinks later, she was fully dressed. In her hand, she carried a duffle bag. Rahshaan took the bottle with him. Normally, he didn't drink on the job, but he needed something that night. Who he needed most rejected him.

Driving with an open bottle set the tone that he was willing to break all of the rules that night. During the ride, Shanae talked a mile a minute. She was "so over" Squeak for probably the four-hundredth time. She wasn't keeping the baby. She had an appointment to terminate the pregnancy in the morning, because she heard Squeak was cheating on her. After the seventh time she mentioned Squeak's name, Rahshaan realized that she was fishing for information. It got around to her that Monaysia was Squeak's new love. She wanted Rahshaan to confirm it. He wasn't sure why. The two of them weren't friends. He simply acknowledged her existence because of Squeak and the children she had for him. Nothing he did ever indicated that the two of them were anything other than acquaintances.

They rode into a touristy area to five star hotels. The cars of state officials were parked at the hotel next to the Convention Center. Rahshaan dropped her off in the front and then parked in the back. He was supposed to go inside, but he sat out there drinking the bottle. If anyone found out that he wasn't on his job, he would never hear the end of it. The night's events, though, took a toll on him. He thought of calling

Shameik or Shondell to keep him company, but was more interested in the bottle of Crown Royal.

He wasn't sure how much time had passed, but Shanae was banging on the window. The frown on her face showed irritation.

"Are you drunk?" she demanded when he let her in.

He didn't answer.

"Banger, we can't go anywhere with you like this."

He still didn't speak, just kept on drinking.

"I have to get home before the baby wakes up, Banger."

He kept on drinking.

Shanae leaned back in her seat. "You ain't in a rush to get home? Ever since you started messing with Rize's sister, you can't get home fast enough."

He kept on drinking.

"What is it about her, anyway? She's had y'all open since she moved in with her old black self. I mean, she cute, but she ain't all that. She do got a fat ass, though. Is it the ass? I swear, y'all niggas would do anything for a fat ass." Shanae's mouth went a mile a minute.

Rahshaan finally looked at her. "You got a fat ass, and you can't even get your nigga to help you carry your baby's stroller downstairs, so what the fuck is you talking about?"

Shanae's smile glistened in the night. "You be lookin' at my ass?"

"You know you got a body. That's the only reason why you got this job now." He turned the bottle toward his lips, but it was empty. Disappointed, Rahshaan tossed the bottle in the back seat.

"You want me to go back in and get you some coffee or something?" Shanae offered.

Rahshaan didn't answer her.

She stared out the window, unsure of what to do. It was close to five. In another hour, her children would be awake. With Squeak coming home less and less, she was on her own getting them to school.

"Banger, how long has Squeak been cheating on me?" she seemed to ask out of nowhere.

Rahshaan looked at her. "Fuck you asking me for? That's between you and him."

Shanae tried again. "How long has he been fuckin your baby mama?"

Rahshaan hesitated. "I don't know," he answered truthfully.

"Why are you here?" she wondered. "I didn't think you'd ever move on from Monaysia. I thought you would just be a ho for the rest of your life."

"That's cuz you don't know shit about me," Rahshaan snapped. "I just had to find a girl I gave a fuck about, not none of you project bitches." He reclined his seat. "Wake me up in an hour. I just need to sleep off this Crown. Then I'll be ready to take you home. I'll make sure you get there in time to get the kids dressed." He felt stupid for leaving his comfort to hear Shanae's drama.

The crows were cawing, but that wasn't what woke him up. It was the clinking of his belt becoming unbuckled, the sound of his zipper being undone. In his drunken grogginess, he couldn't figure out where he was or who he was with. His surroundings didn't look familiar. Then he felt his dick being ripped free from his underwear. A warm sensation engulfed him. He struggled to remember where he was and looked down in his lap. Red hair bobbed up and down. The slurping noises stimulated him. He grabbed the steering wheel and looked around frantically. His drunk mind couldn't think straight. He looked down again.

"Shanae? What the fuck?" He pushed her off of him.

"Come on, Banger. You out here with me, telling me how fat my ass is. Your baby mama fuckin my nigga. Why can't I fuck you? We ain't even gotta fuck. I just wanna feel it go down my throat."

"I got a wife, Shanae."

"Nobody ever told that bitch why they call you 'Bang-HER'?" She looked down at his crotch and smirked. "Besides, somebody don't seem to care what you got."

The ride home was long and silent. He let Shanae take Moosie's car back to her, since he was in no state to drive. He walked right past apartment 4F and got in the shower in G-Ma's apartment. There was no way he could face Shatima after what he let Shanae do to him.

Even knowing what he did didn't explain why Shanae thought that made them a couple, so he didn't have an explanation. Then he thought about how things could be perceived.

Giving money to her kids every time he passed them in the hallway. Sending Shatima downstairs to do her kids' hair for free like she was some servant. He felt like shit.

"You're taking too long to answer," Shatima snapped.

Rahshaan had no answer.

"Get out of my house, and don't come back," she told him. "That's two bitches I've fought over you, and that's two too many. Get out."

"I don't wanna wake up Quest," he said pitifully, trying to find some reason to hold on.

"I didn't say Quest had to leave," Shatima snapped. In her mind, she panicked. How was she going to handle that part of the breakup? She couldn't turn her back on him after she promised to be there for him. "You gotta get out my house, though. I'm through with you."

"Tima..."

"Rahshaan, get out of my house, or I'm calling my brother to take you out." The last thing she wanted to do was involve anyone else in this drama, but she had no other choice.

Rahshaan planted himself in the bedroom and refused to leave until she heard him out. There was nothing he could say. Eventually, Shameik came and led Rahshaan up to G-Ma's house. He wanted to come back and say, "I told you so," but hearing his sister cry really just made him want to beat the shit out of his friend. He slept on the pull out couch in Shatima's living room that night and made sure that Rahshaan didn't return. She tried to cover the sound of her crying with Mary J. Blige's *My Life* CD, but Shameik hurt for her as he heard her sob.

By no means did Shatima want NyQuest to think he wasn't welcome in her life. The little boy went through too much for her to take him through another change. After getting off work, Shatima went to G-Ma's house and took him home with her like she always did. She took him and Jabez out to eat. If Rahshaan was there when she got there, she simply ignored him and took NyQuest with her anyway. They brought G-Ma dinner at the end of the night. Shatima always gave NyQuest a choice of where he wanted to stay. If Rahshaan was out working, then he slept in his bunk bed at her house. She made sure to help him with homework and made sure his favorite snacks were stocked in her cabinets. As far as explaining what was going on, she didn't bother. If he wanted to know why his daddy didn't come with them anymore, then he had to ask his daddy. Maybe he'd get a better explanation than the one she did.

By February, Rahshaan had all but given up hope on reconciling. She made it clear every time they passed each other that she had no interest in breathing the same air as him. Seeing her was hard for him, so he stayed away to avoid her. He retreated back to the dark place he lived in before she let him be a part of her life.

"You miss her, don't you?" Mont asked him one day as they sat in his office counting money.

"It ain't hard to tell," Rahshaan said, wrapping a rubber band around a stack of money. "The illest part about her is that even through whatever bullshit me and her got going on, she's still there for my son."

Mont stopped what he was doing and studied Rahshaan. "Can I ask you a question? What made you fuck around with old bird ass Shanae? You knew she'd run her mouth."

"I ain't fuck her. She sucked my dick," came Rahshaan's weak defense. He didn't dare share the exact details. Mont would kill him if he knew how off his game Rahshaan was that night.

"Nigga, whatever-the-fuck. Why her? Was it because of Squeak and Monaysia?" Mont pressed.

"Hell no. I don't give a fuck about them. I just got caught up," Rahshaan said quickly. "But Tima didn't deserve what I did to her, so I'm gonna let her move on. I wish I ain't fuck shit up with her, though. That girl is perfect. She even makes Quest's lunch every day. I fucked up for real."

"Yeah, you did. I know you fucked up about it though, cuz you talking about it freely inside of a building." Mont nodded his head and went back to counting money. He went through several stacks before speaking again. "Take her to the Virgin Islands."

"What?" Rahshaan asked.

Mont counted some more money and rattled off a total for Rahshaan to type into a spreadsheet before repeating himself. "We can swing it. For what you did, it's gonna take a hell of an apology to get her back. That's if she'll take you back at all. I called her and asked about you, and she told me *'If you can't call here about niggaz who actually live here, then don't dial my number!'* and hung up in my face. I ain't never felt more disrespected in my life. I don't know why Chillz wanted a daughter so bad. That attitude would make me hurt something."

The high pitched mimicking of Shatima's voice gave Rahshaan the first laugh he'd had in weeks. "She ain't gonna go nowhere with me though, Unc. I can't even get anyone to mention my name and her name in the same sentence. Shameik is ready to kill me. Even Quest is mad at me. G-Ma ain't speaking to me, and she don't even know what I did. She just keeps talking about how hard she fought that girl to even look my way, and now I got her looking like a fool."

That made Mont laugh. "You don't worry about my goddaughter," he said. "You just make sure you don't pull no shit like this again. I can't be funding hoe-cations every time you backslide. I'm supposed to be kicking your ass myself, but I'm gonna chill out and help you get her back just this once."

Lynn had enough of Shatima moping around the shop, so she canceled their appointments for the rest of the day, grabbed Selena, and took them out for retail therapy. She hated sadness, especially sadness over a man. She understood being embarrassed, but she never experienced it on the level that Shatima did. No woman had ever been crazy enough to come to her job over a man. Lynn wanted to kick Rahshaan's ass herself after the incident in the shop.

"Oooh, Tima. Look at this two piece!" Lynn exclaimed. She

frowned at Shatima dragging her feet behind them through a department store.

"It's cute," she said dryly. "It's also February."

Lynn and Selena exchanged a look that went unnoticed by Shatima. "Oh, you haven't been around the family for long, so you don't know. We all take a girls' trip in February. We need a break from the cold."

Shatima thought of how nice it would be to get away from men. Seeing any of them angered her.

"Go try it on," Selena urged her.

"And here go a sarong to cover that horse ass you got!" Lynn tossed her a turquoise and royal blue cover up. "I don't even understand why you would want to though. If I had an ass like that, I would never cover it."

Selena laughed, but Shatima didn't. "I can't go anywhere. Who will watch Jabez?"

"The same people who watch the kids any time we do anything, Tima. Damn. That's what the fuck grandparents are for." Lynn shook her head and leaned against one of the racks. "You're one of the best mother's I've ever seen - especially for a young bitch - but the way you hold onto that little boy is damn near unhealthy."

Shatima cut her eyes at her aunt, but took the bikini anyway. When she went into the dressing room and tried it on, she had to admit that she looked good in the strappy two piece. She knew if Rahshaan saw her in it, then she wouldn't have it on for long.

Then she was sad. Everything she did made her think of Rahshaan. Trying on the bathing suit took longer than it should have, because she was trying to stop herself from crying. She hadn't been that depressed in months. Looking at the price tag on the bathing suit only depressed her more.

"So where is it?" Selena asked when Shatima exited the dressing room.

"In there waiting for it to go back on the rack," Shatima replied. "I can't afford that."

"Yes, you can," Lynn argued and patted her purse. "I got your uncle's credit card. You can get that bathing suit, your plane ticket, and anything else you want. It's all on him."

"And he does this every year? Just like that?" Shatima wondered, eyeing a pair of denim micro shorts with lace where the side seams were supposed to be. Usually, it irritated her that summer clothes were available at a time when they still had to wait six months to be able to wear them. She walked over to the shorts and held them against her body. Her reflection in the mirror made her smile.

Lynn nudged Selena. She immediately chimed in. "Yup. Every year around this time we go down to Miami for a weekend, and then we spend about ten days in the Virgin Islands." Another odd set of looks were exchanged between Lynn and Selena that went unnoticed by Shatima.

Shatima made a face as though she smelled something putrid. "Ten days? I've never been away from Jabez longer than an overnight shift at work. And with everything going on with NyQuest-"

"Bitch, cut the cord!" Lynn cut off the laundry list of excuses that Shatima was going to try to rattle off. "Now I know that being raised by Hope Thomas—"

"If you can call what she did raising," Selena offered.

"—makes you think that your sun has to rise and set over your child, but you need a break. You're moping around like you lost your best friend, and this trip is what you need to put a smile on your face."

"But what about work? This is really short notice for me to be rescheduling my clients." Shatima stopped looking at clothes and tried to level with the women. A sales associate came by and offered to help them find anything. They ignored her and continued to loiter by the rack.

"What about work? What about this? What about that? What about Shatima?" Selena went off. "All you do is work and take care of kids. You have been an adult for five years now. Have you ever done any of the things that adults enjoy? Have you ever even left the state as an adult? It almost feels like you punish yourself for having a child. What type of shit is that? Shatima, you are not Hope. Nothing you can ever do can make you be the sorry ass type of mother that she was. Stop measuring yourself against her. Live a damn life." Selena's eyes locked with her daughter's. She wanted to make sure Shatima digested every word. In the months since their reunion, she watched her daughter intently. Even though she was very proud of the woman Shatima had become, Selena wanted her to stop letting her twenties slip by.

Lynn's mouth formed an O as she turned to Selena. "My brother was so blessed to have you, because I don't have the patience for all that maternal shit. Bitch, you did that mothering shit."

"When someone is introverted like Shatima, you have to approach her a certain way," Selena explained. "And you're right. You don't have the patience or the tact for that."

"Why are y'all talking about me like I'm not here?" Shatima spoke up.

"Because you've been on another planet for the past few weeks," Lynn retorted. She took a bathing suit for herself off the rack and led them to another rack of clothing. "I know breakups are hard, but you can't let that nigga take you under, especially not over stankin' ass Shanae, that old Cabbage Patch face ass bitch. Now come on. I wanna get some draws from that expensive line Lil Kim used to rap about *if th*ey come in big girls' sizes."

The closer the time came for the trip, the lower the temperature dipped. The day before the trip, the temperature in Sanford County dropped to two degrees. Lynn kept walking around and fussing about how the temperature shouldn't have bothered rising above zero if it wasn't going to make an effort. Shatima thought of not having to wait for her car to warm up and brush snow off — although the boys on the stoop still took care of the latter before she woke up in the morning. She felt guilty leaving NyQuest and Jabez behind, but they were excited about spending the week at Big Grams' house. Haddus took her clients who weren't willing to reschedule. The temperature got even colder.

When she walked into first class on the flight, she almost felt like she wasn't worthy. Lynn and Selena acted like they were used to it, but Shatima wasn't ashamed to marvel over the fine champagne, full meal, and noise cancelling headphones. Not even when she was a little girl traveling with her mother did she get to experience flying like this. Hermes silk pillowcases and Peter Thomas Roth products in the bathroom only added to her amazement. For the first time, she understood why Hope had a hard-on for her father's money.

The Miami weekend was spent in the spa and on the beach during the day and partying at night. Shatima was a better drinker by this time and knew not to mix dark and light liquors as well as when to cut herself off. This afforded her the luxury of clubbing well into the morning. She felt bad for judging those girls who did it before. They were just enjoying themselves. She regretted not learning earlier what fun was. Fun was making up fake names to give to men who wouldn't stop sweating them for their phone numbers. Fun was dancing on top of a bar. Fun was winning a $500 second place prize in a *Whistle While You Twerk* contest (Selena won the $1000 first prize). Fun was watching the rose man in the club follow Lynn around all night and eventually give her all of his light up roses and teddy bears as though they were the equivalent to an engagement ring. Shatima never got to experience anything like that before. She was glad Lynn and Selena talked her into it.

On Monday morning, they ran straight from the club to the airport. The flight to the Virgin Islands was scheduled to depart at six, and they didn't leave the club until four. Somehow they got separated at the security gate. Shatima panicked when she realized she was alone on the other side.

"Aunt Lynn! Where are you? They're boarding for our flight!" Shatima screamed into her cellphone.

Lynn paused. The setup was cruel, but it had to be done. Only one thing was going to put a smile back on her niece's face. "Just get on the plane, Tima. We'll see you back at home."

"Huh?"

A second announcement that they were boarding first class passengers came. Shatima looked at the line. She knew she wasn't going crazy. Over the months, she'd memorized the silhouette of the tall man at the front of the line. His hair, which was pulled into a ponytail, was only that tame because she took care of it. The walk was undeniable. Her heart sank.

"Tima, don't be mad. Just go enjoy yourself!" Selena slurred into the phone, still tipsy.

She sucked her teeth. "Y'all know how bad he dogged me out. What part of maternal nurturing involves you encouraging me to go back to a nigga who cheated on me? I should've known y'all were setting me up with all these slutty clothes and shoes."

"I know, Tima. It's bad. We're garbage for this. Just go to the islands. You've never been there before, right?" Lynn said.

"It doesn't matter. I'm not getting on the plane," Shatima stubbornly insisted.

"Nobody said you had to get back with him, Shatima, but damn! It's a free trip. Get on the plane, or I'm gonna kick your ass myself," Lynn threatened her.

Shatima huffed into the phone. "You better check on my baby every single day, Auntie. I mean it." Letting out a growl, she skulked onto the plane. Men marveled at her ass barely covered by the sundress draped over it and her long legs lengthened by the heels she wore. If she could have flipped them all off individually, she would have.

PARADISE, BEAUTIFUL BABIES, &A DEEP SECRET

A mocha-colored woman, who missed her calling as a Victoria's Secret Angel, and a chocolate man, who looked like he bench pressed Mack Trucks in his spare time, greeted Shatima and advised her that they were taking care of her for the entire flight. They announced that everything on their flight was courtesy of Malachi James, in honor of his top employee and the employee's special guest. First class on this plane was even more luxurious than on the flight to Miami. The man escorted her to her seat. Even though her row was shared with Rahshaan, there was a divider so that the two of them didn't have to touch. The woman took her breakfast order and complimented her on the goddess braids she installed in her hair for the trip. Then she served her a mimosa and advised her that the bar was open and only served top shelf liquor.

"Good, because I'll need it to get me through this trip," she muttered before tying her hair up in a silk scarf.

Rahshaan opened his mouth to speak, but she threw a hand up. "I ain't one of them project chicks you send to my job when you don't like the way I react to you. I can't be bought. All the champagne in the world ain't gonna make up for the fact that you cheated on me."

"Ain't nobody cheated on you," he said softly, sticking with his half-lie.

She didn't respond. He realized that she was wearing headphones and watching her favorite movie, *Brown Sugar*. There was no way he was getting a word in edgewise. Since it was the source of their current position, he declined any liquor. Instead, he fell asleep staring at the side of her face. When he awoke, she was asleep. It had been weeks since he watched her laying next to him. He wished he could hold her or at least touch her. He missed her pretty face so much. In that moment, he realized the depth of his stupidity. This trip wasn't a good enough reason for her to take him back. She'd been his perfection, everything he never knew he wanted, and he threw it away being stupid.

When she got deep into her sleep, the cries for her father and her brother came. He shook her gently at first, but sleep pulled her body went even more limp. He yanked her toward him with his hands firmly gripping her shoulders. Her eyes finally shot open, and she glowered at him.

"People on this plane are looking at you like you're stupid," he half-lied. Only one person besides himself could hear her. "You gotta chill out."

She glared at him and then glared at the ceiling. Somehow, she would manage to stay awake for the rest of the trip.

Her eyes were heavy by the time they landed. She was tipsy from the bottomless mimosas and tired from the night before. All she wanted to do was get to the hotel, take a shower, and get into the bed. She didn't have time to marvel at the fact that they had their own personal car and driver, whose name was Peter. When he announced that he was taking them to lunch, she politely declined. Rahshaan was incredulous. He planned to have her back in his arms by the time dessert came.

"Yo, why did you even come?" he exploded, unaware that she had to be tricked into it.

"Because you and my family snaked me," she shot back. "Do you really think I'd be down here if I knew this was supposed to be some getaway for me and you? I keep telling you I'm not the chicks in the buildings. I can take myself to paradise. I don't need to spend it here with a cheater."

"How many times do I gotta tell you I didn't cheat?" Rahshaan demanded. "Yes, what I did was fucked up, and that bitch should've never came to your job, but how can I tell you I'm sorry?"

"What you just said shows how sorry you are," she quipped.

And there, in between the airport and a luxury ride, they had the argument Rahshaan waited for weeks to have. When she wasn't speaking to him, it dimmed any semblance of hope he had for winning her back. Getting her to react let him know that there was a possibility that she still cared.

Neither of them saw Peter excuse himself and walk away. He made a phone call. Then he quietly walked back and watched Shatima when her phone rang.

"Why you being difficult?" Mont admonished her.

Shatima sucked her teeth. "You got your nerve calling this line. I told you I wasn't dealing with your boy no more. Stop trying to force stuff where it don't fit." She went and stood against a wall, out of the way of people trying to enter and exit the airport.

Being spoken to like he was some kid on the streets made Mont pull rank. "Watch your mouth and show me some respect. In the absence of your father, I am your paternal figure."

"Then why do you have me in another country with a cheater?" she wanted to know.

"Because he's trying to make up with your ass, but you won't give him a chance."

She sucked her teeth again. "Can we speed up this conversation? Only my nights and weekends are free, Unc."

Mont took the time to adjust his attitude. He thought the trip would make her leap into Rahshaan's arms with starry eyes. "Look. I know what he did was fucked up, but don't act like you don't miss that nigga. I see you moping around. Give him a chance to fix what he fucked up."

"And if I don't, you're gonna have your little snitch ass driver report it to you?" She waited for him to acknowledge what she said. When he didn't, she told him to book her an immediate flight home.

"Tima, hear me out. I ain't never seen Banger do better than when he was with you. Y'all was a force. Y'all need each other. He's trying to make up for what he did. He's never had anybody like you." Mont felt like a fool begging on behalf of another man, but if that's what it took he was willing to do it just that once. "If I book you a flight home, then you're catching the bus home from the airport. Hear that man out."

"Whatever, Unc. Get off my phone. My roaming charges are gonna be sky high," she grumbled.

After hanging up the phone, she strutted past Rahshaan and Peter and slammed the door to the silver QX56 behind her. The air conditioning felt wonderful compared to the humidity outside. Briefly, she remembered that she was there to escape the brutal cold of Upstate, New York, and resolved to enjoy herself without reconciling with Rahshaan. Several minutes later, he climbed into the backseat with her, a scowl on his face. They both cut Peter dirty looks.

"Welcome to paradise," the man said sheepishly.

They rode several minutes before Rahshaan's face relaxed. She had to admit that even with that ponytail he looked handsome in his own rugged way.

"I'm sorry," he said in the most sincere tone he could manage.

For a split second, she softened. Then she folded her arms across her chest and stared out the window beside her.

"You can do a lot of shopping here," Peter announced, pointing out the various luxury stores they passed. "You'll be staying in a villa and have access to a private beach. If you want to go to the public beach, then I'll take you there. I'm here for you for the duration of your stay."

"What if I wanna drive myself?" Rahshaan said, glancing at Shatima. If she didn't let down her wall, then there was no way he was going to make her stay with him and fill a car with her misery. The Caribbean humidity made the air thick enough without adding her funky attitude.

"You'll have access to your own vehicles as well," Peter assured him.

Peter chatted away about all the luxury they'd have. Shatima tried to lean on her excitement to keep her awake, but her eyelids were getting so heavy. She barely slept during the weekend in Miami. When she did sleep, she had nightmares that almost induced sleep paralysis. She just wanted to recharge so that she could enjoy herself, regardless of the company she had to keep.

"I hope you like fried snapper," Peter announced as they pulled up. "Hyacinth says she's prepared that for lunch. If you want something else - which, once you smell it, I don't think you will - then I can take you to an oceanside restaurant."

A group of staff met them at the car and unloaded their luggage. Peter led them on a tour of the villa that started with drinks loaded with rum and fresh fruit. He took them straight to a patio out back that was only yards away from the ocean. The white sand was adorned with beach towels, umbrellas, and a small table. Soft waves washed in from the turquoise waters. Taking in that scene made it hard to stay angry. The rum burned off the rest of Shatima's fury.

As they headed upstairs, Rahshaan lagged behind her a few steps and watched as her shoulders released their tenseness. Her walk resumed its normal sway as opposed to the angry switch he'd seen since getting off the plane. He admired the sexy straps wrapped around her calves. Peter showed them to their master suite. Their bags were already unpacked for them, and their clothes were hung in his and her walk-in closets.

"It's supposed to rain this afternoon, but it will be sunny for the rest of your stay," Peter told them. "I'll leave you to get settled in."

When Peter closed the door behind him, Shatima stood and marveled at the room. Rahshaan wanted to do something to break the silence between them while her body language was giving him the green light, so he went to the closet to find his duffle bag. From it, he produced a report with a dinosaur drawn on the cover.

"Quest wanted me to show you this," he told her, his voice gruff. He handed her the report.

"This dinosaur looks a lot better than the one I helped him draw," she remarked as she took it.

Rahshaan chuckled. "Your dinosaur drawing was garbage."

She actually joined in his laughter. He took that as a good sign. She flipped through the report and read the teacher's notes. Most of them made her smile. "He got a ninety-eight?" she remarked. "Two points off for one outdated fact? What a petty bitch."

"Thank you for helping him with that," Rahshaan said to her.

"I think your drawing was what helped him earn that grade. The one he and I drew was tragic," she said to him.

Silence fell between them. She went into the wooden walled bathroom and stepped onto the white tiled floor to wash the flight off of her. There she was given the option of a hot tub, a garden tub, or a three headed his and her shower. She never dreamed of living life so luxuriously, even if only for a week. She opted for the hot tub, because it was filled with rose petals and stocked with a bottle of champagne. Maybe just one more drink would make her company tolerable.

She disrobed and descended into the tub. The bubbles felt amazing on her body after all that traveling. Immediately, she poured herself a glass of champagne and reflected over the past year of her life. In February of last year, she was saving up to get a new pair of snow tires and fighting with the maintenance crew at her job to make sure they had the parking lot plowed by the time it was time for the nine to fivers to end their work day. A year later, she literally sat in paradise. She wanted to travel back in time to tell herself that it definitely would get better.

Rahshaan tapped softly on the door. "Spark one?"

She hesitated and looked around. Topping off this moment with a blunt would make it perfect. "Yeah. Come in."

Rahshaan didn't expect her to be so forward. He thought he'd have to wait until she was done bathing. Her nudity wasn't something he could handle at the moment, not with the way she was acting toward him. "I'm good. I'll just roll up while you wash and get dressed."

"Rahshaan, come in," she commanded. "If we're gonna be here together for the next week, then we should be able to at least be cordial."

Rahshaan wordlessly sat on the side of the tub and rolled a blunt. Bubbles covered everything from her collarbone down. He wanted to get into the tub with her and make love to her until she forgave him. Instead, he lit the blunt and let her take the first hit. After passing it back to him, she took a sip of champagne.

"You wanna slow down with that? You've been drinking since we got on the plane," he admonished.

"I've been drinking since Friday, actually," she snapped. "Definitely haven't stopped since we pre-gamed yesterday, and that was at seven, so..." She took another sip of champagne. "I probably should stop though. Probably gonna have to fight another bitch over you."

He hung his head. "I'm sorry. I never meant for any of that to happen to you."

"Yes, you did, because that's what you're used to. You've had birds trying to fight me over you for years, and it finally happened."

"I ain't want none of that shit to happen to you!" he roared. "Why the fuck can't you understand that?"

"Hmmm..." Shatima puffed the blunt and stared off into nothing. "Probably because you laid up in my bed and told me your deepest, darkest secrets, knowing you fucked somebody else. Now, I can't put Monaysia on you. That was a fight that was probably gonna happen sooner or later. But a bitch came to my job, Rahshaan, and told all my clients and co-workers how many inches long your dick is. She knew that you and I had a fight, and then you came to me trying to have another black love moment like we were in a reenactment of *Love Jones*. What am I supposed to feel for you now?"

"I fucked up," Rahshaan said softly, watching her in the water. "I didn't fuck that broad, though." He got up. "You can take that blunt to the head. I don't need it. It's other bedrooms in here. I'll sleep in one of them. You can take this one." She watched him walk out the room, wishing she could find a way to forgive him. The liquor she drank consumed her body. She wanted him in the worst way, but she couldn't let him touch her again after he betrayed her. Nothing about the water, the weed, or the champagne was relaxing anymore. She threw a silk robe on and climbed the steps to the king-sized four poster bed. Finally, she was able to sleep.

Hours later, she was awakened by the buzzing of her cellphone on the night stand. She reached for it and opened it, but focused before speaking. "Hey, Shameik."

"Mommy just told me where you was at," he snapped. "You want me to send for you? I don't give a fuck what Unc got to say. That's fucked up that they tricked you like that."

She wrinkled her face at the acidity in Shameik's voice. It was weird having such a heavy defender on her team. "Thank you. That's very nice of you to offer. I'm gonna try to enjoy the trip, but I'm glad somebody realizes how messed up this is."

"Say the word, and I'll break that nigga's neck, Tima," Shameik went on.

Shatima wanted to giggle, but she was afraid of her brother's reaction. She leaned back on one of a dozen pillows. "I'm okay right now. We aren't even sleeping in the same room. I think he's at the other end of the house. If I need you I'll call you, okay?"

Shameik paused, unsure. "Aight. I'm gonna have my cell on me at all times, so if you need to leave, then just hit me."

"Thank you, Shameik. I love you."

"I love you too, baby sis."

Once again, her heart was filled. She thought back to a year ago, February 13. 366 days ago was a polar opposite from where she currently sat.

It was a lonely day. She and Jabez walked to the corner store to get him his favorite snack. Despite the cold, she stopped to look at the mural dedicated to her father and brother on the side of the store. If she ever found out who did it, she wanted to do something for that person. Her money was really low, so she probably couldn't afford to do anything more than cook. But the colors were so beautiful. It captured their smiles and the life behind their eyes perfectly. On that day especially, she needed to take it in.

The inside of the corner store was bustling with men buying dollar roses and cards for their valentines. Some of them offered to buy her one, but she declined some and ignored others. She was sad. Earlier, she'd called a prison where Shameik was held only to find out he was in solitary confinement and couldn't have visits. She'd tried to send him the last little bit of money she was able to spare, but it was sent back to her. More than all of the cards, flowers, and candy in the world, she wanted to be able to get in touch with just one member of her family.

"Mommy, can I have a dollar?" Jabez asked, breaking her out of the funky daze she was in.

"All I have is a dollar to get your candy," she told him.

"Oh. I wanted to get you a flower," he said, disappointed.

She shook her head. "Just get your candy. One day, you'll make enough money to buy me a whole garden of flowers." She smiled and winked at him.

They walked home, and she didn't think anything else about the flower.

In the morning, as they were leaving Apartment 4F, Jabez spotted something in the doorway. If he hadn't said anything, she would have knocked it over.

It was a vase containing a single rose.

There was something about paradise that made her think about everything she had gained in the past year. The family. The love. Had it not been for Rahshaan, she wouldn't have it. That couldn't be the anchor of their relationship, though. She had to separate the deed from the man who hurt her, but how could she? He earned his promotion from making cameo appearances in her life to having a starring role. He also broke her heart. Thanks to him, she had everything. She owed him nothing.

Having everything seemed empty without him. She hated to admit to herself that some of the fullest moments of her life were with him. He brought life back to her. It was always her goal to never be consumed by interest in a man. Loving him for the short time that she did didn't swallow her whole. When she ran away from it, she never felt like she was running toward freedom. Instead, she felt like she was running away from something she'd never get again. She wanted a family. He gave her two— the one she lost and the one she thought she could put off until school was over. He made her feel every verse to every 90s R&B love song she listened to.

She ventured downstairs through the home, touching all of the wooden features as she traveled. The white house was every mother's dream. With a five-year-old, she'd never have decor that color. Every room she passed through gave her a view of the ocean. The waves rushing the shore and then retreating made her want to go outside and sit in the water. In a minute, she'd get out there, but first she had to eat something to soak up the liquor she couldn't seem to stop drinking.

Hyacinth, the cook, was a robust woman who shared Peter's coffee complexion. When she smiled, her lips never parted. She invited Shatima to sit at the kitchen island as she put the finishing touches on lunch. "Your husband is still asleep?" She had a much thicker accent than Peter's.

"He's not my husband," Shatima said.

"Oh, he's not? Well the two of you should hurry up and get married. You would make beautiful babies," she pressed as she bustled around the kitchen.

Bashfully, Shatima smiled. "I don't think that's going to happen any time soon."

"He cheated on you?" Hyacinth pried. "He has the look on his face of someone who got caught cheating. How did you catch him?"

For some reason, Shatima didn't mind the woman's intrusive line of questioning. "The girl came to my job, and I had to beat her up."

Hyacinth guffawed. "And did you bust him one good time?" She set down a plate of red snapper and plantains.

Shatima wanted to answer, but the mouthful of food made her eyes roll to the back of her head. It was an orgasmic experience to eat Hyacinth's cooking. "You have to teach me how to make this!"

Hyacinth grinned. "You like to cook?"

"I love to cook, but I don't ever want to live without you again, Miss Hyacinth. I think I love you. Please come back to New York with me!" Shatima begged, smiling and shoveling food into her mouth.

Hyacinth laughed. "New York? I'll never go to that place again. Too cold in the winter."

"You're right about that," Shatima agreed with a nod. "That's the main thing that's keeping me here now."

"That and that handsome man," Hyacinth drove the conversation right back to where she wanted it. "I see how you look at him. Either stab him or leave him, because you're too in love to let him roam the Earth without being by his side."

The dramatic statement Hyacinth made drove Shatima outside quickly after lunch. She sat on the shore in the strappy bikini she bought when Lynn took her shopping. The water came into land and washed itself up to her ankles then left as though it never touched her and made her feel its warmth. The sun mercilessly baked her, turning her chocolate skin to black coffee. With her arms extended behind her and most of her weight resting on her palms, she closed her eyes, leaned her head back and worshipped the sun, silently thanking it for showing up in St. Croix when it refused to do so in New York.

She felt him standing over her. Without opening her eyes she said, "Thank you for arranging this. This is really beautiful."

"I just had to see your sexy ass one more time," he told her solemnly.

Slowly, she opened her eyes. His bare feet digging in the sand caught her attention. "Why are you doing that?"

"I never felt sand before. Wanted to see what it was like," he said sheepishly.

"Oh." She hoped she hid the pity in her voice for living such a sorry ass life that deprived him of experiencing the beach.

He stood over her with his hands jammed in his pockets. His feet kept digging into the sand, scooping it up, and sifting between his toes. He seemed perpetually amused by the sensation. She watched him and became slightly tickled by his enjoyment.

"You're really beautiful," he told her seemingly out of nowhere.

"Thank you," she said slowly, her voice almost saying that she was waiting for the other shoe to drop.

"I'm trying to apologize to you, but I keep fuckin' up." He sat next to her, sand covering and filling his white shorts. "Can a jellyfish come eat us?" he asked her in all seriousness.

"It can come sting us, but it probably won't eat us," she replied. She stared out into the ocean, still amazed by the turquoise water. Suddenly, she turned her head to him and asked, "What made you do it, Rahshaan?"

"What you think happened didn't happen," he replied, "but I did violate. That night fucked me up so badly, and I'm almost embarrassed about it."

Her eyes glazed and twitched, beckoning him to continue.

"I didn't fuck that bitch. I went to go chill with Moosie at a club. We had a few drinks because we were still stressed about Squeak. Shanae was there and asked me for a ride somewhere because she didn't know if Squeak was coming home or not. I felt bad because I knew that Squeak was dead but she didn't, so I gave her the ride. I was drunker than what I thought I was and fell asleep while I waited for her to come outside. Then I fucked up, because instead of just having her drive home when she came out, I slept a little longer. The next thing I know, she's unbuckling my pants, talking about she wants to get back at Squeak and Monaysia, and I was too drunk to stop her the way I should have. I don't know why she came to your job and tried to act like we were in a relationship after that, because I haven't said two words to the bitch since then. That's all that happened." He held his breath. He had a premonition that the follow-up questions would drive them further apart.

"Why couldn't Moosie take her? Moosie obviously likes her."

"Moosie was getting a lap dance."

"So you were at a strip club?"

"Not really."

"How are you not really at a strip club?"

"It's a club, but Moosie brings her own strippers."

"That...never mind. I don't wanna know. Why didn't you push her off of you?"

"I was drunk and didn't realize what was happening."

"How don't you know that you're getting your dick sucked?"

"I said I was sleep..."

"But somewhere in that story you woke up, right?"

"Yeah..."

She poked her head forward, Bucked her eyes out, and bobbed her head around, waiting for him to catch on.

There were no words that could explain his actions, so there was nothing he could say.

"Why didn't you push her off of you?"

"Because I was drunk. Damn. How many times can I say-"

"Did you want to get back at Squeak and Monaysia?"

"Nah. They got what they deserved."

"Then why didn't you push her off of you?"

"I can't answer that question any differently than I already have."

"Did you finish?"

"What you mean?"

"Did you nut?"

"I...I don't remember."

Shatima got up and walked away from him. She couldn't understand this act of masochism she was performing. What about the way he hurt her was so enticing that she needed to know every detail of what he did? If there was a video available, she would have watched that too. Was this a learning exercise? She realized she was digging deep, trying to figure out if there was a way she could prevent this in the future. In the future with who, though? As it was, she wanted to chop up his body and spill his blood in the Atlantic Ocean as a sacrifice for all monogamous women who were conned into joining polyamorous relationships. For a split second, she visualized a shark coming and devouring the pieces. Perhaps she'd chop his feet off and bury them in the sand he was so fascinated with. All roads led to killing the source of her broken heart. How could she be thinking about their future?

Rahshaan dashed after her. Running on sand was strangely

satisfying to him. It calmed his rage to a dull roar. They'd made so much progress. At least she was talking to him. If he could keep her conversing about this, he could get her back.

Or that's what he told himself. He had to have her back.

When he reached her, he grabbed her hand and beckoned her to stop. She recoiled and turned her back to him.

"It's gonna sound crazy," he began, "but to answer your question, I did nut. I sprayed it in her face, smutted her out. I still don't understand why she thought that meant that she and I were together. That shit never would have happened had I been sober, and I'm sure she knows that. I'm sorry for the way I did everything that night, especially for walking out on you. I shouldn't have let you put me out. I should've just told you what was going on."

The sun was no rival for the lava that replaced Shatima's blood. She refused to cry anymore. She wished she hadn't asked. Had the tables been turned — had Rahshaan taken advantage of Shanae while she was drunk — the conversation would be different. This wouldn't be called cheating; it would be called rape. But where did Rahshaan's personal responsibility come into play? Drinking and driving? Was he trying to get himself killed?

"You came back to me like nothing even happened. How could you send me down there to do her children's hair after what transpired between the two of you?"

"Them kids ain't got nothing to do with what went on between any of us," he said. "I just wanted them to look nice for their father's funeral."

She declined going any further down that road. She completely agreed.

"I know you probably won't believe me, but I didn't even really remember what happened until the day I had to come to the shop and pull you off of her," he told her.

"You're right. I don't believe that part. Ain't that much liquor in the world," Shatima said. "So what? Is she pretending to be gay for Moosie so that she can stay close to you?"

A frown dug itself into Rahshaan's face. "Whatever her and Moosie got going on ain't got shit to do with me."

Her eyes studied the frown etched into his face. Arms folded across her chest, she proceeded with caution with her next set of questions. "When you left my house—"

"When you told me to leave," he corrected her.

"Fine. When I told you to leave, *and you left,* it was after 2 am. You went to this strip club where you bring your own strippers, and then Shanae needed to go somewhere... Did she call you? Was she there?"

"She was there serving drinks," he told her. Dread rang throughout each quadrant of his body. If she kept traveling down this line of questioning, then his answers could make him lose her forever.

She nodded her head several times. "So...did Moosie bring her there too?"

"Nah." He shook his head. "She works there as a waitress."

"So then where did she need to go? I know you didn't sit outside of the place where we sleep getting your dick sucked. Not even liquor could make you that stupid." She stood there, waiting for an answer without blinking even once.

"Of course I ain't that stupid. She needed a ride to a job. I asked Moosie to take her, but Moosie ain't feel like leaving. And I knew she was gonna need whatever money she could get, so I took her."

Everything about this conversation hurt, but she kept going. There was a part of her that needed these details. "How did she need a ride to work if you were already at her job?"

Before answering, he considered what was left for him to lose. She already hated being around him. Not even a trip made things better. After all she went through, she deserved the truth. "It was a side job."

"What side hustle could she have that needs her to do it at 3 in the morning?" He didn't deserve the wave of emotion that was trying to come over her. She still needed the whole story.

"That white man was paying four Gs for an hour with her. That's more money than Squeak had given his kids all month, and I knew Mavis was gonna put them out soon as she found out Squeak was dead. I just ain't want them kids to be homeless."

"White man? What are you... Shanae's a prostitute? So what are you? A pimp?"

"It ain't even like that," Rahshaan said softly. He prepared for the end.

"So you just give hookers rides, or was the blowjob your payment?" she demanded to know. Rage boiled over.

"It ain't like that," he repeated, his voice more firm.

She turned away from him. The sun blazed the front of her torso. She regretted leaving her sunglasses in the room. "All this time I thought that you sold drugs, and that was bad enough. But you're a pimp."

"That ain't what I am," he insisted.

"Did you get some of that four thousand dollars she made?" she queried.

"Eventually," he admitted. He had to say something to maintain his reputation. "Look, all I am is muscle. These grown women want to get paid to fuck, so I make sure they do it without getting raped, hurt, killed, or robbed. They dance or serve drinks in a club until they get a call, and then one of us takes them to where they need to go, sit outside the spot, make sure everything goes okay, and then we take them home."

"You ever paid to fuck any of them?" she asked.

"I ain't been lying to you, and I ain't gonna start lying to you now. Before me and you got together, yes, I did fuck a couple of them. But I always strapped up, and it hasn't happened since I kissed you that night. All of them know I got you."

She stared at him. Then she declared, "You're a whore."

He wasn't sure whether or not he was supposed to laugh, so he held it in. "I like to fuck. Making women orgasm is fun as hell. I never liked any of them for more than that, though. They were just something to do."

Both of them thought that was the end of her questioning, but she still needed answers.

"Is that how you met NyQuest's mother?"

Rahshaan didn't see the point of her asking that question, but he didn't dare express that. "Sort of. She was trying to get on, but she acted like she wasn't built for it. First time I took her to a job, she got scared. I thought it was cute, so we started talking. She played me, though. She knew exactly what she was doing, because soon as she hooked me she was fuckin' everything moving."

Another moment of silence passed. The two of them wished that they were having a different conversation on this water and sand. It was too beautiful a scene to be wasting discussing transgressions. There was a lot to digest. Was this how her father got his money? She opened a can of worms with this questioning. She dug her toe in the sand while she weighed which questions she really wanted answered.

"So when you get on that shuttle bus every morning, you're not going to a factory? You're going to drive hookers around all day?" Her tone was sour.

He shook his head. "Nah. I'm going to work at the factory, painting cars, just like I say I am. That's my day job. Sometimes girls get calls in the middle of the day, so I leave the day job to do the other job."

"And when you leave at night you're going to paint cars?" she wondered.

"Until one of the girls gets a call. Then I'm going to the other job. The factory job covers up the other job. That way I have a paycheck stub that explains how I support myself and G-Ma. The rest of it gets paid under the table."

Shatima considered everything he said. "Well, thank you for explaining."

He watched her walk away. The way her ass rocked from side to side in her bikini hypnotized him. He wanted to kick himself for letting her get away. He called her name.

Looking exasperated, she turned to him.

"I fucked up. I love you, I miss you, and I want you back."

It seemed like out of nowhere the rain began to fall, just as Peter said it would. She didn't respond to Rahshaan. Instead, she dashed inside. The bouncing of her ass almost sent him into orbit. He went inside as well, but didn't follow her.

She wanted to take advantage of the rain by exploring the rest of the villa, but she didn't want to run into him. A foolish feeling crept over her. She was actually considering allowing him back into her life. She kept flipping his story in her head to ask herself what would have happened if it were the other way around. What if he saw Shanae laying somewhere drunk and started performing cunnilingus on her? What would that make him? It disgusted her that if that was the truth, then Shanae could get away with it. Her conflicted feelings were going to make her head explode. She climbed into the bed and lay across it. Then she dialed Selena's number.

"Your father cheated on me once," Selena told her on the first ring.

"Um...hello to you too. I was just calling to apologize for blowing up at you earlier," Shatima said. She sank deep into the down comforter that sat atop the bed. "And thank you for forcing me to go to paradise."

"You don't have to apologize," Selena said. "I was wrong for what I did, especially conning your uncle out of a weekend trip to Miami as payment for making me con you." She was delighted to hear her daughter giggle. "But I wanted to tell you about your father for a reason. Hope used to make him fuck her in order to take you on the weekends."

"I know that, and it has nothing to do with me and Rahshaan." Shatima went into the bathroom and retrieved the blunt she put out earlier. She returned to the room and sat on the chaise lounge. The white furniture in the house delighted her without ceasing. She lit the blunt and started smoking.

"You know that? How? You were nine."

"I kind of figured it out as I got older," Shatima said, hoping to avoid a conversation about Hope.

"Oh. Well anyway, your father was really honest about it. I didn't want to believe him."

"So what is the point of this, Selena?" Shatima nearly barked.

"You don't have to feel like a fool the first time. Nobody's perfect, and everyone is going to mess up. If he does it again, then I'll hold him down while you chop his balls off." Both women laughed.

"Well, anyway. I just called to apologize. I'll see you next week."

Just as quickly as it came, the rain left. Shatima opted to go to the indoor pool rather than back out on the beach. The water was warm. Powering through it helped her take away the stress from everything she just learned. She swam laps until her arms and legs ached. She exited the pool room to find something else to do.

"You're very late," Peter told her in distress. "I forgot to tell you that you're having dinner on a glass bottom boat."

"I..."

"Please come."

Peter's words came out in a hurry, so she quickly showered and dressed. In the morning, she was going to do her own thing. She'd had enough grandiose gestures. How could she enjoy St. Croix if it all revolved around forgiving a cheater? The fact that so many people were invested in her love life was bothersome. Boundaries that had yet to be established were crossed. Why did everybody care so much? Her mind stayed glued to that question as she was whisked off by Peter to the boat.

From the outside, the boat seemed tiny. When she entered, she was surprised at how breathtaking the royal blue decor was. Suddenly, she felt underdressed in a black tank top and the shorts she admired during her shopping trip with Lynn and Selena. An orange haze glowed through the window. The sun was setting. At a lone table sat Rahshaan. The champagne that seemed to be obligatory at that point sat chilling in a Bucket in the middle of the table. Rahshaan was drinking Crown Royal. The boat pulled off and into the ocean. They were instructed to take their drinks to the top deck. The moment Shatima saw dolphins leaping from the ocean, she no longer was tired of grandiose. Give her more.

They were then instructed to go down to the bottom where they marveled at all manner of sea creatures. Not even the zoo back home was this captivating. Someone brought them drinks made with Cruzan Rum. When dinner was announced, they went back upstairs to their table to eat fresh caught seafood by candlelight. The glow of the candle made both of them look enticing to each other.

"I know I'm on repeat right now, but I really am sorry for breaking your heart," he said softly.

She couldn't keep her eyes off of his curly hair. She wanted to touch it and remember its softness. Silence fell over her.

"I ain't never been in love before, but I keep on fucking up. All I wanted to do that night was calm down and get back to you. I never meant to hurt you or embarrass you."

She took her eyes off of him and focused on the linen and lace tablecloth. "Have you noticed that every time you say you love me something bad happens?"

"I'm trying to fix that," he told her solemnly.

He let her enjoy her food and didn't say anything else. Instead, he stared out the window at the view and had to admire it. The only time he left his home town was on a bus taking him to prison or to go on trips for work. Now here he was, in the middle of the ocean. It was surreal.

"Is NyQuest okay?" she asked him when she finished eating. "I worry about him every single day. I hate that I told him I'd be there for him, and then I'm not."

"What are you talking about? You're with him every day," Rahshaan countered.

"Not the way that I told him I would be. It's got to be awkward having a bed somewhere and then only going to that bed a few times a week," she pointed out.

Rahshaan considered what she said. "I think it's ill how much love you show him. Anybody else would've said, 'Fuck that little nigga. Me and his daddy ain't together no more,' but you actually stayed true to your word and kept him like he was yours. Thank you, because as awkward as shit is, this is still the most stability he's seen."

"I miss us," she blurted out. It was at that point that she knew the liquor was taking over.

"I miss us too," he said softly. "Every time I see Jay, he asks if I'm ever coming back home. It fucks me up every time. I want to come back home."

"I don't want to be the type of woman who puts her man out every weekend just to let him back in and repeat it the next weekend. I want an actual family. And I want to know what's going on with my family. Don't ever keep me in the dark about anything ever again." She stopped eating and went back to drinking.

He made a face at her glass. "Tima, your liver is gonna be concrete if you don't stop drinking so damn much." He studied her. For the first time during their trip, he saw past her pretty face and saw the anxiety and fear. "You aight? Why you drinking so much?"

She put her glass down and shrugged. "Never been away from Jabez for more than an overnight shift at work. That's all."

He eyed her suspiciously, but didn't want to overstep his boundaries by pressing her.

Seeing that they were at least being cordial to each other, Peter offered to take them to a local party. Shatima got to show out, wining for the crowd as the DJ played Soca and Reggae music all night. They kept praising the "Yankee gyal with the wicked wine." She was in her element. Rahshaan stood against the wall and watched her move like a snake, wishing he was here to enjoy being with her rather than trying to win her back.

He was out of words when they got back to their villa, so he told her good night and slept in one of the smaller bedrooms.

In the morning, Hyacinth had breakfast waiting for them. They gave each other awkward half-smiles as they ate in silence. Hyacinth kept winking at Shatima and muttering something about beautiful babies. Shatima went back to the beach. Upon her request, the staff brought her a mimosa. Then she lay in a recliner and soaked up sun. Rahshaan sat in the recliner next to her.

"I hope you drinking water with all that alcohol," Rahshaan nagged.

She snapped into an upright position. "Rahshaan, you are not my daddy. Stop worrying about what I'm drinking."

"I'm just saying. Alcohol poisoning is real," Rahshaan pressed.

"Thanks. I'll keep that in mind. You should've thought about that when you passed out drunk in a car with a bitch who couldn't beat me."

Rahshaan clenched his jaw. He knew he was wrong, but he was weary of being reminded of his iniquities. He watched her take another sip. When she relaxed the glass in her hand, he snatched it from her and poured it in the sand.

"What is your problem?" she exploded. "Why can't you just leave me alone?"

"Because you been a fuckin' wino this whole damn trip!" he hollered back. "What the fuck is wrong with you? You been drinking nonstop since Thanksgiving."

She got up and stormed back up to her room. The staff stopped and gawked at the scene they made stomping through the house like a pair of lunatics. She kept screaming for him to leave her alone, and he continued to lecture her about her drinking.

"What is wrong with you?" he demanded again, slamming the door behind him. The staff didn't even have to strain to hear them yelling at each other.

"You won't leave me alone!" she cried. "What you don't get? We're through!"

"I understand that, but that don't mean that I stopped caring about you. One more drink, and you're gonna be in detox. Before Thanksgiving, you didn't even drink."

"I'm living my life!" she declared, beating her chest with her fist. "Y'all call me uptight, but when I get crunk, it's a problem?"

"Tell me what's going on with you. I've been seeing a problem since even before we broke up, but I left it alone. Now I'm not leaving until you tell me what the fuck the deal is."

She stood there, frozen. When she woke up that morning, her intent was to do some shopping and enjoy more of the island. Crying wasn't on the agenda, yet she was standing in front of a man she loved but couldn't convince herself that it was time to reconcile. Tears spilled down her face. More than anything, she needed to be held by him. She fit so perfectly against his chest. His arms had super powers, because it felt like nothing in the world could harm her whenever he wrapped them around her. Trying to wean herself off of her love addiction was fruitless when the only solution was the source.

He kept his distance. There was nothing more he wanted than to embrace her, but he felt he was no longer needed. She was strong before he came into her life and fucked it up, so surviving his damage made her titanium. If he touched her, he thought she would turn to glass and break.

"I'm not moving until you tell me what's going on," he persisted.

She inhaled and exhaled. At that point, there was nothing to lose. He couldn't leave her if they weren't together. If they weren't together, then she couldn't care about him judging her for the skeletons in her closet. She inhaled and exhaled again.

"Can we at least go back outside?" she asked.

They walked along the shore of the beach, the water washing up and tickling their ankles. He waited for her to talk. Somewhere during their trek, she reached for his hand, just in case this was the last time he would touch her.

"No one will let me speak to Jabez. They said I'm babying him too much and need to learn to trust other people with him," she said quietly. "Shameik said he went by and checked on him, but I need to speak directly to my son."

"I spoke to him and Quest this morning before breakfast," Rahshaan said. "They're over at Big Grams' house having a ball with her and Unc."

"That's nice," Shatima said with a forced smile. She gazed out at the ocean. "It's not the same. I really need to talk to him and actually hear him say that he is okay. When you told me about Andrew being around NyQuest, I kind of had a nervous breakdown." She stopped walking. A wry smile was on her face, trying to conceal the panic within her. She didn't know how to continue.

Rahshaan stopped walking and examined her face. "I've been trying to ask you about Andrew for a while. Every time his name comes up, you start buggin."

She looked at the sand under the water and started walking again. "That's because I know he killed my brother. He sent me a tape showing me exactly how he did it."

Rahshaan's brow furrowed. "How did he know you?"

She walked, stared ahead into nothing. Her heart pounded so loud that she could hear it. Inhale. Exhale. She took a few more steps. Her eyes moistened. She prepared to lose him for good. "Andrew is Jabez's father."

Hope whisked her daughter away to visit her parents in Richmond, Virginia. Shatima hated staying with the stuffy people who made her feel like children were insignificant. She didn't speak the two weeks she was there.

When they returned to East Sanford, she planned her escape. Hope laughed at her, even letting her go through with going to the courthouse to get her emancipation papers. She knew the family was gone. Staying behind would have been cop-assisted suicide. Every day after school, Shatima looked for at least one of her father's family members. All of their houses were deserted. After a while, she wondered if they were just a figment of her imagination.

"Nice house," someone said to her after school while she stood in front of Chillz and Selena's house, as though a clue would drop out of the sky.

She saw the red BMW before the driver. The windows were tinted and only slightly rolled down. She ran to it and flung the car door open. Shock slapped her in the face when instead of any of her family members, she saw a striking yellow man with saltwater blue eyes and wavy hair. The navy blue pinstriped suit he wore made him look important.

"I'm so sorry," she finally managed to say. "Your car... I thought you were someone else." She backed away from his car and slammed the door before she started to cry in front of a stranger.

"Wait a minute now. I bought this car from the family who used to live in this house. They had a huge sale prior to a rather abrupt departure. I'm thinking about purchasing this house. You wouldn't happen to have any contact information on them, would you?"

She shook her head and started to walk away. He got out of the car. "I'm sorry, Miss, but if you don't mind me saying, you are stunning."

"Thank you, Sir, but I'm only sixteen years old," she said with her back turned to him, wiping away tears. She quickened her pace.

"Sixteen? Wow. You carry yourself as though you're far more mature than your years." He followed her. "I don't mean to pry, but you look like you can use a friend. You say you knew the owner of this car? Would you like to ride in it for old time's sake?"

The man introduced himself as Andrew. That ride started a short friendship that escalated quickly. He picked her up from school every day, took her shopping, took her to his townhouse where she cooked for him, and then he dropped her off at home late at night. He told her it was the relationship of his dreams. She kept reminding him that she was too young for him. He persisted, citing that she seemed unhappy in her home life. Whenever he dropped her off at home, her shoulders drooped with dread. He proposed that she run away from home.

"Your mother won't care. You stay out with me all night as it is, and she never even looks for you."

Little by little, she packed her clothes and books and moved them into his home. At the age of sixteen, she believed the man when he told her she was mature for her age, and that he enjoyed their conversations. Andrew provided her sanctuary from the pitiful stares and whispers at school and the sea of t-shirts with her father's face on them. They got those t-shirts because they went to the funeral. Rumors swirled around that she thought she was too good to go to her father's memorial service. She wanted to drop out of school and get her GED, but Andrew insisted that she tough it out during the day. He always had gifts and flowers waiting for her when she got home from school. In turn, she cooked dinner for him every night. He raved over it and told her that he could never live without the meals she made. His favorite was her fried chicken. He said it reminded him of his college meals. His appreciation delighted her.

Her life with Andrew was strange. She waited for him to state the conditions of her stay, but he never did. He told her daily that he was attracted to her, but he never touched her. He never even kissed her. With everything she had going on in her life, she didn't have time to explore sexual desires. It wasn't for lack of offers. She was considered one of the prettiest girls in her school, but boys either called her stuck up or a ho because she never gave them a chance. Andrew, though, was a gentleman. He told her that her conversation and companionship were enough stimulation for him. He even slept in a separate bedroom. Andrew provided the solace that a mourning girl needed. She never would have gotten that staying at home with Hope.

"Baby girl," he said to her one night while they sat in the living room watching movies. He never used her real name. "How do you feel about me?"

The question put Shatima on the spot. Her ability to feel anything but sorrow left with her father.

"I feel...thankful that you rescued me," she said.

He stared at her. "Baby girl, I've fallen for you."

She tensed as she wondered how that could be. If anything, she felt like he was a babysitter for her. Handsome he was, but she wasn't particularly attracted to him. He told her that women his age wanted him because of his light skin, wavy hair, and blue eyes. His eyes scared her, if she were being honest. Due to their difference in age, they couldn't go anywhere to create any memories that would sway her feelings about him. In her mind, he was just a nice man. The conversation dropped out the blue. She didn't really want to have it.

"I want to start a family."

Her head jerked upward. She studied his face, waiting for him to start laughing. He never did. "I still have a year of high school to finish," she reminded him. "I won't even be an adult until next year."

Andrew got up and strutted around the room like a peacock. Walking around in front of the plants whose leaves cascaded from the mantle made him look like a wild man on a cartoon safari. It was like he was performing a monologue. "A son! I want a son, and I want to name him Jabez. You've heard of Jabez from the Bible, right? 'Oh Lord, enlarge my territory!' That's what I want to do: enlarge my territory or, in this case, my family."

She thought of how nice it would be to have someone who had to love her. Life wouldn't be lonely anymore, because she'd be too busy raising a baby. Then she went back to her original thought: she still had a year of high school to finish. She asked Andrew to wait. He said he would try.

Instead of waiting, he entered her bedroom that night. Her father visited her in a dream for the first night of many to follow. The dream started off pleasantly, and then she watched him being gunned down. Her screaming made Andrew run to her bedroom. His response was to sit at the foot of the bed and remark that her sobs were poetic. She cried to him about the details. He waited until she finished crying, and then he moved toward her and kissed her. To her, it felt forced and not like anything that would make her want to do it again. He ignored her reluctance to reciprocate and started undressing her. He never attended to her bleeding afterward or asked her if she enjoyed it.

For a month, this was their ritual. She screamed herself out of her sleep, he entered her room and fucked her back to sleep, and then she slept until she screamed herself out of another sleep. He he retreated to his bedroom before she knew what happened.

By the time her senior year of high school rolled around, she was ending her first trimester of pregnancy. The clothes Andrew bought her didn't hide the weight she instantly gained. Her eyes had purple rings around them. That started another slew of rumors. Everyone knew the man in the red BMW was the father of her child. Her schoolmates made up stories about him beating her. They didn't know the half. She held her head high, despite it all.

In her second trimester of pregnancy, she went to her old neighborhood. Something about carrying a child made her want to reconcile with the woman who birthed her. She asked Andrew to drop her off at a bus stop and pick her up there. She didn't know what her mother's reaction would be to a man old enough to date her impregnating her daughter. Hope wanted nothing to do with her. She left Shatima on the doorstep and voiced her shame before threatening to call the police to have her removed from the home.

Her ride wasn't due back for a while, so she decided to reconnect with her childhood friends. They wanted to check on her, but they didn't want to be seen with the weird, moody, pregnant chick. That day she seemed happy. April and Nicolette felt bad for turning their backs on her. They gifted her framed copies of the obituaries from her father's and godfather's funeral. They gave her all the details that they remembered, citing that both caskets were close, and the focus seemed to be on her father more than her godfather. The three of them promised not to separate again.

A silver Dodge Neon pulled in front of Hope's house. The three of them watched the handsome boy hop out and walk up the short brick path to Hope's house. Shatima held her breath. She wanted to call out to him, but she didn't want her mother to know that she was still in the area. April and Nicolette marveled over the Jordans on his feet and the Nike sweatsuit he wore. Around his neck and wrists were gold Figaro chains. They watched him knock on the door politely and then bang on the door until Hope answered.

"How many times do I have to tell you she doesn't live here anymore?" Hope hollered at him. "She ran away, and I don't know where she lives, but she's never welcome in my house again!"

"Please, Miss Hope," Rize pleaded. "I just need to find my baby sister."

"She's your half-sister," Hope said icily. "And if you do see her, I have the feeling you'll be sorry." She slammed the door in his face.

Deflated, Rize's head hung as he made his way back to his car.

"He came back for me," Shatima whispered. For the first time in months, she felt something besides the sorrow that burned a hole in her heart.

"Is that your baby daddy, Tima?" April questioned, her loud voice carrying across the street.

Rize heard April's loud mouth and looked up. He dashed across the street to get his sister. For the first time, she felt self conscious. What was she doing? In a month, she would be seventeen. In six, she would be a mother. She tried to position her body so that her stomach was hidden. Even with the large shirt she wore, her swollen breasts and the fat around her face gave it away.

"What the fuck? Who did this to you?"

It killed Rize that his sister was pregnant and wouldn't disclose the father's identity. He felt bad enough that they left her behind. He wanted to take her away, but she refused to leave, saying she couldn't do to the child's father what Hope did to hers. Rize almost had her convinced that leaving was the best thing, but then his tune changed. He got a three-bedroom townhouse on the South side. Shatima insisted on staying with her child's father. Rize prepared a bedroom for her and one for the baby as well. He started picking her up after school and not dropping her off at a bus stop near the townhouse until late at night.

"Where do you go when you're not with me?" Andrew questioned her after several weeks of this behavior.

"To my brother's house," she replied. "He came back for me."

Andrew noticed how much happier she was with her brother back in her life. He hated it and didn't miss a chance to voice it. Sometimes, he would pace around the house grumbling about her no longer needing him. He accused her of using him. She didn't know how to handle his possessiveness. She thought he'd be happy that she wasn't so depressed.

"He wants to take you and my son away from me," Andrew insisted. He always called the baby his son and never left room for the other possibility.

"No, he doesn't," Shatima argued. "He just wants to be there for me. He is my brother. Anyway, I'm not leaving you. You were there for me when I had nothing and nowhere to go."

"So you're just here out of obligation?" he exploded. "You don't want a family?"

With every syllable, he stalked closer to her. He stood over her and repeatedly punched her in her chest. She fought back as best as she could, but his grown man strength superseded her teenage girl strength. They fought until she found an escape path to her bedroom. She locked herself in the room for the rest of the night and stayed up in case he tried to come in.

"Baby girl," he whimpered. "Baby girl, I'm sorry. Please let me in. You have to know how hard I've fallen for you. Please let me in." After some time, his whimpers turned to yelling, and he pounded on the door. "You don't lock doors in my house, bitch! I'll end your homeless ass life!"

Early in the morning, she heard his car pull off. She caught the bus to Rize's apartment. For a week, she stayed there without going to Andrew's house or school. She ignored all of the messages Andrew left on her pager. After that beating, the doctor declared her high risk and put her on bed rest. A Homebound tutor came to the house on weekdays to make sure that she graduated on time. That was better for her. She was able to avoid the rumors and the whispers of her schoolmates.

When she finally worked up the nerve to go back to Andrew's house, she had Rize drive her. All she wanted was the stuff she came with. He could keep all of his gifts. She wanted nothing else to do with him. The disappointment on Rize's face when he took her to the townhouse just outside of the Caesar Chavez Projects confirmed that she would keep the identity of her children's father a secret forever. He was almost afraid to find out who this phantom boyfriend of hers was, but he promised himself was going to kill the man for what he did to his sister.

Everything she owned was in trash bags on the curb when they reached Andrew's townhouse. The locks were changed. In her book-bag he left a note:

Baby girl,
I can't stand to live without you, so I'm not going to.

I'm sorry that you didn't love me.

The cryptic note burned in Shatima's hand. Did it mean that he killed himself over her? Why? Did he really expect her to stay after beating her up? Rize loaded the trash bags into the car and took her home.

Throughout the rest of her pregnancy, she wondered what became of Andrew. She checked the paper every day for an obituary, but none were for him. Being pregnant by a man she knew so little about — especially whether he was dead or alive — made her feel like a fool. Rize begged her to tell him who the sorry nigga was, but she convinced herself that it didn't matter. He was gone, but she couldn't bring herself to feel sad.

In her final months of pregnancy, a rash of kidnappings broke out. Boys disappeared from Chavez, Nat Turner, and the Frederick Douglas projects. As time for graduation grew closer, the kidnappings spread to the lower income areas on the other sides of town. The class of 2000 dwindled. The vanishing boys made Shatima think of her child's father and how he disappeared. She wondered about the note he left behind. Did someone put him under duress and make him write that letter? Was it forged? When the first boy's body was found in a dumpster, sodomized and emaciated, she was even more frightful.

The closer she got to her due date, the more restless Rize became. The two of them started marking the days until graduation on a calendar. He left early one Saturday morning. She never knew where he went, but he always returned with food. That day, she couldn't do anything except sleep. She lay in front of the TV, watching the disturbing news reports about the kidnappings. Rize didn't come home after dropping off her lunch. She made it through one terrifying night alone.

That Sunday, Rize still wasn't there when she opened her eyes. She was a wreck. Rize came into the house close to the afternoon with chicken and waffles he said he'd made at their cousin's house. He sat with her until she was able to go to sleep. She wasn't sure how long that was, but it was dark the next time she opened her eyes. The news reported that a boy from her school had not been seen since Friday. A red BMW was seen driving around the school. Its driver was approaching students.

Her doorbell rang. When she answered it, the missing boy from her school stood on her doorstep, holding a nameplate with her name on it. He demanded to know why it was in his boyfriend's house. When she asked him how he got her address, the boy punched her. She tried to fight back, but she wasn't strong enough to take him. He punched her in both of her eyes and then tackled her. Another person — the force made her presume this person was male as well — kicked her face. She heard some other people run into the house, breaking glass, knocking over furniture, and throwing things. Some neighbors came to help while others called the police. The boy and whoever else was with him were gone when the emergency responders got there. Shatima was unconscious.

When she awoke, she was in the hospital. Rize sat by her bedside, begging her not to die. She was in pain and no longer pregnant.

"You had an emergency c-section," Rize explained to her. He assured her that the baby was fine. It was her they were worried about. She had so many questions, but Rize demanded one answer from her.

At long last, she told him who the father of her child was. She didn't expect him to explode the way he did. Andrew seemed like a random man, not his father's sworn enemy. The hunger for murder in his eyes and seeping from his pores were unfamiliar to see coming from him. Rize was always so laid back. He could find a way to smile at everything she did. Procreating with the man who was responsible for their father's death — as he screamed in the hospital room — meant that he would never smile at her again. Pain surged in her body as she tried to get up to calm him down. He was talking like a crazy person planning a murder. A fresh wound opened her hurt. She ached like crazy, but she had to get up. She wanted Rize to understand that she didn't know what an awful thing she did. She wanted to beg him not to hate her. The morphine dripping from the bag inside of her bloodstream put her in a hard sleep. She thought she heard Rize say he was going to retrieve Rico and Shameik before sleep won the battle it raged against her.

The next time she woke up, Andrew was standing over her. She told him he had to leave, that her brothers were coming to fuck him up. She threatened to tell the police everything he did to her. He smirked at the threats. A nurse wheeled in their baby boy, and they laid eyes on him for the first time together. Shatima asked the nurse to have Andrew removed, but the nurse looked at him and scurried out of the room *without responding. Andrew waited for the nurse to leave before walking over to the bassinet.*

"He's perfect," he remarked. "I'll be back for him when he grows a little bit. You can cook for us while I love on him. We'll be a family like you promised."

A sour taste filled her mouth, and her stomach wrenched when she figured out what he meant. Her mind recalled the classmate who came to her door holding her nameplate.

"You won't touch my son," she swore to him, fists clenched. He left without responding to her vow.

Later that night, she watched the news as she fed her baby. The boy who attacked her was reported dead. His body was found on a path behind Nat Turner. The news reported that his body had been defiled before and after being murdered. Shatima held Jabez to her bosom and sobbed.

When she was discharged, she called Rize nonstop, but never received an answer. Something wasn't right. Angry or not, he wouldn't just leave her at a hospital with a baby. She panicked from the time she took the cab to a ransacked house, to the days when she had to sit in an empty home and wait for a brother who was never returning, to the days later when she had to take her baby and move into a home for teen mothers.

At that home, she was reunited with a pregnant Nicolette. Her parents put her into that home before they could be tied to such a scandal. No one visited her. The father of her child didn't even call. Shatima didn't want Nicolette to feel as lonely as she did. She resumed her position of best friend and stayed by Nicolette's side. It was going to be hard to be teen mothers, but she insisted that they would lean on each other through it all.

Instead of going to their graduation, Shatima stayed behind and held Nicolette's hand as she went into labor. Her child's father came to the home carrying balloons and flowers, making a big deal out of celebrating the birth of his child.

His blue eyes danced a sinister dance when they locked with hers. "Keep that baby growing for me. I'll be back for our family before you know it."

He abandoned Nicolette when he found out that she had a daughter. Shatima kicked Nicolette's ass.

After that, she was put out of the home due to assaulting Nicolette. She still didn't know what happened to Rize. A social worker took her to tour each of the housing projects. As they drove through Nat Turner, she saw a mural with her father's face on the side. Adjacent to it was Rize's.

The week after she settled into her apartment, a manila envelope holding a video tape was placed in her mailbox. She wished she threw it away instead of watching it. Her brother's rape and murder was recorded. The father of her child laughed into the camera as he did unspeakable things to the only person she had left in the world.

The story left Rahshaan's feet planted where he stood. His lips were fused together. Shatima braced herself. She was sure he was going to knock her head off of her shoulders. She waited for him to blame her for Rize's death. The words never came. She waited for him to call her a snake bitch and mush her head into the water until her lungs were so full of saltwater that she could no longer breathe. Instead, he lugged his heavy legs over to the sand and sat. She just stood there and waited for him to tell her he never wanted to see her again. Maybe he wouldn't say anything at all. Maybe he'd just disappear forever. She was sure that he'd never touch her again. His soul penetrating gaze made her nervous.

"Your pops never told you to stay away from anybody named Andrew?" His voice sounded desperate for logic or reason.

"I...don't remember if he did. That wasn't a name I ever heard when I was with him," she replied.

Rahshaan nodded. "Of course he wouldn't. You're a girl. He didn't think he had anything to worry about with you." He didn't say anything else for a minute. Then he said, "Jay don't look nothing like him."

"Please don't look at my son different because of who his father is," she pleaded. "He doesn't even know the man's name. Please don't ever let this get out. I've never told anyone who Jabez's father is."

Rahshaan made a face at her. "Fuck you mean? *I'm Jabez's* father."

Her heart stopped. "Huh? After what I just told you, you still want..."

He couldn't answer her. Mentally, he was processing everything that finally made sense. The mother/son bond that he envied was one of survival. She couldn't afford to relax for one day. He felt horrible for dragging her so far away from her son. Then his mind ventured back in time to the day when she thought NyQuest was missing. He wanted to kick his own ass. How could he put her through that? Cheating on her seemed like a minor offense juxtaposed with the trauma she suffered at the hands of the life he lived.

It was time to start moving differently. This thing that she shared with him was something that changed the state of their relationship forever. She trusted him with something that could have ended her. He wanted to ask her how she could be so stupid, but that wasn't fair. It occurred to him that her father shielded her from this because they had such little time together. He didn't want his daughter to know what kind of life he really lived. Rahshaan knew that was a mistake. He had to be transparent about everything with her. They were a unit. Nothing would work between them unless they were completely open.

"Come sit down next to me," he commanded, his voice soft but firm.

She hesitated, sure he was going to kill her for being the reason his best friend was dead. "Shameik told me he would send for me. I'll leave if you want."

"Shatima, please come sit down next to me." His tone suggested that he wasn't going to ask again.

She obliged.

He put his arm around her and pulled her closer to him. By then she was visibly quaking. "How many times has he threatened you?"

"Only once. The day I got fired was because I punched him

in his nuts for asking me what school Jabez goes to," she replied. "Before this year, I hadn't seen him since Nicolette went into labor."

"You ever went to the police about the statutory rape or him beating you?" Rahshaan wondered.

"I tried. They said the person I was trying to file charges against didn't exist." She sighed and nestled her face into the space between his collarbone and his shoulder. "You might be the only person who understands what it's like to be afraid that your child's other parent is going to hurt your child."

His mind flashed back to his prison sentence when he sat in a cell, waiting for one of his family members to tell him they found out where Monaysia took NyQuest. The number of visits dwindled. He thought they were tired of him asking about his son. The reality was that they were vanishing too. He shuddered and snapped himself back into reality.

"From this minute, we don't keep nothing from each other." He reached for her hand and locked fingers with hers. With his other hand he turned her face toward his. "*Nothing*. Even if somewhere down the line we break up, we remain friends, and we don't keep anything from each other."

Then his mind flashed back to when he learned of Chillz's death. Since he was of no blood relation to Chillz, he wasn't released from jail for the funeral. Lynn and Selena went to the prison to deliver the news. Selena sat across from him, begging him to tell her if he knew why it happened. Chillz always said it was for protection, but Rahshaan thought about how unfair it was that Selena was left to piece things together for herself. How could he love her, he wondered, if he would let her be blindsided like that? Chillz and Selena embodied the love that he wanted. Finding out that Chillz never told her that he knew there was a murder plot on his life shattered his image of them. He stayed angry at Chillz for many years after that, and there was no way to resolve it.

"Rahshaan I'm still mad at you-"

"Tima, let that shit go! Damn!" he thundered. "I apologized. I told you what happened. With the shit that you just told me, none of that shit matters."

Neither of them admitted that the sun was baring down on them. They stared out at the ocean and took in the smell of the salty water. The air around them was heavy. The ocean pushed itself ashore and then retreated back out, wanting them to come play in it. The sound of the waves beckoned them to come be a part of their bliss. Paradise wanted them to enjoy it.

Shatima stared out into the ocean. "The morning after you kissed me was the first day I wasn't angry that I didn't die in my sleep. I don't know what it was, but I just knew my life was going to be different."

"Then why did you run from me?" he wondered.

She shrugged. "I didn't think I'd ever be able to get this close to anybody. I got your best friend killed. Need I go on?" The ocean's serenade brought her tranquility. Suddenly, she jumped up. She didn't want to dwell in sorrow any longer. It seemed like she was forgiven. "Can you swim? I want to go swimming. It's been forever since I've been in the ocean."

He gazed up at her while she grabbed his arm and beckoned him to stand up. In the sun, her smile and skin gleamed. Seeing those dimples deepen and the corners of her mouth turned upward again was worth everything he had to go through to get back to that point. The two of them ran into the ocean like little kids who had nothing to do but enjoy life.

Hyacinth filled them with roti and coconut rum for lunch. She beamed at them and never stopped talking about the beautiful babies they'd have. This time, they sat next to each other at the table, Shatima practically in Rahshaan's lap. Peter chattered on and on about all the places he could take them, but he knew they didn't hear him.

"Let's go to the room and spark one," Rahshaan whispered to her. They dashed upstairs.

He sat at the edge of the bed and got ready to roll up, but she stripped her bikini and let it fall to the floor. Watching how her ass sat atop the long legs that strutted into the bathroom made him temporarily for get what he was doing. Before every sexual encounter he had with her, he thought about how nervous and insecure she was their first time. Never would he understand why she was so apprehensive. Everything about her from her head to her toe screamed "Fuck me!" She was his addiction. Living without her was out of the question.

"I missed you," she said to him as he climbed into the hot tub with her. He responded by kissing her mouth, neck, collarbone, shoulders, and her mouth again. She wrapped her arms around him and put her fingers in his hair. She missed touching the soft, thick mass on top of his head. Her fingers went from the back of his head down the nape of his neck, being careful not to touch his scar. In the hot water, he ran his hands up and down her frame, stopping to appreciate her curves. He kissed her neck then whispered that he loved her in her ear.

"It's too soon for that," she told him, waving him off.

He scrunched his face. "How long do we have to be together before I can say it?"

She shrugged her shoulders. "Please don't love me. Everybody who loves me leaves me."

He leaned in and kissed her. "I ain't going nowhere. Now do you love me or not?"

She was sure she did, but she wasn't going to be pressured into saying it. She climbed out of the tub without bothering to grab a towel. The windows were open, and the air was so hot that the water would dry immediately and be replaced by sweat. Rahshaan approached her slowly, carrying a bottle of her bath oil. At first, she tensed under his touch. Then she relaxed and obliged when he told her to lay on the bed. Sleep coaxed her to return, but his lips on the back of her neck woke her up again. He kissed her from the nape of her neck to the heels of her feet.

Then he turned her over and performed the ritual on the front of her body. Her moans encouraged him to keep going.

"I swear to God, Ma, I'll never hurt you again," he pledged his allegiance to her, staring directly into her eyes. "I'm never leaving you. I'm never keeping anything from you again. I love you."

His bass voice tickled her ear. When his tongue licked her collarbone, she shuddered. It felt so good to have his sturdy, muscular frame over hers again. She ran her hands down the ripples in his back as his tongue moved from her collarbone to her nipples. The way he sucked on them put an arch in her back. She squeezed her eyes shut.

"I love you, Rahshaan." Her voice was barely a whisper, and her words got caught in her throat. The lower his tongue went, the better it felt.

He kissed her navel. "Say it again."

"I love you, Rahshaan."

His head traveled down between her legs. She gripped the comforter on the bed and tried to move away from him. He locked his arms around her legs, stabilizing her. The oil he previously rubbed on her body mixed with her natural scent aroused him. The more she moaned, the more he wanted her to moan. The timbre of her voice was an alarm for his dick. It woke up and wanted to be inside of her, but her taste was an aphrodisiac. He couldn't stop sucking, couldn't stop licking until he felt her shaking.

After the shaking started, her vision went blank, and she temporarily went deaf and mute. When she came down from her high, he was suspended over her. She reached out and touched the smooth nine and a half inches that he declared belonged only to her. It had been too long since he filled her insides with his rhythm and made her gush. She tried to pull him down on top of her and coax him inside. At the last minute, he changed his mind. Instead, he picked her up and carried her out onto the balcony.

"What are you doing?" she demanded in a panic, her legs clamped around his waist.

"Some shit I always wanted to do, but would never have a chance to in them raggedy ass projects."

He turned her around and placed her facing forward, instructing her to hold onto the railing. With her legs spread and her ass arched, he entered her from behind. Upon feeling him, she squealed and then exhaled. He pushed himself in deeper until he couldn't go any further. Immediately, he felt her cum. Her legs shook. He grabbed her hips and steadied her before he started pounding her. Her walls gripped him and refused to let him go.

"I love you, Rahshaan!" she screamed, forgetting that they were in a fully staffed establishment.

He smacked her ass. "Say it again." He thrust himself in and out of her, his speed increasing as he felt her cum.

"I love you!" she called out again.

"You leaving me?" he queried, deliberately slowing his stroke.

She tightened around him more.

He felt like he was drowning, but didn't want to come up for air.

"I ain't going nowhere," she grunted. Then he hit a spot that made her repeat it, but in a louder, clearer tone. "I ain't going nowhere!"

Her mouth longed for something to bite down on while she orgasmed. As though reading her mind, he withdrew himself from her and laid her on the balcony floor. It was uncomfortable on her back, but she was more concerned with climaxing than comfort. Her mouth found his collarbone and sucked on it. Then she grabbed his head and nibbled his ears. She kissed his face and sucked in his groans.

After coming down from being satiated, they spent most of the day holding each other and not wanting to let go. They were afraid that there would never be a more perfect time. How many people could say their love was declared in paradise? The obstacles life took the two of them through made it impossible to think they deserved happily ever after, but there they were. No longer were there insecurities or the desire to run. When they left St. Croix, they carried with them the will to work on what was given to them. They promised they would travel the rough road called life together.

————

Santarez and Hope sat at her dining room table making eyes at each other. Kimborough rolled her eyes while Andrew stomped around them. They all ignored his tantrum. While the three of them were concerned with making money, he had much bigger fish to fry. His father's legacy was at stake, as were the safety and freedom of him and his sister.

"Miguel, I need you to tell me the questions that Derrick asked you. All of them," Andrew pleaded.

Santarez looked irritated that Andrew wanted to take his attention off Hope. "For the last time, he asked me why I was the first to arrive on the scene when the boys were found in that apartment."

"And what did you say?" Andrew pressed.

Santarez sighed. "I told him that he was an informant on a drug case that I was working and that he called me because he was having second thoughts about snitching."

"Did you feel that he believed you?" Andrew wanted to know.

"Of course not, but what can he do? He works kidnappings, and he's just upset because he wasn't the one to make the discovery."

"Miguel, you're not making me confident. Derrick is a close follower of Chief Lyles', and you know they both have personal vendettas against my father," Andrew worried.

"Andrew, he's the lone detective working missing persons cases! Leave this alone!" Santarez barked.

Andrew eyed Miguel. "Now did you ever stop to ask yourself why a kidnapping detective would have so many questions?" He stood over Miguel. "I recruited you and Shannon, because the two of you seemed the most loyal to my father. Loyalty to my father means you must extend the same loyalty to me. At the moment, I don't feel that you are taking any of this seriously."

Without responding, Santarez took Hope's foot in his lap and massaged it. Andrew concentrated his efforts on Hope.

"Were you and Loretta able to get everything taken care of at the pharmacy?"

"Yes, Andrew." Her words came out with an exasperated sigh. "The changes to the medications have been made, just as you asked. It will have a gradual effect, but within a week to ten days we'll see results."

Andrew nodded. "Good. I just don't see how we can accomplish anything without using the girl as our way in. She'll fold if we start applying pressure to her loved ones. Soon enough, she'll lead us to Mont."

THE GOD FORCEFIELD

"You still mad at me, ugly?" Lynn asked as Shatima leapt into her SUV to escape the blustery wind.

Rahshaan tried to stuff their luggage into the trunk as quickly as he could. The transition from paradise to New York's impersonation of The Tundra was a shock. "I am," he interjected. "Why did y'all tell me she knew that I was gonna be there? What if she got me down there and killed me?"

"Then you just would've been killed, and you would've deserved it," Lynn quipped. "You a dummy for even thinking she was going for that." She pulled into the airport traffic. "We should've made this a family trip. I sure could've used some more time out of this cold and shit. Matter of fact, lemme book a trip when I get home. Got the nerve to be two punk ass degrees out here."

Lynn's fussing fell upon deaf ears. Rahshaan and Shatima softly murmured to each other about their living arrangements. She didn't see a point in him moving his stuff downstairs if they were going to start looking for a bigger place immediately. He didn't see the point in them having separate addresses another day. They spoke in hushed tones about whether they wanted to live in a duplex or single family home. Selena glanced at the two of them in the back seat and smiled at their young love.

"Tima, what's that on your finger?" she wondered aloud.

Shatima looked down at the pear shaped diamond Rahshaan purchased their last night on the island. She tried to hide a smile. "A ring."

Selena smiled and shook her head. "Hood niggas only know two speeds. They either string you along forever, or they move at the speed of light. There's no in between."

They all got a laugh out of that.

"It's not *that ki*nd of ring," Shatima corrected. "It's an... 'I'm sorry you popped your jewelry beating the shit out of a bitch trying to compete with you' ring."

Everybody but Rahshaan laughed at that.

Jabez was the first one to run from Big Grams's house to Lynn's car. Shatima clutched her son and held him as tight as he would allow. For once, Rahshaan didn't tell her to stop babying him. He understood and agreed.

It was supposed to be the first day of being a family. A load of clothes was in the wash. The boys sat at the dining room table doing their homework while Shatima sat at the computer, catching up on the assignments she'd missed while she was away. Dinner was in the oven. Lynn, Shameik and Selena were on their way over. Rahshaan went to see if his grandmother was eating with them, or if she wanted them to send her a plate of food later on that night. One of his cousins came barreling down the stairs carrying her son before he could start up them.

"Banger, something's wrong with G-Ma!" she exclaimed. "She's breathing funny and talking crazy!"

Rahshaan took the eight flights of steps two at a time and practically kicked down the door. His grandmother was sprawled across her couch, clutching her chest. He panicked and dropped down at her side, begging her to say something to him.

"Ashley, why the fuck y'all ain't call 9-1-1?" he demanded when his cousin caught up to him. "How long has she been like this?"

Ashley stuttered, but gave no real response.

Shatima appeared in the doorway behind him, followed by Shameik and Selena. Instinctively, she called 9-1-1 while Rahshaan tried to get her to answer him.

"Tell them don't be taking all day to get down here either! I don't give a fuck that we in the hood!" he roared as Shatima screamed for them to send an ambulance.

G-Ma continued to grip her chest and groan about the pain. Her breathing turned shallow. Shatima stayed on the phone with 9-1-1, dictating their instructions to Rahshaan. Selena and Shameik looked around. There were about twelve children there that day. Many of them appeared to be under the age of five. All of them needed to be dressed and more than likely had yet to be fed. It didn't occur to them until that moment just how much the woman did. Without Rahshaan there to help her for the past ten days, she was probably in over her head. Rahshaan ignored the guilt and barked at his cousin instead.

"Call everybody and tell them to come get their kids!" he roared.

Ashley hung her head. "I don't even know some of their mamas' and daddies' numbers. You know I don't mess with Tasha like that, and-"

"Ashley, I don't give a fuck who don't fuck with who! Get on that phone, and tell them to come pick up their damn kids!"

Shatima pointed in the general direction of the kitchen and advised Ashley that there was a board with each child's name, parent's name, and contact information hanging there. She called Lynn and asked her to meet them at the hospital.

The next hour was mass hysteria. Between the multiple calls to 9-1-1 and trying to get people to the apartment to pick up their children, Rahshaan thought he was going to lose it. Seeing how his family took advantage of his grandmother made him want to disown them all. None of them seemed to care that she was going to the hospital, just that their evening plans were being inconvenienced. He didn't have time to decipher who was really being put out and who just wanted to run the streets. All that he knew was that things needed to change.

Selena and Shameik stayed behind and tried to help Ashley locate parents while Rahshaan rode in the ambulance with his grandmother. Shatima followed behind it in her car. Thankfully, the boys on the stoop kept it cleaned off and dug it out of the snow every day while she was gone. Otherwise, she would have been stuck shoveling it out of the parking lot. Trying not to panic as she maneuvered, the icy roads consumed her mind. Under her breath, she cussed about South Ridge always being left for last. The salt trucks should have been down there to treat the streets earlier. Thinking of how poorly poor people were treated brought another thought to her head. With one hand on the wheel, she picked up her cellphone and dialed Rahshaan's number.

"Don't let them take her to any hospital with the words 'community' or 'general' in the name," she instructed. "They'll treat her like crap there, and it'll be hours before they even see her."

That drive was the quickest she ever got across the bridge. The ambulance stopped long enough for the driver to point his thumb out the back window at Shatima's car. She zoomed past the disappointed looking officers and tailed the ambulance to Sanford University Hospital. Kassidy and Big Grams were already in the lobby when she arrived. She breezed past them and went to Rahshaan.

"What did they say in the ambulance?" she asked him.

"Heart attack," he told her. "She probably ain't been taking her pills."

Shatima shook her head. "I doubt that. She's never missed taking those pills as long as I've known her."

It was a long night of waiting. G-Ma was under too much stress. That much was apparent when the parents of the children she watched came down to the hospital. For them, the question was, "When will G-Ma be able to watch our kids again?" rather than finding out if she was okay. The more they piled up, the more irritated Rahshaan became. Until that day, he never vocalized how much it bothered him that she just sat holed up in that apartment, watching children. He didn't think he had the right. After all, he stayed there for twenty years because his own mother didn't take care of him. But these people took advantage of G-Ma because their parents did. It had to come to an end.

"I just wanna know why Charlene got all these children with her every single day," Big Grams said, pacing around the room. "Y'all the parents. Y'all don't never collect your children? Ain't but a handful of y'all working, but you'll have them kids at Charlene's house all week and my house on the weekends, and for what? Y'all don't never check on her, see if she needs help feeding your kids or washing your kids' asses? Do you even give her money?"

"Nope!" Rahshaan spoke up. "Me and Tima the only one who pay her anything."

Ashley shot at him, "Nigga, shut up! You damn near thirty, still living up under your grandmother."

"Making sure she don't kill herself taking care of y'all kids! Who the fuck you think gets your kids dressed every morning and gets them to school? It ain't you." Rahshaan hopped up defensively. "My girl go over there every night to clean up after y'all kids and make sure G-Ma eats because she went hungry making sure your kids had meals. I help bathe them at night. You better be happy my damn near thirty ass is there."

Big Grams' eyes bugged out of her face. "Charlene letting people take advantage of her like that? Well, I'll tell you all one thing. That's all over now. Y'all let Darlene set the wrong example." She glanced at Rahshaan to see if he took offense or had a reaction.

While Rahshaan didn't have a reaction, Darlene Bailey herself stormed in carrying a Bible and a lot of attitude. She sized up every person in the waiting area. Her gaze stopped at her son. She waited to see if he was going to defend her. When his lips didn't part, she shook her head at him.

"Only God can judge me," she declared. She looked around and pointed her finger at the circle of family. "How dare all of you not tell me that my own mother was in the hospital? And then you have the nerve to talk about me behind my back?"

"Ma, this ain't the time for your bullshit," Rahshaan grumbled. He took her arm, encouraging her to take his seat.

"What y'all oughta be out here doing is praying, but you'd rather talk about Darlene's past transgressions like y'all are any better." She stuck her index finger in Big Grams's face. "How often do you go down to the slums to check on your sister, Aunt Jewel? How often do you ask her if she needs help with any of these children? You know how my mother is. Even after she walks out of here, she's still not gonna stop being the neighborhood nanny. Why don't you just help her instead of sitting up in your mansion?"

Big Grams slapped Darlene's finger away. "Darlene, you'd better get your finger out of my face," she commanded. "Now you the last person who needs to be down here criticizing anybody."

The circular fight continued for hours. No resolution came. Rahshaan and Shatima kept dipping in and out to see if there were any updates. The surgery continued. It was too much for Rahshaan to not know if the woman who was responsible for his survival was going to live. After a while, it felt like he was drowning in a sea of words that didn't matter. He couldn't believe his family was acting like that when a woman might have been dying.

In the wee hours of the morning, Shatima called Pastor Candle to the hospital. He was down there in no time. He tried to calm the family, but they were too far gone. Underneath the fluorescent lighting of the waiting room, they blamed each other for being more horrible to G-Ma than the next. Shatima led her pastor off to the side, and Rahshaan followed.

"Well, Rahshaan, it's been some years since I've seen you. Your grandmother tells me about you all the time, tells me that you've turned into a fine young man. I'm glad to see that our prayers were answered about your son," Pastor Candle said.

Rahshaan was a bit taken aback. He didn't think the man would remember him and was surprised to hear he knew anything about NyQuest. Church wasn't Rahshaan's thing. When he was old enough to tell his grandmother he wasn't going anymore, he stopped going. She didn't believe in forcing God onto anyone. She thought that God was something people had to find for themselves. Of course, she hoped that Rahshaan would one day believe; she felt she had enough faith to carry him to Heaven when his time came.

"Seems like it's just one thing after another for you two, doesn't it?" Pastor Candle asked the couple. "Never a moment of rest."

"It ain't about us right now. I just want G-Ma to be okay," Rahshaan dismissed the impromptu counseling session.

Pastor Candle nodded. "If I know Charlene Glover, then I know she's going to pull through this. What did you and Rize used to say she had around her when you were little, Rahshaan?"

Rahshaan's face hinted that it was trying to smile at the memory. "The God forcefield."

"The God forcefield," Pastor Candle repeated. "It's gonna protect her from this attack of Satan, too." He looked behind him. "But you all have to get that under control. There's no reason that woman should be giving up her life to take care of a bunch of kids when all those able bodied people are around."

The two of them nodded in agreement.

Pastor Candle took long strides to the center of the argument. He was a tall man with a commanding presence. "We're gonna stop all this arguing, and we're gonna pray," he announced. "Now I've seen almost each of you in the church with Mother Glover at one point in your lives or another. I've even baptized more than a few of you, so you know what needs to be done in this situation. You oughta be ashamed of yourselves, using this woman like this and then not even being there for her in her time of need."

A hush fell over the crowd, bringing relief to the staff and the other hospital visitors.

Pastor Candle prayed fervently for what seemed like hours. When he said amen, a nurse came out and announced that G-Ma was asking for her grandson and granddaughter.

"Which one? There's a lot of us out here," Ashley remarked.

"She asked for the ones who take care of her," the nurse responded. "Who brought her down here? I'm assuming that's who she was referring to."

Rahshaan and Shatima walked hand in hand to the recovery room, dodging the jealous remarks that came from the family. Pastor Candle promised them he would do his best to keep the family under control. Shatima felt Rahshaan's hand shaking in hers.

"She's all right," she assured him. "She asked for you."

"I don't wanna move unless she can come with us," Rahshaan said. "I'm not leaving her."

"Of course not," Shatima agreed. "So we'll look for a duplex or something. That way she'll have her own space, but still be close enough to take care of."

They walked into the sliver of a room. G-Ma, who was already short at 5'4," looked tiny lying in the recovery bed. Oxygen pumped into her nose through tubes. Her hands slightly trembled. Rahshaan kissed her.

"Boy, you better not be crying over these old bones," his grandmother admonished him. "Your G-Ma is gonna be all right."

Shatima took one of her hands and rubbed it. "You gotta slow down. You can't take in the whole world's kids anymore."

"Aw, here y'all go. Everything is gonna be fine," she told them. "The doctor told me somebody put something poisonous in my medications. It's not watching the kids. Everything is gonna be just fine."

"Yeah, it is, cuz everybody is coming to get their damn kids out your house," Rahshaan declared. "And everybody is coming over there to help you clean up that damn house. Tima ain't doing that shit by herself no more."

"Rahshaan, stop all that cussin," she admonished.

"Nope. *Everybody i*s gonna come pick up their kids and clean your house. Now, if you wanna charge them by the hour, then that's fine, but your crib ain't about to be a free drop off spot no more."

The family was encouraged to go home. Rahshaan, Shatima, and Big Grams stayed behind. While Big Grams went into the room to see about her sister, Rahshaan gave them strict instructions to go to Mother Glover's house and make it spotless. Begrudgingly, they followed his orders. Pastor Candle and Big Grams went into G-Ma's room to sit with her. Shatima and Rahshaan stayed in the waiting room, while Lynn went back to G-Ma's apartment to make sure Rahshaan's orders were being followed.

Darlene lingered behind. "That's real good what you did for your grandmother. I hope you only show me a tenth of that care when my time of need comes." She glared at him and then clutched her Bible tightly to her chest and did an about face toward the exit.

In the morning, Shatima's alarm went off, signaling that she had to get the kids ready for school. Selena called her and offered to take them since they stayed with her that night, but Shatima wanted to see them. She wanted them to know that everything was okay with their G-Ma. They didn't need to go to school with that stress hanging over their heads, especially NyQuest.

It was still dark when she exited the hospital. The snow stopped falling. A plow rode around in the lot. Some of Rahshaan's family was still out there. She couldn't believe they still found things to argue about at the break of dawn. Some of them cut her nasty looks. Under their breath, they mumbled, asking why she was so special that *their* grandmother wanted to see *her* before any of *them*. She ignored it. The most important thing was that G-Ma was going to live to see another day.

She walked to her car and almost didn't notice the wet slip of paper on the windshield. Her heart skipped a beat when she saw it. Everybody shook their heads when she asked if they saw who put it on her car. Cautiously, she opened it.

"Granny's just the beginning."

Her mind contemplated whether she should run back in there and tell Rahshaan right then or wait until later. She looked at her surroundings. There was a processional of cars pulling out of the parking lot. She pulled hers in between two whose drivers she could make out. Hopefully, no one would try to hurt her in the midst of all of those people. She went and tended to her children, and then she went back and showed Rahshaan the note. No secrets was their promise, and she adhered to it.

Against her wishes, the family took G-Ma to stay with Big Grams upon being discharged from the hospital. She hated everything about her little sister's huge house. Her high rise apartment was just fine. She didn't want anyone fussing over her, but everyone did. Sheila, Uncle Mont's mother, was her personal nurse. When she couldn't be there because she had to work, she had a hand selected team of nurses at her disposal. G-Ma was too independent to let that go on for too long. As soon as she was healthy enough to go up and down stairs by herself, she was going back to Nat Turner.

"We've been meaning to talk to you about that," Rahshaan said to her one night when he and Shatima went to visit her. "We're moving you out of there."

"Without asking me?" she retorted. "I have one little heart attack, and suddenly my grandson thinks he runs me."

"G-Ma, it was more than a heart attack. Somebody fuck—

messed — with your medication. We're moving out the projects, and we don't want you there by yourself. Not where we can't watch you and make sure you're safe. We want to take care of you ourselves," he tried to reason.

"I don't wanna be sitting up in y'all house listening to y'all fornicating," she shot back. "It don't make no sense for y'all to make me sit up in your house of sin."

Rahshaan and Shatima cackled at that. They couldn't deny the accuracy of her accusation.

"We're gonna get a duplex," Shatima explained. "That way you can live downstairs in your own house, in your own space, but we'll be right upstairs if you need us."

"So I gotta live *under your* fornicating?" she grumbled.

They laughed again.

"I don't know why everybody wanna move me somewhere. I've been in that same apartment since it was built. My rent is cheap, and I don't do nothing but pay my tithes and mind my business." The old woman smoothed out the lace comforter that lay on top of her. Then she made a face at it. "My sister dress up her house like white folks. I gotta get back to my own bed."

Rahshaan sighed. "You need to stop being stubborn and let people take care of you."

"For what, Rahshaan? For years, the only people who gave a damn about me are sitting in this room. If it wasn't for the two of you, I'd be starving and probably naked. Now everybody wanna worry about getting me better because who's gonna watch their kids? Why can't I just go back to my apartment and be left alone? I like my little simple life. I like it even better now that Tima takes me out to get crab legs once a month." A sneaky grin spread across her face.

"But that's just the point. You don't get to live your own life," Shatima said. "Aren't there things you'd want to do with your days if they weren't spent changing diapers and making twenty thousand meals?"

"I sure would like to play those slot machines at the casino a couple of days a week," she admitted. "I know I could get me some good money out there."

"Then do that," Shatima told her. "Why don't you let me send you to Vegas for a little while after you get better?"

G-Ma considered this. "You gonna come with me?"

"I can't. I can send your sister with you though," Shatima told her.

"I don't wanna go with her." G-Ma turned her nose up.

"Then take one of your friends from church," Shatima said. "Just figure out who you want to go with and get out of here for a little while. Then when you get back, we'll have you all moved out of that apartment and into your own house."

"I'm not moving," she insisted. "Now, I'll go out of town and come back rich, but I ain't never leaving that apartment, and that's that."

Seeing that the woman wasn't going to give in, they settled on sending her away. Rahshaan and Shatima retreated to the back yard to talk. They felt defeated.

"I guess we're gonna have to stay in our apartment," she concluded.

Rahshaan just scowled. "She's so damn stubborn. Who doesn't want a free house?"

Shatima thought of the patients she took care of when she was a CNA. "Sometimes moving people is bad for them. A lot of the elderly people I used to take care of would die as soon as they were moved from one floor to another." She clasped her hand over her mouth when she saw the horror on his face. "I wasn't saying she was going to die. I was just saying that maybe she knows something we don't. Maybe we should just let her live the way she wants to live."

Reluctantly, Rahshaan agreed.

"At the very least, she'll be better off away from here," Shatima said, more for her own benefit than his.

Their minds worked overtime trying to assuage the premonitions the situation presented. Who was the next target? If it was maternal figures, then Selena was definitely on the list. What about Big Grams? Lynn? It was time for them to talk to Mont about everything that happened.

As if mentally summoned, Mont came trudging across the back yard through the snow. He was bundled up from head to toe.

"G-Ma is looking pretty good for a woman who just had a heart attack," he remarked, giving Shatima a hug. "She's also talking about Vegas. Who put that idea in her head?"

"I did," Shatima replied, wondering why he was questioning her. "I thought it would be nice if she got away and got to enjoy her life for once."

Mont assessed his goddaughter. She was so sure of everything. He wondered what it was like to only have two people to consider in life. He wouldn't say he was jealous of her, but she definitely made him curious.

"And I'm paying for it with my own money, so I don't know why you're out here questioning me about it," she snapped. "I would give that woman the world if I could. If she wants a week in Vegas, then that's what she gets."

Mont stared at her. No one spoke to him the way she did. "Rahshaan, can I get a moment alone with my goddaughter please?"

Rahshaan looked from one of them to the other. Then he slowly walked away.

"What's up, goddaughter?" Mont said to her, feeling obvious tension. The cold was no match for her attitude.

She turned her back on him. "You tell me." She started walking deeper into the trees, touching their snowy trunks. He followed her.

"Why do I feel like there's a beef between us?" he wondered. "The first time we linked up, you seemed so happy to see me. After that, I don't get nothing but attitude from you." He walked ahead of her and then stopped in her path so that she was forced to look at him.

"I don't like being told what to do with my life, especially from someone who's been absent for so long," she said through clenched teeth. "Now, you can run all these niggas around here because you've been here for them, but if you knew the half of what I've been through, then I don't think you'd be coming to me about anything that I do with my life, my time, or my money."

Mont felt like all the wind was knocked out of his lungs. He was so used to people singing his praises that the idea of someone resenting him seemed foreign.

"Goddaughter," he began. "I fucked up when it came to you, and I apologize."

"Why didn't you ever send for me after that day?" she questioned. "Do you know how much trouble I could have avoided if you would have just been there for me like you promised my father that you would?"

He didn't expect her to be so direct. Her questions felt like jabs. "There's a lot you don't know about what happened between that moment and now."

"Same over here," she retorted. "The difference between you and me is that I didn't just show up expecting you to throw me a parade and bow down to me.

"Look, Unc. All I want to do is live my life and enjoy my family without having to ask someone else's permission."

"It's not that easy, Shatima," he said.

"You think I don't know that? I've got police following me and threatening me, because they think I can bring them to you. I just don't want anyone else getting killed because of me. So if that means sending Rahshaan's grandmother across the country to keep her safe, then I'm gonna do it. That woman could ask me to send her to the moon, and I'd do it in a minute."

He peered at her. "What you mean you don't want anybody else getting killed because of you?"

She froze. She thought for sure that Rahshaan told him about her dirty secret. "Everybody already knows I was the last person Rize was seen with before he got killed. And the only reason why he got killed, was because he came back for me when you told him not to."

"That's not entirely true," Mont told her.

Her thoughts briefly dipped into that time in Virginia she spent with people who clearly despised her existence, the days when she wanted to be comforted while she mourned. She thought that in her father's last days, she showed whose side she was on. Why was she the one who got left behind? She never understood how a man who had so many resources couldn't find one person. She wasn't buying it.

"So tell me the truth then," she told him with a shrug. "It's about time I knew anyway. All these people who are supposed to be my family have their preconceived notions of me."

"Do you mean Rico?" he asked. He took her silence as a "yes" and said, "Rico is an asshole. You two are a lot alike. Rico's way of dealing with his brother's death is to blame somebody."

"I wouldn't be the one to blame if you wouldn't have drawn that line between us," she shot back.

If only she realized how much her words hurt. They were in a verbal boxing match, and Mont was going down. That lock in a sock he kept hearing about her using couldn't hurt more than the way she cut him down in his grandmother's backyard.

"And the most messed up part about all this, is that I've got people attacking me from both sides. Everybody's looking at me, trying to feel me out and see if I'm a snake or not. Nobody stopped and thought if I felt that maybe y'all were the snakes."

"That's a serious word you're using," he warned her.

"Oh, I know, and I mean it," she told him. "You left me for dead, and I know my daddy didn't want that."

Mont hung his head. "So how we gonna fix it?"

She shrugged. "Can it be fixed, or do you just want me to fall in line like everybody else out here?"

"I don't know. I'll let you make that decision," he said.

She shook her head at him. Until that moment, she didn't

realize how much resentment she had for him. "Deep down inside, I know that if you really knew everything that I went through when you were picking and choosing your favorites among your best friend's children, then this conversation would be a whole lot different. So the decision is really yours to make." She started walking away from him. "If I can't book the trip for whatever reason, then you're going to be the one to tell her."

Mont stared after her, wondering how she managed to knock him out without touching him. He thanked the Lord, once again, for never giving him a daughter.

After all was said and done, G-Ma got her trip, and Big Grams went with her. There was an unspoken tension between the two women that the family hoped would be fixed upon their return. Maybe then, G-Ma would move in with her sister, and no one would have to worry about her. She was, after all, the true matriarch of the family.

With her gone, Rahshaan and Shatima wanted to have a new house immediately. They opted for houses that stood next to each other rather on top of one another. That way, she wouldn't be able to complain about hearing their fornication. Everyone had plans for the old woman, but she had plans of her own.

———

The worst part of Derrick's job was interviewing families of missing children. It took a piece of his heart every time he had to tell a parent he was going to do everything to bring a child back, knowing the chances of that happening were slim. He walked up to a colonial style brick house and rang the doorbell. A sobbing mother answered the door.

"Did you notice anyone suspicious traveling around the neighborhood the day Antoine disappeared?" he asked the mother after introducing himself and exchanging pleasantries.

She wiped her face with a tissue. "The only thing unusual was the unmarked cop car that kept circling the block. I hoped that increased police presence meant my baby would be safe. It has been days since I filed the missing child report. Why are you just now coming? My baby could be dead or worse."

"I know you feel like just another number at the DMV, and for that I apologize," Derrick told her. "The cases are coming in faster than I can investigate them. I want to discuss the car you just mentioned, though. Do you remember what the driver looked like?"

"She was a white woman with red hair. I remember, because my husband asked who she was supposed to be intimidating. He said she looked lost and goofy."

"A white woman with red hair?" Derrick sat back in the chair he was given. "Did you see anyone else in the car?"

"A man. A real real fine man. Tall. Good hair. Might've been Puerto Rican or Dominican. He got out of the car when we were leaving the house and greeted my Antoine by name. My son said he was the D.A.R.E. officer at his school."

Derrick's eyes shot up. "What school was that again?"

"Thurgood Marshall Middle School," the woman replied. "The school said that he never showed up that day, but he and I walked to the bus stop together. My bus came a little bit earlier than his."

Derrick wrote down the information and went back to the police station to confirm that Miguel Santarez was the D.A.R.E. officer at Thurgood Marshall Middle School.

HOW G-MA GOT HER GROOVE BACK, BEAUTIFUL BABIES, & JUST IN CASE GOD IS REAL

"Hello?"

"Shatima, where is Rahshaan?" Big Grams asked. "I need him to talk some sense into his crazy grandmother."

"He should be on his way home from work right now, Big Grams. He probably isn't answering because he's driving. What's going on?" Her heart skipped a beat.

Big Grams ran her hand through her hair. "Well, I'd really like to talk to Rahshaan, but I can't get in touch with him. Do you think you'd be able to level with her?"

Shatima sat back on her couch with the cordless phone cradled between her ear and shoulder. Something told her this was going to be good. "I should be able to."

"Well, Charlene is trying to do something crazy," Big Grams said.

Thoughts of the woman going overboard at the slot machines made her grin. "What is she doing?"

"She's getting married."

It took Shatima a minute to find her voice. "Excuse me?"

"Yeah, girl. Apparently, she's been waiting for the right time to reconnect with some man, and since she's not allowed to babysit anymore, she said to hell with us," Big Grams went on.

Shatima sat there, not knowing what to say. "Um...Stay right there by the phone. I'm gonna have Rahshaan call you right back."

"Okay, but hurry. She's on her way to some little cheap chapel. I just don't understand her."

Like clockwork, Rahshaan walked in with Shameik, Lynn, and Selena at seven. Shatima wasn't sure if Rahshaan would share in her laugh, but she thought the situation was hilarious.

"Call your grandmother's hotel room, please," she said as she started getting plates ready for them.

"Why? What's wrong with her?" He dashed for the phone.

"I don't know. Just call her." To the rest of the adults she mouthed "Watch this."

"Hello, Big Grams? Where's G-Ma? Is she okay? She what? Put her on the phone, please? G-Ma, what you mean you're getting married? Who is this nigga?"

Shatima exploded with laughter. Lynn, Selena and Shameik stared incredulously.

"Married? Ain't G-Ma like ninety-two years old?" Shameik remarked.

"Boy, shut up. She's only like seventy," Shatima corrected him with a playful slap. "And I don't see the problem. If she wants to get married, then she's grown."

"But when did you ever learn how to use the internet?" Rahshaan asked. "My mom came over and showed you?" He whispered curses at Darlene under his breath.

At the end of the conversation, G-Ma was getting married, and there was nothing anyone could do about it. She didn't know if she was coming back or staying. All she knew is she had a life that she was going to live.

They found a home five blocks away from Nat Turner in the Southview neighborhood. That way G-Ma was within walking distance, if she decided to return. Rahshaan still couldn't believe that his grandmother could make such a life altering decision, but he was happy for her. She gave at least the last twenty years of her life up. She deserved whatever made her happy. And as much as he wanted to interrogate the man who stole his grandmother from him, he knew it wouldn't do any good. So he moved his family into a ranch style house. The landlord was someone from Shatima's church who knew and loved G-Ma. It had the big yard that he wanted for his children.

Decorating their house was a second job for Shatima. She dragged Rahshaan to Lowe's, Home Depot, Bed Bath & Beyond, and Pier 1 Imports several times in the weeks leading into their move. The way she brought the small home together was deserving of a show on HGTV. He hated those stores, but loved how happy she seemed while commanding him to measure the windows for Roman shades. As long as she was happy and was thinking about life with him, then he had no complaints.

Their new neighborhood was a lot quieter than their previous one. Not having a stoop or boys standing on it took some getting used to. Most of their neighbors kept the same hours as them, leaving early in the morning to take their children to their bus stops and not returning until after five. Many of them weren't friendly. Their noses stayed in the air when they passed the Thomas/Bailey family on the streets. They had an air about them that said they were just outside of the projects, but "better than them project niggas." As long as they didn't vocalize that thought, Shatima had no problem with keeping to herself.

Since returning to work, Shatima's clientele increased. She knew word got out about her fight and thought people were coming in to be messy, but she didn't care. The more money came in, the more she could drag Rahshaan to the stores he hated, to spend ridiculous amounts of money in. She had a special surprise planned for the spare bedroom. While she told him she was saving it for a room just in case G-Ma came back, she planned to make it into a man-cave for him. He was always so exhausted when he came home at the end of the night. When his friends came over, she wanted them to have a place away from the children where they could relax and enjoy a football game on a flat screen TV.

By the middle of the week, Shatima's hands ached from sewing in what felt like a million multi-colored weaves. She began to wonder if there was a special occasion. She didn't have to wonder for long, because Moosie came in for her standing Wednesday appointment.

Shatima squirmed every time she was near Moosie. Moosie found Shatima's discomfort with her sexual orientation entertaining. It dawned on Moosie that the aggressive manner in the way she approached Shatima in her pre-Rahshaan days played a part in that. The catcalls she used to make at Shatima were some of her best work. She should have been offended by Shatima's fear, but she looked past it because of Chillz and Rize. Moosie knew Shatima's attitude would have been different if Chillz raised her.

"I know you loving how I got all my girls coming to your chair," Moosie said as Shatima combed her hair out.

"The extra money is appreciated." She tried to be as tight lipped with Moosie as possible.

Haddus stood off to the side, glaring at their exchange as he did every Wednesday. He was a lot less tolerant of Shatima's intolerance of Moosie.

"Yeah, I gotta get these girls ready for this party this weekend. My nigga is coming home after doing a long stretch. Banger ain't tell you?" Moosie went on.

"Nah. He hasn't mentioned any parties," she replied absently.

"It's gonna be a big one. Me and Shondell are throwing it for our boy Tiggs. He been locked up since '99, so I had to make sure we had top notch hoes for him when he got here. You and Banger should come through," Moosie suggested.

Shatima stopped parting Moosie's hair. "Now why would I come to a party with a bunch of hoes?"

"To be the entertainment," Moosie quipped and flicked her tongue at the air.

Shatima popped her in the head with the rattail comb she was using. "Respect the hairdresser, please."

Moosie laughed. "I was surprised when Banger told me he wasn't coming through though. That nigga never misses one of me and Shondell's parties. I guess what they say is true."

"What do 'they' say?" Shatima wondered, beginning her first braid.

"That once you get something real, these hoes don't matter," Moosie replied. "I was trying to get that with Shanae, but after I saw how she tried to break up you and Banger, I started looking at her different. She ain't shit but an opportunist, but those kids deserve better than that. I just want her to get her shit together for them."

Shatima didn't know what vibe she gave off that made Moosie think she was some sort of confidante, but she realized she didn't mind it. She missed having girl friends. She began to soften her attitude toward the woman. Then she started to pity her. She spent the majority of her time with men and then went home to Shanae. That showed the need for an outlet.

"I think it's real decent that you take care of those kids," Shatima admitted. "They got dealt a bad one. Not saying anything bad about Shanae as a mother, because before we had our dealings, I always saw them with her, but losing their dad and their home must have been crazy."

Moosie was shocked that Shatima had more than a one sentence response for her. "It is crazy. Squeak was my nigga, but he barely paid them kids attention, and they still talk about how much they miss him."

"Well, Moosie, you know I don't get down like that with your girl, but if you ever want to bring them in here to get their hair done or cut, it's on me. We'll just keep it between us." She smiled at her client who was slowly turning into her friend.

"Well, what about homework? You think you could help the older ones with their science? That wasn't my thing in school, but Banger always brags about how you help Quest with his homework, and the oldest really need it."

"Of course. Just let me know when you want to bring them by."

"Thank you, cuz I don't want them kids to fail because of me." She let out a sigh of relief while Haddus eyed them strangely.

"We're family. I'd never let another parent drown, especially one who volunteered for the job." That day started an unbreakable friendship.

On the first Friday night in their new home, Rahshaan lay on the couch with Shatima watching *From Dusk Til Dawn*. Although he claimed it was his favorite movie, he seemed to be on another planet. She suspected it had to do with the party. All week, she was so happy that he opted to stay home instead of going somewhere that could potentially get him in trouble. The last thing she wanted was another woman coming into her shop claiming that she was replacing her. If that meant that he had to stay home and be miserable, then so be it. She asked him a question then another. Both went unanswered. With the kids asleep, she thought he'd want to strip her down and make love to her from one end of the house to another. He just lay in her lap, his mind on another planet. Tired of being ignored, she got up and started vacuuming.

"I thought we were watching a movie?" he called out to her over the vacuum.

"That movie has been off for an hour, and you haven't paid me any attention in twice as long," she snapped, turning off the vacuum. "If you wanted to go to that party so bad, then you should've just went."

"Tima, if I wanted to see some ass clapping I would've put a pole in the middle of the bedroom and let you do your thing!" he hollered. Immediately, he paused. His eyes Bucked out of his face as he realized his mistake.

"First of all, lower your voice," Shatima warned him. "Second, who said anything about some strippers? I ain't stupid. I've been doing their hair all week, and all they keep asking is why Banger ain't coming to show no love. You need to go out there and see some naked ass then go." She stormed into their bedroom and slammed the door.

Several minutes later, he slid into the bed and spooned with her. "Baby, you love me?" he whispered, grinding his crotch into her ass.

"Not as much as you would love to be with those strippers," she snapped.

He snatched himself away from her. "I already said I wasn't going, so what the fuck you giving me this attitude for? You should be happy that I'd rather be here with you."

"Nigga, please," Shatima dismissed him, though she wasn't sure why she was in such a sour mood.

All week long, she was tickled to hear about people's disappointment that "Banger" was no longer a whore. People speculated about the ring she wore, and she didn't correct them. It put an extra switch in her step as she strutted around the shop to know that her man belonged only to her. Instead of apologizing for being so flippant, she got out of the bed and went into the bathroom. When he heard the tub water running, he made a dash for the door.

The party wasn't worth leaving the house. He had seen those women, even been with a few of them, but they just weren't who he wanted. He stood around Shondell's townhouse wondering what was wrong with him. Once upon a time, he lived for this. That night, though, he just wanted to go home and be with his family. After tossing some money at some of the dancers just to be polite, passing two blunts and drinking a Heineken, that's exactly what he did.

When he got home, Shatima was asleep on the couch. A half eaten Cup of Noodles sat on the floor in front of the couch. It was an odd choice for a midnight snack. He distinctly remembered her telling him how much she hated them. Often, they were the only thing she had to eat when she stayed in the teen parenting home. Even more than that, he knew she hated clutter. He threw away the cup and washed the fork she used before placing a blanket over her and then going to bed. As hard as she was snoring, he didn't dare wake her up.

For the next few days, she tried to do that thing where she acted like he didn't exist, but he wouldn't allow it. He didn't feel he did anything wrong, and her attitude toward him was unfair. So when she tried to walk around him, he stopped her, kissing her face until she gave in. When she tried to ignore his texts and phone calls, he showed up at her job. Her moodiness bothered him. They were supposed to be enjoying the life they created. Instead, he had to deal with her holding petty grudges. His patience was wearing thin. He tried to give her space to work out whatever she was going through, but it was hard when he had no understanding of it.

Business didn't die down for Shatima, though she certainly needed a break. Her hands ached from braiding and sewing daily, and her attitude toward everything sucked. All she wanted to do was stay home in her bed. Not even going to Bed Bath & Beyond after work put a smile on her face.

Two new clients sat in the waiting area patiently waiting for their appointment time. They buzzed with conversation about their weekend. Shatima wished they'd shut up, but they kept right on chattering.

"Peaches, girl, that party was the livest one Moosie and Shondell threw yet. I made three months worth of rent," the first girl said.

The other girl checked out her chestnut complexion in a hand mirror. "Girl, I know, but we would've made more if Banger had been tossing out money. You know I heard he's a family man now. Did you ever think you'd see the day, Cream? Back in the day, I could've sucked his dick and got my car note paid too. He didn't buy not one dance. Good for his wife or whatever, but this shit ain't working out for me financially."

Lynn walked behind Shatima and gently coaxed the curling iron she was about to launch out of her niece's hand. "Go take a break before you catch a charge," she whispered.

Feeling like the sky was falling, Shatima retreated into the supply pantry. All weekend long, Hyacinth was on her mind. Rather, the fried snapper that she cooked on the first day of their trip to St Croix was on her mind, but that made her think of Hyacinth. Her life needed a rewind button. She needed to go back to the tranquility of the private villa. Her soul begged for turquoise water and white sand. Never was her anxiety eased as much as when she sat at the edge of the Atlantic Ocean and let the water wash onto her. She wished teleportation was a thing. Since it wasn't, she stood where she was and forced herself to stay there until she could get a grip.

"I've never seen a woman get mad because her man *didn't* *c*heat," Lynn fussed as she joined her niece and shut the door. She leaned against a shelf and then knocked over a couple of bottles of conditioner. After returning them to their proper place, she asked, "Is everything okay at home? Do you need to talk or something? I wish you would just start coming to me when you have a problem instead of moping around like this."

Shatima sighed. "I'll be okay. Me and Rahshaan just got into it because he snuck out and went to that party, so I was just waiting for some yamp to come in here and need her ass whooped."

"Yamp?" Lynn repeated with her lip curled. "What the hell is a yamp?"

"A young tramp," Shatima replied.

Lynn cackled, and Shatima joined in.

"Stop calling your customers names and go do their hair so we can get out of here. I'm gonna call Selena. We'll do dinner or something, because you ain't about to be moping around here another day."

The trio went to a Chinese buffet. Shatima piled her plate with lo mein. That got raised eyebrows. She passed by the fish and thought of Hyacinth again. Why the woman she only knew a week was on her mind so much was a mystery. Then the phrase the woman kept saying popped into her mind.

"Beautiful babies..."

As she ate her lo mein, Shatima thought of the last time she purchased pads. Two weeks before St. Croix.

"I need somebody to take me to the store," she declared suddenly.

They got to-go boxes and went to the Dollar Tree next door. Quietly, they followed Shatima around until she found what she was looking for. Then in a quiet voice she asked if they could go back to Lynn's house. No one said anything during the ride. They held their breath as they watched her go into the bathroom.

"Beautiful babies..." Hyacinth's voice sounded in Shatima's head again as she sat and awaited her fate. Five minutes later, she walked out of the bathroom with her bottom lip scraping the floor.

"I'm pregnant," she announced sadly.

The two of them stared at her wordlessly. Then Lynn said, "Duh, bitch. Your titties have grown two cup sizes in the past month, and your hips are spreading."

Selena peered at her. "Why are you sad?"

If she started telling the story, they would have been there all day. The two of them were already far gone, squealing about buying baby clothes. She had to get out of there, but she didn't want to go home.

"I didn't want anymore kids," she simply stated.

"Why not?" Selena asked, her tone sounding like she took offense. "We missed Jabez's baby years. We deserve a do-over."

Lynn turned to Selena and looked at her like she was crazy. "She gotta have a baby because we don't have kids? Bitch, what are you even talking about?"

Selena's face turned red. She looked around at all of the pictures of the children she raised as her own. Instantly, she was saddened.

"I lost my baby," she told them. "I had a miscarriage right after the wedding that never happened. My baby joined his or her daddy up in Heaven." She paced around the living room. "You asked why I didn't come back for you. It was because the losses were too much for me. I...had to go away for a little while."

"Selena, we ain't about to guilt her into wanting a baby," Lynn told her.

Shatima looked from her mother figure to her aunt. She felt terrible for driving this confession out of them.

"This isn't about that," Selena said. "I would never manipulate my daughter like that, and forgive me if it seems that way. I've just been feeling a way since Christmas, when she asked why we never came back for her. I don't mean to make this about me. I just want you to know the truth. I was in a mental institution, and Lynn was making sure that I was taken care of. Your aunts were the only ones who knew."

Tears stung Shatima's eyes. "I'm so sorry."

"There's nothing to be sorry for. You wanted to know, and you deserved to know," Selena said.

Lynn went to the dry bar in her living room and broke out a bottle of wine. She stopped when she realized what she was doing. "This night is calling for some Crown or at least a bottle of Red Cat, but you can't drink, Tima. I don't know what the fuck to give you."

Shatima laughed. Her aunt rarely kept anything non-alcoholic in her house.

"So anyway, I made this a real sad moment when it should be happy. I might be a grandmother in a few months." They started gushing over buying baby clothes and baby showers all over again.

Hyacinth's voice came to Shatima again. "Beautiful babies..."

It was close to the kids' bedtimes when Shatima made it home. Rahshaan sat in the living room fuming. He was tired of the cold treatment he received. Something wasn't right, and he wanted to take care of it. How could he do that if she avoided him?

She dragged herself through the door with bags under her eyes. The last thing she wanted to do was have that conversation, but it was unfair to him not to. They said they weren't going to hide anything from each other anymore. Mentally, she pepped herself up for the conversation.

"You worked late or something?" he asked her. The question was pointless. They both knew that he drove by the beauty shop after she ignored his calls.

"I had a long day. Aunt Lynn and Selena took me to clear my head. Did the kids eat?" she wondered. She went directly to the kitchen to heat up her leftover lo mein in the microwave.

He wanted to argue with her, but her ass was magnified by the yoga pants she wore to work that day. It was a strange choice of attire. She always scoffed at people who wore the tight, stretchy material in public unless it was just a quick grocery store run. Her hair was in a doobie wrap with the pins still in. He wondered what had her mind so preoccupied. His eyes followed her as she went from the kitchen to the dining room. There was something different about her, something alluring.

"Yeah, we ate," he replied. "I took them to get pizza."

"That's nice," she remarked.

"I spoke to G-Ma today. She said she's coming home soon."

A smile spread across her face. "Good thing we kept up that apartment then. Is she bringing her husband with her?"

"She didn't say."

The quiet lingered in the room. Shatima wondered how she would bring up her news.

"You had a good time with Lynn and Selena?" he pressed.

She shrugged her shoulders. "I had a time with them. Selena had to get something off her chest, so I had to listen, and then I felt messed up for being mad at her. So I spent the rest of the night apologizing."

He nodded his head and clasped his hands together. "So am I gonna get an apology next?"

"An apology for what?" she snapped, her head jerking up. "I ain't the one who snuck out the house like Kid n Play in *House Party*. All you had to do was say you wanted to go to the party, and I would've had to trust you."

He cut his eyes at her. "You still don't trust me, and you know that."

"How can I when you're a grown man who sneaks out the house?"

He didn't have an answer for that. Instead, he walked over to the dining room table, laughing at how silly he was. He made a face at her noodles and asked why everything she ate lately involved some kind of salty noodles.

She sighed. "Because you got me pregnant."

Rahshaan's heart skipped a beat, but his face puckered. "Why you say it with so much animosity?"

The last thing that she wanted to do was associate him with the father of her first child, yet that was the sole reason for her angst. In her mind, fatherhood drew a line of demarcation between who men pretended to be and who they really were. So far, Rahshaan was a dream. Life with him was everything she missed when she rejected love. He was perfect for Jabez and NyQuest. What if more children meant choosing a favorite? What if pregnancy made her ugly again, and it diminished his love for her? She didn't want what happened between him and NyQuest's mother to happen to them. She wanted their love to grow. With a baby in the picture, she wasn't sure that it could.

Instead of answering him, she shrugged her shoulders.

"You're keeping him or her, right?" he asked. Slowly, he reached out to her and placed his hand on her stomach. He imagined what it would be like for her to have a swollen belly instead of the six pack that was currently there.

She stared at him, surprised that he asked the question. He didn't take his hand off of her belly.

"I know exactly when it happened: on that balcony in the islands." His smile grew. "Something told me I shot the club up."

A laugh that she didn't mean to let out escaped her mouth.

"Why ain't you excited about this? We're gonna have a baby," he sang.

"It's so soon, Rahshaan. We're moving so fast," she told him.

He shrugged. "Time ain't shit to me as long as I'm spending it right doing the right thing. Ever since me and you got together, I've been pretty much doing the right thing."

His words surprised them both and touched her. She wanted them to cure any doubt that she had. In the back of her mind, though, she couldn't help but focus on the what ifs. Most importantly, what if he died, just like Rize and Chillz? That was one thing he couldn't guarantee. Since he was so happy, she kept this thought to herself. She looked toward the door of the room she was building for him. Maybe another time, in another house, she'd be able to give him his personal space. That room was going to be a nursery.

After finishing the lo mein, her stomach tumbled. He instinctively followed her to the bathroom when she hopped up and rubbed her back when she sacrificed every noodle to the toilet god. It felt like she'd never stop puking. She wanted to curse Rahshaan, but every time she tried to say something, more food came up. He continued to rub her back. She caught a brief glimpse of him smiling, excitement flickering in his eyes. Her arms were too heavy to lift. Otherwise, she would have socked the grin off his face.

The moment she woke up, she spent a half hour losing a battle to morning sickness. Rahshaan was there, rubbing her back again. She wanted to shatter his wrists.

"You know, I was thinking you could stay home from school and work today so that we could pick out an OB/GYN together," he suggested.

She stopped vomiting to peer at him. "I'm gonna use the same OB/GYN I've been using since I started going to one."

"You made an appointment yet?" he interrogated.

"I've known that I was pregnant for five minutes. Can her office open please?" She hurled more into the toilet.

When she was finished, the boys were dressed and ready to go to the bus stop. Rahshaan walked beside them happily, a smile on his usually stoic face. He greeted every person they passed and showed no offense when they declined to respond. Nothing could break his spirits. The girl of his dreams was having his baby.

"Tima, why is Daddy smiling so hard?" NyQuest whispered to her as Rahshaan peacock strutted ahead of them.

"Because he's a Looney Toon, baby. Pay him no mind."

After the kids were on the bus, Rahshaan insisted they spend at least part of the morning together. She didn't think she could take any more of sugary sweet Rahshaan, but her phone rang.

"I'm at the airport. Who's coming to pick me up?"

Shatima paused. "Mother Glover?"

"What is this 'Mother Glover' nonsense? I'm G-Ma to you now, granddaughter. Now come get me from this airport."

She hung up the phone and turned to Rahshaan. "Your grandmother needs a ride home from the airport." Her voice was incredulous.

The smile on his face grew. His favorite girl was pregnant, and his other favorite girl was back home. Sun broke through the gloomy clouds of late winter and tried to give him a blue sky to go with his mood. 2005 was the best year he remembered living. He turned the music up in Shatima's Maxima, not caring that she was listening to yet another CD from the '90's. Mentally, he resolved to put a better stereo system in her car and thought of a million other things he wanted to buy for her. He would give her the world if he could. She was carrying his baby.

G-Ma was sitting outside of the airport when they pulled up.

She carried only one suitcase. The mystery husband was nowhere in sight. Her hair was in a French roll. Her nails were perfectly manicured. The clothes that she wore were fancier than any of her Sunday church attire. Somehow she looked about ten years younger. Her skin was dewy.

"G-Ma got her groove back," Shatima said under her breath as she watched Rahshaan put her suitcase in the trunk. She went to get in the back seat, but G-Ma waved her off.

"This your car, baby," she told her with a smile. "These old bones will be just fine sitting in the back."

The car was filled with an awkward silence. Rahshaan and Shatima wanted to ask the woman about her trip, but knew she was going to tell them to stay out of grown folks' business.

"Rahshaan, stop at the store and get Shatima some fresh ginger," G-Ma instructed. "I want some pancakes, too. Y'all got time to take an old lady out to breakfast?"

They went to the store as they were told and took G-Ma to the pancake house as she requested. No one asked her any questions, but there were a thousand of them on the tips of their tongues.

"Now, Tima, you gotta get up early and steep that tea in boiling water and drink it before that morning sickness sets in," G-Ma instructed after they'd placed their orders. "Otherwise, you're gonna be fighting morning sickness all day. And get some olive oil and start rubbing it on your stomach in the morning and at night, too. I'd hate for that pretty skin of yours to get ruined by stretch marks."

Rahshaan and Shatima watched her as she spoke with bewildered looks on their faces. Finally, she acknowledged their wild expressions.

"I had a dream about fish every night for the past week. Me and Tima was at a river watching salmon jump, and we caught about three of them, and brought them inside and made us some filets. Then we went and fed our three pet goldfish. So I had to come home, because it wasn't no way I was missing my babies expanding their family. I gotta be here to help." G-Ma grinned at the two of them. "After all this time. Who woulda thought?"

"G-Ma," Shatima said when she couldn't take it anymore, "what happened to your husband?"

G-Ma waved her off. "He died."

"Seriously? Are you okay?" Shatima poked out her bottom lip sympathetically.

"Girl, stop being so dramatic. He was eighty. That's when people die. He led a full life, left me a little bit of money, and now I don't have to be bothered with his ass thinking I'm gonna fry him chicken every night." She stuck her nose in the air. "I told him, back home, my grandchildren cook for me. I don't know when the last time I had to make a full meal was. He ain't like that too much, but to hell with him."

The incredulous stares came back.

Rahshaan started laughing and leaned back in his chair. "What else did you do in Vegas, G-Ma?"

"Minded my business, and I'd appreciate it if you'd mind your manners and stop asking about things involving grown folks. Now eat your pancakes."

On the day of Shatima's first prenatal appointment, there were four people ecstatic about the baby. She wasn't one of them. While the ginger took away her morning sickness, she hated its taste. It felt as though she was juggling a set of bowling balls in her t-shirt. Everyone who knew kept talking about how great she looked, but the vain part of her was just waiting for the ugly that came during her first pregnancy. Every morning, she looked for the purple rings around her eyes. Every morning, her skin looked dewy, and aside from the heavy, sensitive breasts, she felt fine. She sat around and waited for it to get awful and for Rahshaan to flip out and leave her.

Rahshaan escorted her into the doctor's office as though she was made of glass. If someone would have offered them a wheelchair, then he would have taken it for the woman carrying his precious cargo. He sat her down in the waiting room chair like he was throning the queen. Then he tried to fill out her paperwork himself, but was at a loss when he didn't know any of the insurance information. He strutted through the office as if he were the first man in the world to get someone pregnant. The women in the office looked at him with hearts in their eyes. Shatima just wanted him to sit down until she knew he was going to be this excited for the full nine months.

Dr. Tawny was a brown, thick bodied woman who stood no more than 5'2" but carried herself as though she were nine feet tall. She was knowledgeable and had a sweet demeanor. Two black male medical residents accompanied her. They looked like bodyguards. Their presence put Rahshaan on the defensive.

"These niggas coming in here to look at my wife's pussy?" he asked when they were introduced.

That got a laugh out of Dr. Tawny. "No, they're going to look at her *vagina*," she corrected him. "You guys are here because *you* *t*ended to her pussy. Now we're here to tend to her vagina and uterus. Totally different things. Totally different feelings."

One of the medical residents shook Rahshaan's hand firmly and spoke up. "I'm Dr. Gilead. I understand if you don't want Dr. Stackhouse and me here. We can step out during the examination. My sister is pregnant, and her OB is a man. My brother-in-law wasn't keen on that either."

Rahshaan eyed the resident. "So is he okay with it now?"

"Hell nah," Dr. Gilead replied. "He wants to fight the doctor every time they go there. That's why I offered to step out."

That got a forced laugh out of everyone. Rahshaan continued to peer at the residents. Shatima just rolled her eyes. She realized Dr. Gilead's eyes were on her and Rahshaan and tried to straighten her face.

She was eight weeks pregnant, which, in Shatima's mind, meant that when Hyacinth was walking around mumbling about "beautiful babies," she was casting a fertility spell on them. It was too soon to detect the heartbeat. After her blood work, Dr.

Tawny announced that Shatima's enzyme levels were elevated. That could mean twins. Shatima wanted to walk to St. Croix and punch Hyacinth in her face. Rahshaan danced around, praising himself for his "super sperm."

"Rahshaan, it was very nice to meet you. Can you please excuse your wife and me? I need to have a one-on-one counseling session with her. Standard procedure," Dr. Tawny said with a smile.

Rahshaan had no problem with going back to the waiting room. He had to go tell everyone that he may be having twins.

Dr. Tawny sat and looked over Shatima's chart. Then she turned in the little stool she sat on so that she faced Shatima. She looked at her patient's hair. "I've been meaning to come down and have you do something with this fro," she said, just to open a conversation.

Shatima smiled at the woman's shiny hair. "Your afro is beautiful."

Dr. Tawny patted the soft, shiny, kinky halo atop her head and smiled. "Thank you. I'm ready for something different. I'm gonna call the shop and make an appointment this week. But, girl, let's talk about you. Your face has been longer than the month of March since I confirmed your pregnancy. What's wrong?"

Shatima shrugged. "It's nothing. I'm just being silly." Her frown deepened. Girl talk in a paper gown wasn't how she wanted to spend her morning.

"You sure?" Dr. Tawny peered at Shatima through her black framed glasses. "Right about now, you look like you'd rather be anywhere but here."

The paper gown started feeling like a straight jacket. It tightened around her neck. "You remember how my pregnancy was with Jabez?"

The doctor opened her chart and reviewed her notes from nearly six years ago. The woman sitting before her was entirely different from the teen who was dropped off at her office with no clue about what she was doing. Back then, Dr. Tawny had no clue how the girl wound up in that situation, but she suspected the child didn't voluntarily become a mother. She never met the father to confirm. She tried to get Shatima to go to counseling, but Shatima refused. She said she didn't believe in someone getting paid to care about her. It was an odd view. The young girl had so many obvious reasons to be depressed.

"I remember you were in mourning, and I remember being very concerned about how that would impact the fetus," Dr. Tawny stated. "I also remember Jabez's father's identity being a mystery. I remember you being high risk, and I remember putting you on bedrest after someone assaulted you. The man that you are with today isn't Jabez's father as well, is he?"

Shatima clasped her hands over her mouth. Hearing someone else vocalize what she was feeling made her feel awful. Rahshaan was not Andrew. She couldn't live in the same fear with him. Her thoughts took her back to that day in paradise, which she was certain was the day of conception. Juxtaposed with whatever day Jabez was conceived, she was living a fairytale. She wasn't some pawn in some twisted game being played by some sadistic, manipulative child molester. This was a family with a man she loved, who loved her back. While she was no clairvoyant, she could be assured that her life as a parent wouldn't be the same as they were for the first five years of being Jabez's mother.

"No. He's the total opposite of Jabez's father," she answered. The paper gown began to loosen.

"Then what's wrong? Because I can tell something is very wrong. Do you just not want this pregnancy? Would you like to talk about terminating? It is your choice, you know." Dr. Tawny got up and put her hand on Shatima's.

"I know it is. You've always made that clear," Shatima said softly. With more strength in her voice, she said, "I just want— I moved really slowly to get with this man, and then when we got together, it was like BOOM! Let's declare we love each other and we're gonna be together forever for the rest of our lives, let's move in together, become parental figures to each other's children, and now oh! Let's throw a baby in there too. I just don't want it to be this whirlwind and end, you know?"

"Did you see how that man looked at you? I don't think he wants it to end." Dr. Tawny winked at her.

"Yeah, but let's see how he feels when my pregnancy weight and the stretch marks and those ugly rings around my eyes get here," Shatima grumbled.

The laugh that erupted from Dr. Tawny's mouth startled her patient as well as people walking by the door. With wide eyes, Shatima sat and watched the woman. She seemed to be having some kind of fit.

"*That's w*hat this is about? You're worried about him thinking you're ugly? Oh girl." She laughed some more. "That's cute. I really don't think you have anything to worry about if you take better care of yourself than last time, but sometimes pregnancy has adverse effects on women. Your focus should be the baby, especially since you snapped back right after delivery last time.

"So if you need to talk, I can still recommend a great therapist if your feelings about that have changed. And if not, I'll see you next time."

Rahshaan's new favorite part of the day was making the ginger tea his grandmother prescribed. He took Shatima home to make some before taking her to work. He insisted on driving her there daily.

"You know you gonna have to teach me how to cook so that you don't have to be on your feet so much when you come home," Rahshaan said as he brought her the tea. He sat next to her on the cream sectional, lifted her legs, and turned her so that she could rest them on him. "I don't know how to make nothing but survival food, and with the way you cook, Quest and Jay ain't going for that."

"What is survival food?" she wondered.

"Eggs, fried bologna sandwiches, and sandwiches," he replied and then laughed. There seemed to be a permanent smile etched on his face. It was almost cute. "So can I ask what you and the doctor talked about?"

"You leaving me because of how ugly I'll be when I get good and pregnant," she replied, staring straight at him and not cracking a smile. She put the tea on a coaster and folded her arms across her chest.

"What the fuck? What be going through your head?" he asked.

"I don't know. I don't get time to think about it, because everything moves so fast with us," she snapped. She was trying to be more cognizant of her attitude, but it was useless. Something about him made her want to take his head off every time she saw him.

"You feel like I forced you into this?" he asked incredulously. "I thought we was in this together."

"No, it's not that, and calm down!" she snapped. "I'm just waiting to see how you're gonna treat me when I'm fat and ugly and your friends can't say 'I can't believe you got bad ass Shatima,' because I know it's gonna change."

"You carrying my baby. I don't know what could make you badder than that," he replied. "You buggin' out right now, but I know it's the pregnancy, so I'm just gonna let you drink your tea."

This depth of her vanity surprised him somewhat. He watched how much attention to detail she put into her looks every day, but he thought she knew that she was naturally beautiful. With the way that she sneered at people for complimenting her, he thought she would appreciate them not having any comments for a while. Did she like it, or didn't she? It was confusing, and not in that way that made her so complex and sexy. He was almost annoyed. He'd never say it, though. For the remainder of the year, he'd blame everything on her hormones.

"I don't know why you're acting like this about being pregnant. You got paintings of fucking fertility goddess hanging over our bed," Rahshaan went on.

Shatima Bucked her eyes and then knitted her brows. "Since when does hanging pictures mean you want to be pregnant? My social worker from the parenting house gave me those paintings when I was feeling bad about being a teen mom. She told me to look at them every morning to remind me that I was created for this mothering shit. Isis is the goddess of motherhood."

"Motherhood and fertility," Rahshaan said.

She smirked. "Oshun is also the goddess of purity and love."

"And sensuality and *fertility*," Rahshaan finished for her. Then they laughed together.

On Sunday, Rahshaan watched as Shatima got the boys ready for church. He listened as NyQuest fussed about having to go, Jabez talking him into how much fun Children's Church was, and watched as she lovingly put cocoa butter on both of their faces. Then he stood in the doorway and admired Shatima as she put on her makeup. She was a magician, because he never could tell what she did, but she somehow looked even prettier than before she put it on. Extra time was spent looking in the full length mirror in the hallway. Every day, she checked to see how fat she was getting. So far, you had to squint to notice that she had a little pouch.

"What are you up to today?" she asked. On Sundays, he normally left early in the morning and didn't return until later in the evening or at night.

"I was thinking about going to church with y'all," he replied. "It's still come as you are, right?"

Her head jerked in his direction. She looked at his plain white t-shirt and crispy Girbaud jeans. "It is..."

"Then let's go."

G-Ma could have kissed the sky when she saw her favorite grandson in the driver's seat. Like a gentleman, he helped her into the back with his children. Everyone he loved most was packed tightly in that Cranberry Maxima. As soon as he could, he was buying them a bigger car.

While church wasn't a place he wanted to appear regularly, that one time felt pretty okay. He owed Pastor Candle a thank you for his visit to the hospital. The man wasn't a hypocrite, like most preachers. The same couldn't be said for the congregation, who whispered about Mother Glover's "drug dealer" grandson, but he wasn't there for them. Lately, he was full of joy. Save for Shatima's hormonal war on him, nearly everything in his life was perfect. He had to thank the God he only half-believed in for giving him this family, just in case God was real.

"Where you been at, nigga?" Mont asked as Rahshaan entered his office later that afternoon.

Walking into Mont's office always felt like being called to see the principal after getting in trouble in school. It took forever to walk down the corridor past the boiler room to get there. Rahshaan sat in one of the folding chairs and waited for his instructions. Shameik and Shondell sat there counting money.

"Church," he replied.

Mont looked at him and let out a laugh from the center of his gut. Shameik and Shondell stopped counting money to join in.

"No. Where was you at for real?" Mont pressed.

"I was at church. Ask Big Grams. G-Ma couldn't wait to get on the phone and brag about her grandbaby getting right with the Lord." His voice rose to a falsetto octave, mocking his grandmother.

"My sister got you whipped like that?" Shameik quipped, his voice seasoned with residual anger from the way his friend hurt his sister.

Rahshaan let it go. As long as the love of his life forgave him, he couldn't worry about Shameik's feelings.

"With that baby coming, I'm sure you gonna need some extra

cash," Mont cut in before Shameik made another comment. "I got an out of town job for you to do. Gonna take a few days."

Apprehension set in. After their conversation on the beach, Rahshaan and Shatima didn't mention his line of work again. He wondered if she could handle him being gone for stretches. "Where we going?"

"Albany," Mont replied. "You know what that means."

"Politician money," Shameik offered. "We could all use that kind of money. When do we leave?"

"Lynn's getting the girls ready to go tonight," Mont replied. "You, Banger, and Moosie need to be ready to go by eight." He stopped when he noticed the fear on Rahshaan's face. "What's the problem?"

"With Tima being pregnant, I would feel more comfortable if me and Trigga weren't gone at the same time," he replied.

Mont sucked his teeth. "Nigga, I'll keep an eye on your family. You actin' like a real sucka ass nigga. Don't forget, this is the time you need to be stackin as much as possible. You can't sit up under her the whole nine months."

Rahshaan dreaded going home. The day started off so well. When he came back with this news, he knew it looked like a setup. He tried to convey that to Mont, but he was in boss mode rather than family mode. There was no sympathy for his relationship issues. Shameik and Shondell chuckled under their breath at how scared Rahshaan looked. He blocked them out and focused on how to deliver the message.

The month of April gave them a warmer day, so it was no surprise that Shatima was outside with the boys when Rahshaan got back. He thought of the day he told her he wanted a back yard for them to play in and was glad he was able to give them that. They had their own swing set, which was a step up from the graffiti covered equipment they played on in Nat Turner. His mind conjured things he'd be able to buy them with the money from this trip. Slowly, he convinced himself this was a good thing.

Shatima greeted Shameik and Shondell and offered them dinner. Of course, they ran into the house to tear into the food, hoping it was fried chicken.

"What's wrong?" Shatima asked Rahshaan when she saw his long face.

They sat at the patio table after Shatima fixed Rahshaan's plate. He looked exhausted. She felt sorry for him.

"I gotta go out of town for a few days," he told her after finishing his chicken thigh. "Unc got a job for me to do."

Shatima's eyes dropped. Right after Rahshaan revealed his true employment description, she put it out of her mind. It still sounded like he was a pimp, and she didn't want to think that she'd fallen in love with one. "Oh. When do you leave?"

"In an hour," he told her.

"An hour?" she repeated louder than she intended. She lowered her voice. "Well, I guess you gotta do what you gotta do."

He felt those icy walls going up, so he stopped eating and reached out for her to come sit on his lap. He needed to hold her before he left. "What's on your mind?"

"Nothing," she lied. Then she cleared it up by saying, "Whatever it is, I'm pushing it out."

"I know you got a question or two," he pressed her.

"You won't answer them, so there's no point in me asking."

He pulled in air through his nose and then let it out slowly. "I told you no more secrets."

"Where do you stay while the girls are doing what they do?" she asked.

"Depends on the setup. Most times in a room next door."

Shatima shook her head. "I can't do this. I really don't want to know or think about this." She hopped off of his lap and waved one of her hands as if she could wave off the situation. "Just please don't have me fighting at my job again."

"Tima, it ain't— This is my job. I ain't going to do nothing to break us up ever again. I told you that. This is all business. I don't know if this is gonna make you feel any better, but ain't none of them gonna want me neither. They all know you. They know who you are to me, who I am to you, and they ain't checking for me. They're all about their money, and I can't even give them half of what they'll make at the end of this trip."

"I can't believe you used to pay for sex," she remarked, sniffling. She hoped she wasn't going to start crying, but if she did she'd blame it on the hormones.

"Don't say it like that..."

"No, but really. You're *Banger.* It wasn't too long ago that girls were trying to fight me over you at the gas station. You could have any chick you wanted. Why were you buying hookers?"

"I wasn't," he snapped. "But at the same time, if I fuck somebody, I ain't gonna let them go home broke. That goes for the chicks at work *and th*e project chicks, and whoever else." Something snapped and then fizzled in his brain. Nothing he said helped his case. It was obvious when he paid attention to the tightening of her mouth and the infrared beams darting from her pupils that he said too much. "Can we forget I said any of what I just said?"

"I think we should." The heat from her eyes didn't decrease.

"I ain't gonna say another word, because everything I say about this comes out fucked up. Just know that I love you, and I ain't doing nothing to fuck us up ever again."

She finally relented. "I'll go pack some clothes for you. Finish eating."

———

Moosie pulled into the pharmacy's drive-thru and waited for someone to come to the window.

"Pickup for Charlene Glover."

The clerk smiled, retrieved the prescriptions, and came back to ask, "Any questions for the pharmacist?"

"Uh, yeah. These are for my grandmother. She said they

tasted funny when she picked up her prescription last month and wanted to know if there were any changes to the manufacturer?" Moosie watched the clerk's face for any signs of guilt. The clerk kept a smile on her face and announced that she was going to get the pharmacist.

A few seconds later, a brown woman with long, curly microbraids appeared at the window. "I hear your grandmother is concerned about this prescription. How may I help you?"

"Are you the one who made the prescription last month, uh..." Moosie leaned forward to read the name on the woman's tag. "...Sarita Grungy, are you the one who made the prescription last month?"

Sarita's neck and shoulders tightened. She peered into the car and saw that Moosie was accompanied by Shameik and Shondell. Their faces held disturbing smiles. She didn't see past them to Rahshaan sitting in the very back, caressing his gun. "I just started working here this week."

Moosie chuckled. "Good answer."

At the end of her shift that night, Sarita asked for store security to walk her to her car. She practically ran to the coupe and let her lead foot carry her home. On a dark road a quarter mile of the way away from her job, her car wobbled uncontrollably. She heard a hissing noise coming from it. When she got out to inspect, she realized the front passenger and rear right tire were both completely flat. Trembling, she tried to retrieve her cellphone from her car but was instead met by the barrel of the same gun she missed Rahshaan caressing from the back seat earlier. Before emptying the round into her face, he made sure that she saw in his eyes how much he wanted her dead. His hatred was apparent even in the dark. Her body dropped. Moosie pulled up behind him, and Shameik hopped out. The two of them bagged the body and put it in the trunk.

"Stop at that farm a couple of exits ahead," Shameik instructed Moosie. "I know a man who pays by the pound for pig slop."

BANGER TAKES A BUSINESS TRIP, SOBA NOODLES, &WEALTH

Moosie drove a minivan with Rahshaan, Shameik, and three women in designer dresses who were dolled up with Lynn's signature touch. The trip up the thruway never took more than two hours. Usually, they sat in silence due to Rahshaan's sullen mood. Those trips were long, nearly unbearable. That night there was a slight smile on his face.

"Banger, I heard you had a baby on the way," Peaches said to him from the third row. "Congratulations."

"Well, congratulate me twice, because the doctor said it might be twins," he told her.

"Two more little boys," Cream commented.

Rahshaan scoffed. "Nah. You see how pretty my wife is? I need at least one girl. If she's half as pretty as wifey, we gonna put her in some commercials."

Peaches and Cream settled in their seats. They took their sights off of Rahshaan and thought about the big money they'd be making in just a few hours.

Moosie drove at exactly the speed limit. Her eyes checked the rearview mirror several times.

"What's wrong with you?" Shameik asked her.

"That Lex has been following us since we left South Ridge,"

Moosie said under her breath. "Looks like an undercover." She kept driving until she got to a rest stop. Then she pulled off and watched to see if the black vehicle pulled off behind her. It kept going. She and Shameik got out of the car. Shameik filled the tank. Moosie walked around inside and bought a pack of gum. Rahshaan kept his hand on the gun he had stashed under his seat and checked his surroundings. When they were sure the car was long gone, they pulled off again. Moosie got off the thruway and took the interstate instead.

The interstate highway wasn't lit in some places, making the ride even creepier. Rahshaan hated taking that route, because the lack of lights meant they couldn't see the cars around them. His hand didn't leave his gun once they left the rest station. He imagined Shameik similarly poised behind him with Peaches and Cream asleep on each of his shoulders. In the front seat, Melinda, the third woman employed for the job, hummed along to the music on the classic R&B station Moosie played. In times like these, they were happy for their line of work. The news always told stories of sex workers being raped by police after being pulled over. With their crew there, there was little to no chance of that happening.

Albany wasn't an aesthetically pleasing city. It didn't seem that the amount of money they were promised for their stay was realistic. For the most part, it looked like a never ending series of abandoned factories until they got to the Capitol building. Then, in a sea of limousines and luxury foreign cars surrounding the convention center, the numbers started to add up. The owners and renters of those cars were willing to pay upwards of the amount of their cars' values to satiate their fetish for black pussy. Moosie checked the address on her GPS. The streets around the building, as well as the parking lots, were filled to the brim with cars. Moosie listened to the GPS again and let it take her to the back of the convention center. She and Melinda exited the car. Peaches and Cream woke up and touched up their hair and makeup. Rahshaan and Shameik looked around for the black

Lexus and any other car that may have followed them to keep watch. They watched Moosie introduce Melinda to a silver haired gentleman in a tuxedo. Their conversation was brief. He handed them what appeared to be a set of keys and went back inside.

Moosie looked in the back at Peaches and Cream. "All right, ladies. Go suck some free healthcare and extra food stamps outta those dicks. The hood needs you."

Peaches and Cream giggled at Buck's motivational speech.

Once the silver-haired man arrived at the small two story home with a few other older men, the work began.

Swelling hands and feet forced Shatima to take her third break of the day on Tuesday. Pregnancy slowed down her productivity. She hated it. Lynn brought her water with cucumbers in it. Drinking it by the liter meant peeing by the half hour, but Lynn swore it would take down some of the swelling. Shatima was willing to do anything to gain back her braiding speed. She wasn't desperate for the money, but she wanted to stack a healthy savings while she could. After the babies were born, she wanted to spend as much time with them as possible.

When her cellphone buzzed, she dove for it. She hoped it was Rahshaan. He was only able to talk to her in brief spurts and through text messages. Wednesday couldn't come quickly enough. She needed to see her man. She'd even try to be nice to him when he got home.

"Oh. What's up, Unc?" Her flat tone was more out of disappointment that Rahshaan wasn't on the other end than Mont being the caller.

"Goddaughter, what's good? What you craving? I wanna take you out to dinner tonight. Spend some time with you." His voice was cheery. He hoped it encouraged her to reciprocate.

"Oh, that's nice of you, Unc. I've been on a noodle kick lately. I think the baby wants soba noodles."

"Cool. I know the perfect place. Meet me in North Sanford when you get off. I'll text you the address."

For the rest of the day, she could just taste the soba noodles on the tip of her tongue as she worked. The promise of food served as a stimulant. Being pregnant started to delight her. Having people cater to her cravings was fun. Her first pregnancy did not afford such a luxury, as they always ate whatever the man brought home for her to cook and a side of ice cream. Thinking about that made Shatima want ice cream. She chuckled and thought about what kind she would get.

After work and her Tuesday night class, she put the address Mont texted her into her GPS. Driving out of the South Side always gave her mixed feelings. Sanford County boasted about being the "chocolate city" that DC used to be. While that was true of her old neighborhood in East Sanford, South and West Sanford were left behind. While it was good that the children had access to the same education and meals while in school, there was a dramatic difference between what they went home to, depending on their side of town. East Sanford was always first in line for cosmetic upgrades to their streets and parks. South Sanford damn near had to have a riot just to get potholes fixed in their streets. Nat Turner had been promised a new pool and playground for years. The businesses where Shatima lived always got excuses instead of the grants the ones in East Sanford received. And North Sanford, which was where she was headed, looked like something out of a Hollywood film. Meanwhile, the poverty stricken blacks and latinos of the town were forced to look at abandoned homes and sorrow.

She turned on the radio and listened to the news, something she hadn't done in awhile. Another mother in the Chavez Projects cried over her missing son. It was always the sons who went missing. It turned Shatima's stomach. For the first time in a long time, she thought of the boy who came to Andrew's door when she went looking for him. His emaciated body haunted her mind for weeks. Her skin crawled when she thought of Andrew. His return and the missing boys were no coincidence.

The next report was about Malachi James. He was meeting with the mayor about the kidnappings. He wanted to know what she planned to do to keep the children safe. The person who interviewed him tied it into the boys disappearing primarily from low income neighborhoods. She reported that Malachi James wanted to know that the boys wouldn't be forgotten the way their neighborhoods were. It was good to have someone with capital influence on their side.

Shame clouded Shatima's mind when she stopped in front of the black marble water fountain, as directed by Mont's text. A woman wearing a pair of shoes that cost more than her car exited the vehicle parked in front of her. The restaurant's dress code called for much more upscale attire than her yoga pants and flowing shirt. She snatched down the visor in her car and looked in the mirror. At least her hair wasn't a mess. Quickly, she touched up her makeup. Hopefully, they'd forgive her appearance. She looked for a parking space, but instead she was approached by a red jacket wearing gentleman.

"Miss Thomas?" the boy who couldn't have been more than eighteen addressed her, tapping lightly on her window.

She rolled her window down. "Who are you, and how do you know my name?"

"Your party is waiting for you inside. I'll park your car for you." He handed her a ticket. Another young man appeared and escorted her inside. A beautiful woman dressed in all black lace smiled and greeted her. Not once did she make a face at Shatima's defiance of their strict dress code, which was displayed for all to see in the foyer.

"Mr. James is waiting for you. Right this way."

"Mr. James? I think you've got the wrong person. I'm here to see—"

"Right this way," the woman pleasantly repeated.

The woman led her past indoor waterfalls, which resembled

the one in Hair Revolution, and along a stream that seemed to never end. Dim lighting set the mood for romantic dinners. It was the perfect place for someone to propose marriage. At one of the tables, a major business deal went down. It was obvious from all the hand shaking and liquor pouring happening between the smiling men and women in three-piece suits. All that she wanted was a bowl of soba noodles. This exceeded anything she had planned.

They finally reached a private room in the back that was concealed by black lacquer doors with golden accents. They were a perfect match for the front desk at Hair Revolution. Even in the upscale atmosphere, there was something familiar about the place. It felt like home. She walked through the doors to see a man in a gray suit examining a fish tank in the walls. Several servers surrounded the table. The door closed behind her, and she was confused.

Mont turned around and smiled at her. "Hello, Shatima Lynn Thomas."

The sound of leather ripping across bare skin and then a man howling in pleasure caught Rahshaan right before he dozed off. He hated knowing the fetishes of old, rich white men who sat around deciding if abortion was okay. It seemed that they should be okay with abortion with as many as they'd paid for on behalf of the girls in there spanking them. He sat up against the wall and listened for any signs of foul play. That black Lexus had them on high alert. They were sure it was more than a coincidence that someone drove behind them for that long. He texted Shatima. She texted him back to tell him that she was on her way to dinner with Mont. That put him at ease.

"You really in love with my sister," Shameik remarked. Residual anger peppered his voice.

"Nigga, I told you that. You can stay mad at me forever. I don't give a fuck. Long as she's good, then I'm good," Rahshaan snapped. He missed Shameik's friendship, but refused to apologize to him. It wasn't Shameik's business.

Shameik glanced out the window. "It feels like we're being watched."

Rahshaan shuddered. "Yeah I've been having that same feeling since we left the rest stop. Think we should go walk around and check it out?"

They got up and went downstairs. First they looked for surveillance cameras. Recording by their clients was a prohibited and punishable offense. When they were satisfied that their contract wasn't being violated, Shameik went around the back while Rahshaan went to the front to check out the outside. The house was at the dead end of a street. There appeared to be no one in either of the neighboring homes. Once outside, there was no sign of the black Lexus. No other people or cars were found. They went back into the house and up the stairs.

It still felt like someone was following them.

"Sit down," Mont instructed her, "and close your mouth before something flies in it."

Shatima did as she was told. The image she had of him when she was younger came back. He seemed to be much taller and regal. Perhaps it was the suit. It must have been personally tailored by God's hands, because not even in *GQ Magazine* was a finer garment seen. He flashed his smile worthy of a toothpaste commercial and waited for her to order food before talking to her. She came in wanting soba noodles, but the menu boasted cuisine from all over the world.

Once the servers cleared out of the room to prepare their orders, she hissed across the table, "What are you doing?"

"Bruce Wayne did it. Why can't I?" he joked. "For real, though. You ain't know?"

"That *you are* Malachi James? How was I supposed to know that?" she whispered.

"Why you whispering? This room is soundproof. Your pops designed it." He smiled again.

Shatima almost wet herself. She tried to stop herself from squealing and fan-girling. Every time his name was mentioned by the news, she wished she had someone like him in her life; and the whole time he was her godfather. Her mind began to wrestle with whether or not she should be angry. She settled on being starstruck.

"Your attitude is pleasant today," he remarked. "Can't believe you didn't catch on all this time that this is me."

She thought back over the months of luxuries. How could she be naïve enough to think any boss liked Rahshaan enough to gift him trips to islands and sections in VIP? He was the poster child for antisocial misfits. No way did his performance outmatch his personality.

"Last time we talked, you seemed like you had some animosity toward me. You wanna discuss that?" he asked.

She was still trying to come down from the high that she actually knew the greatest philanthropist in the city. "Not really," she said.

"Well, can I get something off my chest? Because I've been fucked up in the head ever since that day."

She looked into his eyes and saw a man pleading to be understood. He wasn't crying, but his eyes were a little moist. She waited for the servers to bring out their soup and leave again before she told him to go ahead.

"I did wrong by you," he told her. "You have every right to feel how you feel about me abandoning you. I should have done more to find out where you were and how to reach you."

"Unc, I went back to my daddy's house every day," she interjected. "It's not like I went into hiding."

"That must have been after the funeral then, because if you went to the funeral, then you were definitely coming with me. I promised your pops that."

"It was," she admitted. The soup's gingery broth reminded

her of the tea she drank in the morning. She was sick of ginger, but relied on it to enjoy her meals. "My mom took me to her parents' house in Virginia, and when she brought me back, the house was empty. Everybody was gone." Sadness swept over her as she remembered the loneliness she felt when she wondered if everyone was real or not.

It was quiet in the room decorated with fish tanks and black hyacinths. Mont felt at ease sitting there, eating with his goddaughter. His best friend would be proud of the woman sitting at the table. She turned out to be everything Chillz wanted to raise his daughter to be: beautiful, smart, independent, a good mother, and a good businesswoman. He thought of how happy Chillz was when he found out Hope was pregnant with his daughter. He had so many plans for their family. It was a shame that none of those plans got the chance to take flight while Chillz was alive, but he was lucky that the end turned out just the way Chillz wanted.

"So now that I see all of this," Shatima swept her hand around the room to indicate that she was referring to her surroundings, "you know I'm gonna ask you again. You had the resources. Why didn't you come find me?"

He finished his soup and thought about how he was going to explain things to her. All morning, he had practiced it in his head, but at the moment he was unsure. "Because I had to fake my death."

She stopped eating her soup and pushed it away. The spoon hit the table and stained the silk tablecloth. "Huh?"

"Look. You know that man you punched at your last job?" He seemed to forget he told her that the room was soundproof, because his voice dropped to a whisper.

"Andrew Jones? Yeah, what about him?"

"Well, he's responsible for your father's death, and he came back to town to make sure that I'm dead. That's probably why he attacked you," Mont said.

Shatima's chest tightened then closed. She tried to pick up

her water goblet, but her palms sweated. She stammered but couldn't make any of the questions she wanted to ask come out of her mouth.

"He's here to try to stop the woman who's running for county executive from winning the election, too. She was never supposed to make it this far. If she does, then the perverted shit him and his pops do is coming to an end," Mont continued.

Once again, Shatima thought about the boy who came to her house to attack her. It made her skin crawl. Her scalp burned.

"How do you know him?" she asked.

Mont told her, "He was your father's roommate in college. He was weird, but your father was nice to him. He pretended to be poor. Me, your father, and your Aunt Lynn really were poor. We linked up with Joy Gilead, who's the new County Executive, and started a…business of sorts."

"Was it the same kind of business that Rahshaan's out of town for now?" Shatima wondered.

Mont nodded. He watched Shatima fidget as she sipped water. Her constant movement concerned him.

"That's a pretty big scandal," she said after downing the rest of her water. Within seconds, a server entered the room, refilled her glass, and then left once more. "Why didn't Andrew leak it to the news to stop her from winning?"

"Because while we were in college, we found out about an even bigger scandal that he and his father created. What do you know about your grandparents?"

Shatima threw a hand in the air, wondering why it mattered. "Nothing about my paternal grandparents, not even their names."

Mont nodded his head as though he expected that answer. "Your grandmother — Shareefa Revolution — was the first civilianTennessee murdered after becoming chief of police. He killed her while she was trying to remove a teenage boy from the back seat of his car. He uses the police force to kidnap kids and then blame it on innocent but marginalized people. Your grandfather — Jeremiah Revolution — was executed behind it," he explained.

Gripping the edges of the table, Shatima popped straight up in her seat. "My mother has nine million awards on the mantle in her living room for a story that she wrote about that man kidnapping kids and stuffing them in basements all around Sanford County until they could be sold as sex slaves."

"*That man w*as your grandfather, and your mother writing that story is the reason why your father left her. Him being your grandfather is the leverage that she used in court to get full custody of you and keep your father out of your life." His heart broke as he watched Shatima's palms go to her face. He couldn't reach out to comfort her yet, so he told her, "I'm not trying to stress you out. I just need you to know the unfiltered truth.

"Andrew pretended to be poor, but we didn't trust him to get in on what we were doing. So Chillz just took care of him to keep him from asking questions. He fed him from the hot plate that he snuck into the dorm. Andrew took that to mean that Chillz had feelings for him, but Chillz explained to him it was just something he did for everybody who needed it. In return, Andrew introduced him to Hope. Chillz was crazy about that looney bitch and saw himself spending the rest of his life with her. Andrew introduced me to Loretta, but I had better options than her at the time. She was in her feelings about that and tried to get me locked up but wound up setting up your father instead. That's when Chillz went to jail, and Hope and Loretta fell off. They was best friends before that.

"Andrew got real jealous when Hope got pregnant with you and started acting weird. He stopped coming to the dorm after class. A little bit before you were born, he got caught trying to take a little boy from his parents in a department store, so we all thought we agreed to stop fucking with him all together. While your father was in jail, she had Andrew over at her house trying to explain his side of things. She wasn't going to listen, but he took her some information his father gave her that he said would guarantee her the anchor position at Channel 3. The story was all lies saying that Jeremiah was responsible for a human trafficking ring involving adults as well as children. It sent him to Death Row.

"On the day of Andrew's visit, somehow Nyir got a traumatic brain injury. To this day, we don't know how, but Andrew went to Chillz and apologized for it. Nyir's been in and out of hospitals because of it his whole life. He can't remember what happened, and Hope's story about it changed every single time she was asked.

"After they both got kicked out of Chillz's life, they became friends again. Tennessee had Hope putting out bullshit stories in the news about the kidnappings. Sometimes she said they didn't happen at all. Sometimes she blamed it happening on a group of people who couldn't afford to defend themselves against the social aspect of it, mostly gay people. We knew that, though, and when Joy Gilead got elected, she was gonna expose the truth. She's gotta move carefully, though, because he can expose her as well. Tennessee Jones went as far as to blackmail her and make her pay money to keep what she did a secret. With me and Chillz both dead, though, he can't get money from her. If I'm alive, though, he thinks he can make bank.

"Those muthafuckas control everything in this county— the politicians, the media, the money, the minds of the people. They need money to do it, though, and their source of income is the boys they've convinced the people don't matter. Tell me something. Growing up in East Hills, when boys disappeared, what was said about them?"

Without hesitating, Shatima robotically rattled off the explanations she heard the adults give for boys disappearing by the dozens:

"Their parents couldn't afford them, but were too irresponsible to practice abstinence, so they got rid of them. They ran away. Their parents were lying. Their parents sold them." Her voice wavered with every explanation she recited. She never believed them.

"Down in South Ridge, we knew the deal. We were the ones suffering the most from it. In East Sanford, Tennessee Jones paid the mayor to look the other way. That's why they get taken care of so well while we get cut off by a bridge. Some of us tried to fight him the right way. Your Uncle Derrick and his father Sedrick and his friend Sam — the current chief of police — thought that they could infiltrate the system, expose the wrongs, and change the system from within. That just got Sedrick executed on the 11 o'clock news. After Tennessee killed Shareefa and burned my father to death in my childhood home, though, fuck the system. It's been war ever since. They killed Shareefa, Sedrick, Chillz, Jeremiah, my father, and Rize. They won't get no more."

He watched Shatima gnaw on her acrylics while she rocked back and forth in her chair. The soba noodles had gone cold. Her eyes blazed. He couldn't decipher if it was anger or sadness making her body quake. Mont was at the edge of his seat, waiting to hear what she thought of his actions making her a target.

"These people steal children," Shatima finally said, her teeth chattering. "Unc, there has to be a bigger reason behind this than just knowing each other's secrets."

Mont let a half smile creep across his face. "You're a smart woman, Shatima Lynn. It's all about power. This thing goes back farther than my generation. Your great-grandfathers, Amin and Hezekiah, worked for the founders of Sanford County. This was supposed to be a community. Instead, Tennessee wanted a taste of that power that he was denied as a Black man wherever he was from. Working together to take care of each other made him sick to his stomach when there were people to exploit.

"We tried to stay in South Sanford and mind our business, but he couldn't being denied the rights to being a dictator for the whole county. He tried to put drugs in the town. We just turned around and taxed the hustlers and redlined the zones where they could be sold. He hated that shit. So did the hustlers, obviously, but it is what it is."

Shatima wrinkled her face. "Is *that wh*at street tax is?"

"Yup. Anybody wants to do something illegal, they gotta do it where I say they can do it, and they gotta pay me to do it. That's how I pay for all the coat drives and the Thanksgiving dinners," he said.

"Oh." Shatima fingered a clean section of the tablecloth and then concentrated on the flickering candlelight. She looked to the side at the brightly colored fish swimming in the aquariums on the wall. Tears started spilling from her eyes without her permission.

Mont leaned forward. "What's wrong? Did me bringing up Rize upset you? I know you thought that was your fault, and I can't let you think that anymore."

"But it was my fault." Sobs took over her body. She slammed her fists on the table and screamed, "I can't believe I got a baby by this muthafucka!"

Mont sprang from his seat and demanded, "You got a baby by who?"

She cowered as she watched him coming toward her.

"Answer me!"

"Andrew is Jabez's biological father."

Mont froze. He didn't know how to react. He wanted to kill her for doing something so stupid. He had to calm himself down.

"How could you let this happen?" he bellowed and threw a plate across the room. It shattered against the wall. Its contents stained the runner.

She rose from her chair. "How could *I l*et this happen? Nigga, you left me! You let Hope drag me off in a car. Did one person run after me? I know you didn't."

This time, she couldn't cut him down with her words. The way he stalked toward her was reminiscent of the way parents move toward their children en route to physically disciplining them. The last person to try that got laid out on her front yard. She was sure she couldn't beat her godfather, but she wasn't going to let him hit her either. In preparation for his swing, she reached into her purse. He grabbed her by her wrists and pulled her toward him.

"I wasn't asking you that question. I was asking myself. And I'm sorry. I thought they killed you that day."

She threw her arms around him like a little girl and told him her story. After hearing exactly how diabolical the man was, she regretted her mistake even more.

"You can't look at Jay any different after this, Unc. Promise me, please? It's not his fault."

"Of course not."

They sat back down at the table. Neither of them had much of an appetite.

"Let me ask you something, though. The whole time you were gone, Hope never went looking for you? Never filed a missing persons report?" Mont wanted to know.

She ran her hands across the silky material of the black table-cloth. "Nope. Not that I know of. I'd think that if she did, then the parenting home I moved to would have at least mentioned it."

Mont nodded in agreement. "That bitch set you up."

"Set up her daughter to get pregnant by a man the same age as her? Who does that?"

"Hope does that. That bitch was in on this from the start. Believe that."

"So what made you tell me all of this today?" Shatima wondered.

"I had a conversation with Selena and Lynn. You needed to know," he replied. "When you cussed me out the last time I saw you, I felt more fucked up than I did when I found out who you were, and *that fu*cked my head up."

"Why?"

"Because it reminded me of how out of touch I am. I can't go to the hood, because everybody there thinks I'm dead. These niggas sat up under me daily and talked about the dime from 4F."

"Who?"

Mont sucked his teeth. "That's what they called you. That was your apartment number in Nat Turner, wasn't it?"

She frowned. "They're so ridiculous."

"Anyway," Mont cut her off. "They never used your real name, so all that time you were working for Loretta, I could have saved you from that bitch. *That's a* scandalous bitch."

She refused to think of the days when Loretta used to torture her.

Three days and thousands of dollars later, Moosie had everyone back on the interstate, headed home. They tried not to fall asleep, but three days of being on high alert had them groggy. They couldn't wait until the two hour ride was over. They left during rush hour in order to blend in with regular traffic.

Melinda refreshed her makeup and checked her hair in the mirror. She squinted at something in the reflection.

"Moosie, that Lex that was following us on the way up there, was it a Land Cruiser?"

Moosie glanced in the rearview mirror. "Yup."

"It's behind us again," Melinda said.

Rahshaan sucked his teeth. All he wanted to do was go home. He clutched the gun under his seat.

Moosie kept driving. She switched lanes to see if the driver would follow. They tried, but couldn't get anyone to let them in. Moosie laughed.

"That ain't Elroy," Melinda said, lining her eyes with black liner. "One of them looks real young. It's two boys in the front seat. Can't see if there's anybody in back."

"Fuck it then. If we need to know who they are, then we'll find out later. Let's get back to the crib," Moosie decided.

Rahshaan didn't take his hand off his gun.

WHEN THE BURIED PARTS OF YOUR PAST RESURFACE

Without Rahshaan there to hold her at night and wake her up when she started screaming, Shatima's nightmares became more intense. They started off strange. She, Rize, and Chillz walked around the park in Nat Turner for a while. The air was frigid. That detail stuck out to her the most. They shivered all throughout their journey around the park. Rize kept asking her to do something, but she couldn't hear what it was in the dream. All of his other words came out clear as day, especially the "Promise me you'll do this, Tima," but whatever it was that he wanted her to do was drowned in the blowing wind.

They walked from the park to the corner store and stood under the mural. Chillz pointed to it and said, "Make sure Banger keeps Jabez off of there." Then Hope walked by with a dog that had Jabez's face. Chillz pointed it out to Shatima.

The dream then flashed to Chillz's and Selena's wedding, as it always did, but instead of Chillz being gunned down, it was Jabez. Shatima couldn't wake herself, and the dream was on a loop until morning when her alarm clock sounded. She was exhausted for the rest of the day.

There was nothing Shatima wanted to do more than go home and get off her feet, but Rahshaan called her and told her he was taking her out after work. She fussed at him and whined, but he insisted. When they got home, he was cutting the grass. She and the boys ran to him. To outsiders, they looked like a family from an ABC sitcom. He stopped mowing the lawn and hugged his children. Then he went to Shatima, unzipped her jacket, pulled up her shirt, and kissed the small round belly that was quickly growing.

"Do I get one of those too?" she asked with a smile. She had missed him so much that she was temporarily finding his antics adorable.

"Shhh! I'm talking to my baby!" he whispered and went back to kissing her stomach.

"Tima, do me and Jabez get to kiss the baby too?" NyQuest asked.

"Not while your daddy's around, apparently." She smiled down at Rahshaan, who was still whispering to her stomach.

"What did the doctor say?" he asked her.

"About what?"

"Is it one baby or two?"

A devilish grin spread across her lips. "You'd know if you were there instead of at 'work.'" She put up air quotes when she said the word work. She went inside and ignored him calling after her.

They hadn't seen Marcus in a while, so when he showed up for dinner, they invited him to tag along. Rahshaan wanted to go to the mall and buy something for the baby. G-Ma told him to slow down, that buying things before the second trimester was bad luck, but he shrugged off her superstitions, as always. He wanted the house to be so full of things that there was no need for a baby shower, even though he planned to throw the ultimate baby shower.

Marcus was the only one not moved by his brother's behavior. He remembered Monaysia's pregnancy and how over the top he was for her, and he didn't think Rahshaan liked Monaysia very much. While seeing his brother in love was weird, seeing him buy everything the mall sold was expected. There was something about new life that humanized his older brother. Marcus normally saw him as a cold bully. He didn't know what it was about babies that brought Rahshaan so much joy, but Marcus wished Shatima would give Rahshaan a child every year for the rest of his life. Then he'd be more tolerable.

For a Wednesday, the mall was unusually crowded. Every few feet, they had to stop and speak to one of Shatima's clients or someone Rahshaan knew. With an ice cream cone in her hand, Shatima didn't object to being dragged from store to store. The boys picked out whatever toys they wanted while Rahshaan looked at educational toys. For an Aunt Annie's pretzel and lemonade, Rahshaan was able to coax Shatima into going into a sneaker store to buy Jordans for their unborn child or children.

"Can we have dinner after we leave here, please?" she begged while they were in Foot Locker. She sat on one of the fitting stools as he asked for six pairs of matching Jordans, one pair each for Jabez and NyQuest, two pairs for newborns, and two for toddlers.

He slung a Finish Line bag over his shoulder and looked bewildered at the Mrs. Field's cookie he had to buy Shatima to get her to come along with him into the second sneaker store. "You eating a whole lot."

Her face clouded up. "I'm pregnant as hell, and you won't let me have dinner."

Looking at her through beady eyes, he bargained, "I'll take you to dinner if you tell me whether we're having more than one baby or not."

"Okay. You got me." She threw her hands up. "The doctor said we were having more than one baby."

Marcus turned to them and raised his eyebrows when Rahshaan let out a whoop and leapt around the store. He couldn't wait for Shatima to give birth and make Rahshaan even happier.

Shatima's cravings had moved from noodles to cheeseburgers, so that's what they had for dinner that night. As they sat in the restaurant and waited to be served, Marcus looked around. He needed something to do, someone to keep him company. Watching his brother kiss Shatima like she was the last woman he ever wanted to put his lips on made him want to be in love too. He looked around the restaurant once more. A peculiar feeling told him that something interesting was about to happen.

No sooner than that thought crossed Marcus's mind did a woman with eyes the color of new pennies walk through the door. Marcus had a thing for women with light eyes, and that woman was a beauty. Something about her looked fragile. She held the hand of a little girl with the same color eyes and her hair pulled in two ponytails. A cloud of doom surrounded them. Sure he could brighten their day, Marcus grinned when the mother and daughter were seated at the table across from them. He didn't even wait for the hostess to walk away before he slid over to them.

"What's up, sexy? My name's Marc. I wanna pay for your dinner."

The woman looked past Marcus and peered at Shatima and Rahshaan.

"Tima...?" she said timidly.

At the sound of her name, Shatima looked up and eased Rahshaan's face away from hers so that she could identify the owner of the familiar voice. Her head hurt as she wondered what else the year was going to bring back to her. When she looked at those shiny eyes, she rolled her own.

"I'm ready to go," she said to Rahshaan.

Marcus continued to smile at the woman. "So you know my sister-in-law, huh? Why haven't I seen you before?"

"Sister-in-law? Tima, you got married?"

"No!" Shatima insisted. "Nicolette, could you please just stay at your table, and I'll stay at mine? I really don't wanna have to beat your ass again."

Rahshaan's head perked up. "That's the bitch?" He turned to get a good look at her.

"Mommy, you said a bad word!" Jabez admonished.

Shatima didn't mean to ignore him, but she was seething.

Nicolette's eyes lit up. "Jabez? This is your son? He's gotten so big!"

"Nicolette, please!"

"I just want my daughter to know her brother, Tima! Damn! Just because you hate me doesn't mean our children have to suffer! You're doing the same thing to our children that Hope did to you and Rize, and honestly, you're better than that."

The ketchup bottle went from Shatima's hand to Nicolette's face within five seconds. She didn't take the time to think about what she was doing or that there were children present. People at tables around them looked to see what was happening. Shatima paid them no attention. Someone was trying to destroy her peace and needed to be dealt with accordingly.

"Tima, chill," Rahshaan said to her, pulling her back down.

Even after the embarrassing hit to the face with the ketchup bottle, Nicolette persisted. "Shatima, I have been trying to contact you for months, and you attack me."

Shatima buried her head in her hands. She tried to drown out the sound of NyQuest and Jabez asking her about their sister. Why didn't the discarded parts of her past stay that way?

"Tima, please. I am begging you for just one conversation. After that, I will leave you alone forever, but I am desperate. I have asked April to find you. She told me how mean you were to her. I know you're still angry, but I just need a tiny bit of your time. Please, Shatima?"

It was comical that this woman felt she could ask Shatima for anything after the way she betrayed her. After missing her prom and all of the other senior year highlights, all she had left to look forward to was graduation, and she sacrificed that for a serpent.

"Please, Shatima?" Nicolette beseeched.

The tears in Nicolette's eyes could have been what moved

Shatima, or maybe it was the desire to let Nicolette know that she had better friends than her snake ass. Whatever it was, she dragged her feet over to the table and sent Marcus away. She sat next to Nicolette's daughter. Curiosity made her peek at the little girl. It was strange to her that neither of Andrew's children inherited his blue eyes. Save for her mother's light brown eyes, Nicolette's daughter looked just like Jabez. Once she noticed it, Shatima couldn't stop staring.

"You've got until my burger gets here. Now what do you want?" Shatima's tone was harsh, but her eyes didn't leave the little girl. She even had Jabez's dimples.

Nicolette sighed. "I really need more time than what you're giving me, Shatima. We have a lot to hash out."

"We don't have anything to hash out," Shatima corrected her. "I said everything I had to say to you after your baby dropped. What more is there to discuss?"

"You never listened while I apologized to you," Nicolette told her. "That man... I didn't know that he was like that."

For the first time since sitting at their table, Shatima looked at her former friend. "Why did you know him at all. How did you even meet him?"

"He came around the way looking for you," Nicolette replied, her head hanging down as she spoke. "He said you left him. He was crying. He thought something happened to you, so he gave me his number and asked me to call him if you came to school the next day. You didn't come to school at all that week, so I called him and told him that. He asked me if he could come get me, and I'd take him around to some places where we used to hang out. I told him that we didn't really hang out like that much after you left to go live with your father, but I could think of some of the places we used to go. Instead of looking for you, he offered to take me shopping. Then he took me to dinner, started crying over you leaving him. Then we went to his house. I didn't know that man, but he had spent so much money on me that I didn't feel like I could leave."

"Did he tell you that you couldn't leave?" Shatima asked. Her tone sounded like she was accusing Nicolette of something, but Shatima really wanted to know if he was as possessive with her friend as he was with her.

"He never offered to take me home," Nicolette quickly said. "After I told him he could take me shopping, it seemed like I had signed some kind of deal with him without knowing it, you know?"

"Go on..."

"He cried and cried and cried over you for most of the night. So I went to him and started patting him on his back. He started promising me all these things like sneakers and jewelry, and I remembered how fly you were in school, and I was jealous. Somebody was always buying you something, and I'm not gonna lie, I hated on you so bad. I was a child. I thought I was cuter than you, and that you didn't deserve half the stuff you got."

"Half the stuff that I got came from my brothers," Shatima pointed out, annoyed by the conversation.

"I know that, but still. Even after they were out of the picture, somebody was always taking care of you. Even right now, somebody's taking care of you. Look at that ring on your finger."

"Nicolette..."

"Tima, please. Just let me finish," Nicolette begged. "I may never see you again, and I have to get this off my chest." She watched Shatima fold her arms and sit back. Convinced that she still had the woman's time and attention, Nicolette went on. "I thought you were dumb. That man was obsessed with you, buying you stuff, and you just walked out on him. So I figured I'd pick up where you left off. But he didn't have any interest in me after that night. I called him so many times to tell him I was pregnant, and he said, 'Well, I can't do anything about it until the baby is born, so keep me updated, and call me when you go into labor with him.' So I asked him what if it's a girl, and he told me it'd better be a boy and hung up the phone."

There was a pause in her story, as though she was waiting for some *Oh girl, no he didn't* commentary, but Shatima's face was void of any emotion. She couldn't even gather the desire to feel sympathy for this tragic story.

"My parents wanted to know who this boy was who got me pregnant, but I couldn't even give them a last name. They thought I was lying to protect him, so that's why they put me out. I stayed in that parenting home and hated you the whole time I was there. It wasn't fair that you got to avoid it. So when you showed up there, I thought it was karma coming back to bite you in the ass."

"Karma for what, Nicolette? I didn't do anything to you." Shatima stared at Nicolette's daughter to keep her from throwing something else. She was drawn in by the dimples that mirrored her own. The little girl smiled at her shyly. Her smile tugged at Shatima's heart.

"You bounced back from everything, Shatima. I hit rock bottom, and you were out living it up. Your mama put you out, you went to go live with your daddy. Your daddy gets killed, you get a rich boyfriend to live with. Then you don't even appreciate the rich boyfriend and go live with your brother who's apparently got a little bit of money too."

Shatima got up from the table. It wasn't in character for her to assault people in front of children, but she was going to hurt this girl.

"Shatima, wait. Just let me get this off of my chest."

"I'm not here to appease your jealousy of me, Nicolette. You're sitting here telling me you want me to fail, and I'm supposed to be okay with that." She refused to give Nicolette the satisfaction of knowing her suffering.

"I didn't want you to fail. I just wanted things to be better for me. Getting pregnant pushed my life downward." Desperation was in Nicolette's voice.

Shatima sat and waited for her to go on with her story.

"I know I was wrong for sitting in your face and acting like we had some bond when you came to the parenting home. You even missed graduation because of me, and that's when I really felt bad. But I didn't even think I was going to see that man again. When he came up there with all those balloons and flowers to take me to the hospital, I didn't know he was going to do that. And when he treated you like you were nothing to him, it made me happy. Finally, you were getting your nose rubbed in something."

"My daddy dying wasn't enough?" She waited for Nicolette to address that, but she never did.

"That man didn't come into the hospital with me. I had to give birth by myself. He came up to visit the day after I delivered and spazzed out because she was a girl. Then he started cussing me out because he just knew she wasn't his. I kind of knew she wasn't his too, but I never told anybody until after we got the blood test confirming that she wasn't." She paused again, wanting Shatima to ask her the father's identity.

"So you wanted to sit me down to tell me that I whooped your ass for nothing? Because you still screwed him for vengeance for some animosity that I don't even understand," Shatima pointed out.

"That's not why I wanted you to sit down." Nicolette curled her lip and sneered at Shatima as though her former friend was dumb for not catching on. "I wanted to tell you about this the day that I came back to the parenting house, but you were so angry at me that you were willing to get kicked out over your anger."

"What is your point, Nicolette?"

"There was only one other person who could have been the father, and that was your brother Rize."

That was the moment that Shatima stopped believing in coincidences. Every single thing in life was part of a design. This newest revelation joined her past life with her present life. All the days that she sought out who she was supposed to be never prepared her for the joining of her two worlds.

"Wait...what? When did you even meet my brother?" She racked her brain trying to think.

"There were plenty of times when I could have met him, Tima. You were stuck so far up your own ass that you didn't even notice he was checking for me. Those days when you were dissin' me and April after school to go see him, he was looking at me. He never really said anything to me until that day you came back around the way to see your mother. I got his number that day. We talked for a little bit, but he got killed before I could call him my boyfriend or anything. So Rize and Andrew bumped heads a whole lot more than just over you." She lifted her chin and fidgeted with an R medallion dangling from the gold chain around her neck. The shine caught Shatima's eyes and made her blink a thousand times.

"Nicolette, you're acting like you just threw down the Big Joker, but I don't even know what it is that you think you have over me. You have a baby by either my brother or the same dude that knocked me up. So what? What do you think you win?"

Nicolette's face soured. This day wasn't going the way she planned it in her head. More than anything, she wanted them to go through single motherhood together, help one another up, but as usual, Shatima had it all. She stared at the pear shaped diamond on Shatima's finger, and her heart sank.

"I'm not done with my story. Can I just have a little more of your time? I promise there's a point to all this." Her lip started quivering. She didn't intend to be obnoxious. There was a lot of anger and jealousy still inside her though, that decided to work itself out there.

Shatima threw her hands up. "Might as well."

"Look. I don't know what that man did to you to make you leave him, but I know now that he was an abusive piece of shit, and I apologize for ever judging you for doing what you had to do. Because after Anaijah was born, I didn't hear from him for a very long time. He was distraught over the fact that she was a girl."

The mother in Shatima kicked in. She cut Nicolette off once again. "Hey, pretty girl," she said to Anaijah, who was sitting there listening to her mother's every word. "Can you do something for me? Can you go sit at that table with my sons and color with them, please?"

Anaijah looked to her mother for permission. Her mother nodded her head, so the little girl hopped down and skipped over to the table.

Nicolette gave Shatima a half smile. "So anyway, he cussed me out in the hospital and started threatening me. I had to call the hospital security to get him out of there. I wanted to file a restraining order or something against him, but didn't know his last name. I felt really stupid. He reached out to me for the blood test some time later. I don't know how he got any of my information. He just showed up at my doorstep and told me he had to know the truth. So I figured hell, it ain't like he's been a father. I was doing it all on my own, and I didn't know Rize was dead, so whatever. I thought Rize just dissed me to be a deadbeat, but I should've known better than that. Your brother was way better than that. I didn't think Andrew was gonna care whose baby it was, but the way he flipped out in that court room, I really did need a restraining order. It was so weird, because he acted like he actually cared about our child. So I had to have the police escort me out of the courthouse. Then, after that, I went home and thought it was over.

"For months, he bothered me. He sent me a sadistic videotape of him murdering your brother. He was calling me, threatening to kill me, telling me he was going to do me what he did to you. And at the time, I didn't know what that meant. But nothing ever happened to me, so I thought he was just talking shit, you know? And after a while, it died down. But last year, I went back around the way to see April when she came home, and I saw him coming out of your mother's house. I didn't even know him and your mother got down like that. I didn't want him to see me, but he did, and he started threatening me again. We had to get April's brother to get him off of me."

"He attacked you in broad daylight?" Shatima asked, her mouth hanging open.

"He was really upset," Nicolette told her. "I couldn't figure out why he cared so much, but he kept yelling about me not giving him the son I promised him. So me and April went out clubbin' that night. I didn't really feel like it, but she promised that her brother had my back. Whatever, so I went. I went to the bathroom for one minute, and this nigga jumps on me in the bathroom, and it felt like he stabbed me, but there wasn't a lot of blood coming from where it felt like he stabbed me. And then he left me on the floor. The club was kind of dead, so it was a while before somebody came in there and saw me laying in the floor. They thought I was drunk until they saw how he busted my lip. They called the police. The police make me go to the hospital. They're asking me all these questions, taking my clothes—"

"Your clothes?" Shatima asked.

"Yes, girl. He violated me again, and then he stabbed me with a syringe."

"Who carries syringes around?" By then Shatima's appetite was gone. She no longer cared about the burger.

"A nigga who wants to infect you with AIDS. That was his revenge on me for not having his son. He said since his daddy got infected with it, everybody he hated was getting it too. That man is crazy and shouldn't be walking the streets, but I guess you do what you want when your daddy used to be the chief of police." She sat back and studied Shatima's face, trying to see how she would take this all in.

Shatima's face dropped. Nobody deserved what Nicolette told her. "So what are you saying?"

"I'm saying that he wanted to make sure that he infected me with this shit, and he did."

"So why did you want to see me to tell me this?" Shatima

wondered. "I'm very sorry that you're going through this, but what can I do?"

Nicolette unraveled her silverware that sat in a black, cloth napkin and played with the napkin between her thumb and forefinger. She started sniffling. "I only spoke to Rize a couple of times after I got pregnant, but he told me that if I ever needed anything for Anaijah, that you would do it for me on the strength of him."

"Well, what do you need from me?" Shatima asked. The dream where she couldn't hear Rize started to replay in her head.

Nicolette's gaze traveled far away. While her body was still present in the restaurant, her mind was not. "I need you to take her."

"Take her where?" Shatima asked.

Nicolette sighed. "I need you to take her and raise her."

With her brows knitted, Shatima turned and looked at Nicolette from one curious eye. "Why would you want me to do that? She's your daughter. Is it because of the disease? Nicolette, there are many people who are parents living with this disease."

"I don't want to live anymore," Nicolette said quickly. "Anaijah deserves better than me. I can't find the right cocktail of medications to help me function. I'm depressed all the time. Most times, I don't even want to get out of my bed. My body is full of sores. I can't do anything for that little girl. That man is threatening to kill her, and I can't keep her safe. I'd never be able to live with myself if I let him kill my daughter."

Shatima stood up and told Nicolette to follow her. She told Rahshaan to give her burger to Anaijah. Anaijah just sat there coloring. She looked after her mother but didn't say anything. They walked until they found a quiet spot by a wishing fountain. As they walked, Shatima remembered the days when she felt the way her estranged friend did. Jabez was the only reason she stayed alive during that time. She couldn't imagine leaving him in a world where Andrew could get to him. She put her hands on Nicolette's shoulders.

"What are you doing? You have a daughter. You can't just give up."

"Tima, I gave up the day they told me that he put that disease in me. If I continue to live, what else is he going to do to me? That man tortures me, and there's nothing I can do about it. I don't have anywhere to go. He finds me. My family won't help me, because he's threatened them too. It's too much." Tears spilled down her nutmeg colored face, pushing down black eyeliner. She started to look like a wet raccoon. "Rize said that if I ever needed anything, then you would do it for me."

"Nicolette, how do I even know that's my brother's baby? It's not like he's here to do a DNA test. And you snaked me. Why should I trust you now? How do I know I'm not being set up? You still talk to my mother?" Although she fired off those questions in rapid succession, her heart and mind were already set on what she was going to do.

"I've seen Hope around the way. She's a terrible person. I see why you stopped fuckin' with her when you were old enough to get away," Nicolette said. "There's always police at her house, and my mom said Andrew is over there a lot too. I just don't understand how she could do you like that. You're her daughter."

Shatima shrugged. "Lots of people who are supposed to be down for me do me dirty, but they all come to me begging for something." She hoped that dig hurt Nicolette as much as she wanted it to. "Nicolette, I have a whole family now, and I'm pregnant. What if I don't have room for your daughter?"

Nicolette shrugged but answered a question that Shatima didn't ask. "I dream about your brother all the time. It feels so real. We just kick it and talk about how we'll get that chance to do things right soon. He asks me to come with him. He's always like 'Leave Anaijah with Tima. She good.' And I know you think I'm crazy, but I can't put that little girl through this shit that I'm going through."

"What makes you think that Andrew isn't targeting me too? I know you've seen the news," Shatima pointed out.

"Yeah, I did see that." Nicolette laughed. "It felt like you were getting revenge for both of us."

They sat there, staring at all the loose change discarded into that fountain. Hopefully, someone's wish came true, because neither of them got to fully embrace what that felt like.

"Why don't you ask April to take her? April's her godmother, right?"

Nicolette guffawed. "That damn girl is so damn out there. She's a college girl. She's doing her last semester abroad. She doesn't have time for a baby, and besides, she's a buy sneakers and outfits, maybe take her for an hour type of godmother. Look at you, Tima. Once you had that baby, you were so in love. And I don't know who that other little boy is, but he was looking at you like you were his mama. I can't give that to my daughter. I know you will on the strength of your brother."

Shatima sighed. "I wish you would stop saying that. You can't prove to me that that's Rize's baby."

"Look at her face, Tima. She's got my eyes, but that's it. The rest of that face looks just like Rize, looks just like Jabez. She looks more like you than she does me when she smiles."

"Nicolette, Rize was about four years older than us..." Shatima bucked her eyes and shook her head.

"I know, Tima. I know. I lied to him about how old I was. I told him I was eighteen and taking a gap year. He didn't find out the truth until he came to the school to pick you up one day. Remember when you got those purple rings around your eyes and had to go to the doctor to see what they were...? The day I was crying and told you I was pregnant, and you told me I could come live with you guys if my parents put me out...?" She hung her head low.

Shatima narrowed her eyes. "So you're saying my brother was a creep like Andrew, preying on teenage girls?"

Nicolette's eyes widened. "No, Tima! Rize was...Well, you know your brother was the truth. He's just someone I lied to, and I'm not really sorry that I did. We didn't have much time together because of everything that was happening in your lives, but the times we were together were everything to me. You can never compare him to Andrew, because how can someone in his early twenties tell the difference between a seventeen and an eighteen year old? I told Andrew numerous times how old I was, and he still did what he did."

Shatima sighed again. "All I wanted when I woke up this morning was a cheeseburger and to go back to bed. How did today even happen?"

They walked back to the restaurant slowly. Nicolette linked her arm with Shatima's. Her energy transferred, and instantly Shatima felt as gloomy as her former friend looked. She didn't want Nicolette to think it was her illness that was turning her off, so she allowed her former friend to violate her space. She became a crutch to her, and Nicolette's weight was heavy to carry. As they walked, Shatima tried to reason with Nicolette. She told her she would help her in any way she could, but Nicolette had made up her mind. Both her fight and her flight were gone.

"Rahshaan, do you remember Rize saying anything about having a baby on the way before he got killed?" Shatima asked.

Nicolette looked stunned. She didn't expect Shatima to be so forthcoming with such personal information.

Rahshaan thought about the last time he saw Rize. He assessed Nicolette and decided that with her skinny frame and button nose, she was exactly his type. "He visited me once when I was locked up and said he thought he might have gotten a shorty from the East pregnant, but she didn't know, and they had to wait and see." He looked at Nicolette then Anaijah.

"I told you that little girl looks just like Jay," Marcus remarked.

Rahshaan continued staring. "Word. Rize couldn't deny that little girl if he was here to do it."

But Rize wasn't there to do it, so it was Rahshaan's responsibility to take care of her. He waved to her. She locked her shiny eyes on him and smiled.

The conversation about these circumstances couldn't be had in one night over cheeseburgers. There were legal documents that needed to be drawn, lawyers that needed to be consulted, and space that needed to be considered. Through dental records, they were able to confirm that Rize was the father. Trust had to be gained, because the situation felt like a setup. Nicolette had to explain to the court why she wanted a woman she once pressed charges against to be her child's legal guardian. Rahshaan and Shatima would do anything for Rize in life or in death. At the end of the spring, they had a daughter whose biological mother gave up on life. Nicolette said she didn't want to see her daughter as her health declined, but Shatima took Anaijah to see her anyway. It was a mistake, because Nicolette was just a sliver of a person, and it only upset Anaijah. Shatima wondered if Nicolette left out part of her story.

A GRADUATION, AN ASSHOLE APOLOGIZES, &SHATIMA'S FAVORITE SONG

As spring turned into summer, the news was talked about so much that it didn't matter that they didn't watch it on television. Everyday the front pages of newspapers were full of pictures of either missing children or corpses. The chief of police begged someone to come forward with information. He pledged to the county that his entire career would be dedicated to finding out what was happening to the boys of Sanford County. Everybody knew, though, that some of the police were responsible for it. In turn, they questioned how the Chavez Projects of West Sanford remained unaffected by the crisis. How was it that every other low income area was targeted except that one?

The disappearing boys were just the surface of the deteriorating police department's problems. Tennessee Jones' final days gave way to a war between his soldiers and the ones who believed they had a duty to the community to reform their system.

The police department's civil war didn't mean anything to the citizens of Sanford County. A cop was a cop. They just wanted their children returned to them and the people responsible for their disappearance to be dealt with severely. During the day, they rallied at the police department's headquarters and demanded answers. At night, they hugged their sons tighter and prayed it wouldn't be the last time.

At the crack of dawn on the last Saturday in May, Rahshaan ushered children who were half asleep out of the house to give Shatima free reign while she got ready for her graduation. Lynn and Selena were there with more curling irons and makeup than he ever paid attention to in his life. He knew those two would have her looking like Miss America by the time she was done.

"Daddy, why can't we go to the graduation?" Anaijah wondered with a yawn as he secured her in her booster seat.

Having one extra voice calling him Daddy made Rahshaan's heart melt. This one struck him in a way he'd never experienced before. The little girl had become the center of his heart.

"It's gonna be long and boring. You gotta stay at Big Grams' house and help her get ready for the party, okay?"

She smiled and nodded her head. Every time she did, he saw his deceased best friend.

"I hope Tima likes the cake we made for her," NyQuest added. "She deserves a nice cake."

"Oh really?" Rahshaan Buckled his seatbelt and looked at his son sitting in the passenger's side of his Jeep. "Why is that?"

"Cuz she works hard. She goes to school *and* work, and she loves us. I would give her a million dollars if I could," NyQuest told his father.

"Well, I would give her a billion trillion dollars!" Jabez piped.

Rahshaan chuckled at them and headed down the road, trying to figure out which route he was going to take. He wanted to take his time getting back, in order to give Shatima and Lynn enough time to do whatever girly stuff they needed to do. He opted to take the city streets rather than jumping on the highway. The city was quiet with the sun barely up. He drove through Nat Turner, turning up Lloyd Banks' *Warrior* as he passed a few boys on the stoop of G-Ma's building. He waved to them. They gave a half salute. It felt funny not living there anymore, but he was glad to have moved on. He wished his grandmother would come with him. He missed being able to look at her every morning and make sure that she was okay. She was too stubborn.

The black Lexus Land Cruiser didn't start following him until he was almost out of the South Side. He was sure of it, because he'd been checking his rearview mirror frequently. The twist in his heart he felt during the ride to and from Albany returned. He reached under the seat to make sure his tool was still there. Nothing was going to ruin this day for Shatima, especially after she told him about missing her high school graduation. If he had to kill someone in broad daylight in order to get to her ceremony and take her to her party, then he would do it twice without blinking. The children kept on with their chatter. They were used to his quiet. Anaijah and Jabez sang a song while NyQuest covered his ears and screamed for them to stop. According to NyQuest, they'd been singing the song since the night before. Unfortunately, Rahshaan wasn't there to confirm it. He was at work. He was always at work.

In the rearview mirror, the Land Cruiser tried to seem inconspicuous with the increasing Saturday morning traffic. Rahshaan kept catching glimpses of it. He slowed down, so that whoever it was could catch up to him. Then he remembered he had a car full of children. Was it undercover police? Normally, his stomach dropped when the police followed him. The feeling he got when this car was behind him was a different feeling, a creepy feeling as though a maniac in a horror movie was following him.

Right outside of Big Grams' gated community was where his stomach dropped. Red and blue lights flashed in the rearview. He pushed the gun into the glove compartment, took out his registration, locked it, pulled over, turned the car off, and rolled down the window. He waited for the officer to approach his car. He knew he'd done nothing wrong.

A white woman with red hair stepped out of the driver's side. "Kind of early for you to be out, isn't it?"

Rahshaan dodged her question and instead asked why she pulled him over.

"Routine traffic stop, sir. May I see your license and registration please?"

"Soon as you tell me what I did that made you pull me over," he insisted as he watched another car pull up behind him. This one was black. Its red and blue lights flashed as well.

"We don't see too many cars like this in this neighborhood," she explained. "Looked kind of suspicious. Where are you headed?"

He bypassed giving her attitude, just to get on with his day. "To drop my kids off at my grandmother's house." NyQuest being in the front seat was reason enough to give him a ticket, but he hoped she'd overlook him.

She peered into the car and stared at the children. They stared at her with quizzical eyes. "You looked like you were headed to that gated community over there."

"I sure was," he declared.

"Seems strange. We don't normally see a lot of cars like this in this neighborhood."

"Jeep Cherokees?" Rahshaan's tone urged her to say what she was alluding to. "I've seen at least five in the driveways up here."

The officer ran her hands over her red hair and stalled for something more to look for. A broken taillight, anything. Both of his smaller kids were in booster seats, so she had nothing to give him a ticket for. "Get to where you're going quickly."

Rahshaan pulled off. When he got to Big Grams's house, he called Kassidy to come get the kids. The Land Cruiser had him on high alert. He hoped no one was following him to plant anything in his car. It was just too big of a coincidence that the police appeared after the Land Cruiser disappeared.

Pregnant belly, glowing skin, and nose contoured to mask the fact that it was spreading from one earlobe to another, Shatima looked marvelous in her cap and gown. She couldn't stop looking at herself in the mirror and smiling. There was still no sign of the purple rings around her eyes. Lynn and Selena cried like babies as they draped Shatima in her black gown and drab hood. Over and over, they gushed about wishing her father was there to see it. She fussed at them, telling them to stop before she ran her makeup. Rahshaan and Shameik just looked at them and shook their heads.

"It's time for us to get a van," Rahshaan remarked as they piled into his Jeep. After his run in with the police that morning, he didn't want to chance them going in separate cars.

"Okay, so we'll take your Jeep to be traded in on Monday and look at vans," Shatima said, and looked away so that he wouldn't see her laughing.

Rahshaan turned around and sneered at her sitting in the seat behind him. He and Shameik took the front. Lynn, Shatima, G-Ma, and Selena were stuffed in the back row. "Why we gotta get rid of Charlene?"

"Why we gotta get rid of my car?" she shot back. "I just got done paying it off. I don't want another car payment."

"Can y'all little ugly asses argue about this later? Damn! Tima's hips are taking up the whole back seat." Lynn shifted around.

"She needs big hips to carry my twins," Rahshaan declared.

The women in the back seat rolled their eyes at him.

They were among the first to get to the convention center. Rahshaan wanted seats right in front. Shatima walked around with them to see where they decided to sit so that she'd know where to look when she walked across the stage. They ran into a news crew setting up.

"Oh excuse me. I'm so sorry. I—" Shatima frowned and looked into her mother's face. She sucked her teeth.

Hope took in her daughter. She wasn't expecting to see her there as a graduate. The belly was too large to go unnoticed, but the pear shaped diamond was what really caught her eyes. It was reminiscent of the one Chillz gave her back when he wanted to give her the world. Shatima was a baby then. Hope hadn't seen her daughter as more than the reason that she would always have Chillz. Looking at her that day, Hope saw a beautiful woman who defied all odds to accomplish greatness. She wasn't sure whether it was the pregnancy or just all around joy, but her daughter had a glow that no bronzer could mimic. Looking at her hand joined with this man's, she saw everything Chillz ever wanted to give her.

"Shatima, I had no idea you were..." Hope's voice got caught in her throat. She surveyed Shatima's belly, the diamond, and the cap and gown.

Shatima stood there looking at the woman, waiting for the insults to start. Her hair was wrong. She wasn't wearing enough makeup. The gown made her look fat. The cap made her head look big. Nothing was said. They just stood there, staring at each other.

Shatima held her head a little higher as if to say, "Yes, bitch. I'm still standing."

"Well, thank you," Hope choked out. Finally, she said, "Congratulations." Her eyes went from Shatima's cap to her honors hood to her belly to her ring finger. Indigence flashed in her eyes.

"Well, thank you," Shatima returned, beginning to slightly recoil under her mother's gaze. It was the first time she realized how much her voice sounded like her mother's. She stepped around her mother and led the crowd away. Hope's eyes were on them until they were out of her sight.

"I always hated that bitch," Shameik mumbled as they walked away, making sure he was just loud enough for Hope to hear.

"What is she doing here?" Selena hissed, her skin turning red. She kept looking over her shoulder to make sure Hope didn't follow them.

"The news covers the graduation every year," Shatima

replied. She could feel Hope's stare, even though they were out of her line of vision.

"Mmm-hmm." Selena looked over her shoulder once again. "And she just so happened to be the one covering it."

"I read that the man delivering the commencement speech just bought the news station where she works and is looking to replace everyone with younger reporters. I *think that*," Shatima said, "she's only here on business. She seemed caught off guard that I was here. You saw her face. She didn't even know I was in school. She thought I was some lost cause with no direction in life. That's what she wanted me to be." She looked directly at Selena. "Please don't waste today focusing on her. Today is supposed to be a happy day. Okay?"

Selena nodded her head. "Okay, baby."

"I mean it," Shatima said sternly. "We're here for the graduation. I know it's easier said than done, but I'm just naive enough to think that lady didn't think enough of me to have something planned for today."

With that sad statement and seeing that her family was sitting in the third row, Shatima joined the mass of people whom she never really got to know. She felt that she should have felt regret for not networking more. The faces blurred themselves and faded with the struggles of the past five years.

As Shatima sat in the sea of graduates, her mind couldn't help but wonder about Hope's presence. Her eyes and mouth rounded when she saw Shatima. Those were certainly signs of surprise. A strange part of her felt joy in her presence. Her biological mother, who didn't think she was capable of accomplishing anything, was there; as was her *real mo*ther, who thought the sky was the limit on Shatima's accomplishments.

"All that's missing is you, Daddy," Shatima whispered to the sky.

When her name was called, announcing that she was officially finished, she wasn't prepared for the amount of noise coming from her small section. She tried not to cry, but a year ago, she wasn't even going to attend the ceremony. She had no one to root for her. But there were five people who really loved her, cheering on her accomplishments. The tears spilled, and the waterproof makeup and setting spray did their job. With her hand on her growing belly, she said, "We did it, babies. Uncle Rize is so proud of us."

"I want ribs," Shatima declared when they were back in Rahshaan's Jeep.

"Tima, this back seat ain't gonna be able to hold you if you eat another thing," G-Ma joked. She reached for Shatima's cap. "What did you do to your hat?"

Shatima smiled. "I just decorated it." She flipped it over so that everyone could see. "It says 'I did it for you' and put all of your names, Unc, Daddy, and Rize. Then I ran out of room and put 'my kids'. Then, with the way this year is going, I put an ellipsis, just in case I had to adopt another child."

Everyone laughed at that.

She watched Rahshaan drive back toward the bridge. "Where are we going? I wanted to go to..."

"You said you wanted ribs, right?" Rahshaan cut her off.

"Yeah."

"Then quit back seat driving."

Rahshaan wasn't sure if Lynn and Selena were able to keep the party a secret or not, so he didn't know what to expect when they pulled up to the Steve Biko Legion. Shatima asked if they were at a carnival, so he knew that they were good for keeping the secret. He pointed out the royal blue and gold decor. Slowly, it came to her.

"Aw y'all gave me a graduation party?"

"Why are you crying?" Lynn demanded.

"Nobody's given me a party since I was nine!" She started sobbing with happiness. They all gave her pitiful expressions.

The smoky smell of slabs of ribs, chicken, burgers, hot dogs, smoked sausage, and seafood wafted through the air when they exited Rahshaan's Jeep. As they walked through the field outside of the three story building, they passed through tables full of gifts and cards. How she would be able thank all of these people was the only thing on her mind as she went through the crowd.

"I hope you don't mind this being a baby shower too," Rahshaan whispered to her. "Somebody said it was tacky to have too many parties where gifts were expected in one year."

"Oh, I don't care about that. This is just one of the happiest days..."

"Don't start crying again," he admonished.

"I know I'm being a big baby, but this time last year it was just me and Jabez, and now..."

"And now, you realize you should've let me be your man a lot sooner." He looked down at her and smirked.

That made her laugh.

After she ate, she was summoned upstairs by Uncle Mont. She was surprised that he was there, but he was in a room on the third floor, watching the party through a window and eating a plate of ribs. Some handsome, tall, light brown boy sat in the room with him, also eating. From the doorway, she could see his profile. He seemed familiar. He mumbled congratulations with a mouth full of food but didn't turn toward her. She smiled and thanked him then continued to Uncle Mont. Butterflies were in her stomach.

"Goddaughter!" he scooped her up into a hug that lifted her off of her feet. "I'm so proud of you." He apologized for not being able to be there, but they both knew the apology wasn't necessary. "I know Chillz and Rize are looking down, even more proud than I am." He motioned for her to sit. She kept trying to catch glimpses of the man sitting with his back to her.

"I'm proud of you too, Tima," the stranger said. "And I'm sorry I cussed you out and said all that fucked up shit to you and hated you for so long."

"Rico?" Shatima guessed while turning her full attention to him. Timidly, she watched him come to her and embrace her.

She tensed, waiting for him to shoot or stab her. Maybe he'd do a combination of both. "You came to see me?"

"I said I'm sorry. Don't make me say it again. I don't apologize too much, but I was wrong about you. I didn't know you went through all that, and you shouldn't have had to."

She looked at Uncle Mont. "You told him?"

"Just the highlights," he said.

Rico's face dropped. "You mean it's more to that story?"

"More than you'll ever wanna know," Uncle Mont told him.

There was an awkward silence between them as they fished for something to say to each other.

"I met your seed earlier," Rico finally said. "My nephew. I gotta get in the habit of calling him that. That's who he is. Yo. He looks just like Pops."

Shatima smiled and nodded. "Yeah, he does. I wish I would have named him after Daddy."

From the picture window in the room, they could see the whole party. Before them a sea of people with smiling faces ate, laughed, and danced. They were all there in celebration of her and an end to her struggle. She didn't want to cry again, but the tears were coming. She'd never been happier.

"What the fuck is that on your finger?" Rico asked, pointing at the pear shaped diamond.

A quick flashback to St. Croix's turquoise waters made her smile. "It's just an 'I'm sorry' ring. Your boy did me dirty and thought he could buy me back."

Rico reached out and rubbed her belly. "Looks like he did."

Feeling her brother's affectionate touch filled her with warmth. "Nah. He just...did all the right things and made everything almost perfect." She stared into the ring, fully immersed in thoughts of turquoise water and white sand.

"Look at your face. You look like Mommy when Daddy asked her to marry him." Rico pointed at one of the corners of her mouth and noted how high up it turned.

"Y'all go outside and enjoy the party," Mont told them. "Tima, I might stop through after if that's aight with you."

"You're always welcome at my house, Unc."

There was never a day in her adult life when Shatima was happier. Her heart was going to burst from the joy that surrounded her. All that time she was alone, there were really people out there who loved her and wanted her to be a part of them. Dwelling on the past should not have been her thing, but she couldn't believe what a stark contrast this scene was to her life last year. Hell, not even a full year ago it was just her and Jabez, maneuvering life as much as her loneliness and depression would let her. But when she really let go and allowed herself to be loved, she found what she denied herself.

"Stop before you shake my babies outta you!" Rahshaan called out to her as she danced in the middle of a circle, a rib in her hand. The people surrounding her cheered at the way she moved despite being pregnant in the late spring heat.

She giggled at him and blew a kiss. The man who walked her to her car every morning was more than what she thought she postponed for a degree and a career. He was the perfect gift.

That party went down in history as one of the best ones the family ever threw. No one wanted to go home when it was time for the event center to close. The family took the celebration to Rahshaan and Shatima's house. While the children ran around the yard, they sat on the porch and talked about everything. Shatima got to know Rico and his girlfriend, Nichelle. Ken-Ken and PeeWee were drunk and had endless stories. Normally, Shatima found Shondell too arrogant to be around, but he was delightful that night amongst the rest of their crew. Moosie and Shameik cracked jokes while Lynn and Selena just sat there laughing. Even Marcus was tolerable that night. Usually, he spent his time chasing women, but he quietly sat and passed a bottle of Crown Royal with Kassidy. Donned in a hoodie, Mont sat on the darkest part of the porch with them and experienced what it was like to just hang out.

"So lemme get this shit straight," a drunken Rico slurred, standing in the middle of the walkway and holding a Corona with one hand and pointing with the other. "You tryna tell me that little girl out there is Rize's seed, and we just now finding out about her?"

"How many times you gonna ask that question, nigga?" Rahshaan growled. He glanced across the porch at Shatima. "I forgot I got one more gift for you, but you better not start crying."

"What is it?" she wondered. She was exhausted, but she didn't want the perfect day to end. Something inside of her worried that after she closed her eyes, she'd never feel this level of perfection again. Scattered about her house not only were her own children, but nieces, nephews, and Moosie even brought Shanae's children so that they could feel like they were a part of something. She wanted all of those children and their parents to stay in that picture perfect moment with her as long as they could.

"You know her ass is gonna cry!" Mont teased while watching them leave.

In the garage, Ken-Ken and PeeWee were setting something up. They quickly departed when Rahshaan and Shatima entered, holding hands. PeeWee teasingly whispered something about Rahshaan being pussy whipped. Ken-Ken snickered. Rahshaan laughed at them both and flicked on a light switch. She stared at a canvas for a long time before speaking. Her favorite song, *Forever My Lady by* Jodeci, played softly on the small stereo she kept out there to keep her entertained while she washed clothes.

"I figured you missed staring at it everyday since we ain't in the hood no more," Rahshaan told her of the painting of her father and her brother.

She looked at him. "*You?* Rahshaan, if I would have known you were the one who did the mural, then I probably would have given you some the first day I moved down there." She turned her focus back to the painting. It wasn't the exact same, yet it was obvious that it was done by the same artist. "I really love it."

He stood behind her and kissed the back of her neck while he wrapped his arms around her. "I got one more gift for you."

"What is it?" She spun around and looked at him through the tears that glazed her eyes.

He took a ring box from his jeans pocket. "Be my wife?" He took the pear shaped diamond from her left ring finger and transferred it to the right. In its place, he put a VVS1 cushion cut. He dropped down to one knee. "Will you marry me?"

She looked from the ring to the canvas and finally into his eyes. "Rahshaan, I have never been as happy as you make me. If I could say yes to being your wife every day for the rest of my life, then I would."

"Does that mean that I get some pussy?" His eyes twinkled.

"What? Our whole family is here," she whispered.

"Then we gotta be quiet and quick."

Before dawn, the men and Moosie left with plans to return later that evening. Lynn and Selena took Shatima's bed, while Nichelle and Shatima slept in recliners. Not wanting to wake up anyone with her insane screaming from her nightmares, Shatima stepped into the garage with a load of clothes. The sound of footsteps startled her. Jabez was in the doorway.

"What's wrong, baby?" she asked.

He smiled. "Nothing. I just wanted to see you."

The sun was starting to rise. She hoped that didn't mean the rest of the children were going to start waking up. They hadn't been to sleep for very long. Jabez walked over to her and climbed on top of the storage cabinet between the washer and dryer.

"Did you like your party, Mommy?" Jabez wondered, stretching.

"I did. Thank you. You're good at keeping secrets." She measured liquid detergent and poured it into the washing machine. "Are you having fun with your cousins?" She rubbed her hand in his braids and watched him nod his head. Then she moved him over so that she was sitting next to him on top of the metal storage cabinet. He put his hand on her belly and then kissed the part of it that he could reach.

"Mommy, I'm glad that you're not sad and lonely anymore," he remarked. "I like seeing you happy."

She held him against her. "I was never lonely; I had you."

"Yeah, but you were always sad. I just wanted you to have some friends, and me too. You never used to let me stay the night anywhere or go anywhere without you."

Quickly the sun rose. The birds were up singing their songs.

It never occurred to her that he wanted to be away from her. "So you're saying you like it better the way it is now?"

"Yeah, because now I get to play with my friends. I got a brother, a sister, and a daddy to keep you company while I go play."

She laughed at the little boy. "When did you become such a social butterfly?"

He looked at her quizzically.

Before she could explain what she meant, she saw a black SUV pull into the driveway. Nausea rushed over her, causing her to run outside of the garage before she spilled the food she ate the night before in the ditch that separated her home's property from her neighbors', she hurled until her stomach ached and her throat was raw. She felt herself being watched, but couldn't look up to see who was in the SUV. Silently, she cussed Rahshaan out for not being there to make her tea that morning. Jabez ran behind her and tried to rub her back the way he saw Rahshaan do it one morning, but his arms were too short.

"Are you okay, Mommy?"

"Yes, baby. The babies must not have liked something I ate last night," she told him. She tried to see if there was any sign of the SUV, but it was gone. She and Jabez sat on the porch for awhile and waited for her nausea to go away completely before she went inside. The SUV was forgotten. It was probably just someone who got turned around, she convinced herself.

Later in the day, Nichelle rode with Shatima to the grocery store to get some food to throw on the grill that evening. Shatima really liked the short, brown woman her brother chose to be the mother of his two children, six year old Tiara and four year old Quentin. It was wild to Shatima that she and two of her brothers had babies at the same age who took that long to meet each other. She always wanted a big family that she could trust for her child.

Rico and Nichelle had been together off and on for a few years. They met shortly after Nichelle graduated from high school. They were more off than on, but were currently in a good place. He followed her down to Virginia after Chillz's murder, but they currently lived at separate addresses. Their relationship worked better that way, according to Nichelle. They were considering moving back to Sanford County, but she was almost certain they would remain at separate addresses, no matter what they decided.

"I think it's dope that you adopted Anaijah," Nichelle said to Shatima as they walked to the butcher's section of the grocery store. "She's so cute, though; I don't see how you could have said no."

Shatima gave a half smile and rubbed her stomach. "Well..."

Nichelle chuckled. "Well, yeah, but besides that. It's nice that you did that. I gave my first daughter up for adoption."

"Really?" Shatima's head turned from the meat selection to Nichelle. "What made you do it?"

"I was too young to have a baby. I got pregnant in high school. I'm surprised you don't remember. You and me went to the same one. Everybody used to talk bad about me for it." She picked up a bottle of marinade and examined the ingredients.

"I'm sorry. If I was one of the ones who said something bad about you, then I apologize. I really don't remember too many people from high school. That time is a blur to me outside of very specific events." She looked at the marinade and shook her head in disapproval.

Nichelle put the bottle of marinade down. "I understand. Rico says the same thing. I remember you, though. We were on the track team together until I got pregnant. You were always quiet and dressed really nice, but people didn't like you because you were with loud mouthed April and thirsty ass..." Her voice trailed off when she looked at Anaijah. "I talk too much. I'm sorry."

"It's okay." Shatima's tone was even. "I guess I really did have my head up my butt, because I didn't realize a lot of people didn't like me because of them. I just used to always hear them call me stuck up, and I don't have time to correct people who don't get to know me, so I just let them think what they wanted." She went to the butcher and placed her order. "May I ask you a question about the adoption?"

"Sure," Nichelle encouraged her.

"Do you ever wonder what happened to your baby and how she turned out?" Shatima was still having a hard time reconciling with Nicolette's request for Shatima to never bring Anaijah to see her again.

Nichelle fished around in her purse for something. "Oh, I keep in touch with the family who adopted her. They send me pictures, and sometimes I talk to her." She pulled a small photo book with Winnie the Pooh on the cover. "Her name is Nakimah. She's seven now."

Shatima cooed over the brown girl with the thickest, kinkiest hair she'd ever seen. She had bright, round, dark brown eyes just like her mother's. "She's a doll." She flipped through the pictures.

"She's smart, too. I couldn't have given her a better life myself." Nichelle put the photo book back in her purse. "I'm going to see her tomorrow. I go visit her twice a year. Every time I see her, I hope that she doesn't ask me why I didn't keep her. I know she's gonna ask me one day, and I don't have an answer that makes sense, especially since I have other children now."

Shatima didn't know what to say to that. She was curious about why people felt so comfortable opening up to her. Since she had no response to that, she changed the subject. "Do you think you and my brother will ever get married?"

Indignantly, Nichelle shook her head. "Girl, me and your brother just try to make it to the end of the week and take it from there. We fight much too much, mostly about my oldest daughter. He wanted me to go back and get her once I told him about her, but that ain't his baby to make that decision. I did what made sense for me and her at the time. I'm not about to shake up that little girl's life. The people who adopted her are rich, and they have a lot of kids that love her, and that's her family." She took the order from the butcher and started loading it into their cart. "But I guess it was good for me to come up here and meet you, because seeing what you did for Rize proves that he would have done the same thing for me. He probably would have taken her and raised her right, just like you do for all of your children. It seems like that's just how y'all are, from Big Grams to Banger's grandmother down to Selena, and now you. I don't know if I have the heart y'all do to take in other people's kids."

Shatima called out to Anaijah and Tiara, who were trying to wander off to find the candy aisle. The girls came running back and took her hand. They picked out some snacks for the kids and made sure that they had enough paper products before leaving the store and loading the car. A black SUV was parked next to their car. An ugly feeling spun around in Shatima's stomach and weakened her knees. She dropped onto the pavement and crawled far enough away from her groceries to keep them clean before she vomited again. The black SUV ripped out of the parking lot.

For the second night in a row, Mont came over to spend time

with the family. They loved having him in the midst of things for a change. Whatever he had to go through to get across that bridge unnoticed was more than appreciated. The more the family came together, the more they wanted it complete again. They were willing to go to war to have it.

It was another perfect night. The children ran around in the backyard playing while the adults sat on the back patio, slapping mosquitoes and calling the children back so that they could spray another layer of bug repellant on them. The humid air tempted them to go inside, but they enjoyed sitting under the stars too much. Ken-Ken and PeeWee served as the night's entertainment. The two of them had endless stories that kept everyone laughing until they cried. At the moment, they weren't worried about children being kidnapped or any of the other bad news they heard around town. It was the break they needed.

PeeWee was in the middle of a story when they heard glass shatter in the garage. Everyone jerked their heads to the sound. The adults drew their guns. As they ran towards the front yard, they saw a black SUV speed away. Moosie said she was sure it was the one that followed them to and from Albany. Shatima knew it was the one that parked next to them at the grocery store. Nichelle agreed. Shameik, Moosie, and Shondell jumped into Shondell's car and tore off into the night. The remaining women gathered the kids and rushed them into the house. Uncle Mont took post outside of Shatima's bedroom where she herded the children. Shatima and Nichelle tried to get them to go to sleep, but they were too afraid. Shatima instructed Nichelle to take them into the windowless family room turned on a movie in hopes that it calmed them.

While Nichelle and Selena got the children settled, Shatima went into the back of her walk-in closet and retrieved a locked box from her top shelf. She hadn't touched it since the night she pulled it on those girls in her apartment. Rahshaan came into the room and called out to her. She told him where she was, and he entered the closet behind her.

"I forgot you even had that," he remarked.

"Good. I don't want the kids to know it's here either, but I'll use it if I have to."

Rashaan's phone rang. He walked outside to meet Shameik. Shatima went into the family room with the children and sat in a recliner in a corner. She hoped none of the children saw what was sitting beside her. Lynn caught Shatima's eye from across the room; her hand was in her purse. Selena sat in the back of the room with one hand behind her back. Nichelle didn't even hide her gun. She kept it in her lap and told the children to pay attention to the movie, not her.

Uncle Mont walked into the room, startling the women. He held his hands up and asked them to meet them outside after he made Marcus take post with the kids.

Shatima waddled into the garage to assess the damage with Rahshaan. Two My Buddy dolls with bricks tied to them were what shattered the glass. Both had the seats of their pants and the stuffing ripped out of them. One had no head. The brick tied to the headless doll had Rize's name painted onto it. The other brick had Jabez's name painted on it. Shatima got nauseous all over again. Her skin crawled when she realized who the culprit was. For years, she knew that the father of her child would return, but she never formed a concrete plan on how to handle it. She thought she'd be alone when it happened. Being surrounded with family did nothing to make her feel safer.

Lights came on at the houses on either side of them. Neighbors stepped outside in pajamas and bathrobes. Some stepped lightly to the edges of their yards and timidly asked what happened while craning their necks. Others stood at the curbs with their arms folded while they shook their heads and mumbled about "South Ridge trash" bringing gang and drug wars to their doorstep.

"This ain't that kind of neighborhood," one man wearing a stocking cap fussed at them, his slippers sliding across the grass. "Take your gang activity somewhere else."

"Gang activity?" Shatima yelled. "Somebody just threw a brick through my window, and you think my family is in the wrong?"

Rahshaan stepped in front of her and told her to chill out. He politely asked the man to leave so that they could take care of his family's issue. The man kept charging toward them, telling them they needed to take their violence out of "his" neighborhood. People looked on. No one was bold enough to vocalize agreement, but no one was in a rush to defend Shatima and Rahshaan either.

"Look at Tima's car!" Rico called and rushed down the driveway. "They slashed her tires and smashed the side of it." He turned to the crowd outside. "What are y'all out here for now? You ain't have nothing to say when somebody was out here fuckin my sister's shit up?"

"Rico!" Mont called from the doorway. "Fuck them folks and get over here before we have to fuck somebody up, and we all end up in jail tonight."

Mont called Derrick, who had a small group of officers coming to take a look at things. Mont then had Marcus drive him home before his face was seen. Rico, Shameik, and Rahshaan walked around with Shatima to look at her car and see if anything else was damaged.

"I can't believe that out of all of these people standing out here, ready to crucify me for being attacked, nobody saw who did this!" Shatima cried out, hoping that her tone would make them back off. The people were more concerned with knowing how long it would be before she cleaned up the glass. No one offered to help. They just stood around and sneered, as if to silently ask when she was going to move out and give them back their peace. It didn't pay to be the so-called princess of the hood if the title was non-transferrable.

Three cop cars pulled up, followed by an unmarked black Chevy Impala. Derrick hopped out of the Impala and went to Rahshaan. He introduced himself to Shatima as Rico's godfather, but Shatima wasn't in the mood for a family reunion. While everyone else ran to Derrick to give him their version of the story, Shatima retreated and let Rahshaan do the talking. She couldn't keep her eyes off his badge and what it represented. Her family seemed so sure that he'd be able to do something about what happened that night. She wondered why they thought the report would even get filed.

Derrick and his small team looked around the house and assessed the damages, noting things the family missed previously like the words "GIVE ME MY SON!!!" etched into the passenger's side of the car. The more damages they rattled off, the more she wondered how those people were able to get away with so much without one person noticing.

A fourth cop car pulled behind the others. From the look on his face, this car wasn't a part of Derrick's team. He cursed under his breath and approached the car. When the driver got out, Shatima saw her mother's boyfriend and the redhead who tried to recruit her. She and Kimborough caught each other's eyes. Kimborough's lips contorted into a wicked smile. Shatima returned it with a dirty look.

"Hello, Santarez. Kimborough," Derrick greeted them. "You weren't called for this, so how may I help you?"

"We figured we could help you," Kimborough told him before Santarez said something dirty.

Derrick looked at his team. "We've got it covered. I'm sure you have other things to do."

Santarez stepped forward. "I think we can help you take a look around, question some people. Maybe your investigation will help ours." He started toward the house.

"What investigation would that be?" Derrick challenged him, stepping in front of him. "Would it have anything to do with the townhouse you rented out a few months ago in Midtown that had the missing boys in it?"

Santarez froze. Everyone watched the match of wits between the two men. He narrowed his eyes and glared at Derrick.

Considering what he was up against, he backed down. "Check the house for drugs!" he shouted. "I know there's drug trafficking going through that house, and I don't think the good people of this neighborhood want to deal with that."

The neighbors standing around in their robes, pajamas, and slippers exchanged concerned glances. Their lips turned downwards in disapproving frowns. They pointed at Rahshaan, saying they knew he was a drug dealer. He was used to the assumptions and let them roll off of his back. Shatima, however, was not about to let them talk about the man who gave her everything like that. Her pointer finger shot out, and she stalked toward him.

"Don't you come down here lying on my family. You're probably responsible for all of this. How did you know to come down here anyway?"

Derrick raised his eyebrows in anticipation of his answer.

"This isn't even your area to patrol!" Shatima continued. "Don't you need to be down in Nat Turner, making sure no more boys get kidnapped, or are you over here doing *somebody's dir*ty work, trying to see if you can *expand your territory* and find some new meat to snatch up?"

Santarez turned bright red under the street lights. "You don't know what you're talking about, so close your mouth, little girl."

Derrick stepped in front of Shatima to shield her and then guided her backward with his arm. "The question is valid. What are you doing here?"

Kimborough spoke up. "We heard a call. We responded to it. Now do you want our help or not?"

Derrick eyed her. "We've got it under control. Stay in your zone. I'd hate to hear someone got kidnapped or murdered because you guys weren't there to prevent it. That's what we're here to do, right? Protect people, not make unfounded accusations."

Santarez and Kimborough planted themselves in the middle of the street, their expressions apathetic.

"Okay. Come on. Poke around. See what you can find," Derrick called their bluff. "Make sure you turn your report in to Chief Lyles first thing Monday morning. He's the one who sent me down here."

Kimborough turned on her heels and got back into her car. Santarez stalled a little before following her.

As the police investigated, Shatima packed bags for her family. Then, she helped Nichelle get her kids' things together. She and Rico were staying in a hotel, so Shatima figured that she would book a room there too. That way, the kids would be distracted by being surrounded with cousins. They'd think it was a mini vacation. Rahshaan, her brothers, and their friends could pack up the house and put things in storage during the day. She could look for a new house when she wasn't working.

Rahshaan's mind was on a different plane. They went to G-Ma's house. Shatima and the kids stayed in one room. Nichelle and her kids stayed in another. G-Ma got the kids settled down while Shatima and Nichelle went outside and stood on the stoop with Moosie and the men to see what was going on. All of their eyes were burgundy, blazing with anger from the attacks and accusations. The night air was thick and sticky. Sweat poured down Moosie and Shondell's heads. Their white t-shirts were drenched.

"That was definitely the same truck that followed us out of town, fam," Moosie insisted, stomping her feet. "I'm telling you."

"Well what happened to them?" Shatima butted in.

"Derrick got 'em," Moosie replied. "He'll be through here in a minute."

Derrick drove up and stopped his car in front of the stoop. "They said Andrew hired them," he told them. "They're from Chavez. Gasoline and lighters were found in the car. They said they were working alone, but we've got cars patrolling the house for the rest of the night. Make sure you get everything you value out of the house in the morning. You can't go back after that. It's not safe for your kids there."

In the morning, their landlady beat them to the house. The short woman wore an acidic expression on her face and hands on her hips. Her bottom lip poked out as she looked at them through one open eye.

"I expected more from you." Her pointer finger was extended in Shatima's direction. "You sit on that third pew with Mother Glover every week, crying and carrying on in church, and then you lay with drug dealers the rest of the week."

"Get your finger out of my face," Shatima told her without blinking. "I expected more from you, too. You sit in that church every week and judge people you don't know. I expected to live in a neighborhood where my children would be safe. Instead, we got met with victim blaming and unfounded accusations. Not one drug or drug dealer has passed through these doors since we've been living here. But maybe you can tell me who these people were that did this to the house I was supposed to be living in comfortably with my family. Seems kind of strange that I could live in the projects all that time without anything happening to me, but the minute I move into this fake bougie neighborhood, I'm in danger."

Rahshaan stood off to the side, waiting to interject, but he was so impressed by the way Shatima spun the whole thing around that he became a spectator. Every time the woman hurled an accusation at her, Shatima volleyed with their tenants' rights in New York State. When the argument went on for too long, he asked the woman how long it would be until they saw their security deposit. She didn't have an answer, so Shatima told her they would see her in court. He'd never witnessed anyone cussing someone out without actually cussing. The already short woman looked half her height by the time they left her that day.

They split their belongings between Selena's and Lynn's basements and alternated between their houses and G-Ma's apartment while waiting for Mont to tell them when and where they could move. Mont never cared for the stiff Southview neighborhood they chose when they moved out of Nat Turner. This time he wanted somewhere better for them, somewhere that felt like an actual home.

———

Andrew and Loretta sat by their father's bedside, watching him struggle to sleep. His chest rattled when he inhaled. He seemed to be shrinking by the minute. Hope entered the room and stood off to the side with her hands folded reverently. The scent of her perfume must have awakened Tennessee, because he opened his eyes and looked directly at her.

"You were always my favorite," he told her.

"Oh, that's very sweet of you, Tennessee. You know I've always had the utmost respect for you." She pushed her way in between Loretta and Andrew and smoothed out their father's comforter. "The girl has sent her daughter to live with mine. Soon we'll be able to confirm that Mont is alive."

"What if the girl runs her mouth to the wrong people?" Tennessee asked.

Hope smiled at Andrew. "Well, Tennessee, you would be very impressed with your son's fear tactics. Andrew has that girl too afraid to breathe her own breath, let alone tell what we did to her."

"And the last shipment made it out okay?" Tennessee stared at the ceiling.

"Miguel shipped the boys down to California, and the money for them was wired to Channel 3's advertising account yesterday. Loretta deposited it into your account this morning," Andrew reported.

"Good," Tennessee remarked, never looking in Andrew's direction. "There's a chance I may be able to die rich and innocent after all."

In the midst of everything that happened, it was important for Shatima to make sure Anaijah transitioned smoothly. Having a daughter brought on a new insecurity. She wanted to be the opposite of what Hope was to her: critical, stifling, and abusive. The little girl never asked about her old family, and Shatima found it odd. With each passing day, she looked more like the reincarnation of Rize.

Anaijah clung to Rahshaan more than Shatima. Whenever he came home, she was the first to run to him and hug him. She couldn't sleep until he came home. Sometimes, Shatima had to hold her and promise her that her daddy would be back by the time she woke up. When he went on overnight trips, Anaijah didn't understand. She didn't think she was safe unless her daddy was there to watch over her. But she also loved spending "girl time" with Shatima, where they would leave the boys at home and go do things like get their hair and nails done or take ballet at Selena's dance school.

The bonding was more for the mother's sake than the daughter. Shatima was slightly jealous of how Anaijah's relationship with Rahshaan was. She thought that Anaijah's magnetic clinging to him would result in a second generation of what she went through with Hope and Chillz. The last thing she wanted to be was a mother whose daughter despised her. If Anaijah one day decided that she didn't like getting her nails done and going to dance classes, then Shatima would find something else for them. She just wanted to be as much of a friend as she was a parent. Through the transition, she never wanted her daughter to be lonely.

Anaijah came running into Hair Revolution ahead of Selena. Everyone smiled at the cutie pie in her pink leotard and tutu. From her station, where she was curling a woman's hair, Shatima threw her mother a sidelong glance.

"You just had to get the pink one?" She smiled at her daughter. "You look pretty, Ny."

Anaijah smiled. "Thank you, Mommy."

"Mommy" was still weird to Shatima. She thought the little girl would call her "Tima" just like NyQuest did, but she followed Jabez's lead instead. It was like the little girl didn't want to remember that she had a life before the day she got dropped off in the hamburger restaurant.

"Ny, come here and let me paint your nails *pink* like your tutu!" Antoinette knew how much Shatima hated pink and used that as a moment to tease her. Shatima cut her eyes at Antoinette but smiled.

Selena sat in Lynn's chair. She thoroughly enjoyed her grandmother role, although she opted for the kids to call her "Lena" rather than Grandma. She was way too young and fine for her official title. "Have you heard from your Uncle yet?"

"Please don't ask me about that nigga." Shatima's tone soured instantly. She looked at Selena and apologized. "I didn't mean to take that out on you, and I know it's not really his fault either, but I am so sick of living out of suitcases and three different houses."

"Bitch, we know. You make it known every time you come through one of our doors," Lynn piped up.

"I apologize. It's just that I was ready to start decorating the nursery. Every time I ask Unc, though, he tells me he needs more time, and I'm so tired of not knowing when I'm gonna have my own address." She parted the woman's hair and curled it with the iron.

"I just can't get over how much you've gone through this year," Selena went on. "Unc can't either, which is why he's trying to set up something nice for you. You definitely deserve a peaceful house if nothing else. I mean, you took in somebody else's children."

"So did you," Shatima pointed out. "Five of us."

"Yeah, but not like you did. You beat up both of their mamas, and now their kids call you Mommy." Selena looked in the mirror and tried to decide what she wanted done to her hair.

"Yeah, Tima, I don't know if I could drop a ho and then have to sign her child's permission slips," Antoinette chimed in. There was no such thing as a private conversation in Hair Revolution.

"You'd leave a baby out in the world, Antoinette?" Shatima wondered.

"I would," Shatima's client piped up, and everyone laughed.

"I don't know," Antoinette replied. "I just know that you got a real good heart."

"Yes, Miss Tima. God is gonna bless you. Just you wait," Haddus agreed as he mixed a fiery red chemical for his client's hair.

"What you know about God, Haddus?" Shatima asked without looking up.

Haddus gave her a look that she didn't notice. "What you mean, what I know about God?" His Southern accent stood out, showing that he was offended.

"You're gay. You can't be gay and serve God." Everyone looked at her like she'd lost her mind as she absently pinned her client's curls. She looked around at all the eyes on her and frowned. She saw nothing wrong with the question.

Holding his rattail comb as though it were a machete, Haddus glared at her. "Now look here, you homophobic heffa. I put up with your dirty looks and you acting like that lesbian that sits in your chair every Wednesday has a disease, but what you won't do is act like I don't love Jesus because I'm attracted to men. I watched you beat the shit out of a bitch over a nigga that you ain't married to, but you think I *can*'t serve The Lord because of who I sleep with? Fuck you, Shatima. You ain't no more Christian than me, and it would do you some good to remember that. Now, I've put up with you because you're Miss Lynn's niece, but I'll cut you if you ever question my relationship with God again. Do we have an understanding?"

Stunned, all Shatima could do was nod her head. She wasn't expecting to be told off like that, especially not by Haddus of all people. He normally steered clear of her bitchiness, whether it was directed toward him or not. It occurred to her then that he picked up on her homophobia and was offended by her ways.

The thick air in the shop took hours to dissipate. No one commented on how Shatima had been told about herself except Lynn, who stood at her station cackling obnoxiously. In between manicures, Antoinette kept looking at Shatima, wondering if she'd ever be able to pick up her face off the floor. Nobody messed with her BFF.

Toward the end of the day, the shop was back to buzzing with its normal gossip. Someone who looked like he stepped off of a magazine cover came into the shop. The man with Hershey bar smooth skin and baby dreads was so fine that he seemed to be moving in slow motion. He smelled of cocoa butter, sandalwood, and Heaven. Every rip and chisel that made his upper body was exposed by the fitted white shirt he wore. Antoinette charged twenty-five dollars to create eyebrows as perfect as his. With his legs taking long strides, he walked toward the back of the shop. Antoinette waved at him.

He said, "Hey sexy," but it was obvious he wasn't talking to her by the way he patted her on her shoulder and kept going. He stopped at Haddus and pecked him on the lips.

"You look good," Haddus told him. "You must have had a shoot today?"

"Oh, baby. I don't look half as good as you," the god on Earth returned the compliment. "You got time to tighten my dreads? I do have a shoot tomorrow, and I wanted to spend some time with you."

"Well you know you're always welcome to spend time down here in the shop with me, but my chair is only for paying clients. Take me out to eat - somewhere expensive, of course - and I'll do your hair tonight."

Shatima sat there and watched as the mold for the entire male species stood there rubbing Haddus' head while Haddus talked to him like some trick off the streets. She couldn't get over how handsome the man was. Juxtaposed with him, Haddus wasn't too bad to look at either. As they stood there embracing, they looked like the picture of black love, and Shatima was surprisingly okay with it. There was still a lot that she was missing, though.

"Well, I'm gonna go get some coffee while I wait, because this is a long day for me. Can I get anybody anything?" He left the shop and went to the cafe down the street.

"Haddus..." Shatima hissed as she watched the door close behind the man's fine physique.

Haddus signaled for her to stop with his hand. "Don't peep me because you can't be me." He turned to her. The smirk on his face was purely diabolical. "Didn't think I could pull one better than what you got, did you?"

"Boy, please. You know it don't get no better than what I got at home." She said it to save face, but she was still stuck on how attractive Haddus' man was.

"Miss Tima, please." His use of her nickname let her know that they were cool again. "Banger aight, but until you cleaned him up, he used to walk around looking like he got into a fight with the whole world. Jacoby - that's my baby's name - is perfect and polished."

"But he don't act like..." Her voice trailed off. In an attempt to not offend him again, she chose her words carefully.

"A sissy?" Haddus finished for her.

"No. I don't even use that word," Shatima said. "I just thought that-"

"You *thought th*at all gay men walked around shrieking, giggling, and crossing our legs like little ballerinas, didn't you?" He waited for her to deny it. "Well, while there are some femmes, I'm not attracted to them."

"Then how do you know who's the man and who's the woman?" Shatima wondered.

Haddus looked at her like she just licked the school bus window. "Tima, it is a man on man relationship. Ain't no woman! Ain't no need for somebody to play the role of a woman if nobody's attracted to women."

Shatima considered this. "I still don't understand."

"That's because you're still stuck in what you were taught is normal. If you opened your mind, you would see that ain't nothing for you to understand cuz it ain't your business. Everything ain't about the way you're used to seeing it." He forcefully added, "And while we're on the subject, all gay men ain't child molesters and kidnappers."

"I know," she said, her head hanging low as she wondered what she did to make him feel the need to say that.

"Good. Because with everything that's going on in this town and in your life, I don't want you to get the wrong idea." He walked over to her and gave her a tiny hug. She felt bad about him coddling her after she insulted him earlier. "You good peoples, Miss Shatima Thomas. I like your little swag. You just gotta stop being so uptight and realize my life and lifestyle are nothing for you to understand or accept. They just are a part of life, just like yours."

"What a long day!" Shatima exclaimed as Rahshaan helped her

into his truck. "Sure would be nice to be climbing into *my own bed* and getting my feet rubbed in *my own bed*."

Rahshaan looked to the sky for help. When she was tired, she took it out on him. Lately, she seemed tired all of the time. The August heat only added to her meanness. "What did the doctor say this morning?"

"Well, if you were there, you would know that she said I need my own bed so that I can go on bed rest," Shatima snapped. "In the beginning, you were damn near going to the appointments for me. Now, you can't be bothered."

An alarm went off in Rahshaan's head while he ignored her accusation. "Bed rest? This early? What's wrong?"

She waved him off. "I'll be in my third trimester next month, and my blood pressure was high this morning. I told her it won't be high once I'm in *my own bed,* in my own house, so call your uncle and tell him that. Maybe things will move a little bit faster." She waited for him to strap Anaijah in her booster seat and get behind the wheel. "It would also be nice to have a car that can hold all of our children, since I don't have one."

"Are you done?" Rahshaan blew each word out of his mouth slowly.

She shifted her weight in her seat. "No, but I can hold if you have good news for me." She looked at him from the corner of her eye.

He shook his head and laughed at her as he pulled away from the shop. Nagging him about the new address and new car seemed to serve as a sexual stimulant for her, because after the kids went to sleep, the insults stopped, and she climbed on him, refusing to get off of him until he was completely drained. It didn't matter that they were in other people's homes. The trade off from the crazy woman to the sex deviant was well worth all the attitude. For fear that the sex would decrease once the source of anger decreased, he almost wanted to wait until the babies' birth to move and replace her vehicle.

They pulled into the familiar parking lot in Nat Turner.

Negative air bled from Shatima's nose and mouth. She tried not to say anything. Their living arrangements weren't Rahshaan's fault. He was doing the best that he could with their circumstances. Thinking about how many flights of stairs she had to carry her babies up lit a match within her.

"Rahshaan, please look at me," she started on him.

Slowly, he turned his head to her and waited for his nightly decapitation.

"How are you doing?" she asked, instead of cussing him out. "I know I've been very mean to you, and I'm sorry. I'm just worried about everything. You especially."

"I'm good, Ma. You ain't got nothing to worry about." He took her hand and kissed it. "You and Ny can wait right here. I'm going to get Jay and Quest."

"Where we going?" She started dancing in her seat.

He tried to stifle his smile. "Just wait until I get back."

The drive to The Valley took no more than five minutes. It was a little livelier neighborhood than their previous one. Despite it getting dark, children were still outside playing. Parents sat watching them on porches. One family had a game of Spades going and drinks set in front of them. Rahshaan kept driving until he got to a stucco and brick Spanish style house with a freshly mowed lawn and a turquoise minivan. She marveled at the candy paint, rubbing her hand along it.

"Why would you?"

"Because you were in your feelings about having to get rid of your punk ass Maxima, so I had to do something to make your van sexy. I ain't giving up my Jeep. That bitch been with me through some hard times."

She sucked her teeth and continued toward the house. Its backyard was even bigger than the last house's. The kids' swing set was there, and their patio furniture sat on a deck. There was enough room for an above ground swimming pool. From the outside, she was in love with the house.

The kids ran inside. Shatima and Rahshaan strolled behind

them, holding hands. Her feet were swollen, but she wanted to see as much of the house as she could. She started to laugh when she saw how he tried to put everything the way she had it in their last house. This house was different, though, bigger. She could do even more decorating. Walking through the foyer, she planned to put 10" x 13" pictures of each of the children on the walls. There was a fireplace with a mantle. The painting Rahshaan gifted her sat in the perfect place on top of it. This was the most at home she had felt in a physical place in her life.

The first floor of the house continued to impress her. For the first time in her adult life, she had a separate kitchen and dining room. There was a dishwasher, and she kissed Rahshaan right there for that. He tried to wash dishes before going back to work in the evenings, but she hated going to bed with dishes in the sink if he didn't finish. He told her there was a bedroom on the first floor and two in the basement. She'd figure out what she wanted to do with them later. She really wanted to finish the tour of the home, but her feet were killing her. The important thing was that they had their own address. Finally, she could sleep in her own bed. She insisted he take her to their bedroom.

"It's turquoise," she remarked excitedly, squeezing his hand. "You painted it all by yourself?"

"Hell no." He led her to their bed and took her shoes off. It was a ritual for him to rub her feet every night before she went to sleep. "Rico and Shameik helped. Me and the whole crew have been coming over here for a few hours every day getting shit together."

"I didn't even have to make one phone call about a house. You're a dream man. Marry me and have five of my babies, please?"

He laughed at her and told her he was going out to get them something to eat. She'd be asleep by the time he got back, but she'd eat later. Before she dozed off, she called Mont and told him that her father chose the greatest man in the world to look after her in his absence.

In the middle of the night, Rahshaan came home to find Shatima sitting in a rocking chair in NyQuest's room. He imagined she'd been in each of the kids' rooms, watching over them the way she was watching over NyQuest.

"Why you still up, sexy?" he asked her.

"Couldn't sleep, so I was just waiting for you." She got out of the rocking chair and followed him down the hall to their bedroom. "Do you see these floors? I never thought I'd have a house like this."

"Didn't you grow up in a house like this?" he remarked.

"Not really. There was no love in it. This house is full of love." She ran her hands against the walls and stopped to look in Jabez's room and then Anaijah's. The tears came. She laughed at how silly it was that she cried about everything, and then she cried some more. "I wish my daddy was here to see how happy you make me."

Rahshaan walked ahead of her before he started crying too. They climbed into their bed together. He rubbed olive oil on her skin just as G-Ma instructed him. "Your pops the one who taught me how to be a father."

"He did an excellent job." With her eyes closed, she exhaled the pleasure she felt from him rubbing the oil on her belly.

"When Monaysia was pregnant, he sat me down and wrote a list of everything it would cost to take care of a baby. He could see right through her and knew we weren't going to last, whether Quest really was mine or not, so he tried to make sure I didn't get caught up the same way your moms did him. I guess it worked out in the end."

"Yup. I guess it did," she agreed. "Or maybe... Maybe he was preparing you to be the father to his grandchildren. I don't believe in coincidences anymore. Everything that's happened this year was the culmination of something..." Her voice trailed off and gave way to snoring. Rahshaan kissed her belly, told the babies he loved them, and went to sleep alongside her.

———

Dressed in a tight black shirt that boasted the little bit of muscles he did have and a pair of Levis, Andrew shyly entered the club. He preferred quiet evenings spent reading and listening to classical music or at the theater, but those weren't places he could pick up dates. Every now and again he went out to see what kind of people he attracted. Once upon a time, someone he deeply admired told him women checked him out. He wondered, then, why they didn't approach him. Out of the two women he had in his lifetime, it was his job to make the first move and impress them. That type of unfairness made him decline women, though he certainly found them attractive.

With a book in his hand, Andrew sat at the bar and ordered a Screwdriver. He watched the bartender, who was dancing while making his drink. He pulled club-goers up on the bar to dance with him in between filling orders. The bartender seemed to be so loved by everyone. Andrew wondered what it was like to be the center of attention like that.

"Reading at the bar? Who forced you to come out here?"

Andrew looked into a face carved from onyx and a head adorned with baby dreads. "I needed a drink and some atmosphere but didn't necessarily feel like participating in the festivities."

"I heard there was something else that you look for when you come out to this place." The man sat down next to Andrew. "My name is Jacoby, and I'm looking for work."

"What type of employment are you seeking, and what makes you think I can provide it?" Andrew asked.

"Oh. My apologies. I see you down here in this bar every week and thought you were a recruiter. I was merely offering my services."

Andrew sipped his Screwdriver. When he looked up, he was met by the flaming retinas of the bartender.

"OOOH, NIGGA, YOU AIN'T GONNA BELIEVE THIS SHIT."

Rahshaan and Shatima got a permanent address at the perfect time for Derrick. He called a mandatory family meeting at their house. At the door, he was met by Shatima's frowning face. He was already annoyed that talking to Rahshaan meant that he'd have to stand outside in the heat rather than in the air conditioned house. Dealing with the young lady Uncle Mont generously described as cold was another obstacle to get around. He wanted to like her, but she looked so much like her mother that seeing her face made him angry. It was probably for the best. Him being a police officer meant that she'd never fully trust him.

"Rahshaan's not here yet," she told him.

"Did he tell you I was coming?" Derrick was hopeful.

She nodded. "Go ahead to the back. He's probably on his way. I'll call him to see how far away he is."

After finding out that Rahshaan was five minutes away, she took a Heineken out to Derrick and wordlessly set it on a coaster in front of him. The two of them sat at the wooden patio table in silence. He snuck little peeks at her here and there. Each glimpse he caught of her diminished her mother's features and amplified her deceased father's. After a while, she looked like that baby Chillz couldn't be seen without. The bitterness he previously felt toward her diminished. It was his job to protect her.

"Aunt Lynn is bringing Mommy over," Shameik came into the backyard and announced. "Somebody's been calling her house looking for you and hanging up when she tells them you're not there. It sounded like your mother."

"How the hell did my mother get her number?" Shatima wondered. "And why the hell is she bothering Selena?"

"Because the bitch is fuckin looney," Derrick declared. He looked at Rahshaan. "Do we need to go out further in the back, or can I start talking?"

Rahshaan looked out at the kids playing. He didn't want to disturb their fun. Throwing a hand in the air, he said, "Go ahead."

Since they were already on the subject of Hope, Derrick opened with her. The Land Cruiser that trailed them was rented in her name. It was unclear what her goal was. There seemed to be an interest both in what Rahshaan was doing and where Shatima was. Right before the bricks and dolls shattered the window, Hope called the police and reported the vehicle stolen. She came down to the police station, causing a ruckus about the stolen vehicles many times within the weeks following the incident.

The boys were still in jail for the theft. No one posted their bail, and they had prior arrests. Both denied knowing who Jabez was or why they were vandalizing someone's house. They were both living with drug addictions and were provided with them as long as they carried out jobs. One said they were doing it for Hope. The other claimed they were working with someone else. They trembled at the thought of being released from jail, but wouldn't say why. Both of them were from the Chavez Projects and were terrified to go home.

"I've got somebody pumping them for more information. I thought they were some missing boys, but they're both over the age of twenty. That's not Andrew's normal targeted demographic. I checked their names in the missing persons registry, and neither of them were listed. There's a rumor floating around that Andrew has been poking around the gay clubs, paying for people to help him snatch up young boys. People he asks to do it are turning up dead or missing before I have a chance to confirm that, though."

"So that's it? After weeks of wondering, this is all the information that we get?" Shatima's outburst wasn't meant to be as ungrateful as it sounded. "Andrew is targeting my son, and—"

A chorus of whoas sounded around the table.

"Tima, how do you know who Andrew is?" Shameik demanded.

Rahshaan ran his hand over his face. "Oh, nigga. You ain't gonna believe this shit," he said under his breath. His comment took the attention off of Shatima for a split second.

Shatima clenched her fists and put them in front of her face. Rahshaan wouldn't be able to fight them all off, and she wasn't sure he'd want to. She wrung her hands. "Andrew is Jabez's biological father."

"Call that shit what the fuck it is!" Rahshaan exclaimed. "You were sixteen, and he was like 40. That nigga raped you. That nigga came into your room and forced himself on you until you got pregnant, and then he told you he was coming back for your baby to do the same shit he did to you."

"Nigga, you knew that shit and ain't tell nobody?" Shameik exploded.

"Shameik, could you please chill out?" Shatima begged. She gave Rahshaan a stern look, wondering why he blurted that out at a time when emotions were already high.

Everyone around the table just sat there staring, unblinking, unmoving, not sure what to make of the news. Rahshaan turned to Rico, his glare implicating his friend of his past crime. Rico turned his back to them.

"Rize knew, and that's why Rize is dead," Rico said to nobody in particular. He peeked at his sister then looked away. Neither wanted to revisit their argument from the year prior.

"Y'all better not look at my son no different," Shatima said firmly. "I'd hate to have to beat one of your asses for looking at my son side-eyed."

Quickly, they assured her that they'd never blame her or Jabez for where he came from.

"Damn. That nigga was so obsessed with Pops that he even went after his daughter," Shameik surmised. "We thought the women were safe."

Derrick sat there, writing down everything Shatima told him about her encounter with Andrew. It felt strangely cathartic. After her prior ordeal with trying to report him to the police, she never thought she'd receive justice. Her thoughts went to Nicolette. She didn't want to bring her into it unless she agreed to it.

"Excuse me, Derrick. I have a phone call to make. I promise it's related to this. I'll be right back."

She excused herself and went into her bedroom to get her cell phone. As she climbed the stairs, Lynn led a crying Selena through the front door. For a second, Shatima felt self conscious about having company before she had her house picture perfect, but there was something more important going on. Selena's hair stood on top of her head, her golden complexion replaced with the color of cardinal feathers.

"It's happening again," she whispered. "It's happening just like the day your daddy was murdered."

With Lynn following them, Shatima grabbed Selena's hand and took her upstairs. Her fingers trembled as she tried to dial Nicolette's number and rub Selena's back at the same time. Somehow, she finally got the number to go through. Nicolette was nasty to her when she answered the phone.

"Tima, I just want this shit to be over! I don't want to hear that man's name anymore!" Nicolette coughed and sputtered.

"I'm spitting up blood, Shatima. Blood! What else do you want from me?"

"I don't want anything *from* you, Nicolette. I want justice for you. For us. For our children." She ran her hands through Selena's hair. It was amazing to her that she wasn't breaking down with the rest of the women.

"I'm sorry, Shatima. I don't have the same luck you do. I'll never be able to bounce back like you. Between him doing this to me and your mother—"

"My mother?" Shatima sat up. "What did my mother do to you? Nicolette? Hello? Nicolette?" She was met with the announcement that Nicolette ended their call. When she dialed the number again, it went straight to voicemail. Over the next few days, it would do the same thing until Shatima figured out that Nicolette blocked her number. She was sure then that Nicolette left out a huge chunk of her story when she gave her Anaijah to raise. Though their friendship ended long ago, Shatima felt a responsibility to find out exactly what Hope and Andrew did to terrify Nicolette into choosing death over her own daughter.

"Mommy, you have to pull it together." Shatima held Selena's face between the palms of her hands and encouraged her to breathe. She looked at her aunt to make sure she had her attention as well. "Now we're going to go outside and listen to what Derrick has to say, but I have to tell you something first. Everyone out there has already heard it."

Selena's head bobbed and eyes glazed while her face paled. Shatima gave her a condensed version of her dark secret. Her mother looked like she was melting before her eyes. Lynn, for once, was stunned into silence. Suddenly, Selena bounded down the stairs and into the back yard.

"Tima must have told her," Shameik remarked, watching imaginary smoke coming from her nostrils.

"That redheaded bitch that was there the night Tima's car got fucked up. Was her name Shannon Kimborough?" she demanded of Derrick, removing a small pink journal from her purse. The journal was full of everyone she spoke with about Chillz's death from the day it happened until the present. The names of police officers, doctors, phone numbers she was given, depression medications she was prescribed, and even the people responsible for his funeral were written in it. Her records resembled medical research in complexity.

"She's been harassing me since last year," Shatima said as she waddled behind Selena. "Same one who told me Andrew didn't exist when I went to press charges against him."

Selena opened the journal and flipped through the pages. "I asked her about Chillz's car several times, and she told me it was destroyed. Now Shatima is telling me Andrew had it. If I give you the VIN, can you trace it to see if it was the same car? Derrick, when we went back to the house to get our stuff, a *lot of* it was missing, and we never found any of Rize's."

Derrick nodded. "This shit is falling into my lap too easily. There's an internal investigation going on with her and her partner regarding Squeak and Monaysia's deaths. I know it's all related."

Mont came to the back dressed in another hat and a hoody tied around his face to conceal it. After hearing everything that was going on, he told everyone to prepare for their business to close after Labor Day. He said that they were at a point where no one could be trusted. Their clients were tied too closely to the police, and there was too much violence for them to conduct business safely. He wanted there to be no way the current crime wave could be attached to him or his business, especially since he planned to do a lot of killing in the next few months.

After everyone left, Rahshaan thought about the long days he had ahead of him. The violence was out of control in the projects. The younger boys from the stoop reported that they had to fight the boys in the Chavez projects in school. There were drive-by shootings in Nat Turner that made Rahshaan worry about his grandmother getting hit by a stray bullet. Then there was the danger his immediate family faced. He doubted the change of address would keep their attackers away for very long.

He went out to Big Grams' house with Mont to talk about their next moves and how they would stay one step ahead of what Andrew was doing. With Andrew's police resources, it seemed impossible. Derrick was on a decades-long mission to find out which cops were Tennessee Jones loyalists and which ones were on the side that wanted to serve and protect. For the first time, Rahshaan felt overwhelmed by the way he lived. He was ready to retire from the never ending DMX song that was his life.

When Rahshaan got home, he saw Shatima dozing off in a rocking chair in Anaijah's room. Gently, he coaxed her out of the chair and made her come to bed.

"You gotta get some real sleep and stop staying up, waiting for me every night," he told her.

"I gotta make sure you come home," she protested, climbing into the bed. "Besides, your babies wake me up hourly to use my bladder as a trampoline, and then one of them is having a kickboxing class or something with my ribs."

Rahshaan place a hand on her belly and felt for movement. He smiled at the rumbling happening inside of her. "I'm always coming home." He moved down and kissed her belly.

"You better." She put her hand on top of his. "Because we need you to. We started this family together. I don't know what I'd do if I lost you, and today just shook me. Did you see Selena's face? That's exactly how it looked the morning of hers and my daddy's wedding."

Rahshaan kept kissing her belly. "It's all gonna be over for good soon. Stop worrying." He was talking to himself more than her. "I'll tell you what. Tomorrow, let's take the kids somewhere and do something after you get off work. Anything. Whatever y'all want. We can go out of town to a water park overnight, just something to take our minds off of all this. Even if it's just for a day, it'll be good for us."

In order to keep from going crazy, Lynn spent the following weeks focused on expanding the salon. She wanted a full service spa. With Shatima able to handle the business side of her plan more efficiently, Lynn was ready to move forward with phase one. They spent the day interviewing estheticians and reviewing independent product lines. After being abandoned by her sisters' needs to pursue other avenues, she didn't think she'd ever see the day where she was able to get her goals accomplished. Standing alongside her niece, vetting potential employees for skill, professionalism, and likable personalities, was the happiest Lynn had been in a long time.

Toward the end of the day, Erika announced the sexiest man in the world had just entered the building. She ran to the back, fanning herself. Haddus quickly went to the front with her to check the man out and came back to report that he agreed.

"Well, unless he's here for a job, then he needs to make an appointment for another day," Shatima grumbled at them acting like horny teenagers.

"I told him that. He won't leave. He's asking for you, Shatima," Erika announced.

Shatima sucked her teeth. As she waddled to the front, she started feeling nauseous. When she stood face to face with Santarez, she understood why.

"How do I book a happy ending?" he asked. He was dressed in a plain polo shirt and khakis. If he wasn't a dirty cop, Erika might have been right about him.

"What do you want?" Shatima snapped at him.

"I just told you." He grinned with one side of his mouth. "I know this is where you keep your hookers and drugs."

"Oh really? Well, where do you keep yours?" she asked. "Probably at a middle school, huh? Seems like a good place to enlarge your territory."

Santarez's eyes widened. He drew back slowly. "I'll have to tell your mother she did a horrible job raising you. You never seem to know when that mouth has gotten you into too much trouble."

"You do that, and I'll make sure to tell Chief Lyles you stopped by." Derrick told Shatima that mentioning Chief Lyles' name was always a surefire way to get Santarez and Kimborough to back off. Their whereabouts were never known to their superiors, so if the reigning chief got word of what the former chief's loyalists were doing, there would be a full on investigation launched against them.

Just as Derrick said, Santarez left. Shatima went to the back and washed her hands. Lynn eyed her niece.

"That was my mother's boyfriend. He seems to have some kind of ideas about what's happening in here, and I don't know why," Shatima whispered as her aunt joined her.

Lynn called Derrick. In the past, the end result of police presence around her workplace was the death of someone close to her. Her return to Sanford County was contingent upon her not losing anyone else she loved. Derrick's promise seemed to be breaking right in front of her face.

After work, Shatima couldn't wait to leave town. Santarez's presence made her want to be as far away from everything as possible, even if it was only for one day. Rahshaan already had bags packed and was waiting at the door for her when she pulled into the driveway. The two of them rode to G-Ma's house to pick up the kids. When they got to Nat Turner, Shameik and Moosie were standing on the stoop. They sprinted toward the van before it came to a complete stop.

"We got a problem," Moosie informed Rahshaan.

Shatima buried her face in one hand while she opened her door with the other. Disappointment sank her heart down to her toes.

"Tima, go upstairs with G-Ma as quick as you can get up

there," Shameik commanded her. When she didn't move fast enough for him, Shameik roared, "Run your fat ass up the stairs!"

Before she could move again, a series of pops sounded from the far end of the alley. Screams from people whose late summer days were ruined covered them all as they hit hit the ground. Rahshaan scurried over to the passenger's side of the car and shielded Shatima. She trembled as she tried to protect her belly without putting all of her weight on it.

"Don't get scared on me now, baby. You Chillz's daughter. You ain't built to let some gunshots bother you."

She hated how true that was.

Ken-Ken and PeeWee came running around the corner. Blood soaked Ken-Ken's shirt.

"Oh my God!" Shatima cried out.

"I'm good, Tima," he assured her. "This ain't my blood."

"Whose is it then?" she asked, unable to relax.

"Niggaz from Chavez snatched Meechie," Ken-Ken reported, his head hanging low. "It was two of them. I got one, but the other one pulled off with Meechie in the back seat."

Shatima wanted to cry. Instead, she silently prayed. The day was like something out of a '90's hood movie, and she wanted the credits to start rolling. When she was sure it was safe to get up, she climbed the flights of stairs to make sure her children and grandmother were okay. They were all huddled in G-Ma's room. Tears dropped from the old woman's eyes.

"I should have moved when y'all told me to. It's been like this all day." She shook her head. "Moosie brought Shanae's kids up here and came and sat with me until a little bit before you got here."

"Well, I'm glad you had someone to help you, but you're right. You really should move. It's not safe over here anymore. Pack some clothes, and get in the car. You're staying at my house tonight."

"Take me to get a new t-shirt?" Ken-Ken requested of Rahshaan once Shatima was indoors.

Rahshaan motioned for him and PeeWee to get in the van. Shameik and Moosie joined them. They passed the t-shirt to one of the younger boys on the stoop so that he could put it in the incinerator in the building. Then they headed to a shopping center where they could get cheap clothes. On the way there, they stopped in an alley. PeeWee hopped out, grabbed something from the bushes, and then hopped back in. He ran into the store and bought his friend a t-shirt, and then they went to Shondell's townhouse in the next neighborhood.

"What the fuck is the deal?" Shondell greeted them with his face balled up in anger and threw his hands in the air. He stalked toward them. "Niggas been riding through here, shooting all day. I know it was them bitches from Chavez. I just had to send a team over there."

"A team? What the fuck for?" Rahshaan demanded.

"Them bitchass niggas from Chavez came around here tryna snatch some little boys off the bus on their way home from school." Shondell's hand stayed close to his waist, his eyes looking in all directions. Every few seconds, he perked his ears and turned around in anticipation of having to draw his gun. "School just started, and these kids can't even go safely? We gotta do better for these parents than this. The pigs sure ain't!" He hollered at a police car as it sped by.

"I know, nigga!" Rahshaan roared at Shondell's lecture. "The fuck you think we came over here to get you for?"

They trekked through the Frederick Douglas high rises and townhouses and listened to parents crying for their children. At the end of their tour, they found out that four were missing in all. That was four boys too many. When the police arrived, they made themselves scarce and went out on their own mission to find the missing.

The men and Moosie searched every abandoned building, alley, and car for Meechie and the other boys whose names and pictures were plastered on the news only to be forgotten by the time the morning traffic report aired. This was the most important part of their job: taking care of their neglected community. While Mont posed as Malachi James and put financial pressure on the powers that be to care about people who weren't rich enough to grease their palms, the people he called his niece and nephew traveled and did what the police claimed their purpose was. It was them who got the shooting to stop and shook down people for information that they could take back to Derrick to help move his investigation along. He was so close to proving that some of his co-workers were orchestrating the kidnappings, but it was hitting too close to home.

G-Ma, Lynn, Nichelle and her children, and Selena joined Shatima in her home for the night. They tried to keep the frazzled little ones entertained, but calming children when they didn't know if someone they loved was going to make it home in the morning was hard. Shatima spent most of the night in Anaijah's room, keeping her daughter from looking out the window for her daddy and eventually falling asleep in a rocking chair, holding the nervous little girl. Shatima waited for Anaijah to scream that this was too much and cry for her real mother. Instead, the little girl secured her arms around Shatima's neck and begged her to protect her. Shatima took her three kids into her bed and lay there staring at the ceiling until sleep finally took her children under. It never visited her. She cried and prayed for Meechie and the other boys to come home.

In the morning, when Moosie and the men came stomping through the door, everyone was exhausted, but everyone was in one piece. Neither they nor Derrick and his small team of officers they hoped Derrick could trust were able to find what happened to the missing boys.

Haddus moped around the shop looking like he'd lost everything. His depression left his work lackluster. His clothes started to sag with the realization that his twenty-five-year-old life was falling apart. Many of his friends were either disappearing or murder victims. The missing were brushed off. They were told they were bogged down with the kidnappings of the children and to take a number.

Among the missing was his current boyfriend. As he awaited finding out if his love just lost interest or if his life was taken, his nerves were shot. Not even Antoinette could reach her friend. More time was spent going outside to smoke cigarettes than doing hair. After a few days, Haddus canceled all of his appointments and stopped coming to work. The ladies of Hair Revolution took him food and tried to get him out of bed. He came to work in his pajamas and sat at his station looking forlorn.

"Jacoby didn't seem like the type to just bounce without saying anything," Antoinette remarked when there was a lull in the day's business.

"Yes, he did," Haddus snapped. "He was a broke ass model, and I'm scared that he did something stupid for money since I wasn't giving him any."

Shatima's ears perked as she listened to the two of them. She wished she knew how to butt into their conversations the way they did hers, but she was just getting comfortable with the gossip circuit. Timidly she waited outside of the conversation and waited for the perfect moment to jump in like in a game of double dutch.

"Like what?" Antoinette wondered.

"That nigga was always begging, always trying to count my tips at the end of the night," Haddus went on fussing. "I can't believe I let that nigga in my life with his sorry ass."

"But, Haddus, what do you think he did?" Shatima pressed, interested in hearing the answer to Antoinette's question. "Because it clearly has you scared. You aren't the type to just let yourself fall apart because a man left you."

Haddus sighed. "I think he's either selling drugs or his body to make money. He really thought he was cute enough to lay up under me. I think the fuck not!"

Shatima led her client to the dryer and turned it up high so that the woman couldn't hear their conversation. She walked over to Haddus and handed him a plate of food. "Why do you think he would do something like that? He wasn't making any money modeling?"

"That nigga wasn't shit but a lazy ass pretty face," Haddus snapped again. "And thirsty too. You know I bartend at night, right? Well, when he figured out I wasn't going to support his lazy ass, he started hanging at my job to see if he could find what he was really looking for: a sugar daddy. So we got into it, because why would you do that at my job? Like, he would literally ride in my car, flirt with niggas, and then get in my car and in my bed when he saw nobody in my club was gonna disrespect me like that. But then a week ago, this light skinned creep with blue eyes came in there, and they left together. I haven't seen or heard from him since then, and he was told by several people to stay away from that man. People who link up with him are never heard from again."

Shatima and Lynn looked at each other. Lynn went to Haddus and asked if he knew the man's name. Haddus said that he didn't. Shatima stepped in the back and made a phone call. When she came back out, her face was all business.

"When's the next time you're going to work?" she asked him.

Haddus shrugged. "I guess I better go tonight if I want to pay my rent."

"I need you to drop something off to that blue-eyed bitch for me."

Before she could give him more information, Haddus' friend came running into the shop.

"I've been looking all over for you!" he cried, collapsing on Haddus.

"DeLon, what is your problem?" Haddus recoiled and demanded.

"They found Jacoby in the dumpster behind the bar! His

hands were cut off, and- Haddus, I'm so sorry!" DeLon outstretched his arms, and Haddus fell into them.

Shatima trembled while she listened to the scream that erupted from Haddus. She went to the back and prayed that she never got news like that about Rahshaan.

———

Only a few patrons littered the bar that night. They went in support of Haddus, urging him to drink his pain away. It would take every spirit in the bar for Haddus to be able to wash his troubles down. Earlier that day, he went to Jacoby's parents' house to mourn with the family and was told that under no circumstances was he welcome to come to the funeral. They blamed him for Jacoby's alternative lifestyle as well as his tragic end. Knowing that he wouldn't get to say his goodbyes tore Haddus to pieces. The DJ tried to pep him up by playing his favorite songs, but he just sat behind the bar allowing people to pour liquor down his throat.

The owner was getting ready to close the bar when Andrew strolled in. A lifelong recipient of sneers and dirty looks, he let them roll off his back as he made his way to the stool directly in front of Haddus.

"You got a lot of nerve showing your ass in here," Haddus hissed at him. "I know you're the one behind Jacoby's death. I can't prove it right now, but I will."

Andrew ignored Haddus' accusation and said, "Cherry Cosmopolitan."

Everyone watched as Haddus made Andrew's drink, hoping he put pieces of glass in it. Haddus served Andrew the Cherry Cosmopolitan and slammed a gift bag down in front of him.

"What's this?" Andrew asked.

"I don't know. Somebody asked me to give it to you if you had the nerve to show your face in here. Obviously, they know you. I hope it's Anthrax." Haddus turned his back to Andrew.

Curious, he caught the reflection of Andrew in a steel fixture on the bar. The dance floor's blue strobe lighting behind him made Andrew's jump backward even more dramatic.

From the bag Andrew pulled three manilla envelopes. After opening the first, he appeared to be confused by what he read. He studied each page of the document carefully. Then he read it again. It was a proposal from his father to Chillz that was written back in the eighties asking him to confess to Andrew's kidnapping charges in exchange for early release from prison. He covered his mouth in surprise and horror.

In another envelope was a glossy 8"x10" photo of Tennessee Jones holding a jug of kerosene and throwing a quarter stick of dynamite into the back of a garbage truck that was charging into the back door of one of the Blueberry Hill houses.

The third was a set of medical records. The name at the top was his father's, and they announced that his father had been diagnosed with two chronic diseases. One was throat cancer, just as the news reported. The other, though, was far more controversial. Chief Tennessee Jones had AIDS but didn't want anyone to know it. At the bottom of the bag were three vials of blood and a note that read, *"I know you've been going around infecting women with this contaminated blood, and I know where to get more."*

"You tell me how you got this right now!" Andrew screamed at Haddus.

His shrill voice caused alarm, so Haddus motioned for the armed guards to accompany him at the bar. "It's time for you to leave," he told Andrew. "And don't bring your ass back in here."

Andrew came to the bar unarmed that night. He took the gift bag and scurried out of the bar. Several armed guards followed him to make sure he didn't retaliate on those grounds or come back to take out his anger on anyone else.

Haddus waited until he was sure that Andrew was gone before dialing Shatima's telephone number. Rahshaan answered the phone groggily.

"Hello, Sir. I apologize for calling at such an hour, but this is a business matter. May I speak to Shatima please?"

Rahshaan handed Shatima the phone. "Tell your co-workers don't be calling the house so fuckin' late."

"Hello?"

"Hello, Miss Tima. I took care of that thing for you. Now can you arrange my ride home as promised? I don't feel safe."

"Of course, love. I'll have someone right there to get you. Thank you, Haddus." She hung up the phone and dialed another number. "Unc? That thing you wanted me to do? It's all taken care of."

THE DEAD CROW

Since no one in a position of authority seemed to want to devote the time or the money to finding out what happened to the boys, Mont took over. As Malachi James, he sent money to the county executive to fuel parents with the necessary resources to be able to homeschool their children. That lessened the amount of children who were out there to get snatched from the bus stops. Some communities never received their money from their mayors, though. That occupied the county executive with the task of finding it and allocating it properly. Her being busy, combined with him living silently in the shadows, weakened their plan of attack.

As Unc, Mont sent his family out into every part of Sanford County they could reach to keep their eyes on the police. His crew couldn't be everywhere, but their presence was appreciated by citizens who felt powerless. Their boys were labeled runaways rather than being searched for. Hope sat on the news, pimping stories of boys being recruited into sex work rather than snatched and sold as human cargo. It wasn't until the son of a politician failed to come home that the eyes of the powers that be opened. By then, too many were lost.

In the schools, the staff expressed an inability to keep up

with the violence that erupted in the classrooms. It was everyone against the boys from the Chavez Projects. The rumors surrounding them getting paid to start fights with the boys from the other housing projects around Sanford County, the queer youth, and the latchkey kids were suspected to be true. Once other students caught on, they jumped in to defend and protect their friends. The riots that happened almost weekly resulted in someone's son not making it home. Between the kidnappings and the bullets flying at any given moment, the Sanford County School District was decreased by ten percent a week.

Mont didn't have to assign a mission for Shatima. Every night after work, she dragged herself ahead of mobs of angry and terrified parents to protest either at the South Sanford mayor's office or to the Downtown Sanford Metropolitan area in front of the County Executive's office. She wasn't supposed to be standing out there in the cold, but she knew that somehow Andrew had his eyes on her. She wanted him to know that she wasn't going to live in fear of him taking her son the way she had been for the last five years.

She wished the sign she held every night on the steps of those government buildings was a boulder she could throw through the glass windows. Every night she met more parents who didn't know if they'd ever see their sons again, and all the mayor and chief of police could say was that they felt their pain and were working around the clock to fix things.

In her last two months of pregnancy, Shatima was forced to go on bed rest. Her blood pressure was all over the place. Dr. Tawny worried about the amount of stress that she was under and threatened to have her spend her final three weeks of pregnancy in the hospital if she couldn't stay in bed with her feet elevated.

During the week, G-Ma came to stay with them in the bedroom they prepared for her. She was there to help with the kids and around the house, but Shatima didn't let that stop her from going to the bus stop every afternoon to pick up her kids.

At her size, she was no longer able to fit behind the steering wheel, so she walked.

Rahshaan was stuck putting in extra hours at the factory to make up for the money Shatima wasn't bringing home and putting in work around the city. Between him not coming home until late, the kidnappings, and the killings at an all time high, living without stress was out of the question. Surprisingly, the fact that there were no more direct attacks on her or her property made Shatima uneasy. She felt like there was something major coming. The waiting drove her insane.

At the beginning of November, Shatima wrestled to get her coat and boots over her huge belly and swollen feet. To make things worse, her coat popped open when she finally got it zipped. She overslept. The bus would be there any minute. It was going to take her forever to waddle down the street. Even if she could fit behind the wheel, the van needed to be cleaned off. Damn she missed those boys on the stoop.

Thinking of the boys on the stoop brought Meechie's face to her mind. She said a quick prayer for him and all of the other boys who were still missing on top of the prayer that she could beat the children to the bus stop.

She passed the van and waddled down the street. A delivery truck blocked the sidewalk. If she didn't have to climb a small snow bank to get around it, she wouldn't even have noticed it. Although it was past two in the afternoon, the plow trucks still hadn't made their way down her block. Thankful that she was able to find a pair that fit over her thickened calves, she dragged her swollen feet through over a foot of wet snow in her shearling-lined boots. The wind sliced at the parts of her face that weren't covered by her scarf. The weight of the babies slowed her down. She wished she could home school her children, but she could barely stay awake for more than an hour.

As she struggled to get down the street, her skin started crawling. A few more steps told her why. A crow fell out the sky and died right at her feet. It felt like an omen. Her legs wobbled and grappled against the laws of physics to get her three more houses down to the corner of the street. Parents and grandparents stood out there smiling, wondering why she went through the trouble every day. She looked like she could go into labor any minute. She felt ready to pop, but Shatima didn't care. With the phone calls Selena complained about receiving every day, she had to see with her own eyes that her children were safe.

"Where's G-Ma? It's a good thing the bus is late. You moving slow today, girl!" the woman named Zora who lived next door joked with her.

"G-Ma had to go to the doctor." Shatima surveyed the parents who were looking at her as if to ask why she even bothered. Then, what the woman said dawned on her. "The bus is late?" Bile rose from her stomach and filled her throat. She looked up at the grey sky to see if any more birds were going to give up their last moment of life.

"Yeah," Zora answered. "Probably because the roads are terrible."

They stood there and waited, but the cold and the premonitions filling her head were too much for Shatima to handle. She took her phone out of her coat pocket and dialed the school's number. "Hello? My name is Shatima Thomas, and my children's bus hasn't come here yet. Is everything alright? It's bus four."

The voice on the other end was cheery. "Oh yes. Everything is fine. We're starting to call parents now to let them know the buses were a little late leaving the school today because of the weather conditions. If you'll hold for a moment, then I'll get dispatch on the phone to get an ETA for your children."

Shatima mumbled a dry thanks to the cheery voice while she waited. She tapped her foot.

When the person returned, her voice wasn't as cheery. "Miss Thomas, are you able to send someone down here?"

Shatima couldn't wait for Rahshaan, and she couldn't fit behind the steering wheel. Zora was nice enough to give her a ride down to the school. She called Rahshaan on the way. He told her that he would meet her at the school. As she rode in Zora's car, she wondered why the woman was driving so slowly. Zora was always one of the first ones to follow her to the protests. Didn't she understand that this could mean something bad happened to their children?

"These roads are so icy," Zora complained. She chattered on about the amount of time it took South Sanford to be taken care of being their next protest. Any other day, Shatima would have chimed in, but that dead crow and her children were on her mind.

They finally made it to the school. Shatima barely mumbled her thanks before trying to leap out of the car. The woman came around to the passenger's side to help her.

"I'm sure the children are fine," Zora tried to assure her.

The forced smile on Zora's face and raised tone to her voice finally registered to Shatima. Zora's twitching eyes told it all. She was terrified but pretending to be calm for Shatima's benefit. There were police cars lined up in front of the school. That made her tremble. She took out her phone and dialed NyQuest's cellphone number. When Rahshaan bought it for him, she thought it was foolish to spend money on a Motorola Razor for an eight year old. That day, she was grateful that he had. It went straight to voicemail. Again, she dialed the number. Once again, it went to voicemail. She sent a text message asking if he was okay but didn't wait for a response.

The doors to the school were locked. When Zora pressed the buzzer, a security guard appeared and asked for ID. Instead of standing in the cold and fishing through her purse, Shatima pushed past him and headed straight for the office. Zora followed on her heels.

"I need to see some ID!" the security guard called after them.

"I'll show you some ID when you show me where my children are!" Shatima shot back. She continued plodding down the hall to the main office.

Derrick was at the door with a bulletproof vest over his

oxford shirt and slacks. His badge and gun stuck out to her. He held his arms out for her to come to him. She stayed back, shaking her head.

"Where are my children?" she pleaded with him.

Work boots thudded toward the crowd. The sound was a bit of a comfort to Shatima, because she knew that they belonged to Rahshaan, Shameik, and Rico. Their eyes darted around at all of the police. Rahshaan held Shatima as they listened to Derrick report was information she had so far. It was a moment where Shatima felt she should be screaming, but she couldn't move. The room was spinning, and she left her body to watch the scene play out. A river of tears flowed down her face. This was the day she dreaded since Jabez's birth. The dead crow stayed on her mind.

Within a half hour, children bundled in snowsuits marched into the school. Underneath hats, scarves, and mittens, they looked identical. Shatima's eyes scanned the sea of babies, grateful that they all were safe. She struggled to remember what colors she put on her kids that morning. Usually, she could run down a full description of their outfits. At that moment, she drew a blank. It angered her. Rahshaan started toward them, demanding they took off their hoods, hats, and scarves, but was pushed back by Derrick. They just stood there, waiting for the school to do its job.

A ten year old, curly-haired girl gave her account of what happened. A red truck cut in front of them. Two men bounded onto the bus, waving guns. One of them pointed the gun at the driver's head while the other went to each child, demanding to know which one Jabez was. They pulled off every child's hat. One of the men announced they were looking for a child with blue eyes. The two men argued about that. One insisted that Jabez didn't have blue eyes, and the other seemed upset about this. The students hoped Jabez would keep quiet, but one of the men recognized him as soon as his hat came off. The bus driver moved to pry him away from them and was shot in a struggle over him. NyQuest and Anaijah screamed for them to let their brother go.

"We're missing three altogether," the school cop announced after reading a clipboard.

Principal Phelps shot the cop a stern look for his reckless remark. She started toward Shatima and Rahshaan. Usually, when Shatima came to the school, she paid the principal a compliment for being impeccably groomed. On that day, she couldn't make out any specific details about the woman. Shatima watched the woman approach her. She watched the woman's lips move. She heard the words come out of her mouth, but it took a minute to process them. The number three was the only word that stuck to her brain. Three children were missing.

She put three children on the bus that morning, and not one came back.

Derrick hissed for the two of them not to move. Rahshaan, Rico, and Shameik were ready to tear into the streets and attack anyone who got in their way. Selena, Lynn, and G-Ma came into the school. Another set of three. Three crying women. Their tears irritated Shatima even more than her own. The whole village failed their children.

People came in and took their children one by one. As the crowd of students dwindled, Shatima became hopeful. Maybe theirs were just overlooked. Hopefully this was a twist to her crazy dreams. She knew neither of those were reality. The day she feared her entire adult life arrived. Now people got to see why she "babied" Jabez. They were ushered into the main office, away from the people whose children were going home, safe from harm. Under bright lights, they sat like zoo animals on display. People passing by peeked in at them to catch a glimpse of panicked parents in their natural habitat.

A group of police officers came to the door. Shatima exhaled and hopped up, temporarily forgetting how heavy carrying multiple children was. NyQuest's face was the color of a ripe dragonfruit as he ripped away from the police and made a beeline for his parents.

"Tima, we gotta go get Jay!" he declared, his mouth tightened into a ball of anger.

Bawling, Anaijah was carried by another officer. Her face was an even brighter shade of red. She cried about being thrown on the off ramp and how scary the walk down the highway was. EMTs came in to check on the children. Anaijah had a fit when the strangers tried to touch her.

"That's the man that attacked my first mommy!" she screamed.

"And the man who used to come to Mommy's house with Mr. Squeak!" NyQuest insisted. "He took Jay!"

Derrick came into the room to speak with the children and get more information. They said that they saw Jabez being taken away in a news van. Rahshaan leaned into Shatima's ear and kept whispering how sorry he was. He broke his promise. He felt fucked up because his son was there in one piece, but her son wasn't. His tears fell on her face and neck. She pushed him away from her.

"Just bring him back," she commanded him, Shameik, and Rico.

They awaited the medical team's clearance to take Anaijah and NyQuest home. Derrick told them that Uncle Mont was at Shatima's house waiting for them. She felt like she was gasping for air. The babies did gymnastics in her belly. Rahshaan grabbed her hand and begged her to keep it together. She barely heard him.

Whose car she rode in, Shatima didn't remember. Lynn, Selena, and G-Ma surrounded her in her bed. She wanted to slap herself. Why was she laying in bed when her son was missing? She should have been combing the streets with her gun in her hand, finger on the trigger, steel pressed against the temples of everyone she passed, demanding information on her son.

Marching to the mayor's office wasn't enough. She should have been sitting by his bedside, making him make the choice between swallowing ammunition or bringing her son home himself.

NyQuest and Anaijah asked to be able to lay with her. She invited them to join her. They each climbed in at one of her sides and clung to her. Anaijah whimpered and trembled. She wanted to tell them that everything would be all right, but she knew that nothing would ever be the same. Her children's cries told her that they knew it too.

She wanted to kick her own ass for becoming so lax. As comfortable as being in a relationship was, she never should have put the safety of her son in someone else's hands. The only reason she ever wanted to stay alive was to protect her son from this day. He would have been better off if she wasn't there.

As if reading her mind, Rahshaan came in, sat on the side of the bed, and told her that this wasn't her fault. He announced that the whole family was there, and there were people down-stairs making plates of food for her, but that only upset her more. You bring food after someone has died. No one who lived at that address was dead or dying. Sadness pulled his face down as he reported that they weren't the only ones on the block missing a child. Zora's oldest son was taken from the high school, as well as the sons of two other families from their block.

Rahshaan reached for Shatima's hand. When she gave it to him, he jumped back, remarking how icy it was.

"I've been cold since I left the house earlier," she admitted, then realized she was clinging to Anaijah and NyQuest for their warmth as well as to comfort them.

Kassidy came in and put each of the children in their beds and then brought Shatima a plate of lasagna that Big Grams made. Rahshaan forced Shatima to eat some of it. She was surprised that she held it down. Then he climbed into the bed with her and pressed her body against his. Her entire body was freezing.

"I'm gonna bring him home," he told her. "Just keep my babies safe and healthy."

At that, she pushed out an obnoxious laugh.

"I can't even keep the baby I pushed out of me safe and healthy. How do you expect me to do that for more children?" She shook her head.

The timbre of her voice jarred him. Seeing that she was going crazy, he knew he had to hold it together for the both of them. The dolls that were thrown through their garage door window over the summer came to his mind. He remembered where the stuffing was ripped out of them. The thought pierced his heart and twisted his stomach. Who could fantasize about doing that to a child? Once the thought permeated his brain, he couldn't get it out.

Rahshaan leaned closer to her and whispered into her ear, "Tima, I'm gonna bring him home, and this whole shit is gonna be over. Then you and me can live a regular ass life with our beautiful ass family, and Jay will be there too. You hear me? I love you, baby."

"I love you too, but-'"

"Ain't no but."

The two of them looked up at Derrick and Mont entering the room. Mont's face was wet, his eyes red and puffy. It was hard for Shatima to think of him crying. He didn't strike her as a man who displayed sadness, though his life story showed he had enough to be in perpetual mourning about. He was dressed in war clothes - black hoody, baggy black sweats, and Timbs. Derrick still wore that bullet proof vest, but traded his khakis for sweatpants. Nothing about their dress or facial expressions did anything to ease Shatima's fears for the worst. It wasn't just Jabez's life that was on the line. The culmination of decades-worth of battles evolved into a war that night. That much was apparent when Shameik, Rico, Moosie, Ken-Ken, PeeWee, and Marcus followed Derrick into the room, dressed identically to Mont.

"I just caught your mother outside in a black SUV. She looked like she was trying to get the attention of whoever was driving that delivery truck out front," Derrick announced.

"That truck is still there?" Shatima exclaimed. "It's been out there every day this week when I go get the kids from the bus stop. I didn't think anything of it. I thought one of the parents said they were picking the kids up from the bus stop on their lunch break."

Derrick eyed her. He reluctantly told her, "I had the driver taken to my office for questioning. I don't know if it's gonna amount to anything, but your mother is cuffed in the back seat of a police car. That bitch ain't going home until I know Jabez is home sleeping in his room."

Shatima tried to sit up in the bed, but felt pain and weakness. Rahshaan helped her up and put pillows behind her to take some of the pressure off her back.

Kassidy burst into the room and yelled, "Turn on the news! There's some crazy shit happening!" Instead of waiting, she took the remote from its cradle on top of the TV and turned to a channel that Shatima hadn't watched in nearly a year. Selena came in with two blankets fresh from the dryer and spread them over Shatima.

The rest of them watched footage from the inside of a van. Camera equipment blocked part of their view of the people inside until they came to an abrupt stop in front of a red sedan and a school bus. Andrew and Miguel erupted from the car carrying a near naked Jabez. A leash and collar choked the little boy. Andrew clasped a hand over Jabez's mouth and clamped an arm around the little boy to force him into submission. Miguel tossed Jabez's outerwear and backpack over a highway ramp. The two of them got into the van.

While the van went around the bus and blended with the rest of traffic, Andrew kissed Jabez's dimples and ran his hands over Jabez's long braids. He kept making comments about how pretty Shatima kept him looking. Jabez whimpered and cringed.

When he tried to squirm away from Andrew, Andrew yanked his chain forward so that he could kiss his dimples again. Jabez pushed away and begged him to stop.

"Don't reject me," Andrew firmly commanded, his eyes ablaze and nostrils flaring.

Jabez tensed but didn't move. He tried to hold in his whimpers. Andrew stopped kissing his dimples and ran his hands down Jabez's braids.

"She gave me such a beautiful son. Why didn't she want me? We could have been a gorgeous family," Andrew went on. He looked down at Jabez and demanded to know, "Why did your mother keep you from me?"

Jabez gave him a blank stare. Andrew caressed Jabez's braids through his fingers. He stared admirably at their sheen.

"Your grandfather didn't want me. Your uncle took your mother from me, and then he rejected me too. Your mother rejected me and kept secrets from me. Now it feels like you don't want me either. What is it about Revolution rejection that makes it so addictive?" He gazed down into Jabez's pupils while waiting for the five year old to answer.

The van whipped around a bend in the highway, jerking the passengers to one side of the van. Jabez gasped.

"Stop driving like a maniac! You're scaring my son!" Andrew snapped at the driver.

He rubbed Jabez's cheek. Jabez kicked and screamed for his mother. His crying started to chip away at Andrew. Soon, there were two people sitting in the back seat sobbing.

The driver yelled for them to shut up. Shatima thought the woman's voice sounded familiar. She tried to make it out while they continued to yell, but Jabez's crying turned to screams as Andrew pulled on the chain and demanded to know why Jabez didn't want to be with him. Miguel looked on at the scene with disgust turning his nose at it.

"We're dropping him with the rest of the boys, and then

we're separating. I can't sit through much more of this," Miguel said with his hands over his ears.

The driver continued to tell them to shut up. Shatima tried to recall the owner of the voice, but she was distracted when the passenger sitting in the front seat turned around and slapped Jabez across her face. It made a pop that took her back to a time when she'd been struck like that as a little kid.

Selena sat on one side of Shatima and grabbed one of her hands while Rahshaan grabbed the other. Shatima could barely feel them, because she was distracted by a diamond on the passenger's left hand. The ring on her finger slightly resembled the ring that Rahshaan bought her in St. Croix. A curl fell from the hat she wore on her head. When she slapped Jabez and said, "Cut out that noise, little boy," Shatima traveled back in time to the week after her ninth birthday when she was beaten for crying about wanting her father.

"Why would you do this to your own grandson?" she whispered. In a louder voice she said, "Derrick, that's Hope."

Derrick raised his eyebrows and widened his eyes. "This bitch had the nerve to come here, knowing what she did?"

Shatima nodded her head. "My daddy gave her that ring when I was a baby. She always used to brag about it."

As the footage continued, they traveled into a building with an elevator. Something about it seemed familiar to Shatima, but she couldn't figure out what it was. Watching them go downward made Shatima feel like they were somewhere she'd been before and hated. Before they stepped off, the picture went blank.

A reporter tried not to sound confused and distraught as she came onto the screen and explained, "If you're just now tuning in, we are having technical difficulties. One of the Channel 3 news vans was hijacked earlier today. The culprits have hijacked the Channel 3 signal, and they are broadcasting activity that appears to stem from a school bus hijacking. Three children were taken from the bus. Two were found, and this footage seems to be an explanation of what happened to the third.

"Among today's missing children is six year old Jabez Thomas. He is four feet two, dark brown skinned with black braids that go well down his back. He was last seen carrying a Power Rangers backpack and wearing a matching coat and boots. He is believed to be in a Channel 3 news van..."

Her voice trailed off as the picture came back. Jabez was in what appeared to be a basement in a room that was full of urine and feces. Blood painted a mural on the walls. He was chained to the wall like an abused dog, secured by a choke collar. He was naked and shivering. Scraps of food sat in a bowl in the corner of the room, but the leash allowed him to stop just short of reaching it. He looked so confused and hurt. He did nothing to deserve the torture.

Andrew entered the room. Jabez covered his dimples with his hands. He didn't understand any of what was happening to him, and who would be able to explain it? That morning when he woke up, he dressed himself, kissed his mother, and asked when the babies would get here. Those were his concerns. Now, he was a prisoner.

"Who am I?" Andrew asked the little boy.

When the frightened child shrugged his shoulders, Hope smacked him across the face with a rolled up newspaper.

Andrew crouched over and stared into Jabez's eyes. Jabez shivered.

"Your mother keeps things tucked away in the dark where she believes they can't haunt her, and I'm sure that today she regrets every secret she's ever kept. Unlike your mother, I'm going to be the first honest person in your life. I'd like to introduce myself to you. I'm your father."

Jabez shook his head and said that his father's name was Rahshaan. Andrew screamed and tugged at his wavy hair. Hope shifted, and her eyes grew wide as she watched Andrew's unhinged reaction.

Andrew cupped Jabez's face in his hand and dug his index fingers into Jabez's dimples. Rahshaan clenched Shatima's wrist while Selena leaned forward. She pulled her hair while repeatedly asking where they were.

"Fortunately for me, you're at that delightful age where I can convince you to love me. I waited too long for your mother. I won't make that mistake with you. So let me make my intentions plain." Andrew tried to sit next to Jabez, but he cringed when he nearly made himself comfortable on a pile of feces. "I'm not well received here. I have been building a house for us in California, and I'm ready to take you to live there with me. Your mother agreed to live with us, but she lied. So I'm taking you with me to love you the way that I said I would when she agreed to carry you, before I knew what a liar she was.

"The problem is that you have an uncle named Montell who she told me was dead. I know he's not, and you and me won't be able to live our happy little life together unless he is. So I need you to tell me where he is before we leave. Don't lie to me either. I don't react well to liars, and you're so beautiful. I would hate to hurt you."

Jabez asked him to take the collar off his neck, but Andrew refused.

"Tell me where your uncle is," Andrew said in a plain tone.

Jabez shrugged. Shatima felt Rahshaan and Selena's hands quaking while they held hers. She almost couldn't breathe.

Hope stalked forward and smacked Jabez across his face. "You know exactly where Montell is! Tell us!" She smooshed Jabez's face into the pile of feces.

The reporter whose voice they heard earlier shrieked, "I'm trying! I can't shut it off! Why can't someone from production stop this?"

Shatima's crying fell in time with Jabez's. Through her tears, she searched the background of the scene for clues about where they were. There was something oddly familiar about the room. She leaned closer to the flat screen TV and peered at the shelves on the wall. Something snapped in her mind.

"Those gowns on that shelf in the back left corner look a lot like the gowns we used to use at the nursing home. They're at The Medical Center, in the basement." Then she added, "Loretta had to be the one driving the van."

"You sure?" Derrick asked.

Shatima nodded her head and pointed. "The letters on the door give it away. I worked there from the time I was eighteen until about a year ago. Loretta and the housekeepers were the only ones with a key to that room."

"Then my mother should be able to get us down there," Rahshaan remarked.

As the picture turned black, the reporter frantically announced, "The video that you are watching is from earlier today. We're having technical difficulties. Please stay with us, and please alert the police if you have any information on the stolen Channel 3 news van. It is now being considered part of a crime scene."

The video replayed from the beginning while the reporters and the rest of the news staff tried to get it off the air.

Derrick stepped outside of the room and placed a call to Chief Lyles. They heard him go downstairs. He came back and reported that Hope had confirmed that they took him to the medical center, but that they planned to move him soon. Her being so willing to give up that piece of information made him leery of believing anything she said. Hope was all for self. If she was telling the truth, then they were either being pushed into a trap or being sent to do her dirty work. He went back outside for a few minutes, came back in, and demanded, "Where is Anai-jah's book bag?"

"It should be hanging up in the closet when you first come in downstairs," Shatima said. "Why?"

Derrick thudded down the stairs. When he came back into the room, he dumped out its contents. They all watched him in confusion as he went through all of her belongings. Dissatisfied, he requested Rahshaan take him to her room. They found the backpack she had when she came to them. Stitched inside of the lining was a tracking device. Shatima thought of her last conversation with Nicolette. She wondered what her mother threatened her with to make her use her daughter like that.

Rahshaan looked at all of this and silently gloated that he was proved to not be paranoid. Talking about what they did indoors or in cars could have incriminated them all.

While Derrick spoke with Chief Lyles, Rahshaan, Shameik, Rico, Shondell, Moosie, Ken-Ken, PeeWee, and Marcus went outside and listened intently to Mont's instructions. From the window, they looked like an army, ready for war. Shatima's attention was divided between them and the television. She tried to convince herself that none of this was real. Then, she tried even harder to convince herself that it was. She apologized to Jabez for birthing him into such an awful existence.

Nichelle entered the room and declared, "Tima, you are way too pale." She sat on the side of the bed, touched her, and remarked about how cold she felt. In what seemed like a second, she left the room and returned with a bag. She removed a blood pressure cuff from it and took Shatima's blood pressure twice. She looked up at Selena. "You know her doctor's number? Her pressure's really low."

"With everything that's going on, I really don't trust going to the hospital right now. Remember what happened to G-Ma," Lynn remarked. "Tell Mama to come upstairs. She's a doctor."

"*I'm a nurse.*" Nichelle's neck and eyes rolled as she gave that information. "We can't do anything for her here. She gotta get to the hospital. Call her doctor."

Selena looked around the room "For once, her anal ass is useful," she remarked, picking up a small turquoise notebook from Rahshaan's nightstand. "Everything we need is right here." She didn't mean to holler into the phone, but all of the anxiety from that night came out in her voice. "No, I can't wait! Get my daughter's doctor on the phone now!"

Shatima wanted to laugh at how dramatic Selena was being,

but her vision got fuzzy. First, there were two Selenas, then three. They spun around, calling her name, yelling for Rahshaan to come back inside. She heard Rahshaan telling her to pull through. Shameik and Rico each grabbed one of her hands. Rico apologized for telling her he wished she died and begged her not to. His lips felt hot every time he kissed the side of her face, sending temporary shocks of warmth throughout her. There was the sound of people urging Rahshaan to go to the hospital with Shatima, and the sound of him refusing to let Unc go out there without him. He was going to find Jabez. There was the sound of the ambulance sirens, and the feeling of being heaved down the stairs. Finally, there was the sound of Pastor Candle praying, and the feeling of him anointing her head and belly with blessed oil.

A cold pain surged through her body. She wanted to scream, but her head felt like a balloon that was about to pop. Everything went from pitch black to bleached white. Rize and Chillz appeared and offered their hands. They asked her if she was ready to come with them.

TIMA'S CHOICE

As if the guilt from breaking his promise to keep Jabez safe wasn't enough, Rahshaan had to watch the only woman he ever considered spending the rest of his life with being carried out on a stretcher. All his life, people told him he needed to calm down and think with a clear head. When he tried to do it, those three babies had to discard that night filled his brain.

It was an odd time for him to think of his deceased siblings, but lately they were on his mind. When he got to sleep, they came to him in dreams, smiling and telling him they loved him no matter what, that he would get to meet them one day. He tried to push them out of his head, but he kept seeing their closed eyes and smiling lips. The minute it hit him that their smiling was weird, he heard them screaming as their oxygen was confined to a plastic garbage bag. How was he supposed to keep a clear head with those thoughts swimming in it?

After promising Shatima that Jabez would be back by the time she woke up, he joined Mont in the back yard.

"Moosie got the whips. Ken-Ken and PeeWee are loading them. Derrick got us a nice little setup. We're just waiting on the word from Derrick, and then we move," Mont let him know. "Remember the one rule tonight: *I get* to kill the kid toucher. I don't mean no sucka shit either. Ken-Ken and PeeWee got a couple sticks of dynamite to stick in his mouth and up his ass, but I don't want that shit. I wanna feel that nigga dying in my hands."

The team nodded their agreement. Marcus was the only giddy one out of all of them. Usually he was told he was too young, too inexperienced a shooter. That night, they needed anybody they could trust. He tried to contain himself, grateful that his brother and the rest of his family finally found him worthy.

"Mommy's waiting for us in the back lobby," Marcus reported. "She's gonna get us in the basement."

Derrick came into the backyard followed by a small team of police made up of Chief Lyles, six high ranking officers, and two forensic detectives. All of them wore black hoodies over their bulletproof vests. The handful of cops were victimized by Tennessee Jones in the past. He introduced everyone to each other and told his family that these were the only cops they could trust. Due to the reason they were out there to begin with, it sounded like an oxymoron. They had no choice but to go with whatever Derrick said. There was no telling how much of the police force Andrew had on his side.

Chief Lyles thanked the men for their service. He excused himself, saying that he had a press conference to prepare for. With that, he tipped his hat and left. The crew found the man's presence odd, and his exit even more unsettling, but Derrick assured them that it was a good thing.

The three car police caravan led the vehicles driven by Moosie and Shondell Downtown to the medical complex. After a call from Chief Lyles, plows had finally visited their side of town to clean the streets, making it safer for Shondell to drive at his normal high speed. Often, they joked that he was a getaway driver in a past life because, road conditions be damned, Shondell drove with the skill of a Nascar driver. He was also the one who was responsible for teaching Moosie how to drive. She picked up on his technique, but where Shondell didn't think twice about jerking a car around on ice, Moosie's instincts kicked in and told her to be cautious.

The parking lot at the medical center was full of cars dropping patients off and visiting them. Derrick got out of the car first and introduced himself to the security guards and had a brief conversation with them. The security team made the rest of them uneasy with the way they looked at them while Derrick spoke. Then Derrick went back to them and listened for Mont's plan. Mont was busy gazing up toward the Penthouse Tomb. A single room's light was illuminated.

"Banger, take the reins for a minute. I gotta go handle some business." There was a strange cockiness to his strut as he walked off that was hard not to notice.

Rahshaan watched as his father figure walked away from them. "Nigga, where the fuck is you going?" Rahshaan hissed.

Mont waved him off. "Be easy. I'll be back in a minute. You go find Jay. I gotta handle something for my pops and Jeremiah." With his hands in the front pockets of his hoody, he blended in with the crowds of people entering and exiting and continued walking into the building.

Sheila Drayton was not to be played with, so when she called her co-workers at Sanford University Hospital and told them that her granddaughter was on her way in, they gave her a private suite on the antepartum floor. Sheila and Nichelle barked commands to the team of nurses who jumped to obey whenever one of them opened their mouths. Within two hours exactly, Lynn's younger sister, Adrianne, was there, and the three of them laid down the law. Adrianne worked just under the Commissioner of Health for New York State. Keeping her happy was the hospital staff's top priority.

Still, nothing they did brought Shatima's blood pressure back to normal. Her temperature continued to drop. Her lips lost their pale pink color and turned indigo. Dr. Tawny monitored the babies and looked for signs of bleeding from the amniotic sac. Neither Selena, Lynn, nor G-Ma knew what any of it meant, so they stayed in a corner, out of the way, while watching Shatima. Pastor Candle led them in prayer.

"God, you were already cruel enough to take my husband and my son away from me. If you spare my daughter and grandchildren, and bring my grandson back to us safely, then I promise I'll start coming back to church and believing in you again!" Selena hollered over Pastor Candle's prayer. She meant to say it in her head, but she had no regrets when it came out. She was ready to end her longstanding beef with God.

"Look at you. About a year ago you were asking to come with us. Now you scared," Rize teased Shatima. Those quarter sized dimples amplified when he smiled.

"I'm not scared," she said, not recognizing the hollow voice that came from her. "I just don't want Selena to cry. She's been through so much. We just got each other back. And what about Jabez? Is he here already?" She looked around, but saw nothing but white and her father peering downward. "Daddy, why aren't you saying anything?"

"Can't stand to hear Selena crying. I miss her, but we ain't gonna be together again unless she stops holding that grudge against God." He stood with his back to them.

"Then I guess I gotta go back to tell her that," Shatima said. "Wait... Does this mean I won't see y'all anymore?"

Rize shrugged. "You don't really need to, do you? My boy's taking pretty good care of you." He reached out and patted her pregnant belly.

She smiled. "He's a real good man."

"I know that," Chillz said. "I taught him everything he knows... Well, except that part about walking out on you and getting tangled up with Shanae. I don't know what that nigga was thinking that night."

The three of them laughed.

"Answer my question though, please? Will you guys stop coming to see me every night if I go back?"

Chillz shrugged. "I'm sure we'll come to visit you every now and again, but like your brother said, you don't really need us anymore."

"I'll always need you," she told them indignantly, hugging herself. Though she woke up screaming at the end of them, the dreams always served as an odd source of comfort for her. They were her way of making up for the time that was taken away from them.

"Well, then stay here and think about it a little bit longer. You got time," Rize told her.

All hell broke loose the second the doors closed behind Mont. It started when Marcus' phone rang. Big Grams screamed into it for someone to find Derrick and send him to her house right away. The minute she got home from Shatima's house, a white cop with red hair kicked in her door and led a raid. She instructed the officers who were with her to search for signs that Mont lived there. Big Grams stood against a wall in her entryway with her hands up while they trashed her house and threated to shoot her if she retaliated.

When they weren't able to find any evidence of Mont being alive, she turned the gun on herself and threatened suicide. Big Grams fussed that she had no desire to tell trash that her life mattered in an effort to prevent pigs' blood from spilling onto her floors.

"As a child of God, I'm supposed to extend kindness and love, but I don't give a damn if the bitch dies," Big Grams continued to fuss.

"Big Grams, you know we're in the middle of something important, right?" Marcus reminded her.

"Well, send Derrick to get these bastards out of my house!" As soon as she said that, Marcus heard what sounded like a bullet going through glass. Then the line went dead. Marcus called her back but got no response.

"Shit!" Derrick yelled when Marcus told him what happened. His car's radio sounded off with officers being called to just about every ghetto in the city. Parents decided that night that since the police weren't going to do anything about their missing children, then they would take responsibility for their children's safety in their own hands. Many of them rode down to the Cesar Chavez projects in search of either answers, vengeance, or a combination of the two.

At the edge of the parking lot, Derrick saw a black car moving slowly. He felt like the driver was watching him through the vehicle's tinted windows.

"Santarez!" he guessed and sent one car of his teammates after him. "He's gotta at least stay alive until we get a confession out of him and some answers on where to find the kidnapped boys." He turned to Rahshaan. "After I get you in here, y'all are on your own for a minute. I gotta get up there to Big Grams. I hate to do it like this, but it is what it is, Cuz. Your uncle taught you well. I know the fam is in good hands."

Rahshaan looked at the top floor window and then looked at his team. When this day came, he always thought Mont would be in front of them, guiding their steps. This was the moment Mont had been grooming him for since taking him under his wing. He had to be the leader they needed. His mentor either really trusted him or was out of his mind. Either way, the number one goal was to bring Jabez home in one piece.

He went to Moosie's SUV and pointed in the direction of the car that Derrick just sent after Santarez. "Follow them up to Big Grams' crib, but lay low as possible. Don't do anything unless Derrick needs you to. If you catch the Puerto Rican pig before they do, keep him just at the edge of death. If you see the baby raper before me, hit me. I'm there. We'll get up with y'all niggaz soon as we find Jay."

"Edge of death?" Moosie repeated, a dreamy look in her eyes and slight grin on her chubby face. "I got you, Bro. Say no more." She sped off with Shameik, Ken-Ken, and PeeWee as her passengers.

Rahshaan jogged back to the van where Shondell sat in the driver's seat. He slipped on the icy asphalt but caught himself on the side of the van. "You and Rico circle the parking lot and see if the bastard tried to go out the back. Me and Marcus are gonna take the inside. I'm gonna go see if I can figure out what the fuck Unc doing. And yo. I don't give a fuck what else happens. Soon as somebody hops in the whip with Jay, pull off and take him to Derrick. Don't worry about nobody but my son."

Shondell and Rico nodded, bumped fists with him, told him to be safe, and drove off slowly. So much weight was carried when he returned the words "be safe" to them. Marcus pointed out Darlene, who was standing in the lobby, mopping up the slush, snow, and salt people carried indoors with their boots. Rahshaan pushed Marcus toward her. The mother/son duo looked goofy despite the circumstances. They were just glad Rahshaan trusted them enough to include them in one of the most important events of his life.

Rahshaan went into the building with Derrick. They hoped to run into Mont. Instead, they ventured through a busy walk-in clinic to the eerie quietness of a nursing home and into an office. Six nurses stared at Channel 3 News in complete disbelief. They were startled when they saw Derrick flash his badge and announce who he was.

"Is there a Loretta Jones available for me to speak with?" he questioned them, trying to keep his tone even.

The women's mouths dropped open. Their faces turned pale as their eyes went from the TV screen to Derrick's face. One of them mumbled something about Loretta being untrustworthy, and the others agreed. One of them summoned her downstairs.

Rahshaan stood off to the side in the dark hallway, unnoticed, watching their surroundings. The feeling that he was being watched put him on higher alert. Loretta had home court advantage. She could be sitting in an office, watching them from a camera. Even worse, Andrew could be with her. The thought made him shudder. He reached under his hoody for his Desert Eagle. In times like this, running his fingers along the titanium brought him comfort. The tool was perfect for shooting targets. When he saw Loretta coming down the hallway, he had to resist the urge to shoot her directly between her eyes.

Loretta bopped into the office as though it was a regular work day. In her hands she carried an envelope that Derrick was sure was full of cash. One of the nurses remarked that it was a deposit envelope from the walk-in clinic. The way her face dropped when she saw Derrick let him know that she was expecting someone else.

"Daddy is going to take his last breath any minute now, Derrick. It's over."

"It's not over until you tell us where every single missing boy is. Your friend already snitched and told us that you were the one who filmed the kidnapping and torturing of the boy who was snatched from his bus. How's daddy gonna get you out of that if he's dead?" Derrick asked while he slapped handcuffs on her.

Loretta looked around for God only knew what. Rahshaan kept his distance, but watched from a window until Derrick put Loretta in the back of his car and drove off. Then, Rahshaan went back the way they came in. On his way back, he found an unlit staircase and headed to the basement to see about his son. In the darkness, Mont bounded down behind him.

"He ain't down there. Grab your brother and dip!" Uncle Mont commanded.

"Nigga, where the fuck you been at?" Rahshaan demanded.

"Taking care of something for my pops and Jeremiah," Mont replied. "Let's get the fuck out of here."

At the sound of other people in the basement, Marcus cocked his gun and hid around the corner. Darlene hid behind him. He watched the figures coming toward him in the dark. His heart trembled, and his fingers shook. He'd never had to use a gun on a human before. When Rahshaan called and told him he would need him, Marcus had Mont take him to the gun range to practice aim and accuracy. He hoped that the precision he showed at the ranged translated to being useful during wartime.

Rahshaan hissed Marcus' name. Darlene and Marcus relaxed and walked toward the sound of his voice.

"Jay ain't here no more, but it's about three storage rooms full of boys," Marcus told them. "One of them told us Jay got moved about an hour ago. He said something about a forest."

Mont nodded but didn't say anything else. Rahshaan sent his mother upstairs to report to the nurses what they found.

They managed to make it out of The Medical Center without incident. The lack of violence disturbed them. Marcus informed Mont of the raid happening at Big Grams' house. Mont had no reaction to that except that he knew Derrick would handle it. They waited for Shondell to circle back around and hopped into the van.

"Where my nephew at?" Rico asked, turning around in his seat. His heavily lidded eyes pleaded with them for some good news.

"What's the quickest way to get to Banneker Forest without cutting through Big Grams' crib?" Mont asked instead of answering. "I got a tip that said we needed to head up to cabin number seven."

"You're not telling me what I need to know," Shatima pressed. "If Jabez isn't safe, then it'd be better if I'm not alive anyway."

Chillz finally turned to his daughter. "You know I understand where you're coming from, but what about the rest of your family? You're not even gonna give the babies a chance to live? And what about Rahshaan? I hand picked that nigga for you, prepped him for life with you. You gonna let my efforts go to waste?"

"Word, Tima. That nigga ain't never cared about anyone the way he cares about you. And what about Anaijah and NyQuest? You gonna leave my daughter and my godson?" Rize chimed in.

Shatima sighed. "Just tell me Jabez is gonna be safe, and my mind is made up."

After riding out of the medical complex in silence, Mont

commanded someone to turn on the local news station on the radio. Rather than talking about Loretta's and Hopes arrests, the reporter simply stated that some people of interest were taken in for questioning regarding the latest kidnappings. Instead, the news was focused on the standoff at Big Grams' house. Chief Lyles was there, trying to talk Kimborough out of shooting herself. He assured the reporter and the viewers that the officers in that house were performing an illegal raid and were also involved with the disappearing children. He held nothing back, naming Tennessee Jones as the mastermind behind the kidnappings as far back as the seventies.

While Mont listened to the news, Rico called Moosie and told her to meet them in Banneker Forest. To take his mind off of the fact that Shondell was driving like they were on a roller coaster, Rahshaan looked at the collection Derrick supplied for them. Briefly he debated whether he wanted to take one of the rifles with him but settled on more ammunition for the Desert Eagle that had been so good to him for so long. Mont wanted a battle rifle. He took an M14 from the burlap sack and stopped himself from wondering how Derrick got his hands on such a marvelous arsenal. With Derrick, the less he knew, the better.

Once they were close to the forest, Shondell checked his rearview and slightly smiled when he saw Moosie speed up behind him. They had no idea where they were going once they got to the camping grounds, but the strength they had in numbers gave them a sense of hope.

The green glow on the car's clock let them know that it was nine pm when they made it to the forest. They drove up a path that led to the hilly hiking trails and then pulled off of opposite sides of the road. Snow and silence were their only company as the area they were in was closed for renovations that weren't due to start until the spring. As Shondell parked, Rahshaan saw a figure moving swiftly through the trees then stopping and checking a phone. The tall silhouette and stiff run were vaguely familiar. It was when the figure ran that Rahshaan realized that

Derrick's partners hadn't caught up to Santarez. He remembered watching the police officer chasing down and tackling the hustlers in Nat Turner for years. He had the form of an Olympic sprinter.

Without warning, Rahshaan spilled out of the car and fled in Santarez's direction. He tried to keep in mind Derrick's instructions to keep Santarez just on the edge of death. His foot sank deep within more than a foot of snow, making Rahshaan wonder how Santarez was moving with so much ease. The snow froze his ankles, reminding him of the mother of his children. Anger engulfed his soul while he watched his prey.

Santarez seemed not to know that he had company. In fact, he seemed preoccupied with getting to either a person or a destination. Rahshaan kept watching him and positioning his gun to hit his target. There came a time where Santarez got the cellphone signal and screamed into his phone. The trigger on the Desert Eagle pulled back like butter. Being grounded in the snow kept the gun's power from bucking Rahshaan too far back. With just one shot, Santarez was hit in his left leg. Santarez yelped and leapt forward about a yard. His gun flew from his hand into the snow. He fished for it, but the burning pain in his leg weakened him.

"How the fuck do I get to my son?" Rahshaan demanded when he made it to him.

Santarez rolled around, whimpering. Rahshaan used all of his anger to ram the toe of his Timb into Santarez's nose. The crack of a bone breaking in his face felt deliciously satisfying. After the first blow, Rahshaan's promise to keep Santarez alive was becoming more difficult. Everything inside of him wanted to end the man's life.

Marcus caught up to his brother and put a hand on his shoulder. "Just on the edge of death," Marcus reminded Rahshaan. "Let me, Ken-Ken, and PeeWee take care of him."

"Kill me, and you're all going to jail. You like it there, don't you, Banger? Squeak and Monaysia couldn't send you back, but I can."

Being taunted by the crooked cop sparked an anger in Rahshaan that he hadn't felt in over a year. He sent a rapid series of kicks to Santarez's face, and then he stomped on it in the snow. Santarez begged for him to stop. Flashing back to the three years of his own life that he lost, combined with the eight that he went without seeing his oldest son, caused Rahshaan to draw his gun.

"Do it!" Santarez pleaded.

Ken-Ken and PeeWee were the next to reach Rahshaan. Instead of trying to talk sense into him, they carried Santarez to their vehicle. Marcus held Rahshaan back. His brother was much stronger than him, so Marcus didn't think he'd be able to hold him, but he felt Rahshaan's resistance diminishing as he said each of his children's names individually. Then he reminded Rahshaan of Shatima, laying in a hospital bed.

"What if she wakes up to find out that you ain't coming home?" Marcus talked Rahshaan off the ledge. Snow poured down on them in blankets as he spoke. The wind howled so loud that Marcus had to yell. "You gonna make her single mother all over again? What the fuck was the point of you coming into her life just to leave her? How long did you sweat that girl, and now you just gonna leave her?"

Sanity returned to Rahshaan as he turned around and joined his crew. Marcus put a hand on his back to lightly guide him back to the van.

Moosie drove the SUV around with Ken-Ken and PeeWee in the back seat bringing their brand of torture to Santarez. They stripped him of his clothes and weapons and cut off his middle toe. They asked him about the boys from Nat Turner that they knew of by name and tased him when he told them they were all numbers instead of names. Ken-Ken took a vice grip from the sack that Derrick gave them and clamped it around his dick. Santarez's wails hit every tree in Banneker

Forest. When it became too much, PeeWee punched him in his jaw.

Shondell drove around the series of log cabins until they found one with a seven over the door. Blue tape around the perimeter announced that it was waiting to be renovated. He let them out and found a discreet place to park. He watched for Moosie, who was circling around, waiting for hell to break loose again.

Mont led Rahshaan, Rico, Shameik and Marcus into the cabin. They crept in, not knowing what to expect. The one room cabin made completely of logs was dry and empty. The putrid smell of human waste kicked their nostrils and pulled at their nose hairs. Jabez sat in the cabin, alone and naked. A dull fire was lit in the tiny fireplace, but it was hardly enough to keep him warm. Only the collar remained around his neck. His face was badly bruised, body scratched, but from what they could see, his bones were intact. Rahshaan ripped his hoody from his body and wrapped the shivering child in it. He clasped his arms around his son and whispered a thousand apologies for letting anything bad happen to him. Jabez whimpered and locked his arms around Rahshaan's neck. The smell of kerosene perfumed the little boy's skin and hair.

"Something ain't right about this shit," Shameik remarked. "It's happening too easy."

As soon as those words left Shameik's mouth, a single shot was fired somewhere outside. Shameik and Rico ran outside where Shondell already was crouched behind the van and firing at a small crew of men trying to make their way toward them. Snow fell in blankets, distorting everyone's views.

Rahshaan kissed Jabez's forehead and then handed the shivering, whimpering child to Marcus. Jabez gripped Rahshaan, but Rahshaan promised him that he would catch up with him later.

Marcus took off in search for Moosie. Up the road he found her tearing down a path and jumped in front of the car, waving for her to stop. Moosie just barely missed him.

"Why would you jump in front of a moving car, icy as it is out here?" PeeWee scolded him.

Marcus didn't reply. He climbed into the front seat and wrapped his hoody around Jabez. Then he hugged the little boy to him, hoping he could get him warm. Jabez's teeth chattered while he continued to shiver. He looked in the back seat and saw Santarez. A scream that scalped them all emerged from the little boy. With the safety on, PeeWee drew back his Glock and struck Santarez across the face. He demanded to know what Santarez did to him. Santarez spat blood and teeth in his face in response.

Ken-Ken and PeeWee dragged the man out of the car and cuffed his arms around the closest tree. A series of gunshots rang out. A hopeful look spread across Santarez's face.

Moosie looked to Marcus. "Tell Derrick we got Jay and get Jay the fuck outta here."

Marcus slid from the passenger's seat to the driver's seat. Once he let go of Jabez, the little boy pressed himself against the window and yelled for Rahshaan and Mont. Marcus pulled him down.

"Stay down, Jay! We're going to Uncle Derrick."

Outside, the Chavez boys continued with their fire, hitting none of their intended targets. Shameik and Rico stood behind trees, channeling their father's calm demeanor, waiting for the perfect opportunity to shoot. Shameik pulled the trigger once, and hit the man in front in his belly. He collapsed forward. Rico popped another in the groin. Shondell got in the van and tried to drive so that he could collect his crew, but discovered that someone had either slashed or shot out his back tires. It was a setup. They were either going to die or get caught with a bunch of dead bodies.

"Andrew, bring your bitch ass in here!" Mont called out his enemy in the one room log cabin. Nothing but dry wood and wooden furniture could be seen for hundreds of square feet. "Jeremiah's dead, and so is your pervert ass daddy. This shit over."

The front door swung open. A frigid wind invited itself in. Andrew appeared in the front of the cabin and addressed Mont. "I knew you were still alive!" Andrew cried. "I see you've got your little protégé with you. Thank you for taking such marvelous care of my son and my baby girl. Now you both may join Chillz and give me back my perfect little family." His blood boiled from seeing the two men who were chosen over him. He tried to keep his eyes from twitching and his body from shaking while he addressed them. This was supposed to be the moment that Mont regretted taking him seriously.

Instinctively, Mont cocked his M14, but Andrew had what looked like a jug of kerosene. He spilled the liquid on the floor. Then he looked around. His blue eyes flickered like the flames from the fireplace. His mouth frowned as his neck craned around. He stopped pouring kerosene.

"Where the hell is my son?"

From the back of the room, Rahshaan could shoot Andrew until there was nothing left of him, but his proximity to the fireplace made it dangerous for Mont. The rule was that Mont got to kill Andrew. Mont had to hurry up and figure something out, because the man laying claims to his family made Rahshaan want to empty the Desert Eagle and deal with whatever came after when it happened.

Outside, they heard the gunfire getting closer. They said silent prayers that it didn't reach them before they were rid of Andrew. Rahshaan and Mont hoped whoever Jabez ended up with had enough time to drive off with him. Andrew's ears perked. He smiled and tossed the kerosene into the fireplace. Mont and Rahshaan expected to die right on the spot. The flames spread outward on the wood. Andrew looked strangely at home within them. Rahshaan and Mont retreated backward. Rahshaan tried to back kick the door open but discovered that there was something heavy keeping them bolted in.

With the front of the cabin was ablaze, the wind pushed the flames to grow inward and spread. Rahshaan was sure the blizzard would put out the fire, but was unsure if that would happen before the flames swallowed them whole. The wood was catching fire rapidly. Smoke pushed toward him while he continued to get the back door open. His heart raced as he wondered how he was going to get them out of there.

From what Rahshaan could see, Andrew seemed to be waiting for someone who was never coming. He went from looking delighted to panicking with the realization that he may actually die in the fire in which he previously took pride. Rahshaan kept his gun positioned while he watched Mont pointing his gun at Andrew, trying to put enough distance between the two of them so that he could kill his enemy without killing himself. He screamed for Rahshaan to get out of there, but Rahshaan was trapped. Rahshaan's hands sweated, fingers lost their grip on his favorite piece of steel. Knowing they were better than dead if the flames touched it, he gripped it tighter.

As he continued trying to kick the door out, smoke terrorized his throat and invaded his head. The situation seemed hopeless, but then two men appeared. Andrew seemed not to notice them. Rahshaan's kicks weakened as he wondered if what he saw meant he was transitioning to the afterlife. Rize was behind Mont, positioning him perfectly to kill. Chillz was standing behind Andrew, trying to tell Mont the perfect time to shoot. Rahshaan heard Shameik yell for him to move, and they kicked the back door off its frame from the outside. The door fell into the cabin and onto the floor. Rahshaan ran outside, scrambling to get air.

"Where the fuck is Unc?" Rico demanded.

"He good," Rahshaan sputtered, still gasping for clean oxygen. Its bitter cold made his throat and lungs raw. "Your pops and Rize in there with him." Then he mumbled to himself, "Thank God."

Somewhere far off, there was an explosion. Santarez screeched his way into hell. The remaining Chavez boys continued tearing toward them. Rahshaan turned and fired, glad to finally be able to shoot to kill. Firing the first shot bucked him backward while the bang deafened him temporarily. He got a rush from watching the first boy drop. Then he shot at another one. In the distance, he saw one taking off down the hill. The family took out the Chavez boys and wondered if there were any more coming. Quiet cloaked the woods.

"This shit feels like a fuckin' setup," Shameik remarked in a low voice. "How the fuck ain't none of us get hit, but their whole team dropped?"

"We just gotta hope Derrick gets here before anybody else does," Shondell said out loud, trying to convince himself along with the others.

The flames and smoke left Mont gasping for breath. He thought he was going nutty when he felt someone holding his arms up after they went limp. When Chillz came and stabilized Andrew's arms, screaming for him to shoot, Mont knew he'd lost it. Chillz screamed for him to come to attention, that this was the opportunity they'd been waiting for decades. Rize had the rifle positioned to hit Andrew right between his eyes. Chillz screamed for him to shoot, and Mont took their nemesis down with just one shot. Andrew was launched backward into the flames. Mont felt himself floating — no, being carried —backwards. He lay in the snow, trying desperately to catch his breath.

"Time's running out, Tima. What's it gonna be?" Chillz asked his daughter.

"Why does our time together always get cut short?" she asked rather than answering his question.

Rize took her hand. "We never left you. We're walking with you, and we're always watching over you and the whole family."

Shatima threw her arms around her brother and sobbed into his shoulder. Their father came and embraced the two of them. "I'm gonna miss you two so much!"

"One day, pretty girl, when the time is right, we'll come back and get you. For now, go enjoy your life." Chillz pointed to her engagement ring.

"You got a pretty good one ahead of you. Tell Selena I said stop crying, I'll be back to get her, and I love her." Chillz kissed his daughter's forehead. Rize kissed her cheek. The two of them faded.

Jabez's whimpers drove Marcus insane as he found a discreet place to pull over. He was terrified and didn't understand how his brother could do this for so many years. The gunshots in the background made him want to keep driving without stopping, but he had to wait for Derrick. Once he found a place to park, he stuffed a gun into the door well. Then, he invited Jabez to curl up in his lap. He spoke tenderly to his nephew about taking him to see his parents. He was trying to convince himself that Rahshaan and Mont would come out alive. When Derrick pulled up beside him, he sighed relief.

Derrick wanted to pull out the hair of his low cut Cesar strand by strand. As soon as Marcus told him what happened, Derrick wished his car could convert into a jet. He knew there was a lot to clean up before Chief Lyles showed up. His team rode behind him.

When he saw the blazing cabin, he stopped his car before his heart stopped beating. He shook his head, trying not to cry. Then, in the distance, he saw Rico and Shameik dragging Rahshaan, one of his arms around each of their shoulders. He got out of the car and called to them, "Where's your uncle?"

"Back there with Shondell and them," Shameik grumbled.

"Get this nigga to the hospital before he passes out," Rico added. "He got smoke damage to his brain or something, talking about Chillz and Rize in that cabin."

Chief Lyles pulled beside them in a black truck.

"Where's Mont?" he stuck his head out the window and asked.

Shondell and Moosie helped Mont walk. Mont raised his hand while he dragged them.

Chief Lyles patted the bed of the truck. "I have a gift I'd like you to accept on Roland's and Jeremiah's behalf. It's best if you do something with it before those flames go out."

A black body bag was stuffed in the back of Chief Lyles' truck. He and Derrick helped them carry it to the cabin. Together they threw the dead bastard into the flames with his son.

As Derrick started calling for emergency services, he glanced at the cabin. The fire was being doused in the blizzard. He had to do a double take. He told himself that he was just tired, but he knew what he saw: Chillz and Rize coming out the door, walking away from the fire.

BEAUTIFUL BABIES PART III

"Bitch, don't you ever scare me like that again in your life!" Lynn screeched when Shatima opened her eyes. Selena came over to her, still crying, and kissed her daughter's face. G-Ma shook her head and thanked God over and over that her favorite granddaughter was awake. She hit Shatima's call bell to summon the nurses.

"Hey, niece! You feeling better?"

Shatima attempted to recognize this new person. Unlike everyone else in her family, she was short, but she was shapely like Lynn and had the family's signature dimples. "I'm sorry, but I don't know who you are."

"That's okay. It's my fault. I'm your aunt, Adrianne." She brought her face closer into Shatima's line of sight and gave that smile their family was known for.

"Well, I'm really sorry, but I'll be a lot happier to see you when I get these babies out of me. These contractions have been kicking my ass since earlier this evening. At least it's not cold in here anymore." She pulled the blankets tighter to her body anyway. "Selena, turn on the news. I want to see if that bastard is dead yet."

"Tima, we haven't heard anything–"

"Aunt Lynn, I said turn on the TV. Now unless you're about to give birth, then I suggest you let me have my way," Shatima warned her in a tone that was so even that it scared them.

Lynn dutifully obliged.

Shatima reached for Selena's hand. When she had her attention, she whispered, "Daddy said he loves you and stop crying so damn much."

Selena laughed and wiped the tears from her face.

As Lynn flipped the channels, Shatima turned her head and saw a man sitting in the corner, wearing black slacks and an oxford shirt.

"Hey! Pastor Candle's here, and y'all have just been letting me cuss up a storm." She turned her head again. "Oh, and G-Ma too. Welp. Sorry."

Nichelle and Sheila burst into the room, urging them to turn on the news. Sheila was on the phone with Big Grams talking at the speed of light.

As she sprinkled apologies in for the disturbing footage from earlier, the Channel 3 reporter announced that Chief Tennessee Jones died alone earlier that night in hospice. After that, the city turned to chaos as a gang broke into the room where his body waited to be claimed by his family and stole the corpse. The gang was identified as a group of boys and young men from the Chavez Projects. Reportedly his death signified the end of their enslavement. No longer did they have to rip other boys from their families, which an anonymous source admitted that Chief Jones made them do for decades.

The story cut to a shot of the basement in the nursing home. Families were either being reunited with their children or being asked to claim the bodies of their missing family members.

That story was cut short and went to another scene. A fire was in the background. Shatima's heart sank until the newscaster announced that a little boy had been rescued from the fire earlier. Names weren't being released until they confirmed that it was the missing boy who was abducted from the school bus earlier. Loretta and Andrew Jones, were named as persons of interests.

Another reporter was patched in announcing that Andrew Jones was found dead in the cabin fire, shot by a gun registered to one of the missing boys. Unfortunately, the owner of his gun was confirmed dead as well.

The story volleyed back to the second reporter, who announced that Santarez was found cuffed to a tree, shot in the back of his head by another gun registered to one of the Chavez boys.

The final scene showed boys and corpses being recovered from cabins surrounding the one that was on fire. The reported remarked that the blizzard was the only thing that saved the whole forest from going into flames. A camera followed the reporter to Big Grams' house, where Kimborough and the rest of the police involved with the illegal raid were being arrested.

"Did you get all of that?" Nichelle asked no one in particular. "That bastard and his daddy are dead!" The ladies in the room let out a whoop, while Pastor Candle shouted his praises to God.

"Did Mommy have the babies yet?" Jabez turned his head toward Rahshaan and asked.

"Not yet. She still has a few more weeks before they come, I think," Rahshaan told him. He wasn't sure what would happen after the way she went into the hospital. "Mommy wasn't gonna have the babies without you here anyway."

The paramedics had to work around Rahshaan, because he had Jabez's hand and refused to move. Every time someone came near Jabez he flinched. Rahshaan had to constantly reassure him that no one else was going to hurt him. He wanted so badly to ask him what happened to him that day, but he didn't want to do it in front of the paramedics. There would be plenty of time for questions later.

When the ambulance doors swung open, they were met with the frigid cold. Shameik and Rico hopped out of Derrick's car.

"Nichelle hit me and said Tima's dilating. Go upstairs with your wifey to have your babies. We got Jay," Rico told him.

"Oh, you're having a baby on top of everything else?" one of the EMTs remarked. "Well congratulations."

"Twins, I'm having twins," Rahshaan said, and smiled for the first time in months.

The walkway from the ambulance to the hospital entrance was lined with reporters. He ran the gauntlet of microphones in his face and camera flashes. Little did he know that was the first taste of paparazzi. They'd be hiding outside of his house for months, looking for a story. Hope Thomas was now under police custody, and there was a new anchor position to be filled. He pushed through them and rushed upstairs to make sure the babies didn't enter the world without him.

"AAAAAAAAAAAAAHHHHHHHH!"

"It's just a contraction, Shatima. Breathe through it."

"Fuck you mean it's just a contraction? You ain't got no kids, so you can't tell me this shit don't hurt, Aunt Adrianne!" She winced and clung to the pillow they'd given her. "Just a contraction. Fuck outta here."

Lynn cracked up. "I ain't never heard Miss Goody-Goody cuss like that."

"Oh, this is funny to you?" Her breath was choppy as she came down from the contraction. She turned her head and saw Rahshaan running toward her. Inside, she was relieved that he was unscathed, but her current condition had her angry at the world. "You better have my baby with you, or else you can just go back to wherever the hell you was at."

At first, he was taken aback. He was exhausted and ready to take a nap before starting the next chapter of his life. From the way Shatima carried on, it didn't look like he'd get that opportunity any time soon. "I thought your due date wasn't for a few weeks?"

"It ain't, but there's this little thing called stress that happens when your child gets kidnapped that brings on early labor, and being in a coma makes it a little uncomfortable for people to live inside of me." Her cynicism was so annoying that he wanted to slap her, but something more gratifying happened when she screamed and clawed for his t-shirt. "AAAAAAAHHHHH!"

"Three minutes!" Adrianne called out.

"I'm pissing on myself, you wanna announce that too?" Shatima growled.

Adrianne ignored her and told Nichelle to get Dr. Tawny. Lynn, G-Ma, and Pastor Candle cleared the room and ventured to the pediatric wing to see if they were allowed to see Jabez. Selena and Rahshaan put on yellow gowns while Sheila, Adrianne, and Nichelle served as her nursing team.

As his heart raced, Rahshaan was convinced that no one was more excited than him. This was the first day of his new life. He'd be able to see these babies' lives from the start and be able to see them grow old. No more murders, just life with a beautiful family. Every time Shatima cried out in pain, he shot her a stern look. He'd been through hell. It was her time to hold up her part of the bargain.

"Rahshaan, I don't know why the fuck you keep looking at me like that!" she cried out after a contraction. "You try pushing something the size of a basketball out of something the size of a lemon."

Selena cracked up at the analogy.

Rahshaan walked over to her side of the bed and reached for her hand as though he wanted to arm wrestle while she contracted. "Don't bitch up on me. It's time to focus, nigga!"

"Focus on deez nuts, nigga! We can switch places, and you can tell me what exactly the fuck you're focused on!"

"Shut the fuck up and get ready to push out my babies!" he screamed, his eyes directly on hers. Everyone in the room bursted into laughter. It was a refreshing change from when Shatima initially entered the room.

Doctor Tawny told Shatima to get ready to push. Rahshaan yelled at her the whole time. "Push that baby out! Don't scream!

Push that baby out your pussy so I can see what the fuck we've been blessed with! Bring my baby into this world, nigga!"

The doctor let off a final laugh. "Congratulations! It's a girl."

Rahshaan whooped and jumped around in circles. "My daughter! Aight, what else you got for me, babe?"

The next time Dr. Tawny told Shatima to push, she screamed more than she pushed. Dr. Tawny instructed her to focus on the action more than feeling. Pretty soon, another baby came out. "Congratulations! It's a boy!"

"My daughter and my son! Two girls and three boys!" Rahshaan ran to Shatima to kiss her, happy to leave the end of her that babies came from. Seeing it stretched out for human exit was visually unappealing, although he was glad for the babies who came out.

"Get back down there, nigga. We ain't done," Shatima snapped at him and then started laughing. Rahshaan and Selena looked at her like she was crazy.

"Tima, another one?" Rahshaan nearly passed out.

"Congratulations! It's a boy!"

"Three fucking babies?" Rahshaan tried to steady himself using the bed rail. "How the fuck you gonna keep that from me?"

Had she not been in so much pain, she would have smirked. "Shouldn't have done what you did. And you shouldn't have been out of town when we were supposed to be getting sonograms." She panted.

"Well, I won't be out of town or missing anything else. This shit is over. I'm home with my family from now on," he promised.

The babies were named Rahshaan, Jr., Rize William, and Isis Lynn Bailey. All three were healthy. Rahshaan tried not to play favorites, but the triplets held a special significance to him that only their mother understood.

Hours later, Shatima awoke to a room full of people. She was groggy, but she focused on each of them. They were her family, all in one piece. Rahshaan was doting upon all three of the babies. Over in the distance, she heard a relaxing, swooshing sound. Her head went in its direction. It took a minute for her to get up and get used to walking without carrying three babies inside of her. Once she steadied herself, she went toward the noise. The sight of Jabez's bruised face made her want to cry, but he took off his oxygen mask and pulled her to him. She promised him that he would never hurt again. He looked unsure. His smile was nonexistent. If it took the rest of her life, she would replace his smile with an even brighter one.

Hiding was no longer necessary for Mont, so he revealed himself as city hero, Malachi James. In his new freedom and visibility, he concentrated on advocating for those whose money was too low to speak at high volumes for what they needed. He was able to dedicate himself to his final mission, which was finding out what happened to Nyir and restoring him to who he was before tragedy affected him. In time he brought the young man among his family. Every time the sun rose, it felt like Chillz was smiling down on him and thanking him for taking care of his family.

ONE YEAR LATER...

The bus ride was long, crowded, and loud. Shatima opted to take the bus so that she wouldn't have the opportunity to say forget it and go back home or visit a spa for a day. There were a million other things she could have been doing. Instead, she took this trip. She didn't expect to get closure or understanding. In fact, she went into the day with no expectations. No expectations meant no disappointments.

After being searched, sexually harassed, and treated as though she herself was the inmate, Shatima followed a dozen family members down a long corridor and into a cold room. The wooden tables had the names of previous habitants etched into them. There were very few windows, which made her feel like she was inside of a zoo cage. She made her way over to a ten pound thinner version of Hope. Without the bundles of hair and the makeup, she looked like a totally different person.

As she approached the table, Shatima realized that was the first time she remembered seeing her mother without makeup. She couldn't decide if Hope was prettier with or without it. The eyes that normally dazzled were vacant. The hair that sat atop her head in fluffy curls once upon a time was pulled into a single french braid. The once smooth and flawless skin was marked with many signs of fights she couldn't win. Not even her almost-celebrity status saved her. Not when she was locked up with women who would never see their children and/or grandchildren again.

Shatima pushed the days out of her head when she actually wanted this monster to embrace her. Hope's hands and feet were cuffed to the table. Instantly, jealousy poked at her side. Shatima had the hair, face, and body that Hope was supposed to be sashaying around with. In her mind, her daughter was wasting it being a mother and a wife. She started to shut down. Everything that she wanted to say disappeared. The months of pastoral counseling and sessions with therapists were for nothing.

Shatima slumped back in a hard, uncomfortable chair. She folded her arms across her chest. Immediately, she regretted that move, because her breasts were sore and ready to be pumped. Her eyes stayed on her mother.

"I didn't think you'd come," Hope said.

"Neither did I," Shatima admitted. Her tone was short and cold.

In Hope's letter, she said that she had so much to say. Sitting here with no words between them angered Shatima. She had a family waiting for her. "Well, I'm guessing you didn't ask me out here to apologize."

"Would you accept it if I did?" Hope inquired.

Shatima ran her hands across the damaged wood of the table. Her fingers traced the initials of people who confessed their undying love to each other. "I know you're probably gonna lie or pass the blame onto someone else, but I really want to know what made you do this to me."

"To *you?*" Hope scoffed and then drew back. "I thought, if anything, you'd want to know why I did what I did to your son."

As Shatima shook her head, her hair tossed from side to side. She thought she saw her mother's eyes flash. "Even though I have video proof that you did, I can't bring myself to believe that you, as his grandmother, had anything to do with what happened to him. Today, I'm going to be selfish. I'm going to ask about me. Was it worth it? Huh? Was carrying a life inside of you just to spend 24 years trying to destroy it worth it to you?"

Hope stared at the table that sat between them.

"I don't know what made me come up here."

At the table beside them a woman was crying and gushing about how big her daughter was. She wondered what that woman did to wind up there, and was sure it was nothing like what Hope did.

"I told myself I wasn't going to say anything to you, but I can't leave here without you knowing how happy I am. Everything you ever wanted, I have.

"I used to wake up every morning upset that I didn't die in my sleep the night before. And then I used to turn on the TV and listen to your voice, pretending that it was you calling me to see how I was doing. And I shut myself up into my own little world and told myself that if my mother didn't love me, then I didn't deserve to be loved by anyone else. And then, one day you reappeared in my life and showed me just how shitty a person you were. I hated you so much, but I have to sincerely thank you for that day. I never would have the life that I have with the family that I have if you didn't come into my life and completely fuck up everything for me." By this point, Shatima was on her feet. A guard came to her and told her that she had to sit down or leave.

"I didn't really expect you to have an answer to that, so I'll ask you an easy question. What the hell happened to my brother?" She sat for a minute and waited for Hope to say something, say anything. The words never came.

That night, Shatima went home and kissed her husband deeply. She hugged each of her children individually and told them how much she loved them. When she got to Jabez, the faintest hint of a smile returned to his face. He reached out to her and hugged her back when she squeezed.

ACKNOWLEDGEMENTS

I can't believe it's actually finished. I need to dedicate this to two people: to Jeanette, because she literally saved this book's life; and to my brother Matthew, because I'll never stop missing him.

Fifteen years ago, about two or three weeks before I gave birth to my second child, Shatima, Rahshaan, and Jabez came into my life. They have been through countless transformations, making me get their stories just right. I thank God for showing them to me and for setting things in the divine order that helped me to cultivate these characters properly before passing this story onto you.

First of all, thank God for giving me the gift of writing, and thank my parents for giving me life. Thank you to my parents for making me. To my mother, Denise, thank you for showing me how to survive. Thank you to my hubby, Richard, and my children Jemaine, Shateek, Raymoan, Rahmeelo, and Richara for being the support system that I needed. Sorry about that crazy weekend in October when I was so focused on finishing my revisions that I didn't get up to cook meals. (And thank you, hubby, for cooking them). There is no family in the world better than ours. I love us!

To Pastor Dowdell - You unknowingly gave this book a title. You and your wife have been such an important part of my growth, and for that I am truly thankful.

So many people people have shown me so much support. Jeanette, Courtney, Kim, Lisa, and Stephanie, You know exactly what you did, and this could't have been done without you. To James and Rickey, thank you for showing me what having someone cheering me on is supposed to look like. To 12 Cunningham at Loretto, our years together meant everything to me. Stephanie, whenever you see me, you start with an encouraging word about my writing. I don't know if you realize how valuable this has been to me over the years.

To the Writer's Vibe family, I appreciate all the words of wisdom and inspiration that each of you spoke into my life in the early days. To my Writing Circle Challenge girls — Erica, CC, and Jasmine — thank you for picking me up and making me get back into writing. There was a two year period where I didn't put a pen to paper, and you all broke me out of that rut. Words cannot express how much I truly love the three of you.

To the people who read my work at any stage- Crystal, Dalria, Ashley, & Terri, your feedback is appreciated. Those of you who read the excerpts on MySpace, Facebook, Tumblr, etc., and left comments, I love you for taking the time.

To my brother, Matthew, who rests in Heaven along with our grandparents and Aunt Janie: The day you departed this life, I lost a piece of me. Then I gained an angel. I will never stop loving you and never stop missing you.

There are three women who made this work into art. First of all, Natasha Guy, you have been a blessing since the day you came into my life. The time that you took to edit this and to tell me to stop changing things (even though I changed some things; I'msorryIloveyouIoweyouahedgehog) was invaluable. Davida, the work you did on the original cover was a dream come true. Nicole Watts of Kreations K, the rework of the cover was amazing! Kadi, your attention to detail was the icing on the cake.

And to the R&B and Hip Hop artists of the 90s — Mary J. Blige, Xscape, WuTang, DMX, and The Lost Boyz in particular — thank you for getting me through the hard parts of this novel. Thank you for getting me through the all nighters when I wasn't sure I could "go there" with my writing.

I am so sure that I left out more than a few people. Please charge that to my head rather than my heart. I take no support lightly, and I hope that everyone gains something from the first of many books from Sanford County.

A CHARITABLE CAUSE

The FBI's National Crime Information Center (NCIC) database lists 424,066 missing children under 18 in 2018, the most recent year for which data is available. About 37 percent of those children are black, even though black children only make up about 14 percent of all children in the United States.[1]

$1 from each copy of "Consider Your Ways" that is sold will be donated to Rise Above Property. Please consider making an additional donation at riseabovepovertysyr.org

ALSO BY KIMANI LAUREN

HERE I LAY PART 1
I'VE GOTTA HAVE IT

Available in ebook and paperback.

Chapter One

EXCERPT FROM HERE I LAY PART 1: I'VE GOTTA HAVE IT

Here I lay, taking a deep breath...

When I left my hometown, I had dreams of only coming back as a celebrity guest to light the Downtown Christmas tree. Being back there, dancing on a tabletop and pouring champagne down my friend's throat wasn't the worst thing I could have been doing for money, as I would soon find out. It was just the fact that I was supposed to be in Paris getting ready to showcase a clothing line in Fashion Week, and I blew it.

Weeks ago, it was made known that I had let myself get so depressed that I went from academic probation to kicked out. I shouldn't have let those people at the fashion school that I attended tell me I was too fat, too Black, and too ghetto to sit at their table. I'll own the Black proudly, but my bad suburban ass was far from ghetto. I was from Sapphire Cadre, the place where everyone either owned their own house with a white picket fence, or they were saving for one. Everyone there was a teacher, bus driver, or worked at the post office for ten or more years. I was the jewel of that town. I'd been all over the world modeling, and I left to get a business degree and go to fashion school so that I could launch my own designer label. Ten years later, my label was supposed to be one of the major fashion houses.

Instead, I posed in lingerie for a flyer to entice people to come to this pajama party at the Opal Lounge on the last Saturday night in September. The lace and satin two piece set I wore clung to my curves and just barely covered what the world didn't need to see for free. All eyes were on me. Two sets interested me. First, there was Best. He was the camera man who put me on the flier. Then, there was this dark and sexy stranger standing at the bar. I'd never seen him before, but I was going to know exactly who he was by the end of the night.

A couple came through the door. That added a third set of eyes on me. That set of eyes messed up my whole mood. They reminded me that I had let something defeat me into coming home and modeling for party fliers instead of in ads on the pages of Harper's Bazaar. Foxy Brown and Blackstreet tried to convince me to ignore everything and keep enjoying the way the beat made my hips swung while they sang "Get Me Home," but my friend Brooke just had to point out the couple that just walked through the door.

Who am I? My name is Monaysia Giles. Where did I get the name? Well, if you let my mother tell it, she was tired of every other girl born the same year as me being named Monique or Asia, so she did something different and combined the two. Much later in life, I learned that Monique and Asia were two women my father cheated on my mother with, and he made up the name as his own private joke. All that taught me was that men loved to embarrass the women they claimed they loved, and that was exactly why I was trying so hard to continue rocking to that song.

My friend Brooke climbed onto the bar with me and broke my concentration. "Nay-Nay, I know that's not Miguel coming into your spot with another girl!"

I frowned at her and barked, "Why would you come up here and make it look like I was paying him any attention?"

She recoiled and asked, "Aren't you mad, though?"

I bucked my eyes at her. "Brooke, do you see what I look like, and do you see what the bitch he's with looks like? He lost, not me."

I couldn't help but glance at my ex while he led his new chick to the dance floor to press against her the way he used to do to me. It was a hell of a way to confirm that I was single.

Miguel had been my boyfriend since I was in the tenth grade. He dealt with fast money and was supposed to be stacking some for me to open a warehouse somewhere in New York City. The night before I left for college, he begged me not to go because he was going to miss me too much. Then, he told me to go and get the degree so that he could send me the money to start my line. That was the last time I heard from him, and that was a little over a year ago.

After the song ended, I hopped down from the bar and stomped away from Brooke. She tried to follow, but I snapped at her to leave me alone. My friend Siraya walked with me and asked if I wanted to leave. I looked over my shoulder and shot a dirty look at Brooke. She was standing there with our other friend Yolanda and Siraya's cousin Yvette, trying to look disinterested in guys who approached her to dance. Everything was irritating all of a sudden. Siraya hooked her arm in mine and led me to the bar.

"You want me to run outside and slash his tires?" she asked me.

"Nope. He's dead to me," I replied and took a seat.

Rashad, the bartender, came to us immediately. He made it obvious that he was ignoring Siraya and asked me what I wanted.

"I need five of those top shelf margaritas that you make so good," I told him.

"Aight. I got yours. Whose credit card you putting the other four on?" he wondered.

My face puckered when I answered, "Nobody's. I'm the

whole reason why all these people are up in here. My friends all drink for free."

"No. You drink for free cuz you a dime," he argued.

"My friends are cute too," I pointed out.

"Your friends are high school cute. You the dime. If they wanna drink for free, it gotta be on somebody else's dime," Rashad told me.

I glanced at Siraya, who was too preoccupied to hear the conversation. Instead of paying any more attention to Rashad, I followed her line of sight. The dark stranger was walking with this other fine ass dude. I crossed my legs and told Rashad to go make the drinks.

"Who's paying? Nay, you know I gotta come out my pocket for anything free I give out that I ain't discussed ahead of time," he complained.

"Chill, Rashad. We got them," the stranger said.

"Oh really? What you supposed to be, some type of baller?" I wondered.

"Ugh. Don't tell me you one of them stuck up chicks," he said.

Before I could think of anything else to say, Rashad wondered, "Banger, she talking about buying five drinks. You got all five?"

"Don't disrespect my pockets like that," the stranger said and put down money on the bar. "Make sure it's top shelf, too. I know your boss be telling you to charge top shelf for some dish water."

Rashad cracked up at that and walked away to fill our order.

"Thank you for the drinks," Siraya said.

The stranger said, "My name is Rize, and this is Banger." He had some really cute dimples, but he was nothing like his sexy, rugged friend. He was too friendly. The other one didn't seem interested in drawing attention to himself. Neither of them adhered to the pajama dress code. Instead, they opted for sweatpants and ribbed tank tops. They looked damn good too, but the one named Banger looked slightly better.

"I'm Siraya."

"Pretty name for a beautiful woman," Rize told her. "Your friend got a name, or is she sitting there tryna make one up so that we can't find y'all again after tonight?"

Siraya giggled at that. I gave them my name.

"Which one of these niggas in here looking at you like they want a problem is your man?" Banger asked.

I felt Miguel's eyes on me but refused to look at him.

"Well, I just found out tonight that I'm single after four years, so none of them." I shrugged and said, "Thank you for the drink."

I slid off the barstool. Siraya and I took the drinks back to the rest of the clique. They were dancing with some cornballs that we knew from high school. I was ready to get out of there, but I still had to judge the pajama contest. A room full of bitches who couldn't even dress better than me in their sleep, and I had to give them the prize. I should have been eating baguettes and sketching garments. I gulped down my margarita and went to find my ride.

"Can we do this contest? I'm ready to go?" I asked Best.

His brother Ronnie, who was also his business partner, frowned and said, "We had hoped you didn't see Miguel in here."

"Ain't nobody thinking about Miguel. I just have some work to do," I snapped.

"Nay, I can't leave," Best told me. "You know I make the most money after everything shuts down, and everybody wants to get those last minute pictures in the parking lot."

I huffed.

"I'll take her home," a woman said from behind them.

I backed up a little. This woman's skin looked like liquid gold. She wore a blonde ponytail that perfectly complimented her skin. Her face and lips were shaped like hearts. I wasn't used to there being someone finer than me in Sapphire Cadre.

"I'm their sister Melinda," she said to me.

"I didn't know you had a sister, Best," I said.

She giggled and told me, "I'm the problem child that they try not to acknowledge. I just stopped in here tonight with some friends and bumped into them. It'll be no problem for me to take you home. I'm pretty bored."

I started to tell her that I would walk home, but then I asked, "Aren't you in my sociology class at SCC?"

The smile that she gave me had a warm, sisterly vibe, so that made me comfortable enough to ride with her. I asked Best to take the rest of my crew home, but Siraya came with me.

Banger and Rize stood by a Cadillac Escalade when we got to the parking lot. Siraya tried to slap me five behind her back, but I wasn't ready to celebrate quite yet. Just as I suspected, Melinda got into the driver's seat. Coffee cups and empty mascara tubes were all over the place. That pissed me off, because I would never let a car that nice get that dirty. I also wouldn't bother with community college if I could afford a truck like that, but riding in filth was better than being in the same place as my filthy ex and his new bitch.

"Can we take y'all to get something to eat?" Rize offered while Melinda let her truck warm up.

"I can eat a little something-something. How you feeling, Nay?" Siraya wondered.

"No, thank you. I need to get home and study," I answered.

"Study for what?" Siraya wondered.

"I have a sociology exam on Wednesday," I replied.

She squinted at me and jerked her head forward. "Where do you take sociology?"

"SCC," I replied. "I gotta get my grades up so that I can get out of here."

Siraya shook her head several times before she continued her questioning. "When do you go to SCC?"

"Early mornings and mostly evenings. I go around my work schedule. Before you ask, I work at Sanford Ringer," I snapped.

She shook her head again and blinked. "Friend, how long have you been home?"

I sighed. "Since the end of August."

"And this is the first time I'm seeing you?" she exclaimed. "And you're not just here for the weekend?"

I shook my head and said, "Don't tell the rest of those bitches, though. The last thing I need is them laughing at me."

"You know I wouldn't do you like that," she said.

Rize butted in and asked, "So can we take y'all to get something to eat?"

The front passenger door opened before I could answer. A man with a forceful presence in the physical as well as his overall demeanor hopped into the car.

"Let's go hit The Spot. This shit was dead. Leave it to Sapphire Cadre to have a party where the finest chick in the club was the one on the flier," he said.

Melinda giggled. "That's how it's supposed to be everywhere."

He argued, "Nah. That's supposed to be an advertisement. Like, 'Come here. This girl is gonna be here, and there's gonna be a whole bunch of other girls who look like her.' That shit was like the girl on the flier and then every chick in high school who wanted to be down with her and dress like her so she would be their friend."

"Wow!" Siraya exclaimed.

I couldn't help but laugh as he turned around and squinted at us.

"Leave it to y'all to leave with the girl from the damn party poster. What's really good, ladies? I'm Shameik."

He turned around. Melinda pulled off.

"I ain't wanna be up in there anyway once I saw that nigga from West Sanford in there," Rize commented. "So what's up, ladies? Y'all up for a better party, or you just want us to take you to get something to eat and go home?"

"I really gotta get home to study," I said. "Thank you for the offer, but I gotta get my grades up and get outta Sanford County."

Siraya sucked her teeth. "Stop being a model, and put something on your stomach. You got the whole weekend to study. Depending on who you have, I might have an exam from last semester that I can give you to study from."

Melinda turned around in her seat as though there weren't a steering wheel and brakes in front of her. "For real? Girl, I will pay you for whatever notes you have for that class. That lady ain't no joke."

Siraya nodded her head. "So that problem's solved. Come and get something to eat, friend. We're probably too naked to go to another club."

Melinda took that as a signal to get comfortable with her driving. She jerked that monster of a truck around corners, missed turns, and drove in reverse at one point. I clung to Banger for my life, even though I didn't know him to be trusting him with it. She drove out of our little suburb and to a bridge to get into South Sanford. Siraya and I were always told to stay out of there, but we kept it cool that night. A sheriff standing at the entry made Melinda roll down her window to check her license, but he took one look at that swan neck, seductive eyes, and heart shaped lips and told her to have a good night. She drove forward and gagged.

"What the hell was that? You didn't even do anything," I said.

"Just don't drive down here without your license is all I can say," Melinda warned me.

We went to a 50s style ice cream parlor with black and white checkered floors and red chairs. Rize suggested we get chicken finger subs. I didn't eat too much fried food, but it smelled too good for me to decline.

Instead of sitting in the restaurant, we got back into the car and drove down to the Aliners River, the u-shaped body of water that kept South Sanford separated from the rest of the county.

I'd never been that far down the river, but the water sparkled under the moonlight. We sat and had small talk to get to know each other. Banger hadn't said much all night, but Melinda kept the conversation going. Rize asked us if we smoked. When Siraya and I eagerly said that we did, the guys got out of the car. For some reason, Siraya went with them.

"You like working at the phone company?" Melinda asked me.

"Not really. I like getting a paycheck to get me out of here once I get my grades up," I said. "When I put that with the money I make doing fliers for Ronnie and Best, I get closer and closer."

She nodded. Then she took a bite out of her sandwich. After she swallowed it, she said, "You can make a whole lot more at my job. We're having a hiring event tomorrow if you want to come."

I should have asked questions, but she drove an Escalade. I had none that I could think of.

"It's mostly weekends, and you have to go out of town a lot," she continued.

"Who do I make the cover letter out to? I can use as much time away from here as I can get," I grumbled.

She turned around and studied me with sympathy pulling down the corners of her mouth.

"I don't mean to get in your business, but my brother talks about you a lot. A whole lot. I mean, I don't speak to my family often, but your name has been coming out of his mouth since he was 12 or 13. He's really happy that you came back home, and all he's been talking about is saving up to send you to Paris next summer since your family emergency brought you back here."

"That's what he told you?" I asked.

"Yup."

I nodded my head. "That's a good friend then."

"So anyway, I'll pick you up in the morning and bring you in to meet my boss. We'll be gone all day, so make sure you clear your schedule. And don't worry about having to do this club flyer shit any more either. You're way too gorgeous for this kind of work," she told me.

"Thank you, but I have an arrangement with your brothers. I model for them, and they give me free photoshoots to keep my portfolio updated," I said.

"Oh yeah. Best did say that you were a professional model. Well, I guess that works for you then."

Siraya and the guys came back to the car. Melinda rolled the blunt while Siraya told Rize her whole life story. The way that she was smiling at him and staring into his eyes had me ready to smack her. After what I'd been through that night, she should have been done with men the way I was. Even my attitude went out the window once my fingers touched Banger's when he passed me the spliff. Our eyes linked briefly. Then, I looked away and tried not to die choking.

"Damn. I need to cop on this side of the bridge from now on," I said after I recovered. I stared at the river. The sparkle looked like it was turning to bubbles, and it was creeping me out. I couldn't stop looking at it, though. Siraya tapped my knee to get me to pass her the blunt.

"I'm spending the night at your spot, Nay-Nay. Denise and Edwin don't be in your ass about coming home drunk and high the way Siobhan and Dartanion be in mine," Siraya said when we finished smoking.

Rize asked her, "Do y'all have to go home at all? It's early."

"I gotta be at work at 6 in the morning. What about you, Nay?"

"I might do an hour or so of OT," I said, staring out the window. "It'll keep me out of Denise and Edwin's house."

"Oh. That's too bad. I had a lot of fun getting to know y'all," Rize said.

Banger hadn't said anything, but he and I kept peeking at each other. I couldn't tell what he was thinking about me. Part of me wanted to tongue him down and strip him naked just for the simple fact that he didn't mention those drinks he bought my friends and me after he paid for them. Most of the men I knew would remind me of that for the rest of my life. A bigger part of me just wanted to go home. I was still embarrassed about my ex, and I didn't like it.

We crossed the bridge again. Even though the car smelled like a ganja plantation, Melinda flirted with the sheriff and got us across it quickly.

"We're spending the night at your spot. I ain't going across that shit again," Shameik declared.

Melinda started rattling off what she wanted for breakfast. Her order took the rest of the ride for her to finish. Rize hopped out of the car to walk Siraya to the door. I was surprised when Banger offered to walk with me too. I declined.

"Next time I see you, you better not still have an attitude about a nigga stupid enough to let you go," Banger said.

"And what makes you think you'll ever see me again?" I wondered.

"I'm making sure I bump into you again," he told me. "Good night, Nay-Nay."

I switched my ass through my parents' picket fence and waited for Siraya to give Rize her phone number before we went inside to get fussed at by my parents. It was the first time that I came home from a club appearance smelling like I'd been having fun. I was sure my parents would have something to say. They had so much to say every day since I came back to their house.

AUTHOR'S NOTE

Sanford County is the amalgamation of the cultural epicenter of every place I've ever loved before greed took them over, combined with the attitudes and actions that allowed the greed to bastardize them. I'm talking about Syracuse's East Side, Harlem, Columbia, Memphis, DC, Atlanta, and any other hood that got a bike path before it got a bus route. My hope is that this fictional town will bring an end to classism. I realize this is a tall order, but something has to give. Poverty is a crime, but its victims are not the culprits. If anything within the hierarchy of this place I made up jarred you, then it's time to adjust the way you think and act.

ABOUT THE AUTHOR

Kimani Lauren has been writing since she was a little girl. Although she started with poetry, her true love of novel writing was found one summer when she had nothing else to do but fill some unused pages in a Mead Composition notebook. Her first novel, *Yours, Til the End of Time,* was published by her uncle in 1994. Twenty-six years, three cities, two marriages, six children, one dog, one novella, several "main" career attempts, and one pandemic later, she was able to publish her first full length novel, *Consider Your Ways.*

With the *Secrets From the Bridge* series, Kimani hopes to birth a new sub-genre of fiction called Urban Studies. The goal of the Urban Studies genre is to examine how intra-racial classism mirrors racism. Her hope is for Sanford County and everything it takes to build it to become a staple in Black American pop culture.

Over the years, Kimani has had the pleasure of calling Syracuse, Columbia, and Memphis home. She currently resides in Syracuse with her husband and five of their six children.

facebook.com/kimanilaurenbooks

twitter.com/kimanilaurenppw

instagram.com/kimanilaurenbooks

goodreads.com/kimanilauren

pinterest.com/kimanilaurenbooks

amazon.com/author/kimanilauren

bookbub.com/authors/kimanilauren

NOTES

A CHARITABLE CAUSE

1. Kaur, Harmeet (2019, November 3). *Black kids go missing at a higher rate than white kids. Here's why we don't hear about them. https://www.cnn.com/2019/11/03/us/missing-children-of-color-trnd/index.html*